KELDA LAING POYNOT

Dedication

In Loving Memory
of Carla Halstead Berggren Carr
Mother   Daughter   Sister   Friend
August 31, 1969–August 29, 2020
Your love is missed beyond measure.

Acknowledgments

To the muses who dance through my mind during normal times.

To the Great Spirit who guides me.

Abbey

Amy

Anna-Grace

Bailey

Becca

Cheryl

Joey

Julia

La'Toya

Madison

Mia

Paige

Sarah

My Beloved, Scotty

Chelsea – Your talents exceed all expectations.

Thank you for another beautiful cover.

3PetalsPhotgraphy.com

Part One

Chapter One

"Phina, Phina," Mother called. I ran to her and did not dare dawdle. "There you are, my sprite. What do you wish to know today?" That was the way we started our lessons every morning. After breakfast and the chores, we would walk to gather water from the spring.

Mother taught me everything I needed to know to be a healer like her and Grandmother and Grandfather. She taught me the ways of the great spirit who gave us the ability to heal.

Grandfather and Grandmother, Mother, and I lived apart from the city. By choice or by convention, I did not know. The city was a bustling place where the governor ruled over our region. Our land had been occupied for many years, but it had been peaceful in all my memory. Grandfather remembered well the turmoil and unrest, but he did not speak of it. Since the invasion, healers did not live near the palace. Our invaders knew nothing of healers and healing. They were unfamiliar with our ways, and we were not sought after as often as we had been before.

Even among our neighbors, we were different, and we were accustomed to exclusion. Healers led a solitary life except on the occasions that we were needed. Our darker complexion, black hair, and blue eyes were the symbols of a healer and were believed to hold special powers. Our hair was the color of ravens' wings, iridescent and almost blue in the sunlight. We kept our hair bound as to not draw unwanted attention. What little interaction we had with the invaders was met with apprehension. Their ways were very different than ours, and our appearance only made them wary.

Grandfather's hair had once been the raven's black, but I only knew him to have silver hair. "Why is Grandfather's hair silver and not the raven's black?" I asked Mother.

"He is old and very wise." Mother cut her eyes playfully at her father. "His wisdom is too great to be hidden now."

"When I am old like Grandfather, will I have silver hair too?" I asked in my child's voice.

"Only if you are very wise," Mother said, tapping the tip of my nose with her finger.

"Or incredibly stubborn," Grandmother interjected.

Our hair was not the only difference. A healer's blue eyes were akin to the lapis lazuli. I had the raven's hair and the lazuli eyes at birth, but my eyes changed to hazel upon my third birthday. Before my fifth birthday, my eyes were a muddy brown.

My family feared it was a sign that I was losing my ability to be a healer. To everyone's relief, my eyes still gave me the ability to read and understand a healer's ways. I could sing the healing songs; I could name all of the plants in Grandfather's garden and their purposes without any reminding.

They didn't hide their concern for me. Grandfather consulted the great spirit about the change in my eyes, but he received no answer. Mother asked the great spirit for an answer, too, but she only received the comfort that it would be of use to me. Grandmother said it was a sign of change and a warning that great forces were at work. She claimed it to be the mark of protection that would keep me safe.

"She may be an even greater healer than all of us combined," Grandmother said one night as she braided my hair for bed. I liked the way her fingers combed through my hair. I rested my head against her knees. The fire crackled, and my eyes were heavy as her gnarled hands worked the plaits of the braid. "Perhaps she will be the one to heal this land of its heathen invaders."

"What's a heathen?" I asked sleepily.

"It's a godless man. A man who has no faith in things beyond himself, a man who does not abide in the great spirit's ways."

I tilted my head toward Grandmother questioningly. "Not all men trust in the great spirit?" I asked innocently. She huffed a breath.

"No, child, they do not. You will need to be cautious. Many men have no faith and, through their fear and ignorance, choose to strip faith from others' hearts." I could not imagine not having the great spirit to guide me. Grandmother looked down at me and read the confusion in my eyes. "Sorry, Phina. I did not mean to frighten you. I will sing protection over you. Think of it no more."

***

Erik was nearly ten-and-two when he was apprenticed to Grandfather. I was only five, but I remembered his arrival. He, too, was born with the raven's hair and lazuli eyes. Where he came from, there were no healers left to train him, so he was brought to Grandfather. Young Erik teased and played with me. He entertained and, unlike Mother, sang all the time. He became my brother and protector; he was my very best friend.

Once a week, Mother loosened the binding around our hair, and we washed in the pool that collected near the spring. Mother would gently scrub oils infused with lilac and lavender into our hair. She would sing and brush each strand of our black hair until it shone brightly. It was the only time that Mother sang, and it was the only time, other than sleeping, that our hair was unbound.

When I was a child, I was allowed to sing whenever I desired. As I grew, though, I would only be allowed to sing with Grandfather and Erik. My growing powers were protected when combined with their deeper voices.

Mother was a renowned healer, and her voice carried her words and intentions to the great spirit. Although she had only a few strands of wisdom in her raven's hair, she was the wisest woman I knew. Grandmother even said so.

Mother's mate, my father, was not a healer. He was a soldier who drowned at sea. Mother said their love had created me, but he died before I was born. He knew nothing of me but had named me nonetheless.

"'We will have a daughter, no sons,' he declared," Mother mimicked his deep voice. "He wanted a daughter named Phina, and that is what I gave him. The great spirit comforted me in my loss by giving me you. You are the embodiment of our love."

I never knew loss until I lost everything; I never felt pain and suffering until many changes and many years passed. Mother's strength as a healer had come from her loss. I asked Grandmother once, "Why does Mother not join our songs?"

Grandmother told me how Mother had sung the grieving song after my father's death to close her heart to men. From that moment, Mother would never again sing for a man or join her voice. "It also protects Erik. He is still young and impressionable. He needs to wait for the song of his mate." She looked at me, then, and consternation covered her brow. "Once your womanhood arrives, you, too, must be cautious. A woman's song is a powerful thing, Phina."

Grandmother's tone was different. Grandmother was not as renowned a healer as Mother; her most significant power was in foreseeing. The great spirit had gifted Grandmother with sight. From a young age, she could see glimpses into what was to come. Her words to be cautious were an admonition. I nodded solemnly and vowed to always remember.

I wondered if I would ever be as strong a healer as either Mother or Grandfather. They taught me to govern my words and to choose them carefully whenever I put them to song. The great spirit would hear them and answer my prayers. Their warnings and instruction made me mindful.

Once, I chimed in with Mother while we were bathing at the pool. It was not uncommon for the birds to be curious when Mother sang, but our combined voices brought the furry creatures, too. They gathered along the bank and watched us curiously. Mother hummed and let me carry the words while the fishes and tadpoles swarmed around my feet. I wrapped my hands around a large, green trout. I lifted his body up to the surface of the water and stroked down his shimmering scales. He flicked his tailfin and splashed the water into my face. I squealed and giggled before I released him. As soon as I stopped singing, the allure was broken, and Mother and I were alone again. From that time on, Mother and I took turns singing.

"She called the fishes today," Mother said at supper.

Grandfather's eyes glistened at the news. He was always proud to hear of my accomplishments. Grandmother's eyes were more cautious. She was never as indulgent as Grandfather.

"How big were they?" Erik asked. I put my hands out to show him the size. He nodded, impressed. "Did you think to catch our supper?" Erik teased. I shook my head. That idea had been the furthest from my mind. "I am taking her with me the next time you want a trout for the table," Erik declared.

"You will not!" Grandmother chided.

Erik winked and raised his eyebrows to say he had designs on his next fishing day. Grandfather laughed but then grew solemn at Grandmother's expression.

"Child, this is a wonderful thing, but you know that we only use the great spirit's powers to heal and not for our own gain or advantage. That is why the gift of song is not given to men. We are driven differently than women. Our hearts are not as pure and well-intentioned. Perhaps that is why we have the ability to read men's hearts so that it keeps our hearts in tune with the great spirit," Grandfather speculated. Then he grew more solemn.

"It won't be too many more years before we celebrate your womanhood. Protect your heart, Phina, and keep faithful to one man. A divided heart is a dangerous thing."

I nodded but could not imagine. I looked around the table at my family; my heart was not divided. I loved my family; they were my entire world.

Chapter Two

Rumors of threats and signs of conflict reached us in our isolation. The locals who remained came to us for various reasons, and they brought news and gossip. I rarely left our home except when we were called upon to sing forth a stubborn child from a mother's womb. Those were special times when I left the protection of our home. On even rarer occasions, I went into the city with Erik and Mother.

They didn't go to the city often, either, but they spoke of the changes each time they returned. "They cover their women," Erik protested. "You can't see their faces, only their eyes. How can a man ever choose a mate if he can't see her face?" he complained.

"I will not return to the city again," Mother said flatly. I was saddened by that. If Mother didn't go, then that meant I would not be allowed to go, either.

"But why, Mother?" I pleaded. I rarely begged, but this news disturbed me.

"I will not wear a virgin's veil. I refuse to paint my eyes because I am no longer claimed. Even in the widow's clothes, the men take notice of me."

"It's not safe," Erik said, placing his hand on my shoulder so that I knew not to press my mother for more. Later, while he and I were working in the garden, he explained, "Phina, your mother is a beautiful woman. She attracts men, and it stirs up a desire in them. Most men are strong enough to overcome their urges to take a woman by force, but some have no self-control. I read many men's hearts and intentions today. We must protect her."

***

At eight-and-ten, Erik was conscripted as a soldier. I was deeply saddened at his departure but did not weep. He promised to return and heal alongside me. He was a man of his word, and I believed him. It was never hidden that Erik intentioned to stay with us. I overheard when he asked Grandfather to be joined to me when I came of age. I thought he must be teasing. I was only one-and-ten when he was conscripted, and until my womanhood, I was too young to be betrothed.

The night before Erik was taken by the soldiers who came to escort him to the army, there was music. We took turns playing Grandfather's dulcimer and dancing. We combined our voices and sang blessing and favor over Erik; even Mother sang. It was the last time we all sang together.

Late that night, Erik tucked me into bed. He would be gone before the sun. He leaned over me and promised that he was determined to return. "Don't grow up too fast, Phina; I will come back to you." He kissed my forehead. He was a man, and I was still a child of one-and-ten, too young to understand his intentions, too young to understand his love.

Mother's love for my father made her stronger. Still, a healer's love was not quickly gained, nor was it easily lost. Once a woman healer's love was given, she was forever bound to that man, heart and flesh. We were careful with our words, songs, prayers, and, most importantly, our hearts. Everything we were flowed from our hearts through our mouths and our hands. Our nature was incapable of deception. The great spirit would always know our true intentions.

Male healers were fiercely loyal to their mates. They were protective and able to read the hearts of men. They rarely chose a woman who was not a healer because, through their union, a balance was created. Women healers could choose to love any man whose heart was pure.

***

14

More soldiers arrived, so we kept to ourselves and relied only on what the great spirit provided from the earth and our animals. We were safe as long as we stayed close to our home. I was never allowed to wander far past the bathing pool.

A year after Erik's conscription, Grandfather died peacefully in his sleep. Grandmother woke and could not rouse him from his slumber; Mother and I woke to her wailing. The three of us covered him in a large sheet of linen and anointed his body with oils and spices. Had the soldiers not been so close, we would have burned him on a pyre.

Without the protection of a man, Mother became even more protective of me and our home. She slept with a dagger at her side. She never ventured outside, even to the garden, without the weapon tucked into the folds of her skirt. Grandmother disapproved and said that the great spirit would see to our needs, but Mother was adamant that I learn to protect myself and included those lessons along with my study of herbs and tinctures.

Soldiers were seen more often. They kept to a path a safe distance away, but they were not far enough to please Mother. I sensed a knowing from both Mother and Grandmother. I wondered if Mother was gaining the gift of sight.

Grandmother and I were milking the goat when we heard screams. I dropped the milking bucket and ran toward the house. Grandmother's gnarled hands grabbed me with such force that I was thrown down onto the straw floor. I looked up to her in bewilderment, and she placed her finger over her lips to silence me.

Mother screamed again. My eyes widened in fear; she was being attacked. Grandmother shook her head in warning. I jumped to my feet and ran from the goat shelter toward the house. Grandmother was an old woman, but she was more agile than I knew. She surprised me when she was at my side.

I peeked through the open window and gasped when I saw Mother being accosted by two soldiers. They were strong men with broad shoulders. Mother fought against the restraints of one soldier while the second pressed her against the table. He lifted her skirts and forced himself between her legs. His eyes rolled back into his head in pleasure. "Hold her," he demanded of the soldier who was having to fight Mother's protest.

I gasped, and Grandmother held my mouth closed tightly. I wriggled to free myself from her embrace, but she maintained her dominance over me by pressing my body against her full bosoms. She tried to turn my head away to protect my eyes from seeing, but I was determined to watch and wait for my opportunity to do something to help Mother. My heart beat rapidly in my chest, and I could hardly catch my breath with Grandmother's hand over my face. She tried to pull me away, but I was unwilling to move from the spot.

I knew what they were doing to Mother. Of course, I had never seen the actual act before, but I had been warned. Even Erik had warned me that some men lacked the self-control necessary to honor women. Rape was a threat to all women, especially women who lived in a land occupied by soldiers.

The soldier thrust his hips repeatedly against Mother's body until he leaned forward and moaned with pain or satisfaction; I did not know. He leaned over her and kissed her mouth. It looked loving and affectionate, but I knew it was neither. He mocked what the great spirit intended for good between a man and a woman, what the great spirit designed to create life.

The other soldier laughed. He was amused and eager for his turn. "Hold her. Move away," he demanded.

They must have eased their hold on Mother because she lifted her leg and kicked the thrusting soldier solidly in the temple. He stepped back and touched his head, testing the spot for blood. He sneered down at Mother. She released a stream of curses and spat at him, sealing his fate. He responded with a slap across her face. Blood sprayed from her lip from the force of his backhand.

The holding soldier pushed the thrusting soldier away. They exchanged hostile words. For the briefest of seconds, Mother was free. She turned her face toward the window, and her lazuli eyes bore a hole through my heart.

"Run," she mouthed and willed me to obey. Tears pooled and reflected the deep blue, and I could see her resolve.

My gaze was only on Mother, but I saw the glint of steel from the corner of my eye before she drove her dagger into the thrusting soldier from behind. The holding soldier watched with disbelief as the thrusting soldier clasped at his back. Her blade slid easily from its victim. She rolled and jabbed at the other soldier, but he was prepared to defend himself. The dying man held himself, but he knew his own fate. He staggered and stumbled away from Mother toward the window.

We crouched down, but it was too late; he'd seen us. "There are more," he called just before he collapsed onto the floor.

Mother heard him and called out, "Go!"

Grandmother dragged me away from the window the best she could, but I saw everything. The soldier grabbed Mother and pressed himself against her as if he still intended to do what his cohort had done before his demise. In her desperation, Mother managed to stab her assailant before he pulled out his own weapon and slit her throat.

The soldier ran from the house after us, clutching his side, but he was too wounded to get to us. Grandmother held my hand and ran, pulling me alongside her. She panted at my side and pulled at her chest. At first, I thought it was in grief for her daughter, but once we were safely in the woods, she stopped at the edge of the river.

"Water," she panted.

I ran to the river and cupped my hands to gather a drink for her. She sipped from my hands and sent me for more. My hands were small, and I could only carry a little at a time. I pulled a large leaf from a tree and fashioned a bowl. Grandmother smiled, but it faltered.

"Child," she panted once she'd caught her breath. "Drink for yourself."

I ran back to the riverbank and scooped water into my hands, but as soon as the water hit my stomach, I vomited it back up. The image of Mother's blood and the blood from the soldiers forced the meager contents of my stomach out into the moving water.

Unable to hold myself together, I fell down onto the riverbank in a near faint and let the water pool around my lips. I pulled off my damp head covering and dabbed my face with it. It was refreshing and comforting against my flushed skin. I lay there, collecting myself enough to return to Grandmother.

Her eyes were closed when I approached her. Her hand was still clutched at her chest. I sat next to her, and she placed her arm around me. "Phina," she whispered.

"Mother," I whispered in reply. Grandmother's sigh was heavy and dark. She patted my head affectionately and, with what strength remained, embraced me.

"Phina, my child, keep yourself safe." She hummed a familiar melody and, before long, began singing a song of protection over me. Her voice was weak, yet her words were throaty and filled with emotion, pain, and regret. I cried and sang, joining my voice with hers. Exhaustion overtook the two of us, and I was lulled into a fitful sleep.

When I awoke, Grandmother was no longer lying beside me. I walked toward the river to relieve myself and to drink. Grandmother was kneeling next to the riverbank with her head bowed low to the ground. She had gone to drink and pray alone to the great spirit. She did not stir as I approached her.

It was then that I realized that her eyes were open, but she was unseeing. I knelt down beside her. "Grandmother?" I asked and hesitantly placed my hand on her shoulder. She fell over away from me. "Grandmother, no!" I shook her, denying the possibility that she was lost to me. "No, no, no," I repeated.

I collapsed onto Grandmother's lifeless body and buried my face. The rush of the river carried my wails away in the wind. When my voice could no longer expel the fear that rose up within me, I sat back and wrapped my arms around my knees. I rocked back and forth as the morning sun wasted its rays overhead.

My physical needs won out over my fear, and my stomach growled. The sensation brought me back to the present. I had to figure out what to do about Grandmother. I needed to move on, but I couldn't just leave her there. I knelt beside her and quoted the words of blessing at death. I rolled her into a shallow place on the side of the river near where we had camped. I sang prayers to the great spirit. I could not risk the attention that a fire would inevitably bring, so I secured stones inside her clothing to weigh her down and rolled her over into the rushing water. I didn't linger long; there was nothing left for me.

I cautiously returned to the house. I noticed hoofprints in Grandfather's garden; soldiers and horses had been there. The wounded soldier was not anywhere to be seen. I crept around and peered into the window. The dead soldier, too, was gone. The kitchen had been ransacked, and many of our possessions had been carried away. More soldiers must have come and, finding Mother murdered, collected their dead and wounded and took whatever they wanted.

Before I ate, I needed to do something about Mother. I anointed her body with oils and herbs and wrapped her delicately in a sheet from our bed. I placed her body in a hand-cart that Grandfather used in his garden. It took all of my strength to roll Mother's dead body to the place where we had hidden Grandfather's from the soldiers. Again, I repeated the words of blessing for the dead. I sang a song of thanks for the mothers who had given me life and whom I had lost together on nearly the same day.

The soldiers had known nothing of healers; they knew only violence. They found a woman alone and took advantage of her. I ate and packed what little food remained. The soldiers had taken almost all of our provisions, but thankfully, the chest under Grandfather's bed was untouched. Mother's death was all the evidence I needed that it was not safe to stay there alone. I opened the chest and found Erik's old clothes. Grandfather's dulcimer and his cap were also among his things. I plucked the strings tentatively; I hadn't heard the familiar sound of the instrument in two years, not since before they both left me without their music.

I unwrapped my long, black hair from underneath its covering. I braided it carefully. I put on Erik's short tunic and leggings and soft leather boots he'd had when he arrived with us. I knelt and asked the great spirit for forgiveness for what I was about to do. I wept as I chopped my hair off with Grandmother's sheers. I wept for Mother. I wept for Grandfather. I wept for Grandmother, whose body lay under the stones at the bottom of the river, and finally, I wept for Erik, who had been taken to serve as a soldier and whose fate I had no way of knowing. I laid my long braid in place of Erik's things and traded my past for an unknown future.

The sun had set many hours before, so I allowed myself to rest until daybreak. I packed only what I could carry on my own. I took what little food remained and Grandfather's dulcimer. I took some herbs and Mother's book of remedies. I pulled Grandfather's cap over my bare head and did not look back on what had been my life.

Chapter Three

I foraged and fed myself from the land. For the next several months, I slept near trees and in small caves. I kept out of sight, and when I had to be with others, I wore Grandfather's cap and dressed as a boy. I missed the comforts of our home and the weekly baths in the pool. I missed my long hair.

At first, I rarely snuck into the city; so much had changed. Not just the healers, but all of the women bound their hair. It was unsafe, but I was drawn into the city more frequently. I found that I could play Grandfather's dulcimer for coins and scraps of food.

Everyone saw me as a boy. After all, I was thin and undernourished, and I wore Erik's clothes and Grandfather's cap. My short hair and lanky frame deceived everyone, and my ragged clothes kept others away. I no longer smelled of lilacs and lavender. After so long, I forgot how it was to wear girl's clothes. I hardly missed them, or perhaps memories and longing faded. My songs and prayers to the great spirit kept me safe.

The unmarried women in the market were all veiled. Once they grew into their womanhood, they no longer showed their faces. Claimed and mated women did not cover their faces but instead marked their eyes with a dark shadow that concealed their true beauty. Widows and women past child-bearing years wore no veil at all. Their wrinkled faces held no temptation for men.

For three years, I lived alone, surrounded by strangers. I never stayed long in one place. If a shopkeeper or street merchant noticed me or my face was familiar to them, I would move on and find another location to play the dulcimer and sleep.

When the city became too much for me, I would return to the woods for ease and rest. I would find a place to bathe and wash my clothes. I also needed privacy to cut my hair. Those times also brought me back to the great spirit. I could sing, unabated, renewing my voice and my soul.

Each time Grandfather's instrument earned me a coin or two, I thanked the great spirit that it was enough to keep me alive for another day. As time passed, I became quite good at playing the dulcimer.

With the palace symbol emblazoned on his tunic, a uniformed man watched me play from a distance. The silver and blue threads caught the light at every turn. Even in shadow, the emblem shone brightly. Every time I saw it, it reminded me of Mother's blue eyes and Grandfather's silver hair.

For three days, the officer returned and sought me out. For three days, he tossed a coin at my feet. Finally, on the fourth day, he spoke to me. "Boy!" he commanded. Apprehensively, I met his gaze. "Do you have a family?"

I was confused by his question, but I shook my head and answered honestly. "No, sir."

"Is that your instrument?" I nodded emphatically. I was afraid he thought I had stolen it.

"Come with me," he commanded.

I hesitated but knew I had no choice but to do as the soldier directed. I'd seen others whipped in the streets and brought down for theft and other crimes. I had no place to run, so I gathered up my few belongings and followed the stranger through town. He didn't ask my name, nor did he offer his. I had to take double steps to keep up with his long stride. He wasted no words on me, but I noticed that he looked back a few times to make sure I was keeping up.

To my surprise, he led me to the palace; I followed him into the back entrance. It was not as opulent as the side most citizens saw, but it was still heavily guarded and walled. The man I followed must have been of some importance because he was met with bowing heads and *sir* as we passed.

He went directly to the kitchen. I knew it had to be the kitchen because of the aromas that wafted through the entrance. My stomach rumbled, and I salivated. At that moment, I didn't much care why he had taken me to the palace. I only hoped for a morsel or two for my trouble.

Before he entered the kitchen, he stomped his boots. He then scraped the excess muck with a brush that was secured next to the entrance. He looked down at me and directed me to do the same.

"You'll be wise never to cross *her* threshold without first wiping your feet." I nodded solemnly, understanding. Mucky feet had no place in a kitchen; Grandmother had taught me that from an early age. I also wondered at his implication that I might have cause to cross that threshold again.

"Lucia," my escort called in a loud voice. Several women looked up but quickly returned to their work. "Where's Lucia?" he asked the closest woman to us. The woman gave no reply but gestured with her chin over her shoulder.

We had only taken a couple of steps when a woman rounded a brick partition. She was wearing a long tunic, covered by an apron. "Felix, could you possibly find a more inappropriate time to call?" Her voice was sharp, but I was thankful to know his name. She wiped her hands on her apron in a huff before she placed them on her hips. "What's this? Why have you brought this grimy little thing into my kitchen?" she asked, cutting her eyes disapprovingly toward me. I looked down at my hands. She must have mistaken my darker skin for filth.

By the deference he received when we entered the palace grounds, this soldier was in charge of men, and they feared and revered him. But by the way Lucia looked and spoke to him, he was not *her* superior. I understood why he had taken such care to wipe his boots.

"He plays music. It might help," Felix said low, so only Lucia and I could hear. She pursed her lips and nodded, eyeing me speculatively. Lucia's cheeks were flush like she was in a great hurry, but her face was only slightly creased with age. "See to this waif. See that he's presentable." His words were assertive, but his tone made them sound more like an entreaty than a command. Lucia's expression softened as she considered his request.

"Very well; I'll see to it."

"Thank you," Felix said and then turned to me and pointed his long finger in my face. "Mind yourself, boy, and do what she says," he warned.

"Yes, sir," I replied in a whisper.

Lucia sized me up with incriminating eyes before she called to another woman. "Myrtle, see to this. Make sure he's fed. He needs clothes and a bath. I want to inspect him before he's brought to the governor."

Myrtle curtsied at Lucia's command but then forced me to wash my hands and face in a basin before she sat me down at a table. Another woman placed a bowl of stew and a piece of bread in front of me. I couldn't believe my eyes.

"Thank you," I said, remembering to show my appreciation.

I ate everything set before me. I saved a piece of the bread to soak up the gravy from the bottom of the bowl. I couldn't remember the last time I had eaten an entire meal in one sitting. I thanked the great spirit and, with a full belly, sighed with satisfaction.

Myrtle continued to work while I ate. She chopped vegetables until I was finished. I placed my hands in my lap and waited amid the bustling and clatter of the kitchen. It was a busy place. Myrtle wiped her hands on her apron and motioned for me to follow her.

My apprehension grew as she led me down a long stone corridor. There were no windows, and the hallway was lit by sconces. There was only one way in and one way out. She led me into a room filled with tubs. Panic rose in my heart. I'd lived as a boy for three years. I had hidden my true nature for so long that I hadn't thought about the consequences until that moment.

I stepped back, away from the tub. Steam rose around us, but I knew it would not be enough to give me privacy. Myrtle sensed my hesitation. "It's just a bath, child. I don't intend to drown you," she laughed but soon lost all of her humor when I shook my head, refusing her.

24

She took hold of me, then, and wrestled me from my short tunic. Grandfather's cap came off at the same time. My hands flew instinctively to cover my chest and my head. Myrtle gasped and then laughed with surprise.

I was no longer a child, but my body refused to catch up with its years. I had only the budding of breasts. Again, this had given me protection and had allowed me to be unnoticed by men. In my current predicament, Myrtle most likely saw me as a girl of maybe two-and-ten, not six-and-ten.

"You're a girl!" she exclaimed. Myrtle blinked her eyes and took in my expression; my secret was known. She laughed again. "Won't that be a surprise for the master," Myrtle said sarcastically. She didn't comment on my black hair, but I'd cut it only days before, so perhaps it was too short to notice its exact color. She might not have been able to see anything else after the shock of knowing I wasn't a boy.

Myrtle was slightly more patient with me while she waited for me to remove my leggings and boots. I stepped into the tub and eased myself into the hot water. The old woman scrubbed me from head to toe, using extra force behind my ears. Thankfully, she realized that my skin color could not be removed with force. Her hands were coarse, and the soap she used smelled nothing like lilacs or lavender. A heavy scent of animal fat clung to the suds in the water.

She left me briefly and then dressed me in an elegant linen tunic and a cloak embroidered with delicate blue and silver stitches, identifying me as a palace resident. She covered my head in a matching wrap and placed satin slippers on my feet. My tunic was woven from soft linen, and the cuffs and hem were edged with silver thread. It was a little too big for me, but Myrtle assured me that I looked fine.

"Stay here," she said. "I'll be back for you."

I stroked the smooth fabric of my long tunic and marveled at the delicate stitches. They were lovely, and I liked the feel of the soft cloth against my clean skin. I had only waited a few moments before Myrtle returned with Lucia.

"Come, child," Myrtle said, and I moved toward them.

Lucia looked at me and blinked. "What's the meaning of this? I send you to bathe a boy, and you present me with a girl?" she asked.

"That's what she is," Myrtle retorted with a chuckle.

"What am I supposed to do with this?" Lucia asked. She looked me over and walked around me. Lucia placed one palm on her forehead. "Felix, you're a damn fool!" she muttered under her breath before she sighed in resignation. "What's your name?" Lucia asked impatiently.

"Phina," I said and swallowed nervously.

"Well, Phina, it's Felix's intention for you to play for the governor. If he's pleased with you, then you'll stay on in his service. If you don't, well, I have no idea what to do with you." She sighed aloud like the thought was too heavy a load to carry. "Let's not dwell on that. Come along. Are you hungry?"

I was relieved that she didn't cast me out, but I didn't want to appear too eager at the prospect of another meal. "Yes, ma'am, I am. Thank you."

Myrtle gathered up my boots and clothes in her arms. "If you please the governor, you won't be needing these anymore," she said. "What shall I do with them?" she asked Lucia.

Lucia looked at them distastefully. She wasn't a woman who abided by soiled clothes. "Burn them," she said dismissively.

"No, ma'am, please, not the boots and cap," I begged.

Lucia looked at me and considered. "Very well, put them in her room with her other belongings, but burn the rest."

Chapter Four

I was led back to the kitchen and seated at a different table. Curiously, the other women looked at me as I entered. "This is Phina," Lucia announced. "See that she's fed and watched after."

Again, like before, a bowl was placed in front of me. I ate, but my belly was still full from the meal I'd eaten earlier. I wasn't accustomed to so much food in one day. I placed my spoon down on the table, stuffed and satisfied. Myrtle noticed I'd finished and called from across the room, "Cassia, you have any more of those sweet rolls? This one's all skin and bones; she could do with some plumping up." The woman, Cassia, then offered me a roll with currants and cinnamon.

I was really too full to eat another bite, but the aroma made my mouth water, and I wanted it. "Thank you," I said and took the roll. I had never tasted anything so delicious in all of my days. Grandmother baked sweet cakes for special occasions, but the flavors were nothing in comparison.

My belly was full, and I was warm and relaxed after my bath. My clothes were soft and clean, and, for the first time in a long time, I wasn't fearful of someone knowing my true identity, nor did I have to scrounge for food or shelter. The stew and bread made my eyes heavy, so I leaned my head against the wall behind me, where I fell into a deep sleep amid the kitchen clatter.

Lucia roused me gently. "Phina," she said. I jerked up and sat straight. My eyes were wide, and my body went rigid at hearing my name. I hadn't been awakened like that since Mother. Lucia's gentleness confused me. I blinked before I remembered where I was and why I was there. "Phina, it's time," she said in her no-nonsense way.

"What am I to do?"

"You'll play for him." Lucia must have seen the confusion on my face.

"Who?" I asked.

"Felix didn't explain to you why he brought you here?" I shook my head. She rolled her eyes far into her head. She was either disappointed that I didn't understand or that Felix hadn't explained himself. "Felix found you; he says you play well." I nodded and gave a slight smile at the compliment.

Lucia pulled up a chair and sat down beside me. She spoke low so that no one else could hear. "You're here to play for the governor. Sometimes he needs help settling. Sometimes he has trouble sleeping." I nodded, understanding.

I caught bits of gossip in the city and knew that Gaius Julianus Astur was the new governor. The land had been conquered for a while, but the former governor had died. Now it was to be made over peacefully under this man's authority. I had seen the former governor twice from a distance, but I had never seen the new one. The former governor was an old man with wisdom at his temples and a face leathered by the sun. I wondered if the new governor looked the same.

Lucia explained that the governor liked music. My sole purpose was to soothe the governor, and it was my responsibility to calm him with my music when he was restless and could not sleep.

"If you please him, you will be given a room near his chambers. You will be mindful to pay attention to his comings and goings so that you are always at the ready, ready to play and obey. Do you understand?" I nodded again. "Stand, let look at you."

Lucia inspected me one more time before allowing Myrtle to take me directly to the governor's chambers. I followed closely behind the old woman and paid attention to where we walked. She moved slowly on the staircase that winded its way upward toward his private rooms.

Myrtle showed me the hallway that I was to use so as to not disturb my new master. "Servants are not to disrupt at any cost. You seem like a sensible child, so I won't be telling you twice." I nodded.

Myrtle then showed me the small quarters that I was to occupy. There was nothing ornamental in the room. A small bed was on one wall, and a low cabinet with three shelves stood across the room. Atop the cabinet was a pitcher and basin for washing. The window was small but offered plenty of light and fresh air. My instrument lay on the bed, and the sack holding my meager belongings, boots, and Grandfather's cap lay on the floor beside it.

Myrtle looked me over again. "Be at your best, and you'll be fine," she encouraged. "It's nearly nightfall. Wait here until he returns. Mind that you don't fall asleep again."

***

I heard heavy footfalls and deep murmurs and knew that men were approaching; their boots sounded solid against the stone. I hurriedly checked my head covering and held my instrument at the ready. I stood in the hallway that connected my small room to his. The sconces in his chambers were lit, yet I remained in shadows cast by the setting sun.

The governor came into his chambers in a huff with Felix at his heels. Their voices were loud and angry, causing me to back even further against the wall. Another man followed them into the room. His voice was haughty and weak in comparison to Felix and the governor's authoritative tones.

"As your advisor, sir, I must *advise* you on the best course. You cannot afford such a blunder." The governor rounded on the man threateningly, and without saying a word, the frail little man hastened from the room.

While the governor was occupied with his advisor, Felix caught sight of my instrument in the shadow. Recollection passed through Felix's eyes, and his mouth went up in a wry smile. The governor turned away from us, but I could hear his deep inhale of breath and his even louder exhale, calming himself.

"Sir, may I," Felix began but was abruptly cut off.

"I don't need any more advising, Felix. I've heard enough for one day."

"Sir, you misunderstand." Felix attempted to draw me from the shadows and introduce me, but he failed to get his master's attention.

"Leave me," the governor said abruptly.

"But sir," Felix interrupted.

"Go!" he bellowed, and I jumped. Felix cut his eyes at me apologetically. In his raised eyebrow, I read, *You're on your own, child.* Felix left as he was commanded.

I stood in the corner of the room, too afraid to move. The governor removed his cloak and tossed it over a sofa. He then ran his fingers through his hair in exasperation. He looked into the mirror and washed his face in the basin. When he lifted his face again, he saw me in the reflection. He turned with a start. His dark expression was hard to read, but I was unwelcome.

"What are you doing here?" I swallowed but was unable to speak. I opened my mouth, but nothing came out. "Are you a mute?" he asked impatiently. I shook my head quickly. "Then tell me why you are in my chambers and why I shouldn't cut you down for your insolence."

Instead of speaking, I lowered my gaze and knelt in the same motion that I lifted the dulcimer as an offering. Understanding, the governor snorted a derisive puff of air through his nose.

"Then play," he said, resigned.

I sat cross-legged under the long tunic and plucked the strings to adjust its tuning. I strummed the strings lightly and played. Lost in the music and avoiding my audience's scrutiny, I played to the best of my ability. When I finished the song, I looked up tentatively to assess his reaction. He stared at me with confusion and awe.

"What is your name?"

"Phina," I said in a whisper.

"Who taught you to play?"

"Grandfather and Erik," I said, and their names stung my heart.

He stared at me for a long time "Would you like me to play more?" I offered.

"No," he said. I lowered my gaze, afraid he was displeased with me. Would he send me away or cut me through as he'd threatened before?

"Leave me," he said.

I stood to my feet, scurried to my room, and slumped to the ground, nearly fainting on the spot from fear. My breaths caught, and I thought I might never again take in another full breath. Before I passed out, I remembered the governor's expression. His hair was light but short, clipped tightly around his head like a soldier's. He was younger than I had expected him to be. His hair revealed no traces of wisdom. His eyes were in shadow, but I thought they were brown. His most notable feature was his brow furrowed with creases too deep for a man too young for wisdom. He had not run me through, and I supposed that was by the merciful hand of the great spirit.

Chapter Five

I woke in the night, startled and confused. I heard murmurs and thrashing from outside my room. I blinked in the dark and, in a few moments, found my bearings. I took up my instrument that I'd been clutching in my sleep and tiptoed into my master's chamber. He fought some unknown force in his dreams. The governor's head moved back and forth, and his broad shoulders and muscles tensed and went rigid as he struggled against his night terrors.

I watched him for a few moments before I remembered that I was supposed to soothe him with my music. I sat on the floor at the foot of his bed and strummed softly, not wanting to wake him. I observed him as I played, and gradually, his body eased into a restful sleep.

***

Before the sun was up, I opened my eyes to the toe of a boot and a gruff voice. "Get up; go to bed," the voice commanded over me.

I dared not look up into his face and kept my gaze diverted. I pushed myself up from the floor stiffly. I was accustomed to sleeping on the ground, but I wasn't accustomed to staying up all night playing and watching someone sleep.

I sat up to clear my head. I blinked but couldn't shake the sleep from my eyes. My head bobbed sleepily. I heard my master give an impatient huff, yet I was too sleepy to stand. Strong arms lifted me, but when my feet gave way underneath me, those same strong arms scooped me up and carried me to my bed. He placed me gently onto the soft mattress, and I couldn't fight the exhaustion that took me back into sleep.

When I woke the second time, Myrtle stood over me. "Get up, child," she commanded. "Master says you're to have whatever you need, so apparently, you pleased him enough to stay." Myrtle walked across the room and laid a change of clothing on the shelf. She placed my slippers on the floor next to my boots. Myrtle lifted my sack and opened it, examining the contents. She pulled out Mother's book. "Why on earth do you carry this heavy thing around?"

I stood and protectively snatched the book and sack from her hands. "It was Mother's," I defended, clutching the book to my chest.

"Do you read?" she asked.

"Yes, ma'am," I said proudly.

She eyed me again and almost looked angry, like I was lying to her. "Who'd bother to teach a waif to read?"

"I wasn't always a waif." My tone fell flat, and Myrtle noticed the change in my expression.

She laughed and picked up Grandfather's cap, running her finger into a hole. "This needs mending. I can do it for you," she offered. Perhaps she was kind, or maybe she thought that I'd spent all my efforts on learning to read and not learning to sew.

"I can do it myself. I just need a needle and thread." I wasn't sure she believed me capable, but she didn't argue.

I followed Myrtle down to the kitchen and ate a meal. "You'll come down here and eat," she instructed. "You'll bathe and keep after yourself and stay out of trouble when you're not needed. Lucia can't spare anyone to watch you all day." I offered no reply. I'd been looking after myself for a long time, and I was relatively good at keeping out of trouble. "Stay in the walls of the palace; it isn't safe out there." I felt a wry smile twitch my lips. "No wonder you were hiding as a boy," she remarked. We shared a knowing glance. She laughed, remembering the surprise. "Can you find your way back and forth?" she asked.

"Yes, ma'am," I answered politely.

"Good, be about your business, then," she said curtly and dismissed me.

***

The days that followed were solitary, but that was not unusual for me. I was allowed to sleep in safety and for as long as I pleased. I ate in the kitchen, read and studied Mother's book, and gathered useful things for my room. I was given a needle and thread, and one morning Lucia presented me with a brush and mirror.

I reflexively touched the fabric that covered my head. I felt self-conscious that I had no hair to brush. "Let it grow," she whispered, reading my sadness. A woman's hair was a crown. It was revered, and although healers kept their hair braided and bound, it gave us comfort and strength. Lucia would not know that of me, but still, I appreciated her thoughtfulness.

Lucia was a stern woman who commanded respect from everyone. When her face was at rest or when she was kind, the lines at the corners of her eyes were barely noticeable. Her hands were worn from work but not from age. I wanted to ask if she was a young widow like Mother had been, but I didn't want to offend her or make her sad.

Those early nights were much like my first. I would wait until my master's arrival, I would play a song or two, and then he would dismiss me. By the third night, I didn't go to sleep. I stayed awake, anticipating his fitful dreams.

On the fourth night, I waited until he was in bed and then sat at the entrance to his room and played a lullaby to lull him into sleep. To stay awake and keep my head clear, I whispered the words of the song to myself. The great spirit heard them and brought restful slumber to my master. As long as I played, he didn't stir or fight the unknown forces in the night. A few nights, he even snored.

Sometime between the moon's departure and the sun's arrival, I would fall into a deep sleep. The powerful wave washed over me, and I was helpless to fight it off. After that first morning, my master didn't bother to wake me, and I found myself in my own bed, covered with a blanket. I wept at his kindness and thanked the great spirit for bringing me there and allowing me to use my musical gift. I gave thanks for the regular meals and safety I'd been granted within the palace walls.

My master and I shared no discourse. He had no reason to speak to me directly, and I was relieved. The tone he used with his advisor and even with Felix was unsettling. I feared that if I weren't careful, he'd use that same tone with me.

In many ways, I was still a child, curious and fascinated by the palace. I wandered the corridors and empty rooms and happened upon a room filled with books and scrolls. There was a large table where maps had been laid out upon it. I saw the mark for the palace and traced my finger over the parchment. I touched the river and followed it along to my former home. I rubbed it gently, fondly remembering the cottage and my family, and resolved to pray for Erik, wherever he might be.

I took a large volume from a low shelf. I opened it carefully and began reading. Before the end of the first chapter, the adventure of a great warrior and his horse drew me in. When I heard boots approaching, I slammed the book shut. I hadn't been given permission to be there, and I didn't want to be caught.

I crawled between a sofa and a desk and crouched low. Men's voices carried along with their boots. I strained my ears. It sounded like Felix and my master's advisor, whose name I had learned was Marcus. I wondered if my master was with them.

Their tones sounded milder and less angry, less insistent than usual. Then, I heard my master's voice. "That's a good idea, Marcus. Proceed. Meet with the senators; let them know my decision."

"Thank you, sir," Marcus said, and I heard his boots walk away.

"That was unexpected," Felix said when he thought they were alone.

"It makes sense. I need to make some concessions to appease them."

"Concessions," he repeated disbelievingly, and then his voice was sober. "You seem to have a clearer mind; you're well-rested." His comment was not a question.

"Yes, thank you." There was silence for a few heartbeats. "Her talent is amazing."

"Who?" Felix asked.

"The girl, Phina," my master said. I jerked at hearing my name.

"I didn't send you a girl. If I thought a *girl* could help you sleep, I would have sent you a new one every night."

I didn't like the implication of how those *girls* would have pleased my master. Living on the streets made me wary of men and even warier of women used for such purposes.

"Well, Phina is most definitely a girl, and she plays the dulcimer very well."

Felix scoffed, "I found a waif on the street and watched him play for three days before I brought him to the palace. I sent you a boy; I didn't know." His voice was sharp and defensive.

"It's fine, Felix. I've accepted her and made her welcome. She's a child. She's not a woman, and I want to keep her music."

It amused me that he thought me a child. Until my body decided otherwise, I would have to accept it. A surge of pride rose in my heart, hearing that my master was well-rested and wanted to keep my music. I would continue to do my best to please him.

The two men discussed other topics while I remained hidden. I didn't understand everything they said, but I knew it was important to the region's running. They talked about troops and reinforcing borders. They spoke of men they held in high regard and their accomplishments. Felix reported about the punishment of others who had broken the code of conduct.

I felt sickened at the thought of punishment. While living on the streets, I'd witnessed numerous beatings and a handful of executions. After those occasions, I would retreat to the woods and resolve to stay there forever. Punishment under the governor's law was swift and severe.

It was a long time before Felix and the governor left me. My legs had gone numb in the cramped space. As I struggled to pull myself out, I looked up into the questioning eyes of Myrtle. She grabbed me by the elbow and pulled me up from the floor.

"What are you doing here?" she asked with her hands on her hips; she looked perturbed.

"I found a book," I said.

"Like you even read, girl!" she protested.

"But I do read!" I argued, matching her tone. "Would you like me to prove it to you?" I opened the book and read it.

Myrtle's reaction wasn't as great as finding me out to be a girl, but she was surprised nonetheless. She laughed, and I found that I liked that part of her. She had a way of easing the tension and quickly accepting a situation, even when it surprised her.

"Ask before you take anything from this room," she advised. She guided my chin with her fingers and looked me over. She looked disapprovingly at my face. I didn't know what she saw there, but it didn't please her. "You need some fresh air. A room full of musty old books is no place for a child. Find your way, and take a stroll in the garden. Stay there until you come for your supper."

Upon entering the garden, I was greeted by the smell of grass and flowers. I made my way along the garden path. I stood at the edge for a long time and looked over the wall onto the city below. It was a very different view of the city than what I knew of it. The foul odors of horses and urine couldn't make it past the high walls. The voices of the citizens didn't make it up that high either. There were murmurs, but the words were indiscernible.

I took note of the plants and spoke their names aloud. Many of them were unfamiliar to me, but I was determined to learn all of their names. Surely, there was a book in the vast library that I could consult. I was happy to recall all of the flowers I recognized. They seemed to appreciate hearing their names as well. When I found a small section of the garden devoted to herbs and medicinal plants, I knelt down in front of it and wept.

"Grandfather," I cried his name in thanks and found myself smiling through tears. If I hadn't known better, I would have suspected Grandfather had cultivated that garden just for me. Examining the overgrowth and the woody, mature bases, the plants were old, possibly planted before the invasion when healers were still called to the palace.

"You are for fever," I said, touching the plant whose leaves could be ground up and made into tea. I pointed to three more plants. "You are for pain, you are for stomach aches, and you are for slumber." I wondered if my master would allow me to make a tincture for him to help him sleep. I looked over some of the plants and was surprised to find a long vine creeping toward two other plants. When eaten, the fruit of the vine made a woman fertile, but if a woman had conceived, she would have to be careful of the seeds. When consumed, the seeds would bring on her bleeding and cause death to the child. In milder doses, extracts from the seeds could induce a woman's labor.

On one particular occasion, a woman came seeking healing. It was rare that someone left disappointed, and Mother was deeply saddened by the woman's request. Mother explained that some women did not desire a child and would ask for the seeds to expel it from her womb.

"Why would a mother not want a child made from her love?" I asked.

"I cannot speak for every woman's heart, but there are times," she hesitated, "there are times when a woman conceives a child out of union with her mate or if she is taken by force. Those are times of great fear, and she is left with a constant reminder in her child's eyes."

Mother warned me most gravely that the seeds could kill the mother along with the child if she had carried it more than a few months. "Be mindful of the moon cycles before you allow a woman to use the seeds." Mother had the seeds, but she did not allow the woman to have them. That was not a healer's way. We could not harm more than we healed, and putting that woman at risk would do more harm than good.

Returning to my vine and two of its closest neighbors, I said, "Well, I haven't seen you in a while." The two were rightly planted together. "You can kill, and you, my prickly friend, can save." The tall, beautiful plant held a potent poison from its roots to its petals. The roots could kill, whereas the soft petals only induced deep sleep. Its thorny counterpart was not much to look at, but its powers to heal were in every bit of its fiber. It could expel poison in various forms, renew vigor, and bring life back to someone who had ingested the poison.

There was no fruit on the vine, but I cleared a path for it to crawl and meander its way along the ground where it belonged. I lost myself as I pulled and weeded the small space for hours, taking in the fresh air and the sunshine. The small plot was overgrown and untended, but when I rose for my supper, I was pleased with the progress I'd made.

When I entered the kitchen, Myrtle gasped. "Where have you been, child?"

"In the garden, where you told me to go."

"I told you to take a walk, not roll around in it." I looked down at my tunic and realized my kneeling had soiled it. I had been too excited to remember an apron.

"I was tending to a patch in the garden."

"Well, you're filthy. Wash your hands and eat. You'll need bathing and changing before you return to your room. He can't be seeing you like this."

"Yes, ma'am," I replied and devoured my supper so that I would have time to ready myself for my master's return.

Chapter Six

It was late when my master entered his chambers. He looked exhausted. I was curious to know sometimes where he went and how he spent his days. I had spent my day in the garden, and I felt renewed by spending time with the soil and plants.

I resolved to return daily to the garden and to ask permission to use the library. It took a lot to muster my courage. I hoped that he would be in a pleasant mood and receptive to my request. I had overheard him with Felix and reminded myself that my music pleased him, so I hoped that was enough.

There was a low stool in my usual spot. It was covered with a soft tuft of fabric. Before I sat down, I hesitated and looked up in question at the governor.

"It's for you," he said. "It's better than sitting on the floor all night." His brown eyes were soft; he was doing me a kindness.

"Thank you, sir." I sat and readied myself to play. "Thank you, too, for seeing me to my bed. I can't seem to manage to get there on my own." He nodded like it was of little consequence.

I strummed the strings, bringing the instrument to life. The air in the room settled. He sat at a table and read through scraps of parchment. He nibbled from a plate of food while I played.

I changed the tune and played a livelier melody that reflected my good mood. He looked up from his correspondence and sat back. He crossed his legs at his ankles and his arms across his chest, listening and watching.

"That one is new," he commented.

"Yes, sir. Do you find it to your liking?" I asked.

"Indeed."

I felt he was about to return to his work and dismiss me, so I knew it might be my only chance to ask his permission. "Sir." The word came out in a breathy whisper. I cleared my throat and began again, "Sir, may I make a request of you?"

His brow rose with curiosity as he considered my words. "If it is reasonable and within my power, I don't see why I couldn't." I lowered my eyes and smothered the giggle that threatened to escape. Warmth rose to my cheeks. "What amuses you?" he asked, and I could hear a smile in his voice.

"You are the governor; isn't everything in your power?" I asked, and it was hard to hide a genuine smile.

His broad shoulders relaxed, and he seemed amused with my comment but quickly humbled himself. "That's not entirely so, but within the walls of this palace, my word carries weight. What do you wish?" he asked.

"I wish for permission to use your library."

Without considering my request, he quickly replied, "What would you need in there? It's filled with parchment and dusty, old books."

"I know; I wish to read them, and I would like to find a book about the plants in the garden."

"There is no one to teach you to read," he said flatly.

The same irritation that had surfaced with Myrtle forced me from my stool, and suddenly, I was standing. My hand was on my hip, and the words flew through my lips before I could stop them.

"I can read," I said forcefully. "I don't know what else Felix told you, but I am not an ignorant waif." I could feel angry tears pooling in my eyes.

41

My master considered my words and cocked his head to one side. "Were you in the library today?" I nodded. He set his jaw. "You overheard our conversation."

"Yes, sir."

"Were you spying on me?"

"No, sir. I was curious and happened upon the books by accident. I was reading when you came, and I didn't want to be seen. I was afraid. I'm sorry."

I wished at that moment that I could scurry behind a piece of furniture or run back into my room, but I knew that would not be allowed. I was not free to do my own will, and I would have to accept my consequences.

"Who taught you?" he asked accusingly.

I was surprised by his question. "My family."

"They must have had a great deal of leisure to waste their time in such a manner."

Could he be so foolish to think it was a waste of time to teach a girl to read? I couldn't tell if he was teasing me or provoking me. "They didn't see it that way."

"Where are they now?"

"Dead." I swallowed back the pain that pressed against my heart at the thought of them.

"The same family who taught you to play?" I nodded. "They taught you well." I nodded again.

There was silence between us, then, and I felt compelled to fill it. "The music is what brought me to your palace, but that is not my true gift."

"Really?" he asked skeptically. "What gifts does a girl of so little age and consequence have?" he asked condescendingly.

"I am a healer, or I was intended to be so from birth."

"A healer?" he asked. "You are too young, and besides, women are not healers."

I was young, but no one knew my years. Plenty of girls my age were betrothed, and some already had children of their own. I had hidden as a boy for three years, yet now I was hiding behind my youthful face and slight body.

"Yes, sir. Not in your kingdom, but before the invasion, women were a great many things."

I didn't mean for my words to challenge him, but he lifted his chin, and I recognized the familiar look of displeasure. He'd gone from amusement to annoyance in a matter of moments. I lowered my gaze toward the floor because I knew it wasn't my place to challenge him or the king's authority over our land.

"Phina." I looked up at my name. His brown eyes were kind again. "You may read whatever you like, but with conditions." I held my breath until I heard his words. "You must keep this knowledge to yourself. You may read in your room or alone in the garden, but the library is not a place for you to linger. Do you understand?" I nodded.

"Thank you, sir," I said with emotion. Tears of relief threatened this time. I wiped my cheeks and smiled self-consciously. "You have made me exceedingly happy, sir." My words broke as I choked back the tears that broke free, suddenly flooded by relief and anticipation of new knowledge.

"You're free to go," he said. He could tell it was too much to hold myself together in his presence.

Chapter Seven

I learned a great deal in the early months of my service at the palace. I spent hours at a time in the garden, sometimes reading, sometimes tending to the patch of medicinal plants. Following Mother's instructions, I began harvesting and drying them or grinding them. Lucia had been instructed to give me whatever I might need, and she rarely questioned my requests. She allowed me to take small bottles and other odds and ends that helped me organize and build up my stores. She also allowed me to bring a small table upstairs to my room. It took me an hour to maneuver it up the stairs.

Except for the crones who cooked and tended to the chambers, no other women lived in the palace. There were no children or babies, either, save one, me, and technically, I was no longer a child. My body simply mocked me.

After that night, the night I'd asked to read his books, I found that my master was not obverse to light conversation when I played quietly. He almost welcomed it. I craved the dialogue, and other than the old women's chatter in the kitchen or the bath, I had very little interaction. When he was not in his chambers, I was allowed to read and study and listen to the way of things.

"How does a man with no wisdom at his temples come to such a high position?" I asked as I strummed absentmindedly.

"The spoils of war and privilege," he stated flatly. I did not understand his meaning and looked up into his brooding eyes. "The king is my uncle, my mother's brother," he explained. "While serving as a soldier, I was injured. My mother begged her eldest brother, the king, to give me a position as far from the front line as possible. Little did she know that her request was more perilous than any battle I waged during the siege."

"What do you mean?" I asked

"The governor is forced to deal with politicians. They are more dangerous than any enemy I've encountered, thus. They are back-stabbing and ruthless, constantly squabbling and bickering. I've had men whipped for less dissension and hung for their insolence. At least, I knew my soldiers had my back, and I could rest knowing they weren't undermining my authority at every turn."

"Did you serve with Felix?" I asked.

"Indeed. Felix is a good man and was my commanding officer for a short time before I was promoted. Again, probably a perk of being the king's nephew."

"You did not deserve the promotion?"

He sighed. "I supposed I had earned it to some degree on my own merits, but I was very young when I was thrust into a position of independence."

"I understand." And I did. At the age of three-and-ten, I, too, had been thrust into independence. I concentrated on the instrument, but I could feel his eyes on me. His brown eyes were intense and focused. They sparkled when he laughed and flashed when he was angered, but mostly they just watched.

"What happened to your family?" he asked in a low voice.

I took a deep breath and diverted my eyes. I strummed simple chords to keep the music going, but my heart had left the song. I shook my head, but it wasn't a refusal. The thoughts of them were just too painful. The memory of them was something I avoided, but he was my master and the governor, so I dared not refuse to answer his question.

I took another breath before I spoke. "They were all taken from me. First, Erik was conscripted. He was taken by the soldiers, and we never heard from him again. A year later, Grandfather died. He was very old, and it was his time to pass from this world to be with the great spirit."

Erik and Grandfather were more natural to speak of, but it was still painful. "Grandmother died after she," my voice faltered, "after she got me to safety."

"What of your mother and father?"

My father didn't cause pain to speak of because I had never known or loved him. "My father was a soldier whose ship sank, and he drowned before I was born. I never knew him, but Mother loved him, and from that love, they had created me." I smiled, remembering Mother's retelling, but it was bittersweet.

I'm sure he saw the pain that crossed my expression, and a few moments of silence passed between us before he asked, "And your mother?"

I blinked back the tears that burned and finally gave up the fight. I closed my eyes and let the tears leak down my cheeks. I kept playing until the drops plopped onto my instrument. I wiped my face with my sleeve and then dried the tears that had fallen onto the dulcimer.

"Phina, I don't mean to cause you pain." His voice was low and soothing; he was sincere. I sniffed and dabbed my eyes. "Please, Phina, I would like to know. Look at me."

I nodded, but my throat was closed. I settled myself so that I could speak. I silenced the instrument and mustered up the courage to look him in the eye. I shivered and wrapped my arms around myself.

"It will anger you," I confessed.

Confusion darkened his expression. "I don't understand."

No one knew anything about me or where I'd come from. My master was the only one who ever asked about things beyond my ability to read and play music. Felix, Lucia, and Myrtle knew bits, but this man was the only one who ever asked directly.

"We heard her screaming in the house. Grandmother and I were milking the goats." My voice sounded off. "Soldiers came into our home, and we were without a man to protect us." I left the story to settle my body. I had never spoken the words aloud. I diverted my gaze and shook my head to scatter the images of Mother being ravaged and slaughtered.

"What ill befell her?" he asked.

How could he be so crass and unfeeling? My expression must have been one of shock. I glared into his eyes. "Ill?" I asked incredulously. "No ill befell her! Soldiers, your soldiers, raped her, and when she fought them to protect me, they… they… they slit her throat!" My words were choppy and breathy as my body shook, and I gulped for air. "Had… had… had we not run, they wou… wou… would have come after me, too."

I was right. Anger flashed in his eyes, and I recoiled when he leaped from his chair toward me. "I'm sorry!" I screamed, afraid he'd strike me for my disrespectful tone and for accusing his soldiers of such injustice. I clung to the dulcimer and shielded my face reflexively.

In a breath, he was kneeling in front of me, and his strong hands were on my shoulders. I wailed and tried to move away from him but, in my panic, slid from my stool. He caught me before I fell to the floor. I pushed him away from me, fearful of the anger in his eyes and trapped in the memory of the soldier holding Mother. I screamed.

"Phina," he said sharply and shook me to get my attention. I whimpered and muffled a wail that threatened to escape. "Phina," he whispered. "Shhhh," he soothed and pressed my head into his chest. His muscular frame enveloped me as his arms wrapped around me. He held me securely until the sobs and pants subsided.

It had been so long since I'd been held or hugged that I'd forgotten the comforting touch of another person. He was warm and smelled of sandalwood and myrrh. In my state of hysteria, I dropped my instrument. I clung to him, both arms wrapped as far as I could reach around him. Finally, my sobs abated, but he didn't release me right away.

"Phina, will you be alright if I let you go?" My tears soaked into his shirt. I could feel the dampness on my cheek.

I squeezed him tightly and refused to release him. His kindness continued, and he held me a little longer. Desperately, I clung to him, not wanting to let him go. He pressed his cheek onto the top of my head and shushed me some more. He rocked me slightly in his arms like he was comforting a very young child. I supposed in his eyes, I was.

When he placed his hand on my back and drew me closer, I was flooded by confusion. My stomach tightened with a feeling I had never felt before. My mind was conflicted by the knowledge that the comfort I felt in his arms was stirring something deep within me. I was teetering between childhood and womanhood, and I suddenly fell into the unknown.

Sensing the change, my master eased me away from him and looked into my eyes. He gently wiped the remaining tears from my face. "There, there, you're going to be fine. You're safe here; no one will harm you."

My eyes blinked wide, and I nodded. His words were encouraging. Without his warmth, I was cold and shivered, or that may have been from nerves. I felt small and insecure. Although it confused me, I liked the feel of his arms around me, and I especially liked his warmth. That surprised me; he was warm. It was a strange sensation but not unpleasant.

"Go to bed," he stated. It wasn't a harsh command like he sometimes gave Marcus and Felix, but it was firm and authoritative. I stood and walked toward my room. I was dazed. "Phina," he called after me. I turned, and he offered me the dulcimer. I took it from his hand.

"Thank you, sir," I said, and my emotion leached from the words. My appreciation for him doubled.

"Get some rest. There's no need to come to me. I can do without you for one night." He thought I needed a night to rest.

"Yes, sir." I turned and walked sluggishly to my room. I removed my head covering and brushed through the spikes of hair growing out full and black as raven's wings. I put on the nightdress that I rarely wore and eased myself between the covers of my bed. Sleep crashed solidly down upon me.

***

I woke to a thump and a curse. I heard the sound of water being poured from a pitcher and into a cup. I jumped when I heard a crash. I sat up, startled. The governor was muttering something indiscernible. I heard him get back into

48

bed and settle himself again for sleep. I listened for a long time. I had grown accustomed to being awake at night, so my sleep had refreshed me. Although he'd dismissed me, my fingers were eager to play and soothe him back to sleep, as was my habit and duty.

I crept from my bed and took my instrument. Focused on my task, I didn't think to dress or cover my head. I didn't even bother to find my little stool in the dark. I played low and unobtrusively. Soon, I was settled in the music and knew my master was too.

Chapter Eight

The sun was bright in the sky when I awoke the next day. I stretched my body long and comfortably underneath the warm covers. I scratched my unwrapped head. My thoughts were heavy, and I wondered if I had dreamed the events of the night before. I sat up and realized that I was in my own bed and covered with a blanket from my master's chambers.

Unless I had dreamed the whole encounter, my master had most likely seen me in my nightdress, and he had to have seen my black hair. It would have been an unnatural color to him. Fear gripped me, and I knew instantly that it wasn't a dream. How could I have been so remiss as to forget my head covering?

***

For a week, the palace was in a flurry of preparation. Lucia was more commanding than usual. Myrtle looked flushed and bothered. Cassia baked night and day.

"Why are you preparing so much food?" I asked Myrtle. I didn't dare interrupt Lucia.

"Of course, the feast, child."

"What feast?" I asked.

"The annual Governor's Feast. The palace must be at its best for the celebration. All of the most notable citizens will be present. This is our governor's first feast, and we want to make a great impression. Without a lady at the governor's side, Marcus and Lucia are left to the details. It's terribly consuming. It's also time for the daughters to be presented. If one of them finds favor, perhaps he'll find a suitable mate. He needs a woman to make his life easier. His mother will also be in attendance. She's arriving from the capital tomorrow. She'll see that everything's done right."

Myrtle's gossip was a constant chatter while she worked. She could've called upon me to do something, but Lucia had reprimanded Myrtle the first time she handed me a knife and set me to chopping vegetables.

"What do you think you're doing?" Myrtle and I looked up at Lucia's scolding. Although it had been a while, I knew how to work in the kitchen. I was competent with knives and garden tools. Lucia jerked the knife from my hand and jabbed it, point down, into the wooden chopping board. "She'll surely cut her fingers off, and then where will we be? We can't risk her hands for anything. Do you understand?"

"I can help Cassia with the dough," I offered amid the haste the day before the feast. Cassie looked up, hopeful at the prospect of another set of hands.

Lucia nodded but then warned, "Mind yourself, not too close to the fire."

***

After I kneaded rolls and loaves all afternoon with Cassia, I'd been dismissed. I was given a tray of food and told to stay in my room, out of sight. Nearly every window in the palace was illuminated with a candle or lantern. Torches had been lit all over the gardens and throughout the grounds. It was a magical transformation.

Guests arrived, senators and ladies. Lucia warned me to keep to my room for the evening, so I peered over the wall of my master's balcony to get a better look. It wasn't wholly obedient, but the palace's excitement and flurry made me curious to see more.

I had never ventured onto my master's balcony. I'd kept to my assigned path back and forth to the kitchen, obscuring any view of the garden. From my master's chambers, I could see my little patch of medicinal herbs and plants. The balcony offered shade on sunny days, and fragrant blooms clung to the trellis beneath it. I hadn't imagined it being so near to where I slept. My window was on the other side and offered little view. I looked across the garden toward the other windows and rooms. The library was a floor below and just above the kitchen.

I turned my focus on the guests and celebration below. The female guests were not veiled, and the younger ones had left their hair unbound. I peered more intently to take in all of their elegance and beauty. By the looks of their tunics and headwraps, the women who arrived were wealthy, escorted by men of importance. Their colorful cloaks and tunics showed brightly under the torchlight as they walked together in the garden.

I supposed the men and women who stayed together were mated couples, but the young women whose hair fell freely down their backs and across their shoulders seemed to form their own groups. They all looked about my age, but their bodies were fuller and curvy. They had breasts and rounded hips.

Now that my hair was growing out, I missed the way it felt on my shoulders. Seeing them made me long for things that I didn't have. Envy, I felt envy for the first time in my life. Mother and Grandmother had been bright with laughter, and I'd also spent time with the women in the kitchen, but these ladies were different in many ways. I had never encountered so many young ladies together in clusters. Their voices and laughter carried up toward the balcony.

I felt a pang in my chest at the thought of my master choosing one of those young women to be his mate. I didn't want to harbor ill will toward anyone, especially someone I did not know, so I whispered a prayer to the great spirit that my master would choose wisely.

My master walked into the garden later in the evening and greeted his guests in turn. I presumed the woman at his side was his mother. She was a tall woman with an elegant headwrap that encircled her neck and continued gracefully down across her shoulders. I knew she had arrived, but I didn't know her. The garden quieted upon their entrance, and I could hear his voice clearly as he spoke to his guests.

"Astur, you didn't tell me that Cato would be attending," his mother said as she directed her son toward another group. The man, Cato, stepped forward and greeted my master's mother affectionately. He took her hand and kissed it.

"Madam, you look lovely this evening. Your beauty puts every other woman to shame," Cato said with a flourish.

My master's mother smiled at the compliment and laughed in a way that both accepted and denied his words simultaneously. "Cato, you scoundrel. Your new position suits you. How is life as a young senator?"

"Grueling," he said with a sly smile. "Your son, here, has us at our wit's end. He won't budge an inch. Maybe you could help him see clearly the way of things."

"Oh, no, my dear Cato. I gave that battle up long ago. You'll have to deal with him as the governor, now."

Cato turned to my master, then, and said in a loud voice that carried up and around the guests and into my ears, "Governor, why is there no music in the garden? I can hardly stand the doldrums. Will you be enacting the Governor's Privilege this year?" His comment was met with snickers and giggles. "With so many lovely ladies on parade, surely you'll find one who might suit you."

The kitchen women had gossiped about the Governor's Privilege, a tradition that gave the governor the *privilege* to choose any young woman to spend the night of the feast with him. Other men could also stake their claim on any woman the governor did not select. After that night, the chosen young woman would be sent back to her home with coins and gifts, but she was never guaranteed to have a mate of her own after that.

"Give a cue, sir, and let me know your choice. I'll be happy to take what's left over," Cato said and was greeted with cheers and raised goblets.

"Now, Cato, I'm sorry to disappoint you, but you know that won't happen as long as I'm governor," he said, pacifying the crowd with a smile.

"I know; we all know your upstanding reputation. Word has it, Governor, that you keep no mistress, that you keep no women at all in the palace." I didn't like the tone that Cato implied.

My master gave no reply but allowed himself to appear distracted by some guests passing in front of him. He nodded politely and then finally returned his attention back to Cato. He smiled and asked, "Wherever would you hear such a thing?"

"You know how we senators like our chatter."

"All too well, I do."

Others piped in with their comments. "Why would he need to keep women?"

"The land has never been so peaceful; he's an excellent governor."

"He has no need for a woman."

"I hear he has a muse, a minstrel, who plays all night and weaves slumber songs," an older man jested.

"With sleep like that, why would he need a woman?" a man's voice bellowed in agreement. There was tittering and a few snickers. The small circle of guests was amused.

"I, too, have heard you have your own minstrel. One who plays quite nicely from what we hear," a middle-aged woman with haughty eyes said knowingly.

"A minstrel, you say," Cato said. "How delightful. Well, let the lad play for us."

"Not a lad, Cato, a young girl." The woman's tone eluded to something akin to gossip.

"Perhaps you would share *her* with us all. Since you won't indulge us with the Governor's Privilege, you will indulge us with music."

My master's eyes flashed with anger, but he considered Cato before he said anything. More guests moved closer to investigate. Everyone was eager to hear the conversation. I felt uneasy, waiting for his words.

My master cut his eyes upward toward his balcony. Could he see me? Did he know I was watching and listening to everything below? My heartbeat quickened, and I could feel fear wash over me. No one said anything for a long time, or maybe I couldn't hear because my heart was beating in my ears.

I saw him motion for Felix. He whispered something into Felix's ear, and Felix nodded and left the garden. I lowered myself to the ground behind the balcony wall. I needed to move, but I was too afraid that Felix was on his way upstairs.

If I stayed on the balcony, then maybe, just maybe, Felix wouldn't find me. I had been instructed to stay in my room for the night; I might be punished if I wasn't brought to the governor right away.

I didn't linger long on the balcony. Felix found me in my room with my instrument. I'd already checked my headwrap and tunic. When I heard his boots on the stone, I stood near the door. He looked at me for a few seconds before he spoke. He knew I was waiting for him, but he didn't ask how I knew.

"The governor wishes for you to play for his guests." I nodded. "Are you ready?" I nodded again. "You know, you're allowed to speak to me."

I looked up at him, surprised by his comment. "Yes, sir. I know."

He smirked. "You were a convincing boy. I watched you for three days; you had me fooled, and that's not easily done. Lucia thought I'd pulled one over on her. I wish I'd been in on it." His tone was playful. He smiled down at me. I liked the way his eyes twinkled. They reminded me of Grandfather's when he was amused. Felix had a good heart; I could tell that instantly.

Felix's long strides made it hard to keep up. It had been hard enough in leggings and boots, but a long tunic and slippers made it nearly impossible. "Felix," I panted. "Please, I can't keep up with you."

He turned and looked back over his shoulder. He stopped and waited for me. When we resumed, Felix paced his steps with mine. "Tonight is an important night for your master. Play your best," he encouraged.

Felix led me to the garden, but I already knew the way well. He put his hand on my shoulder and told me to wait until I was called. When the governor saw Felix approaching from the shadows, his eyes relaxed slightly. My master said something that I couldn't hear, and Felix motioned for me to come forward. I looked around and saw the guests who had gathered. The crowd had nearly doubled in size.

When I walked forward, I had to pass in front of Cato. His expression was passive, but his grin made me uncomfortable. I did not want to perform and play for this Cato. Unlike Felix, I did not trust him at all.

As I approached, the comments began. "She's only a child."

"Why, she could fit in the governor's hand."

"I wonder why he keeps her? You don't suppose he indulges himself with a child?"

"Maybe she's his kin."

"Maybe she's a pet, a plaything."

I looked into my master's eyes and blinked. My master could sense my apprehension. Although he didn't smile, his eyes were kind. I stood in front of him, waiting on his direction.

"I wish for you to play for my guests," he said loud enough for everyone to hear. His words were full of authority, and I could not refuse them, but he was making a request of me. He wished for me to share my music.

"Yes, sir," I whispered. Only he and his mother were close enough to hear. "Where shall I play?" My voice stayed small. I was nervous, but I tried hard not to show it.

His mother glanced around and motioned toward an empty bench. The crowd parted, and I walked a few feet toward it. I settled myself and checked the instrument's tuning.

"Astur, she's so young. Wherever did you find her?" his mother asked, but I didn't hear his reply. There was chatter all around me. I blocked out their comments; I'd already heard enough.

I strummed the first chord of an easy song and played the familiar tune. The music was settling for me, and before long, I was lost in it. I closed my eyes and let the garden disappear from my sight and my mind. I breathed in the familiar scents of the flowers and allowed the guests to fade away. I'm not sure how long I played; one song led smoothly into another. I played all of my favorites and many of my master's. Some of the tunes were lively and upbeat, while others were somber.

I felt a hand on my shoulder. I inhaled his familiar scent and allowed the warmth of his hand to penetrate through me. "That's enough, Phina," he whispered and removed his hand.

I ended the song and opened my eyes. The crowd stood around me in awe; there were no comments, just rapt silence. I couldn't read some of their expressions, except Cato's. That man made me feel uncomfortable, so I looked up quickly, seeking my master's approval. I offered him a timid smile. Although he didn't return my smile, his eyes were bright and proud.

"Thank you," he said with all the authority of his position.

Felix was at my side then and motioned for me to leave the garden. He followed behind me, obscuring me from everyone's view. Once I was inside the palace, I could hear the uproar of comments and questions.

In my haste, my slippers stumbled on the stone steps. Felix caught my arm before I went tumbling. I gathered myself but was overcome by a wave of dizziness.

"Are you alright?" Felix asked.

I exhaled. "I was so nervous; did I play well enough?" I asked.

Felix looked down at me questioningly. "Well enough? Well enough for what?"

"Well enough to please the governor and his guests."

Felix chuckled. "I knew you had talent when I found you on the street, but I've never heard anything like you played tonight. I suspect many of the guests have not, either. They'll be wagging their tongues over this one for some time to come. I'd say you played *well enough*," he said wryly.

"Thank you, Felix," I sighed in relief. "I would like to return to my room now."

"That's where I'm taking you."

Once in my room, I undressed and vowed to stay in bed until morning. My eyes had been closed, but I could feel the guests' unfamiliar gaze on me. I could sense their scrutiny and skeptical minds.

Chapter Nine

The governor came back to his chambers late. He waited until every guest had gone. I only dozed a bit because I was not in the habit of sleeping at night, but it was late, even for me. The gray of dawn crept into my window.

"Phina," he called through his chambers into my room. He didn't speak loudly; his voice carried, and it was familiar to me. I hurried to cover myself and wrap my head.

"One moment, sir," I called as I stood from the bed. I tied my robe around myself and reached for my head covering.

"That will not be necessary," he said. I looked up at him. He'd never come into my room like that before. Obviously, he had been in there because he carried me to my bed, but I was the one who went to him. "I do not wish to interrupt your rest for long. Please sit." He gestured toward my bed.

I sat down on the edge and touched my hair self-consciously, pulling the uneven strands behind my ears. He'd seen my hair before, but not while I was awake. He smiled curiously at it but was kind enough not to bring unnecessary attention to my appearance.

"You played very well tonight," he complimented me. His smile stayed, and I thought from his expression that I had made him proud. I nodded, accepting his words, but I didn't smile. "Were you terribly uncomfortable?" I shrugged one shoulder noncommittally and looked away. "Phina, it was not my intention to make you play. If it had been, I would have prepared you."

I kept my gaze diverted and blinked back the tears that pricked my eyes. I wasn't sure why I was crying. My master knelt down in front of me. He took my small hands in his larger ones. Warmth penetrated me, and I closed my eyes. Tears escaped, but I was not able to wipe them away.

"Phina, look at me," my master whispered. I begrudgingly turned to face him. "Are you angry with me?" I tilted my head in question.

"No, sir," I said honestly. He examined my expression for a lie. I wasn't angry at him, but I was disappointed in him.

"Then, what is it?" he asked, still holding my hands.

I blinked slowly and took a deep breath before I spoke. "I did not mind playing for you tonight. I never mind playing for *you*, but I watched the party in the garden from your balcony," I confessed. "I was curious and drawn to the guests."

"That's understandable, but what else?"

The disappointment covered me, and I felt protective of him as if I had any power. "I did not like the way they spoke to you and about you. They said such awful things behind your back. I listened for a long time, and I watched how you were coerced by that Cato. I knew when you sent Felix to get me. How can you invite so much distrust and deceit into the palace, into your home?" I asked. My voice sounded pleading.

He leaned back on his heels and looked deeply into my eyes, searching for something, but I did not know what. "You heard all of that from the balcony?"

I shook my head. "No, some of it I heard in the garden."

"You have a keen ear and are an even better judge of character." That pleased me more than his compliment about my music, and I smiled. He smiled, then, too, and gently squeezed my hands before he released them. He stood and paced the room before he spoke.

"The palace is where I live as long as I am governor. It is technically the property of the people. I am merely the tenant, and as long as I carry that title, I will reside here, but it is not my *home*. I would protect my own better than that. I would never knowingly or willingly invite treachery into it." He was emphatic.

I thought for a few moments. I considered the palace my home, but it wasn't, not truly. I corrected my thoughts. I had settled myself there, playing for my master, but the palace wasn't my home either. I would be careful to remember my place, and my position, too, might be temporary.

In my small room, he walked toward my shelf. He stopped and lifted the bottles absentmindedly. "What is this?" he asked and lifted one of them into the dim light to get a better look at its contents. He placed it down and lifted another to examine it.

"That particular bottle or the whole lot?"

"The entire collection," he clarified.

I walked and stood next to him. "It's my herbs and ingredients for healing," I said proudly. Although my stores were small compared to Mother's and Grandfather's, I was proud of my efforts. I wasn't sure he believed that they had any real purpose.

"Wherever did you get all of this?"

"The garden."

He looked amused again and cut his eyes down at me. "I used to collect insects from the garden when I was your age." I doubted that. At nearly seven-and-ten, he was most likely studying and practicing languages and preparing himself for his military service, but I didn't reply. "Do you like the garden?" he asked.

"Exceedingly. Other than the library, it is the most wonderful place to me."

"Playing music for me isn't your greatest delight?" I shook my head and smiled up at him; I knew he was teasing. "Tell me about your collection." I was a little surprised that he wanted to know.

I took the jar from his hand, removed the cork, and passed it under my nose. I called the contents by name. "It helps with an upset stomach and eases digestion. It's best served in a tea, but you can just chew on the leaves, too."

I passed it to him, and he sniffed. It wasn't an unpleasant odor. He recorked the bottle and set it down as I reached for another. "This one is for fever." He sniffed it and made a face. "I know; it doesn't taste good, either, but it works. When one's fever is high enough, it doesn't matter how bad it tastes."

A strong aroma wafted from the third bottle I opened for pain. My master pressed his hand over it and pushed it away. "That one I know," he said. I looked up at him questioningly, but I hurriedly replaced the cork and set it down. "I've had my fill."

"When you were wounded?" I asked. He nodded, but he didn't say anything else.

I quickly picked up the last bottle and uncorked it. "This one is for sleep." I poured the contents out into my hand. "They don't have any scent until you crush them just before you offer them in a tea or in a warm broth. They are quite flavorful, but again, you wouldn't know that by just looking at them." I rolled the tiny ball in my hand with my thumb.

"If I didn't have your music, I might like to try that."

"I could make you a tea anytime," I offered.

From one shelf, he picked up some drying lavender and sniffed it. "How did you learn all of this?"

"From Mother and Grandfather mostly. I also found out more from some books in your library." I reached for a volume and opened it to show him.

He eyed me and the book speculatively. I wasn't sure if he doubted my ability to read or the fact that I'd managed to do something useful besides play music.

"You found all of this in the garden?"

"Yes, sir. I hope you don't mind my harvesting it. I thought it might be useful to be prepared. Some of the plants have been so neglected that it might be a long time before they produce enough to collect."

He didn't like hearing that anything under his supervision was neglected. "Do I need a gardener?"

"No, sir. I can mind it myself. I mean, if it is alright with you, I would like to continue spending my time there." He looked exhausted from the long night. He held my gaze before he agreed and left me almost as suddenly as he had entered.

Chapter Ten

For the next few nights, I played for my master as usual. Then one morning, Lucia and Myrtle arrived in my room to wake me. They never came together, so I thought maybe I was in trouble.

"Phina, get up," Lucia demanded. I opened my eyes with a start as she placed a tray of food on my small table.

"Lady Gaius requests you play tonight," Myrtle said excitedly.

"Lady Gaius?" I asked sleepily. Myrtle tugged on my arms and practically lifted me to stand before Lucia.

"The governor's mother. She leaves tomorrow and wants to hear you play again," Lucia explained. "You need to bathe and ready yourself, child. There will be guests." She took my face in her hands and examined me. She checked behind my ears and disapproved of my uneven locks of hair.

"You've grown since you arrived," Myrtle babbled as she held up my tunic. I'll find something new for tonight. You need to look your best." She gathered up the sheets from my bed into her arms.

"Trim her hair, too. She doesn't need it growing out like that," Lucia added. "How are your slippers? Where are they?"

I bent down and retrieved them from underneath the bed. Lucia scowled when she saw them. "They fit fine, but they are a little worn."

Lucia huffed, "Find the girl some slippers, Myrtle, and then I'll meet you in the baths." Myrtle curtsied and left the room with my linens. "Eat," Lucia demanded.

I covered myself with my robe and picked up a piece of meat. I took a bite and watched Lucia with big eyes. "Is there something else, ma'am?" I asked.

"His mother is curious about you, and I suppose, to some degree, I am, too. His guests are still gossiping." She scrutinized me again. I took a sip of the tea from my cup and continued eating so that I didn't have to answer her questions right away. "Your unnatural complexion only improves in the sun, your hair is black as pitch, and Myrtle says you read. You collect bits and bobbles, and you've brought the plants to life like a garden sprite."

Lucia's words pleased me. Mother sometimes called me a sprite. I smiled a little as I chewed my food, but Lucia didn't. "It's my job to know the workings of this palace. The governor took you in without question, but that doesn't mean that Felix and I don't have plenty. His mother has her own misgivings, but she wants to secure her son's future. She sees everyone as a threat to his success."

I gobbled up the last two bites of food into one and licked my thumb and index finger. I chewed and swallowed quickly and chased it all down with a big gulp of tea. Lucia waited for my reply.

"Felix indeed found me on the street, but that isn't where I was born. My hair is the same color as the rest of my family's, but they aren't alive anymore to prove that to you. My ancestors lived here since long before there were governors and regions. My *bits and bobbles* are ingredients for healing," I said proudly. Lucia leveled her eyes; she didn't believe me. "I'm no threat to the governor; he's a good master, and I'm safer here than I was on the street. Do you think I'm foolish enough to jeopardize that?"

Lucia placed her hands on her hips and cocked her head back. "To be so young, you're a smart little thing. If his mother asks you anything directly, you'd be wise to answer her with as few words as possible."

I nodded and finished my tea. Lucia took my tray, and I followed her down the stairs and the long corridor toward the baths. She left me there with Myrtle, who trimmed my hair so it would grow out evenly.

I was then left alone to bathe and dress. The tunic that Myrtle laid out for me didn't have the palace emblem on it like the rest of the servants. It was a similar blue with silver trim and woven from silk. I carefully pulled it over my head and allowed it to fall over my hips toward the floor. It felt soft against my skin. The long scarf I was to wear as a head covering was a slightly darker blue yet had the same silver trim.

Myrtle returned and presented me with silver slippers that were more elegant than anything I'd ever owned. "What is all of this?" I asked.

"Master says you're to have something new to wear tonight. His mother is quite particular that she not be surrounded by servants, so tonight, you won't look like one in her presence."

Lucia came down to inspect me like she'd done the first time I was to be presented to the governor. She looked me over, and her discriminating eye was pleased with what she saw. After our discussion upstairs, I wasn't sure if Lucia would meet me with more concern, but instead, she smiled. When she did that, she looked so much younger.

"You were right to go with the silver trim, Myrtle. The silver brings out her eyes."

I returned her smile, and I could feel a flush rise to my cheeks. "Thank you, Lucia; thank you, Myrtle," I said in turn.

"Go upstairs and get your instrument. The guests will be arriving soon."

"Guests?" I asked nervously. "How many?"

"No worries, it's only a few. It won't be the lot you played for at the feast," Lucia said. I exhaled, but I still felt apprehensive.

***

Felix found me once again waiting in my room, my instrument in hand. His mouth went up at the corner in a wry grin. "Lucia did well."

"Myrtle helped."

He shrugged. "I'll let them share the credit, then. You look nothing like the waif I met on the street. You look nothing like a *boy*."

"Thank you, Felix. It's nice not to have to pretend to be one." He laughed and stepped forward as if to go. "Felix," I said before following him. He turned back and looked at me. "Thank you, too, for bringing me to the palace." I had thanked the great spirit for guiding Felix's hand, but I had not thanked the hand.

He nodded, accepting my words, and offered me his arm. I placed my free hand in the crook of his elbow, and Felix escorted me down the main hall to the banquet room.

Felix went in without me. I waited in the hall until he returned. I noticed my reflection in a long mirror that hung on the wall. In the torchlight, my face was in shadow. I stepped forward and gasped at my likeness because it wasn't my likeness at all; it was my mother's. I stood there, staring at myself. My eyes shined brightly beneath the silver trim. They didn't show the muddy brown; they looked almost silver in the flickering torchlight.

Felix joined me in the mirror. His ability to move silently made him a good soldier. He stood tall behind me. My head barely reached the middle of his chest.

"They're ready for you," he said, but he didn't rush me. I looked up into his eyes appreciatively.

I had seen the banquet room in daylight when it was empty. Upon entering, I marveled at the candles and tables. They were laden with food and flowers. Guests mingled around the room with goblets in their hands, and my arrival interrupted their murmurs and laughter. When I hesitated, Felix cleared his throat to encourage me forward.

The governor turned his head toward me and motioned for me to come to him. I avoided the guests' eyes the best I could, but I knew they were all watching me. I was once again a curiosity. His mother's eyes felt piercing, and I heard the familiar snicker of the man named Cato. I bristled at his words even before they were spoken.

"Lady Gaius, is this your doing? Your influence over your son is noted. Astur has never indulged us like this before." He clapped his hands to applaud my master, but his gesture wasn't sincere.

I met my master's eyes then, and reflexively, straightened my back. I set my chin. I didn't mean to appear haughty or proud, but I disliked Cato, and my master read my expression clearly.

"Astur, she doesn't appear pleased to be here," his mother said like I wasn't there.

"No, ma'am, she's pleased, just shy." I think my reaction to Cato amused him. I relaxed my shoulders and lowered my eyes. It would be easier to pretend to be nervous and insecure than to have to explain myself to his mother.

"Where shall we seat her? The guests are growing impatient," his mother said in a whisper, but her smile assured everyone around her.

My master gestured to Felix, and I followed his eyes toward a small sofa in the corner of the room. It was near the banquet table and in direct sight to my master, yet his guests had to look past him or turn around entirely to see me. That would be rude, indeed. He protected me from their stares, their presence, and their curious chatter.

I made myself comfortable on the sofa and readied my instrument. In the light overhead, the silver trim at my wrists glistened in the light. I liked how the sparkles danced through the silk tunic, and I could only imagine the same thing happened each time I moved my head. I had seen glimpses of it in my reflection and was drawn to it.

The guests' attention was on me, and I heard their questions and comments. They were much the same as in the garden. Soon the first course was set before them, and they were drawn into table conversation. My music entertained them while they ate.

I didn't close my eyes while I played. I was under no one's scrutiny, and the few times that my eyes caught my master's, he was smiling. He wasn't necessarily smiling at me, but he was pleased, and I think playing familiar music settled him like it did when he slept.

During their toasts and speeches, I was afforded breaks to relieve myself and eat and drink. Felix escorted me to and from the kitchen. He waited patiently for me before he took me back to the banquet room.

When Lucia passed us, Felix winked at her and complimented her on the meal. "Be sure you get your fill at the table, and don't you be coming around later for second helpings," she warned.

Felix laughed with her. From the first time I'd seen them together, I liked the feel of them. They were both fierce and commanding in their own right, but she and Felix were different together.

I watched them curiously before the question escaped my lips. "Is Lucia your mate?"

Felix rounded on me like I'd attacked him. I stepped back in fear. I hadn't meant to offend him, but he looked angry. "That's not a question you ask in polite company."

"I'm sorry, Felix, I meant no harm. It's just that I can read your heart, and I see that you love her."

It was Felix who took a step back. "What do you mean that you can read my heart?" he asked cautiously. I had never seen Felix shaken or surprised.

"I do not know; I can. Grandfather and Erik could read the hearts of men. It was their gift, but now I see that I, too, have that gift. Maybe it was all the years I pretended to be a boy, but now I see clearly. It's really not that hard."

"Who else's heart can you read?" he asked.

"The governor's, Marcus', and Cato's." I spoke Cato's name with distaste. I didn't like the feel of it in my mouth.

Felix crossed his arms over his broad chest and nodded, understanding. "And what of their hearts?"

"Yours and the governor's hearts are protective and kind. There is good in both of you that is deep." Felix smirked at that, but he didn't deny my words. "Marcus' heart waivers. I have to read his heart each and every time I am in his presence. He is inconsistent, yet not malicious." Felix's expression understood. He was good at reading men's hearts, too.

"And Cato?" he asked.

"Cato is as easily read as you and my master," I said in a whisper.

"But not in a *good* way?" he guessed. His tone matched mine.

I shook my head. "I feel a threat from him all the time. Even when he isn't present in the palace, I sense the darkness in his heart." I didn't know why I suddenly needed to speak my concerns aloud, but Felix was the one man who could protect our master. "Please, watch him," I said urgently. "I do not trust him, and if I had the power, I would banish him."

Felix stepped back and laughed. "I'll be mindful of that, little one," he said, easing the tension.

"So, what of Lucia?" I asked.

"Lucia was claimed by my best friend. We all grew up together. I've known her my entire life."

"And you love her," I said.

"Yes, child."

"And you are her mate."

"What do you know of such things?"

"I know what is between a man and a woman," I defended. I knew of the physical pleasure that men sought from women. I had witnessed my mother's rape, but I had also seen men and women together in the city when they thought they were alone.

Felix scoffed, doubting what I may or may not know on the matter, and then concern covered him. "When you were living on the streets, did a man force himself upon you? Have you been with a man?"

"No, sir," I said, shaking my head. He sighed in relief and hurried me back to the banquet hall.

***

I played until every guest was gone. They drank and raised their glasses for a long time after their meal. Cato and Lady Gaius liked the wine and were showing its effects by the end of the evening. Cato was the last to go.

Their voices carried, or perhaps they were the voices I was just more aware of. "I want Astur to have a wife, Cato. He needs to be settled with a family. Perhaps you can arrange for him to have some companionship, someone to comfort him."

"You know I will do everything in my power to make my friend content, but he keeps to his own company. Felix is always at his beck and call, and now he has his little muse," Cato said leeringly, and I could feel his eyes upon me. I refused to acknowledge his comment and continued playing softly.

"Well, she's a plaything; a child can't offer much companionship to a man, especially a man of Astur's stature and position. Sure, her music is delightful, but she's merely a distraction. He needs to think of his future. He needs an heir."

"He's still young; there's time for that, but if you think it would help, then, of course, I'll do whatever I can." Cato's words dripped with falsehood.

Cato lingered a few moments longer, and then Lady Gaius took his arm and led him toward the door. Her son had walked his remaining guests out. Felix was attending to other business, and I was left alone. I scooted from the edge of the sofa and bent over to adjust the heel of my slipper. When I stood, yawning from a long evening, Cato had returned.

"You are quite the little wonder," he said.

I didn't move; I couldn't move. Cato took a step forward, trapping me in the corner between the sofa and the doors. I lifted my dulcimer and held it firmly in my hand.

Cato blinked and staggered; he was drunk from the wine. Drunk men were unpredictable. "Cato, darling, did you find your cloak?" Lady Gaius asked from the doorway. Cato turned to face her, and she caught sight of me. "Oh, Cato, leave that little thing alone," she said dismissively.

I took advantage of Cato's distraction and ran for the side door of the banquet room. It led directly to the kitchen, giving me access to the staircase to my room.

Chapter Eleven

Soon after Lady Gaius's departing banquet, I was singing low to the flowering plants when I was interrupted by a man's voice. "Well, what do we have here? You're no gardener digging about in the governor's garden. You could lose your hands for touching things that don't belong to you." I recognized the voice instantly. I turned around, horrified, to see Cato standing a few yards away from me.

I shuddered. "You're the little musician," Cato said arrogantly. I didn't answer. I just stared at him. "I know you can speak; I just heard you singing to the flowers. Won't you sing a song for me?" he asked.

I knew there would be consequences, but I shook my head quickly, refusing him. "You may speak. I won't hurt you." His words felt sticky like honey but not as sweet. I remained kneeling, although my insides screamed to run. It took all my resolve to stay put.

Cato took two steps forward, and his shadow covered me. It was a sunny day, and until Cato's arrival, it had been a pleasant one. "I'm curious; if you won't sing for me, who is the audience you seek?" He peered over my head toward my patch of garden. "There aren't many flowers here. I thought girls preferred flowers, but then again, you aren't like any girl I've encountered. If it's not flowers, I'll have to find what you like so that I might entice you to sing for *me*." The smile he offered made me cringe.

He took another step and put out his hand to help me stand. I refused to accept his gesture. I whispered a prayer from my heart to the great spirit.

"Come on, child; I don't bite." But his words did.

My stomach tightened as he leaned over me. He was close enough to grab me, and I could smell his breath. It wasn't offensive, just hot and heavy.

"Cato!" I closed my eyes, relieved to hear Felix's voice. "You were asked to wait in the library."

Cato turned to face my rescuer. Felix looked down at me and could read the fear in my eyes. "Are you alright, Phina?" he asked. His expression was fiercely protective. Cato took a casual step back to give Felix access to me. "What business do you have here?" Felix asked Cato.

"I heard her singing; I wanted to hear more."

Felix stood to his full height and took an intimidating step toward Cato. "Her songs aren't yours for the asking."

"What's the harm in one little song?" Cato asked.

Felix put his hand out toward me, and I took it willingly but released it as soon as my feet were steady. "Are you finished here?" Felix asked, but I took his words to mean, *It's time for you to go.*

"Yes, sir," I said. I dusted off my apron and gave a brief curtsy and nod. "Thank you, Felix," I whispered, but my thanks were genuine. I gathered my gardening tools and was on my way.

"Phina, heh?" I heard Cato say with a smirk. I didn't linger any longer to hear Felix's reply.

***

Once Lady Gaius left the palace, my master's routine resumed. I was glad to see things return to their regular pace. My master left early in the morning and returned to supper in his room. I played for him, and he seemed at peace.

"Felix told me about the garden today," he said as I played. "You refused to sing for Cato, but he insisted that you were singing to the flowers."

I didn't look up, but my fingers hesitated on the strings, stuttering the music. I caught myself and continued to play without answering.

"I understand why you wouldn't sing for Cato, but I've heard you, you know, singing. It's lovely."

I looked up, shocked. I had been so careful. "How?" I asked, shaking my head, denying it.

He did not answer the question. "Please, sing for me; I wish to hear it in my chamber tonight."

His request was friendly but still a command from the governor. I knew better, yet I had to refuse. I remembered Grandmother's warnings. I could sing alone or with the women when we sang a child from the womb, but never *for* a man, only *with* a man. I shook my head slightly and averted my eyes. I couldn't let the song escape in a man's presence. He looked at me, not liking my refusal.

"The songs you hear are not songs for your ears. Those are my prayers to the great spirit. Only the great spirit has ears for those songs." He considered my words.

"Who is this great spirit of whom you speak? Is that your god?"

"The great spirit is the one who gives me the power to heal. My prayers are received and answered. The great spirit leads me, watching over me and protecting me. My songs to the flowers are like that, too. They flourish under the great spirit's songs." I was unsure if my master prayed or had any knowledge of the great spirit, but he didn't deny my words. "I am truly sorry to refuse your request, sir, but I must." He didn't look angry but genuinely disappointed. I reconsidered and countered his request. "I cannot sing *for* you, but I could combine my voice with yours. There is no harm if I mingle my song," I offered, hoping that would appease him.

He scoffed. "No, I do not sing."

"But everyone sings. Did no one teach you any songs?" I asked.

"I know some songs; I learned them as a child," he said proudly. "Mine is not a pleasant voice like yours, Phina; I don't think you'd like the sound of it," he laughed.

I nodded, understanding. I could tell when my master sometimes teased and had a playful tone to his voice. "If you truly want me to sing in your presence,

73

perhaps we could try one song together. I will teach you." I hummed and played a child's song about the woodland creatures. I then spoke the words in time with the melody. His lips went up slightly, amused by the lyrics.

"Do you know this one?" I asked. He shook his head. "Okay, with me this time."

I stated the words a line at a time. He joined my voice in a whisper. I shook my head. "That won't do. You have to sing, or I will remain silent and only be able to hum."

"It's just singing. Why can't you do it alone?"

I lifted my head to his challenge and looked into his eyes. "It is unwise," I said flatly.

"You are a child. What do you know of wisdom?"

"I know enough not to waste my song." My words were sharp, and he glared at me. I had crossed a line by refusing him, and my tone was unacceptable. I lowered my gaze; the intensity of his eyes was too much sometimes. I felt the need to explain. "As a healer, a female healer, my song is powerful. I must be careful with whom and for whom I sing. Once I am a woman, my songs will only be for my mate and our offspring."

He chuckled derisively. "Mates," he repeated and rolled his eyes. "That's all my mother spoke of during her visit."

"Why do you not have a woman to comfort you? Why do you not take a mate? A woman's comfort might help you sleep."

He scoffed again. "Why do you ask me that question? I just don't think you want to sing."

"Sing with me, then, and I won't mention mates or marriage or your mother."

He knew I was teasing. "Very well, I'll sing with you. I'll do just about anything not to have to discuss those topics," he said and did, and from that night on, he sang with me often. I taught him nearly every song I knew, except the grieving song, the marriage song that bound a woman to a man, and the song sung over the dead. I even taught him the songs that I sang to the flowers.

Many nights later, my master confessed something very personal. A new song eluded the topic of lovers. "Phina, it's not that I'm opposed to marriage. Did you know that I once had a wife?"

"No, sir. I did not." I had heard many things about him, but most of them were gossip and hearsay. I reserved my opinions of him by what I experienced.

"She was beautiful, and I begged my father to arrange our union. We were very young and naive, but I believe she loved me, too. I was called away in my soldiering. She was sad and lonely. Then I received word that she was heavy with our child. I happily awaited the news of its arrival, but I lost her for good when she brought our child into the world."

He shared the knowledge of his loss without showing deep emotion. His words were measured and straightforward. He had either reconciled the past or had protected his heart from the intrusion of pain.

"And the child?" I asked.

"He died two days later; I never saw him. I left my wife too often, and it worried her. She couldn't do it without me. I should never have claimed her. She would have been better off alone or with another man."

"Who was her healer?" I asked.

He looked up at me questioningly. "There was no healer."

"There was no healer?" I asked, surprised. "Why did you have no healer present to sing forth the child?"

"Where I am from, there are none such as you. No one speaks or looks like you. I know nothing of you and your ways. Singing forth a child sounds ridiculous." I focused again on the music. "Phina," came my master's voice, "that doesn't mean I do not wish to hear more or that I am not curious about your ways."

I looked up, comforted that I had not displeased him. I watched him and heard his gruffness with others, but thankfully he rarely showed that side of himself when alone with me.

"How long ago was that? How old were you?" I asked.

75

"Five years ago. I was barely twenty." I calculated the years. He was nine years older than me, but I did not divulge that. "Still, you should find a mate. She will take care of you and give you another son."

"I'd rather sing with you than find a mate," he laughed.

"Cato and your mother seem determined."

"Thankfully, my mother is back at the capital, and Cato is not allowed in the palace without guards."

"Why?" I asked, surprised. It might not have been any of my business, but I was curious.

"Mainly because I dislike him." I giggled but read my master's face. "Honestly, it's because of what you told Felix. I don't want him coming here and seeking you out."

"Thank you, sir. That comes as a great relief. I keep looking over my shoulder at every turn, afraid he's watching me."

My master watched me for several moments, probably imagining me scurrying about the palace, but then he asked, "Is it true? Can you read the heart of a man?" I nodded solemnly. "Any man?" I shrugged. I had no idea. The ability had come as a new revelation.

"I suppose so."

"So, what of my heart?" he asked.

I smiled. "Your heart is easy to read, sir, but perhaps that is because I spend so much time with you. You have a good heart. You and Felix." That pleased him.

"And Marcus?"

"Sometimes, but he has a divided heart. I do not always know his intentions."

"Hmmm, I wonder. Can you read when his intentions are aligned with mine?"

"Yes, sir."

He sat back for a few moments and pondered my ability. "Phina, would you do me a kindness?" he asked.

"If it is reasonable and within my power, I don't see why I couldn't," I replied, using his words.

He chuckled, remembering. "Call me by my given name." I looked at him questioningly. "When we are together, you may call me Astur. I grow weary of being called formally: *sir, governor, and master*," he said derisively. "My mother's visit wasn't entirely pleasant, but it reminded me that no one calls me by my name. I would appreciate hearing it in my chambers."

"I will, Astur," I said timidly. He smiled approvingly.

I liked the way his name felt on my tongue. His request deeply humbled me. Names held power, and he trusted me with his. I would weave his request into my evening songs and ask the great spirit to make his name on my lips a balm.

Chapter Twelve

"I have to go away," Astur said one evening.

"How long?" I asked.

"Three weeks."

"Where will you go?"

"To inspect the region, and then I will spend a week at the king's palace in the capital. All of the governors meet there once a year."

"Who will accompany you?" I asked. I wondered if I had to go along, too.

"Felix and Marcus."

"Who will be left to watch over the palace and the women in your absence?" I asked.

He thought for a moment, considering my words. "Are you afraid?" I nodded. "Because of what happened to your mother?" I nodded again. "I'll have Felix see to that."

"And Cato?" I asked timidly

"What of Cato?" he asked.

"Is he summoned to the capitol, too?"

"No, he is not." Astur looked questioningly at me. "Do you think he should?"

"He cannot undermine your authority as easily if he is with you."

Astur chuckled, "Keep your allies close and your enemies closer."

"Yes, sir. I read that somewhere."

"As did I. It makes sense. If you can read men's hearts truly, then you might have a future as an advisor. I'll have to remind myself of that."

Astur retired early the night before his trip. He included Cato in his party. Cato saw it as an honor, but Felix and Astur knew otherwise. Marcus knew nothing. I played all night that night. Astur needed a good night's rest before his long journey.

He rose before sunrise and was surprised, I think, to find me still sitting on my little stool strumming. "Good morning," he said gruffly and stretched.

"Good morning," I replied.

"You played all night?"

"Yes, and you slept peacefully?"

"Indeed." He stretched again and yawned.

I stood and curtsied. "Farewell. I pray that your journey is advantageous and that you return safely." I felt a little sad at his departure, but I didn't cry. I forged a sleepy smile to assure him.

"Farewell, Phina," he replied, and I left him.

After his departure, my days were quiet and settled. I read and tended to the garden. I spent luxurious hours in the library reading. I studied the maps that lay open on the tables. I traced rivers and towns with my fingers.

The women took their leisure, too. We shared supper each night together at the long table in the kitchen. Lucia had them scrubbing floors and doing their regular chores, but she asked me to play my music a few times in the evenings when the palace was at rest. The women sang with me. Their voices surrounded me with great joy, and Lucia, too, enjoyed the music. She propped her feet up and reclined back against the wall. I was thankful to share my music with them all.

***

A year had passed since I'd arrived in the palace; I was well-fed and healthy once again. Even under my tunic, the women noticed my curves and teased me. My body seemed to catch up finally, and my breasts and hips were shapely.

Each day, I saw more changes. My hair was full and soft. It was black as raven's wings and shimmered in the sun.

After seeing my reflection that night before I played at the banquet, I requested a mirror. It made my room appear more spacious, and when the sun was bright, it illuminated every corner. Sometimes when I looked over my shoulder and saw myself working over my table, I smiled. It was Mother there in the mirror, or at least what I remembered of her.

One night while Astur was still away, my lower back ached, and I had a headache. I made myself some tea in the night from my stores, but I continued to be uncomfortable. When I rose at some point to relieve myself, I noticed that my body's changes had also brought my womanhood.

Myrtle came upstairs to check on me when I didn't come down for my meal. "Are you ill, child?" Myrtle asked. Myrtle took one look at me in the bed and placed her hand on my forehead.

"I do not have a fever. I started my bleeding," I confessed.

Myrtle and Lucia were kind, and they showed me the way of things, but they couldn't hide their gloom. They didn't see this as a day to celebrate. They provided me with teas and tinctures and fitted me with a new tunic and veil. I didn't like it because it hid my mouth and made it hard to sing to the great spirit.

Grandmother had promised a grand celebration when I became a woman. I would have been given wine, and Mother would have baked a cake. Grandfather would have played his dulcimer and sang blessings over me. Instead, I bathed alone in the tub and washed the blood from my body. I had requested scented oils and lavender for my hair as it grew out. It was almost to my chin. That day, I longed for Mother and lilacs.

Knowing that I had been the only child in the palace, I also had the knowledge that women were not kept there, either, not young ones, anyway. Deep in my heart, I feared that my womanhood's arrival would change everything. I was of age to be joined to a man. When my womanhood was revealed, would my master send me away?

I returned to my chamber and sang the song of maturity over myself and prayed to the great spirit, singing aloud, the words resounding in my small room. The melody floated out from my window, up and into the sky, directly into the great spirit's ears. I was now of age to be a healer. I prayed for the great spirit to hear my heart's desire to become so.

Thankfully, Astur was still away when it all began. Although I had missed his presence, I was relieved not to have to play for him for a few more days. When he returned, he was tired yet restless from his travels. I waited until he settled himself before I joined him in his chambers. I sat quietly on my little stool and played for him from the corner of the room.

"I wondered when you'd come in and play. Was I gone so long that you forgot me?" Astur asked teasingly.

"No, sir." My voice sounded odd from behind the veil.

He listened in the darkness while I played, but I didn't say anything or ask him about his journey. "Phina, you are very quiet; what is it? Are you well?" he asked and rolled over to face me.

I strummed the dulcimer gently. "Yes, sir, I am." Still, my voice sounded off. I was self-conscious and didn't want him to know the changes that had occurred in his absence.

"Come here," he commanded. I laid the instrument next to my stool and walked begrudgingly toward him so that he could see me. He sat up to take a better look. Even in the dim light, I could see his eyes widen when he noticed my face veiled. I could not read his expression, so I diverted my gaze. "Did the women give you that veil?"

"Yes, sir," I whispered, keeping my gaze lowered.

He sighed, and I heard him run his hands over his short hair. "So, I'm *sir* again." I shrugged. "Phina, look at me." When I looked up, tears flooded my eyes. I had not wept over my womanhood, but suddenly I couldn't keep the tears at bay. I tried to wipe my cheeks, but the veil was in the way. "Does it bother you?" I nodded. "If it bothers you, you do not need to wear it in my presence."

"But I have grown into a woman. It is your custom."

He almost scoffed at the mention of me becoming a woman. "Here," he said as he reached up and lowered the veil. The fabric gathered underneath my chin. "There, that's better, isn't it?" He wiped the tears from my cheeks with his thumbs and held my face in his hands. I nodded and smiled meekly. I liked his touch, and I leaned into his hands.

"It is better, but it doesn't change anything," I said.

His eyes softened as he acknowledged the truth. "Phina, your body has decided to mature, but that does not yet make you a woman. You still have years before you are ready for marriage and children."

I looked down again, suddenly wishing for the veil to cover the blush that rose to my cheeks. He could feel the heat radiate from my face into his hands. "Phina, look at me," Astur commanded this time like he was seeing me, really seeing me. He caught the change and realized his error. "How old *are* you?" he asked. He had never asked me that before and probably thought me of no consequential age.

"Ten and seven," I said, surprised that my voice was steady. He knew it was the truth – shock, pure shock. Astur released me like I was a snake. He stood then and grabbed his robe and covered himself. I stepped back, away from the fear and fury I saw in his eyes.

"That's impossible," he said, but I dared not interrupt or correct him when he was in a temper. "You're a child, no more than two-and-ten, three-and-ten at the most." I did not speak; he would have to make the connection for himself.

He paced the floor for several moments. The darkness of his chambers made his confusion harder to witness. When he was in an ill temper, it was my duty to soothe him with music. My fingers longed to strum the dulcimer and ease the tension in the room. Since I had been the reason for his mood, I wasn't sure I would be able to comfort him.

I wanted to run and hide in my room, but I could not leave his presence unless he dismissed me or was in a deep sleep. He rarely dismissed me, so I stood, unmoving, watching him sort through the facts in his mind. I hated seeing him like that. I closed my eyes and opened my heart to the great spirit, calling forth for calm and discernment. I wanted nothing more at that moment than to sing.

"I allowed you into the palace, into my chambers," he clarified. "Night after night, you've played for me. Your deceit began when you arrived dressed as a boy! You pretended to be a child all this time when you were practically a woman! I should have known you weren't to be trusted!"

I shook my head, denying his words. It wasn't like that. "No," I pleaded. "Please, Astur, please do not be angry with me."

"Leave me," he commanded and pointed toward my room. His words were permanent, and I doubted he'd ever call for me again.

I defiantly caught his eyes and returned his angry stare. I lifted my chin proudly. If I were going to be dismissed, I'd speak one last time. "You're wrong," I said, and it took all I had to stand my ground under his rage. He seemed to double in size when he was angry. "I have deceived no one. I lived as a boy to protect myself after I was abandoned in this life and lost everything. I didn't ask Felix to bring me here, yet I have honored you, served you, and protected you to the best of my ability. When I arrived, no one asked me anything except my name. My age and past were of no consequence to you, just my ability to play music. You are the only one who has asked me anything, and yet when I speak the truth, you doubt my abilities to read and heal." My heart was beating wildly, but thankfully, my tears never fell. My voice stayed steady.

"Send me away, if you must, Astur; I understand, but it would be in your best interest to reconsider and avoid making a decision in haste that you might later regret." He bristled at my words.

"Is that a threat?" he countered.

I shook my head slowly; he'd mistaken my words. Sadness and pity replaced my boldness. "No, sir." Tears pooled in my eyes. "There's just nowhere else for me to go." I blinked quickly to keep the tears at bay. My words deflated his anger, but I could tell he still wanted me to go. I turned and picked up my instrument as I left the room.

Chapter Thirteen

I pulled off my head covering and veil and tossed them angrily onto the floor. I stomped them repeatedly with my slippered foot. I pulled off my tunic and stood in my room uncovered, naked, in the moonlight. I crumbled into a heap on the floor next to my bed and sobbed silently. I pulled at the blankets and wrapped them around myself; I cried until I was spent, finally catching my breath and watching the moon through my window. I heard my master's boots on the stone, and it sounded like he left his chamber.

Knowing Astur couldn't hear me, I sang low to the great spirit. The nightingale joined me, and soon there was a chorus of critters in the garden echoing my song. They often came to me when I sang to the flowers, but they'd never accompanied me before.

***

I woke early, dressed, and hurried down the servant's stairs to the kitchen. After I ate, I went directly to the garden. I spent the entire morning there, only taking short breaks to drink some water. I diligently weeded and pruned and gathered.

The shadow of the balcony crept across and shaded me in the early afternoon sun; it was a welcomed relief. I looked up in that direction, and that's when I saw Astur standing on his balcony, watching me. I had lowered my veil to drink and had forgotten to replace it. I offered him a weak smile, but his expression was brooding. If he were a great bird, he could swoop down and snatch me from the spot.

There was a sudden pain in my midsection that flowed out hot and solid like I'd swallowed coal from the ovens. I lowered my gaze and returned to my work, but I'd lost my passion for the task.

I stayed in the garden until my evening meal. My intentions were to eat and bathe and hide in my room until I was called or forgotten. After reading Astur's dark expression earlier, I felt confident he was deciding what to do with me. He was a decisive man; he wouldn't linger long before he made his decision.

I didn't have much appetite, but I went to the kitchen to escape the memory of his dark stare. Myrtle barked orders to some of the other women and nearly knocked me over as she hurried out of the kitchen with a tray. There was an odd feel to the place. Cassia was bustling about in a frenzy.

"What's happened?" I asked.

Cassia wiped her brow with a cloth and tucked it into her apron. "It's Lucia," she said. She picked up a loaf of bread and ladled stew into a bowl for me. She set it down before me. I could tell she was worried.

"What is it, Cassia? Is Lucia ill?"

Cassia shook her head quickly. "No, child, she's not ill, but she's in a great deal of pain." I looked up into Cassia's worried eyes.

"Take me to her; I'd like to help."

Cassia scoffed, "I doubt you'd be any help; it's best to just leave her and Myrtle to it."

I heard a wail over the kitchen sounds. Cassia's head perked up. "Please, take me to her; I can help." She did as I asked, and we hurried down the corridor to the women's rooms.

As soon as we rounded into Lucia's, I knew something was wrong. Lucia was in a great deal of pain and was lying on her side, wearing only a nightdress. Her hair splayed out from a braid. Her face contorted, and she bent forward, clutching herself. She cried out again and panted.

I ran to her and knelt next to the bed. "Lucia, what is it? Where is the pain?" I put my hands on her flushed cheeks and looked into her eyes. She lowered her hands around her belly, and I placed my hands where hers had been. Her stomach was tight and full. "A child?" I asked, unsure of what I sensed from her. She nodded. I almost laughed in surprise. I was right to think she was a young widow like Mother; she was still young enough to conceive. "Does Felix know?" I asked. She didn't answer me; instead, she closed her eyes and stiffened as another wave of pain attacked her.

"How long has she been at it?" I asked.

"All night. She's exhausted," Myrtle said, and from the looks of it, Myrtle had been with Lucia every minute.

"Get her to the baths," I commanded. Myrtle looked at me and almost challenged me, but my tone was firm. "Cassia, help her! I'll be right back!"

I ran upstairs, straight to my room. I gathered my herbs and a clean apron. Before I left the room, I remembered Mother's book. I'd read it many times, but I wanted it near me. I turned back toward the door; Astur blocked my way.

"Where are you going?" he asked accusingly.

"Downstairs; it's Lucia," I panted, impatient to return to her, but he didn't move to let me pass.

At the sound of his maid's name, he jerked. "What's wrong with her?"

I didn't know what he knew or what I should say. "Please, it's urgent." I moved to go around him, and he flinched away from me. Then, I had a thought. "Felix. Please get Felix. He needs to know."

"Know what?" he asked, but I was already running down the stairs.

"Just get him!" I hollered back over my shoulder. My voice echoed a little, but I was sure he heard me.

Lucia was in the bath, still wearing her gown. Her eyes were closed, and she looked relaxed in the warm water.

"Lavender," I said, and Cassia got the bottle from the shelf and poured it into the bath. "Myrtle, get a cloth for her brow. Lucia, how are you feeling?"

"The water is nice," she whispered. "How did you know?" she asked.

"It's my job to know; I'm a healer," I replied in a whisper. Lucia smiled weakly but didn't argue. "The water helps you relax and relieves the pressure of the pains. Is this your first child?"

Lucia moaned and turned her face away. Myrtle wiped tears from Lucia's cheeks. "No," Myrtle said for her, and from her tone and expression, the child hadn't survived.

"Have your waters broken?" I asked. Both women nodded. "Are you feeling the pain coming again?" Lucia nodded. "I want you to take a deep breath, and when you feel the pain peak, let the breath out slowly. Can you do that?"

She didn't answer me with words but followed my directions. I breathed with her until the pain passed. "Keep your eyes closed and just relax. Before the next pain, I need to feel where the baby is. I'm going to touch you now."

I had attended several births with Mother and Grandmother. I had been allowed to examine a few women during labor. It had been four years ago, but I remembered well enough. I had read Mother's book, and I felt prepared to sing this baby into the world.

I lifted the gown that floated between Lucia's legs. She moaned slightly as I placed my hand low on her rounded belly. She was small, but the baby's head was easy to feel. I continued between her legs, and my fingers extended to measure her progress. She was nearly ready.

"You're close," I encouraged. Lucia muttered a curse under her breath. She didn't believe me. "I'm going to sing this baby forth; your child will live," I said confidently. Lucia rolled her head back and moaned. Myrtle hurriedly wiped her brow.

Cassia brought me mugs of hot water when I asked, and I made teas to ease the labor. Lucia sipped and cried. Myrtle wiped her brow and whispered words of encouragement each time Lucia moaned or moved in the water.

I began singing low over Lucia, and the time passed in waves of intensity and rest. She relaxed, and the great spirit embraced her and the child. After an hour, Lucia panted loudly and cried out. Her belly writhed, and I knew that she was near her time. "Sing with me," I said aloud to Myrtle. "Cassia, call the women; we need to sing." Cassia didn't question me and ran from the baths. Myrtle doubted me. "Sing," I demanded. I began the song again, and Myrtle's low voice joined mine.

The other women came quickly, and Cassia told them to sing with me. I led the song, and after a few verses, they joined me. The women's voices were low initially, but as Lucia floated in the water, her belly tightened and forced the baby down and out. The women increased their volume; their voices echoed throughout the bath, willing the child to come forth.

I carefully observed Lucia, waiting for her time. "Push when you have the urge."

Lucia gripped the sides of the tub, and her legs drew up. She moaned as she pushed through the pain. Myrtle held her upright from behind, singing all the while. I leaned over the tub, anticipating the child. I could see the crown of its head through the water.

With the next push, the baby slid from between her legs and into the warmth of the bath. I caught the slippery newborn and eased it toward the surface of the water. Lucia cried in relief, and the women joined her exultation.

I brought the baby's head out of the water and floated it toward's Lucia's breast. "It's a boy," I said, smiling proudly. Lucia's eyes were open wide and expectant. She welcomed the child with open arms. Tears of joy ran down her cheeks. Everyone was joyful; the room expanded with it. We were all smiling, marveling at the arrival of the child.

Myrtle and Cassia made Lucia comfortable before they returned to the kitchen. They dried her and dressed her before they helped her into her bed. Myrtle gently brushed Lucia's long hair and braided it before she wrapped it. All the while, the baby nursed at his mother's breast, and she gazed lovingly at her son. I made her tea to ease the soreness that would follow. When the baby was finished nursing, Myrtle returned to diaper his tiny bottom. She swaddled him before she handed him over to me. Lucia's eyes were heavy; she needed to rest.

"You can sleep, Lucia. I'll stay here with him until you wake."

I had nowhere else to go, and I honestly preferred to be needed there and not have to face Astur. I held the tiny little boy in my arms. I looked down at him and smiled. His head was covered with blond hair, and his chin was dimpled slightly like his father's. I hummed a song as I rocked him gently in my arms. I whispered a song of thanks to the great spirit. This child had been sung into the world, and he was healthy and safe. He was the first child I had sung forth on my own, and I felt increasingly thankful for Mother and Grandmother's careful instruction. The great spirit deserved all the credit and thanks. I nuzzled his fuzzy head under my chin; he was warm and smelled fresh and new.

A deep sigh broke the silence. I looked up from the infant in my arms to see Felix in the doorway. "Phina?" he asked. His face was flush as if he'd come from a distance. He looked over at Lucia, sleeping in the bed, and then to the baby in my arms. He didn't move; his feet were fixed.

"Felix, come; meet your son," I whispered and gestured for him to come closer.

"Really? A son?" he marveled.

Felix didn't come to me, so I rose and walked toward him. "He's perfect, Felix. Look, he has your chin." Felix smiled and silently laughed. He lifted his hands tentatively but didn't take the child from me. "Would you like to hold him?" I asked. Felix blinked and nodded.

I gestured for him to sit in the chair in the corner of the room. I laid the child in his arms. The little thing's eyes were wide as he looked up at his father for the first time.

Felix was tall with broad shoulders; he was a leader of men and carried that authority well. When he took his child in his arms, though, he eased his large hand around the baby's head with all the affection of an experienced father. I wondered if he'd ever done that before.

"Congratulations," I whispered.

Felix smiled proudly. "I didn't want her to be alone, but the stubborn woman wouldn't listen. She was determined to keep me away. I think she secretly hoped it would happen while we were at the capitol. Thank you, Phina, for sending the governor to find me."

I glanced down at the mention of our master. I blinked hard to hide my emotions; I didn't want to take away from Felix's first moments with his son. "You're welcome, Felix. He's a beautiful child." I smiled and put my attention back onto the baby. "What will you name him?" I asked.

It was customary for fathers to name their sons and for mothers to name their daughters. It was unusual, but that was one of the many reasons I liked the story about my father choosing *Phina* for me. It made me feel closer to a man that I'd never known.

Felix took his time before he answered me. "I will name him Traian after my father."

"That's a good name," I said.

"Felix, I thought I told you to stay away," Lucia whispered. Her words were firm, but I couldn't tell if she was angry with us.

Felix stood with the baby in his arms and winked at me. He wasn't about to let Lucia dampen his joy. "Phina called for me, and, if you recall, the governor gave explicit instructions to give her whatever she asked. We can't go against him, now can we?" Felix asked. His banter was playful and loving.

She smiled sleepily. "You're a fool, Felix."

"Perhaps, but you've given me a healthy son, so you're stuck with me forever."

Lucia's eyes fluttered as she blinked back tears. "He is a fine one," she agreed, "but I can't take all the credit." Felix walked toward Lucia and sat on the edge of her bed. I felt like I was intruding on a private moment between them. Their attention was all on the baby they'd created from their love. I slipped silently from the room; they could manage without me.

Chapter Fourteen

I passed through the kitchen and took a loaf of bread and a cup of wine upstairs to my room. I pondered the day as I looked out the window. The sun had set, and the night was bright. I was exceedingly thankful for Traian's safe arrival into the world. I pulled pieces from the loaf and dipped the bread into the wine, careful not to let the wine drip onto my tunic.

Astur cleared his throat in my doorway. I froze and swallowed the bite that I had been savoring. I placed the bread and wine down on my table and turned to face him. Unsure of what to say, I just stood there staring at him.

"How are Lucia and the baby?" Astur asked.

I smiled, relieved that he knew. "They're fine, and he's beautiful. He looks just like his father," I gushed. "I wasn't sure what you knew."

"I wouldn't be an effective governor if I didn't know the happenings in the region, and I'd be an even worse governor if I didn't know the happenings in the palace."

"True. Is that why you were so bothered last night?"

He shook his head. "Not completely." I didn't ask him for the particulars, and he didn't offer any. I just stood there, awkwardly waiting for him to say more.

The night before, he'd been conflicted, and his brooding continued throughout the day. His brown eyes were piercing me through with unspoken questions. I refused to be intimidated by him, so I lifted my chin and met his gaze.

"Am I allowed to stay?" I asked.

"You cut right to it, don't you?"

"I see that I have no choice."

His brow furrowed, and he glared at me. "Why do you say that?"

"I am in your service. If you dismiss me, Astur, then I'm forced to find a different path. I cannot go home, and it's not safe to return to the street. I'm of age, now, to join myself to a man, but I do not choose that, either."

He was irritated by that prospect; he saw me as a child. "You wish to stay." He didn't ask it like a question.

I looked at him, confused. "Of course, I wish to stay." It was the truth, and I couldn't hide the smile that followed the words.

He didn't say anything; we just looked at each other from across the room. When he finally spoke, he changed the subject entirely. "You did a great kindness to Lucia today." I nodded once, accepting his compliment. "Myrtle can't stop talking about how you came in and took command. 'For such a little thing, she is to be so bold.'" He mocked Myrtle's inflection, and it made me smile a little. Then, his expression grew serious. "How do you know how to birth a baby?"

"I told you; I'm a healer. I come from generations of healers. I read and study, and before I was orphaned, my family trained me well. Nothing was kept from me."

"How old were you?" he asked, referring to my abandonment.

"Three-and-ten."

He quickly added the years in his head. "You lived alone on the streets for three years?"

"The streets, the woods, and a variety of other places."

"How did you manage to feed yourself?"

"I foraged in the forest, and the great spirit provided for me. When I played my music in town, coins found their way to my feet. It kept me alive. I was able to buy bread and other provision."

"Three years," he marveled and shook his head. "It's a wonder you survived."

"Indeed," I agreed.

The struggle was no longer behind my master's eyes; he had decided whether or not to dismiss me. I stood to my full height and braced myself for his words. Either way, they would direct my path. He cleared his throat before he spoke.

"I know you've had a long day, Phina, but will you play for me tonight?"

My usefulness proved itself once again, and the great spirit secured my path. After Astur left my room, I twirled around with relief, thankful, and delighted to stay. Suppertime had already passed, so I waited until Astur settled in his bed for the night. I moved to my stool and resumed my usual task. He'd been without my music for weeks and a day.

At the first strum of the chord, he audibly sighed and rolled over away from me. The shadow of his shoulders relaxed, and he fell into a deep sleep. His light snore comforted me. I had missed him more than I wanted to admit, and his return only made it more apparent. Perhaps at his sigh, he'd missed me too or, at least, my music.

The next day, I checked on Lucia and the baby. Little Traian nursed well. Lucia's coloring was good, and she had rested during the night. Myrtle was seeing to them, and with Cassia's help, Myrtle was managing the household, too. I had little to do except leave ingredients for tea. I promised to return frequently and check on them.

"Please, send for me if you need anything. I'll be in the garden or my room."

"I know where to find you, child," Lucia said, amused. "I'm sorry I didn't believe you before." I lowered my eyes humbly. "Your presence made all the difference."

I looked into her brown eyes. "What do you mean?" I asked.

Her smile was pained. "Years ago," she began and swallowed, "many years ago, my first child died. The pain with Traian was just the same, and I was afraid I'd lose him, too." She looked lovingly into her baby's eyes and traced the outline of his face with her fingertip. "But you changed all of that. You made a difference. For one so young, how did you know?"

"I'm not *that* young," I said in a whisper.

"I know that now, too." I cocked my head to one side, wondering at her meaning. "The governor told Felix, and they thought I should know as well. Your secret is safe, Phina, but I caution you," she said sternly. "Be wise and look after yourself. You're a woman now, a beautiful, young woman with talents. Even within the palace walls, you might not be as safe as you think." I nodded and received her words. She meant them sincerely.

"Cato?" I asked, but I hadn't seen him again since the garden.

"Not only."

"Who?" I couldn't imagine any threat from the women, but there were always soldiers guarding the palace.

She shook her head. "I don't know, but I'd rather you be cautious."

I would heed her words; they'd come from a place of concern for my well-being. "Yes, ma'am," I said before I turned to go.

"Thank you, Phina."

"It was my pleasure, Lucia. He's beautiful; it is an honor to be in your service."

"In the service of a housemaid," Lucia scoffed.

I shrugged. "Housemaids or governors, I like being useful for my friends."

A flash of warning crossed her expression. "He's not your friend, Phina. He's your master, a terribly indulgent master, but still. Please, child, don't mistake his kindness for friendship."

My stomach tightened at her words, and tears pricked my eyes. I nodded reflexively and blinked back the tears that threatened. "Yes, ma'am," I said quickly and hurried from her room.

I had to stop on the stairs to catch my breath. The tears burst through before I could make it to my room. I was confused and conflicted. I didn't understand my feelings, and my thoughts ran in different directions. Had I mistaken Astur's kindness for friendship? No, his heart was pure; I had not misread that. He'd asked me to call him by name when we were alone. Sure, he indulged my requests and comforted my fears, but maybe Lucia was right. After all, he was my master and had the power to keep me or dismiss me. I needed to protect myself and remember two things. This was not my home, and Astur was not my friend.

Chapter Fifteen

The next few months were joyful. Lucia's confinement passed quickly, and she returned to the management of the household with a vengeance. Felix insisted that she and the baby move into his small apartment with him. It was only a short walk across the back courtyard to the kitchen.

Word soon spread throughout the palace that I had assisted in Traian's birth. Within a couple of days, the women came to me for help with a number of ailments: stiff joints, dry skin, and an occasional headache.

The soldiers found me after that. I was most often in the garden, so they came there and shyly asked for my assistance. Their ailments usually concerned chafed skin and rashes, irritable stomachs, and odor in their boots. It was all easy enough to manage, and I enjoyed the interaction. The soldiers were all on their best behavior, but that was what Felix commanded of them. Serving at the palace was a great honor.

Once Lucia returned to the household's command, she most often wore her little one wrapped securely in a sling. I began the habit of taking Traian into the garden with me in the afternoons. It was the time of day when he was fussy, and Lucia was busy preparing supper.

Traian preferred being outdoors. He cooed and made his sweet baby noises up toward the sky. Mostly I wore him in the sling like Lucia; he liked it when I sang to the flowers or read aloud in his presence. His blond hair came in thick and wavy, and his eyes gradually darkened to his mother's brown.

One particularly pleasant afternoon, I heard loud horns blasting. Then the sound of hoofbeats thundered toward the palace, and men's voices rose in a clamor. I placed Traian in the sling and looked over the wall; at least fifty mounted soldiers approached. I was frightened for a moment, thinking the palace was under attack, but then realized they were all wearing the palace symbol on their uniforms.

Flags and banners adorned the front entrance. Astur and Felix and the guards greeted the soldiers from the steps of the palace. Astur stood proudly, dressed in his finest cloak and tunic. The soldiers dismounted from their horses, removed their helmets, and walked in a procession, saluting their governor and commanding officer in turn.

The captain of the men bowed before he walked up the dozen or so steps. Four men flanked him. I gasped at the sight. My body reacted before my mind. My heartbeat quickened; I could hardly catch my breath.

The second soldier to the captain's right was tall. His shoulders were broader than I remembered, but he was still tall and lean. Although it was cropped short, there was no mistaking he had hair as black as raven's wings. His keen eyes took in his surroundings, and without a doubt, his eyes were the lazuli blue.

"Erik!" I panted.

Erik was at the palace! I held Traian securely and ran from the garden. Without thinking, I ran toward the front entrance. I slowed myself as I rounded off the stairs. Guards stood at attention, waiting for their next command. I could see Felix's back, and when I stood on my tiptoes, I saw Erik's brow.

At that, one of the guards recognized me. He quietly cleared his throat to get my attention. Begrudgingly, I looked at him. I could read him easily. The rash on his neck from the ivy was gone. His eyes told me that my presence was unwelcome, and he looked disapprovingly at me. I took note of myself. In my haste, I hadn't replaced my veil. I adjusted it, smoothed my tunic, and checked my headwrap. Traian's eyes were wide and curious. Thankfully, he was settled with me and didn't cry.

The guards moved quickly, and the air in the palace changed. Astur passed in front of me, but I wasn't watching him. Felix turned and allowed the four soldiers to pass in front of him. The captain was first, then the three others, and finally Erik. I couldn't remain still. My delight and relief at seeing him were too much to contain.

"Erik!" I exclaimed, unable to keep his name from escaping. My feet followed my words, and before I could stop myself, my arms wrapped around him. I buried my face in his chest, so thankful. He had kept his promise to return to me; the great spirit made it possible.

The soldiers bristled and turned at the interruption to the governor's procession. A veiled woman with a baby didn't pose much threat, and the palace guards knew me, but that didn't make them any less protective. The sound of unsheathed swords rang in my ears.

At the sound of his name, Erik turned, but he didn't return my embrace. He deftly removed my arms from around him and stepped back, holding me at a distance. He didn't recognize me. I felt everyone's eyes boring into me, but my eyes were only on Erik.

The captain was the first to speak. "What is this?" His tone was unamused and condescending.

My eyes flashed around at the men. Felix was conflicted that I was standing there, holding his son, and Astur looked even more cautious than usual. He lifted his hand to direct his guards.

"At ease," Astur commanded. "Phina, what is the meaning of this?" His tone was measured and calm.

I smiled behind my veil, but he couldn't see that. I hoped he could read my eyes. "Forgive me, sir," I begged. "Please, it's Erik."

That's when I heard Erik's low voice. "Phina?" The confusion was there, too, when I looked up. I hoped he would know me. Tears of joy flooded my eyes when recognition crossed his face, and, for the briefest of moments, he returned my smile. We took a step toward one another; I anticipated the embrace that would make him real.

Suddenly, he stopped, remembering where he was and in whose company. He looked at the child in my arms, and anger flashed in his eyes. I stepped back, reading his expression.

"Erik, do you know this woman?" his captain asked impatiently.

"Yes, sir, she is my relation," Erik replied. His voice was commanding and authoritative. I was relieved that he recognized me, but I'd never heard that tone from him before.

"When our meetings conclude, perhaps the governor will afford you a visit, but this is not the time."

I looked to Astur, hoping he would make it so. He lifted his chin and cautiously examined Erik. Finally, Astur acknowledged my request with a brief nod. His hardened features made me uncomfortable, yet I was satisfied. I had interrupted the governor's business with the army, and I wasn't sure if he was disappointed that I'd been so impulsive or if it was something else. With so many men in my presence, their hearts and intentions bombarded me. I couldn't read them all at once.

"Thank you, sir," I said humbly. "My apologies. I'll be in the garden." I bowed my head slightly and retreated to the garden to wait.

I tried to read. I tried to tend to the flowers, but I was too excited to be still. *Six years!* It had been six years since I'd seen Erik. So much had transpired in the last third of my life. I wondered what he'd been doing all that time. Unable to settle myself, I ended up humming and dancing around the garden with Traian. He enjoyed the movement and music. He always liked the music.

It was nearly suppertime when Felix led Erik into the garden. Traian was sleeping peacefully. In Erik's presence, Felix admired his son from a distance. I wasn't surprised at that, but I was surprised by Erik's expression.

"Will you be fine with him here?" Felix asked, referring to the baby. I nodded.

"Yes, we're fine. Thank you," I replied.

Erik's concern increased as he watched our exchange, but he didn't say anything. I looked up into his lazuli eyes and took a few steps toward him. "Oh, Erik, I'm so happy to see you. It's been too long." He'd left our home just past his boyhood, and now a grown man stood before me. I hoped enough of the boy who was my closest friend remained. I searched his face for any sign of him. "When did you return to the region? How long will you be here?" He didn't answer my questions and instead shook his head in bewilderment. "Erik, what is it?" I asked.

"I can't believe you're here."

"I can't believe you're here, either." The veil concealed my smile.

"May I see you? I want to see your face."

"Of course, I forget."

I fumbled with the fabric and shifted Traian so that I could lower my veil. Erik's response was unexpected. Instead of moving toward me, he stepped back and cursed.

"You look just like your mother," he gasped.

"I know; it surprises me, too. I catch Mother's reflection sometimes and think she's there with me. Then I look closer, and the eyes aren't the same at all."

"No, but they aren't the same as when you were a child either. They're almost silver." He moved in closer, then, and examined my face. "How long have you been here?"

"It's been well over a year, almost two."

"Where is everyone? Grandmother and Grandfather? Your mother?"

My eyes pricked at his question. I took a deep breath; of course, that would be his first concern. "They're gone, Erik. They're all dead." Tears welled in my eyes; I hated giving him that news.

His eyes were troubled, and he shook his head, denying the truth. The flash of anger returned. "How old is the child?" he asked.

I looked fondly at a sleeping Traian and smiled indulgently. I couldn't help but adore him. "He's only a few months old."

Erik's jaw tightened. "I've heard rumors that the governor kept a girl at the palace for his pleasure. How could you?" I didn't like his tone and what it implied.

I was the one to step back then. This was not the reunion I anticipated. "You misunderstand my circumstances, Erik," I said defensively.

"What have I misunderstood?" he asked. His voice rose in frustration, but he didn't let me answer. "After all this time, I find you veiled in the palace. The leader of our army and the governor both honor you with deference. Your eyes aren't painted like a claimed woman, yet you've given him a child." Erik's anger was no longer a flash, and he spat the words.

I gasped, unprepared for his accusations. How could he think that? Then, I realized; Traian had been with me all afternoon. I laughed. "Oh, Erik, Traian isn't Astur's son," I managed between giggles. Erik frowned.

"*Astur*?" he asked incredulously. "You call Governor Gaius Julianus by his given name?"

I covered my mouth reflexively; it had slipped out. I wasn't doing much to defend myself. "Please, Erik, let me explain. He's Felix and Lucia's son. I help with him sometimes."

Just then, Lucia came into the garden. She and Erik eyed one another. She could tell that there was tension between us. She walked deliberately towards me and put out her hands to take Traian. As I passed him over, Traian stirred; it was time for him to nurse.

"You alright out here?" Lucia asked.

"Yes, ma'am. I'm fine. Lucia, this is Erik; Erik, this is Lucia, Traian's mother."

Lucia nodded once respectfully. "Pleased to make your acquaintance," Lucia said politely, but I doubted her sincerity. She noticed our resemblance; there was no mistaking a connection.

Once we were alone in the garden, Erik relaxed. I invited him to sit near me on a bench against the wall. "Erik, it is true that the governor keeps me, but I play music for him; that is all." Erik's features softened, and I took his hand. He looked down at it and stared. "Please, I don't want to quarrel. I have missed you and so many times wished for your return. I didn't know if I'd ever see you again, and yet, here you are."

Erik's eyes met mine again, and tentatively, he lifted his hand like he wanted to make sure I was real. His hand fisted, and he withdrew his other hand from mine. Confusion and anger collided in his eyes.

"Two years ago, I went to the cottage; everything was in disarray and abandoned. All that I found of you was your braid." I put my hands over my mouth, understanding. "I thought you were dead, Phina," he whispered breathlessly. His voice was low as he relived the experience; It had been painful for him. "What happened that would make you cut your hair?"

I looked away across the garden. I hated talking about it, but he needed to know. "Many horrible things," I confessed. "I didn't want to cut my air, but I knew I'd be safer without it."

He frowned at that. "Safer from what?" I shook my head, dismissing his question. I didn't want to talk about that. They were each taken from me, and I was left to fend for myself. Erik was impatient to know and didn't leave me long in my distraction. "What happened, Phina?" he asked like a command.

I composed myself and began the horrid tale. "Grandfather died peacefully in his sleep about a year after you left. We grieved but knew he was with the great spirit." Speaking of Grandfather's passing was naturally sad but not as painful as the rest. I tried several times to begin, but I just couldn't find the words.

Erik sensed the pain that it caused me and released his breath and tension slowly. He waited patiently for my explanation. I took a deep breath and began, "Soldiers came and found Mother unprotected. Grandmother and I ran to her aid, but the soldiers had already gotten to her. She fought them to protect me but lost her own life. We watched as they raped and murdered her."

I didn't look away as I told the story. I wanted Erik to know the truth. "Grandmother dragged me away from the house. We spent the night by the river, and the next morning, she, too, was dead. She had no injuries; the shock

102

and overexertion to get me to safety were too much for her." Erik's eyes dulled, and he sat unmoving as he listened. He refused to accept the pain of my words.

"I sang blessings and thanks over them and hid their bodies the best I could. Your old clothes and Grandfather's dulcimer were all that remained after the soldiers looted us. They protected me for a long time."

Erik said nothing, so I continued, "I lived as a boy for three years, playing music on the street. I retreated to the woods often, but I never returned to the cottage. The great spirit kept me safe, and I was able to earn coins to keep myself fed. Felix found me playing music and brought me to the palace. He thought I was a boy and would be of service to the governor." I laughed, remembering. "They were all surprised to discover otherwise. My music pleases the governor, and so he keeps me." I couldn't read Erik's expression, so I trudged on, "Since my womanhood arrived, I have been able to practice healing. Little Traian was my first to sing forth," I said proudly.

"They allow you to heal?"

"Only a little here at the palace. The women and the guards seek me out. I have a healer's garden over there." I pointed to it. "Here, let me show you."

I took Erik by the hand and led him to the other side of the garden. "You planted this?"

"Oh, no. It's been here for a long time. I've tended to it since my arrival, and it has flourished under my careful hand. The great spirit hears my songs."

Erik turned to me. "You sing for them?" he asked. His eyes flashed with distrust, and I was surprised by his reaction. He knew the ways of a healer's garden.

"Of course, I do. The flowers need it."

"Do you sing for *him*?"

I didn't need to ask of whom he referred. "Erik, I have never sung for a man, and I doubt I will for a long time," I said defensively. Sensing his constant disappointment, my excitement for his presence waned. I lifted my chin and looked into his deep blue eyes. He was a man, and I could clearly read his heart. I was saddened that he couldn't read mine.

He was no longer the young man who had promised to return to me, and although he was the closest thing to family, he was neither my father nor my brother. "I can see your hesitation and doubt. This is not at all what I expected from you. Perhaps it might be better if we resume this conversation another time." I smiled politely to conceal the tears that threatened behind my eyes. "I need to eat my supper and ready myself for the evening." My voice broke as I curtsied and turned to go. I couldn't be there anymore.

"Phina," Erik called after me, frustration poured off of him. I hated leaving him, but I had to get away.

Chapter Sixteen

Astur ate his supper with Erik's captain, and I wondered if Erik was there, too. It was late when Astur returned to his chambers. I heard him come in and get into bed. I sat on my little stool and played; I closed my eyes and strummed. The music settled me, and perhaps I needed it more than Astur did that night. Mine and Erik's conversation in the garden replayed in my mind. Astur was restless and didn't fall asleep at his usual time.

He rolled over and sighed loudly. He muttered a curse under his breath and sat up. "Phina," he said in a whisper.

I opened my eyes at the sound of my name. "Yes?" I answered but continued to play.

"May we talk?"

"Of course, Astur, it would be my pleasure." Knowing he was fully awake, I began a livelier tune that I knew he liked.

He reached for his robe and rose from the bed. He walked toward a bottle of wine and poured himself a glass. He rarely drank wine at night, and I was surprised when he walked toward me and offered me a glass, too.

I placed my instrument against the wall behind me and took the glass he offered. He then offered me his hand. I took it and stood and allowed him to lead me to the sofa at the foot of his bed. I sat down tentatively and watched him. This was a very odd exchange between us. He pulled up a chair and sat across from me. He raised his glass and encouraged me to taste the wine. I followed his lead. The wine tasted good, and I couldn't hide the smile that followed.

"I was curious about your relation, Erik. I spoke with him tonight. He's a good soldier, and his captain speaks highly of him." Astur took another sip of his wine, and I did the same. "Until this afternoon, I had forgotten. You mentioned him when you told me about your family. That was a while ago, but there's no denying it. Your hair is the same color, and I've never seen eyes like either one of yours." Astur knew my hair color well; he'd seen my head unwrapped plenty of times, but he'd never made mention of it. "Did you have a pleasant reunion in the garden?" he asked.

I lowered my eyes toward my glass and took another sip. I didn't know how to answer that. "It came as a shock to both of us. He went to the cottage, and when he found it abandoned, he thought I was dead."

Astur frowned. "I can see how that would be."

"Once the shock passed, he was disappointed more than he was pleased."

I felt Astur's concern for me. "Why would he be disappointed?" he asked.

"He found me here. He presumed the worst."

"What did he presume about you?" he asked protectively.

I glanced at Astur reprovingly. "What could he think?" I shrugged. "He found me in the palace, veiled with a child. He had heard the rumors about your keeping a woman, a girl. I can only imagine what else might have been eluded to in those rumors. It took some time to convince him otherwise. I'm not sure he believes me." I lowered my gaze. "He thought Traian was mine. He presumed that I was your mistress and that Traian was yours."

Astur stood suddenly and poured himself another glass of wine. "I'm sorry."

"It's not your doing. It made sense, but he was mistaken. I think the next time we speak, it will be easier. I regret leaving him so suddenly, but his words were sharp. I hope it wasn't my only opportunity. I'd like him to know me again." I looked hopefully into Astur's eyes. He would be the only one to allow it.

"I disagree."

"I understand." I lowered my gaze again. He had every right to deny me. I blinked hard; I didn't want to cry.

Realizing how I'd taken his words, he began again. "I disagree because it is all my doing. They don't know you, but your reputation is tainted because I keep you. The rumors circulate because gossip is easily afforded, and the senators will do anything to reduce me. I have no power to stop their tongues, and I know Cato and a few others keep their speculations about you flowing."

Astur placed his hand over his eyes and put his thumb and middle finger in at his temples. He then pressed them into his eyes before he let his hand stroke down his face, finally resting it at the base of his throat. He took in a deep breath and exhaled slowly. It was the way he always released the strain of difficult conversations.

"I'm sorry, Astur. I don't mean to upset you."

He looked down at me indulgently. "You haven't, but I am concerned. What will become of you?" he asked rhetorically.

I shrugged. "I hope to remain here and practice my healing."

"He mentioned no plans to take you away?" he asked.

I was surprised by his question. "Who? Erik?" I asked. "He cannot," I said plainly. Astur looked confused and somewhat bewildered.

"Even as your governor, your brother has more of a right to you than I do."

I covered my mouth and laughed aloud, unable to contain it. "Oh, Astur, I can see why you would think that, but Erik is not my brother. We were raised together, yes, but he was apprenticed to Grandfather."

"He is a healer?"

"I do not know. We did not speak of that."

"He has intentions for you, then? Were you promised to him?" Astur's jaw tightened at the question.

I laughed again. "No, Astur, I was not. I was one-and-ten when he was conscripted, nowhere near being a woman. At the rate my body matured, he would have been waiting a long time." Astur understood, and I felt the blush rise to my cheeks.

"Has he proposed?" Astur asked. I couldn't tell his tone.

I laughed again. "No, we all but argued today. Until he believes me, I doubt Erik has any thoughts of that. Besides, I have no elder to arrange anything for me. I'm not sure if the cottage is even inhabitable. I suppose Grandfather's land would have passed to me, but I cannot be sure. Taxes being what they are and all the statutes of your law and land, I doubt I could afford to reclaim it."

"What do you know of those things?" he asked.

"From the books and parchment in your library."

"Why does that surprise me?" He chuckled under his breath.

"I do not know," I said wryly.

"You surprise me, Phina. I thought you might be eager to leave with him."

"No, Astur, I don't wish that at all. Erik was apprenticed to Grandfather when I was five. For as many years as we were separated, we shared our lives. He was once very dear to me, but today, I met a stranger. Six years was a long time to share our lives, but it's an even longer time to be apart. I do not know what will become of any of this. My mind is a muddle, and I do not know my own heart. It may take days to reconcile."

Astur nodded knowingly. "Do you wish to play for me tonight, or would you rather be alone with your thoughts?"

I considered his question. I sipped what remained of my wine and stood, offering him my glass. He rarely asked me to play or gave me a choice. I understood his expectations, and he had only relieved me from my duty a few times. He was honoring me, but I knew that he wanted me to play for him. His heart was always clear on that subject, and I didn't want to refuse him.

"I can think and play at the same time." He smiled, and we resumed our routine.

***

A few days passed. I did not see Erik, and for all I knew, he had not sought me out. Astur was preoccupied with soldiers and army things. I tended to the garden, read, and helped with Traian. I sang for the flowers and did a bit of healing.

One evening before I played, Astur handed me a small envelope. I looked at it in surprise. He'd never given me anything to read before.

"It's from Erik. He asked that I give it to you."

"What does it say?" I asked.

"I didn't read it," he said defensively.

"I didn't mean to suggest you had. I thought Erik may have told you."

Astur chuckled. "I'm his governor, Phina. It took a great deal for him to approach me and ask a favor of me. He's brave and determined. As a soldier, I see his merit, but as a man, I'll defer to your good judgment." I held the envelope in my hand, unsure if I should read it in front of Astur. "I suspect it's an apology and a request to see you. He did ask me that much." Astur nodded toward the letter. "Go ahead; read it," he encouraged. I bit my bottom lip and turned away from him before I opened the envelope eagerly.

My Dearest Phina,

I deeply regret the way we parted. Please, forgive me. I hope to see you again, and I promise to listen and understand.

Erik

Chapter Seventeen

Astur agreed to relay my consent, and Erik came to the palace the following afternoon. He found me in the garden, tending to the flowers. He knelt down next to me and assumed a familiar posture. We had worked side-by-side together like that in Grandfather's garden. I didn't say anything and waited for him to speak first, confident that he wouldn't repeat our last encounter.

"You were always better at this than I was. The flowers preferred your tiny hands to mine," he complimented. His words were almost playful, and I eased at the tone of his voice. His heart was contrite.

"You weren't as patient," I replied.

Erik chuckled. "Grandfather tried, but he didn't quite succeed."

At that moment, Erik resembled everything that was once familiar to me, and I wanted to know him better. "Are you a patient soldier?" I asked.

"I am more patient than most, but there is always room for improvement."

"The governor says your captain speaks highly of you, that you're a good soldier." I purposefully didn't use Astur's name. I didn't want to provoke Erik with my words.

"I serve a purpose, and I do it well." His words carried no arrogance.

My work was finished, so I dusted off my hands and stood. Erik followed me to a barrel of water, where we washed our hands. "Do you like the army?" I asked. I wanted to keep him talking.

He smiled at my question. "Yes. At first, I was not sure. When I left my home to apprentice with Grandfather, I had no doubt that I was on the right path. The first few months of my conscription were brutal, but soon I was content there, too. My ability to read men's hearts has made me a trusted advisor. My captain doesn't question my ability; he simply uses it to his advantage. That, in turn, gives me an advantage."

I led Erik back to the bench where we'd sat before. He waited until I was comfortable before he sat down next to me. "Thank you for agreeing to see me," he began. "I didn't like the way we parted."

"I'm sorry, too. I was confused, and your doubt was a burden."

Erik frowned. "I know; I could tell. May we begin again?" he asked. His words were kind.

"I'd like that. Thank you." I hoped he could read the sincerity in my eyes. My smile was broad behind my veil.

"May I?" he asked. I looked into the familiar lazuli of his eyes. He gestured toward the cloth that covered my nose and mouth. I didn't refuse, so he gently lowered the fabric from my face. "That's better." He smiled, and his boyish mischief returned. "I've been all over this land, and I don't think I will ever get used to that, the veils, I mean."

I shrugged. "I haven't worn it very long, so I often forget. Where all have you been?"

"I was assigned to my captain a few months after my training. He was not a captain then. He was a lieutenant, but as his rank rose, so did mine."

"Do you serve as a healer?" I asked.

Erik pursed his lips and looked away. He didn't answer. Regret poured from his heart. He finally shook his head. "I'm afraid not. My odd appearance and abilities draw enough attention. Besides warning soldiers what not to eat in the woods, I haven't used any of my healing knowledge in years. I'm embarrassed to say that I might have to begin my studies anew."

He stood and gestured toward the healer's garden. "How have you managed to maintain the plants so well?" he asked.

"I took Mother's book from the cottage and read it at every opportunity. For years, it was the only thing I had to read. Since coming here, I have access to the palace library. There are many wonderful books; I have learned a great deal."

Erik eyed me skeptically. "You must be very sneaky to get past the guards."

"There is no need to sneak." He doubted me again. "Erik," I began with gentle reproof. "Why do you continue to question me?"

"Their customs, their ways. I cannot name even five women who can read in this kingdom." He held up his long fingers for emphasis. "Do they know you can read?"

"Yes," I said defensively. "It is not something I flaunt, but the governor knows and a maid or two."

"He did not forbid it?" I blinked at his question. I'd never considered that Astur would do such a thing, but then again, Lucia had described him as indulgent. I supposed he could have restricted my access to books, but he couldn't limit my prior abilities and knowledge.

"The governor gave me access to the library soon after my arrival. He was surprised to know I could read, but he's accepted that about me. He's kind to me and trusts me; my ability to read and tend to the garden pose no threat to him." I smiled encouragingly. "Please, Erik, come and sit with me, or if you prefer, we can walk the grounds. I want to be near you and hear about your time as a soldier." Then I reconsidered, "Perhaps you'd rather talk about our time together at the cottage."

That suggestion made him smile. "I'd like nothing better," he said with pleasure.

***

Over the next week, Erik came every other afternoon to the garden. We spoke of many things. We especially liked reminiscing about Grandfather and Grandmother. We laughed at Grandfather's stories. Erik could mimic Grandmother's reproving voice. "Phina! Erik! Who's been at the apples?" Erik said in his best impression of Grandmother. He made me laugh and brought tears of joy to my eyes.

Erik didn't mind that I kept watching over Traian. I brought Mother's book a few times, and once, he asked that I bring the dulcimer. I was delighted that he'd asked. I hadn't heard Erik play since the night he left.

At first, his fingers fumbled over the strings, but it didn't take long for them to remember. He played a few songs that he'd learned from Grandfather. I had forgotten a couple of them; it was nice to hear them again.

That night, I played one of Grandfather's songs for Astur. He never asked about my time with Erik. I suspected he knew each time Erik came to the palace, but Astur did not question me.

"That one is new," he commented.

I smiled. His ear was attuned to the songs I played. He always noticed when I played something different. "Yes, it was one of Grandfather's songs. I had forgotten it."

"Erik's visits brought it back to you?" he asked.

"I suppose so. Erik knew many more songs than I did when Grandfather passed to the great spirit. Erik came to us knowing how to play. We always had music, singing, and dancing. It was a lively home."

"You play for him?" Astur asked. His voice was steady, but I sensed his hesitation and concern. I should have suspected that it might displease him.

"No," I answered honestly. "He mostly plays for me and perhaps a bit for himself. I had forgotten what it was to hear someone else play and sing for my enjoyment."

"Your playing doesn't bring you enjoyment?" I rolled my eyes. Astur didn't understand.

"It's different when I can just listen and not have to concentrate. Except for the occasions when you sing, Astur, no one else shares music with me." I could hear the sadness in my voice. I supposed Astur could, too.

"Play something else, something you've remembered," he requested. I happily obliged.

***

"Is your heart ever divided, Phina?" Erik asked as we sat one afternoon reading through Mother's book.

Erik's eyes drew my attention and held it. Other than our initial reunion, the time we spent together was pleasant, and I found myself anticipating his visits. "What do you mean?" I asked.

"You study and read, and yet you rarely have use for that knowledge. You garden and plant but have so little to harvest. You waste your music on a man who will never honor the great spirit's gifts or see you as anything other than his servant."

I looked into Erik's eyes and considered his words. "I've never thought of it that way," I finally said. "Nothing I do is wasted. I study and read so that I am prepared when my knowledge will be useful and sometimes to appease my own curiosity. I practice healing some, as you know, and I am gaining confidence. My stores are growing, and I've expanded the healer's garden. In time, those plants will be mature enough for harvesting. We must remember Grandfather's warning, Erik." I raised my finger like Grandfather did when he was making a point. "'Patience and pleasure, young ones, are strange companions. Pleasure is rarely attained without the discipline of patience. Careful to learn that,'" I giggled, mocking Grandfather's wise voice. Erik laughed with me. I liked it when I was able to make him smile. I suspected that he rarely had an opportunity for laughter as a soldier.

"As far as the governor is concerned, I have a safe and comfortable life here. You are right; he knows nothing of the great spirit, but I am free to follow the great spirit's ways. Like you, my abilities serve a purpose, and he has never limited my music or my songs to the great spirit."

There was a mixture of concern and irritation that washed over Erik. I waited patiently for his question. His doubt would find the words. "Have you sung for him?" he almost accused. I was not offended that he'd repeated the question; he was making sure that I had not given my heart to another.

I shook my head. "No, Erik, I have not. I already told you that."

He smiled, trusting my words. He was reassured. "You've changed so much, Phina. You aren't the girl I left behind."

I shook my head. "No, I am not. While we are on the subject, is your heart ever divided?"

Erik stood and walked a few paces, considering my words. "Before my conscription, I thought that I'd serve my time and then return to Grandfather's house to be a great healer like him." Erik smiled and chuckled low. "I saw my life, our lives, simply. I promised to return to you, but the great spirit had other plans than what I imagined."

"What did you imagine?" I asked.

"I saw you in the garden with your mother. I planned it all out. Over supper and wine, I would ask for your hand. There would be a celebration, and on the next full moon, the great spirit would unite us, make us one."

"That is all very nice, Erik, but I never knew you had such intentions for me." I looked away as the blush covered my neck. Warmth covered me entirely. The hope of a different future tapped on my heart.

He moved back to me and tilted my chin with the tip of his finger. "You've grown into a beautiful woman, Phina, and I think I love you more than I did when you were a child."

I took in a quick breath. "You love me?" I asked in a whisper.

"Of course, I do. I always have."

His words were gentle, and his lazuli eyes blazed as he leaned in and kissed me. I liked the feel of his lips on mine. When he put his arms around me, heat passed all the way from my chest to my knees. I leaned into the kiss, enjoying his touch. Physical contact was rare, and I desired it more than I admitted. Unsure how long we were like that, alone and kissing, I didn't want it to end.

Chapter Eighteen

"Phina." I jumped at the sound of my name. It was Felix. Erik released me and stepped protectively in front of me to face his commander. I touched my lips reflexively. I had not been kissed since Mother's death, and I had never been kissed like that. "Soldier," Felix said commandingly, but nothing followed.

Erik stood at attention, lifted his chin proudly, and saluted. "Sir," Erik replied. I gathered myself and replaced my veil. Much like with Astur, I was in the habit of not wearing it in Erik's presence.

"Phina, the governor wishes to see you."

I was surprised. Astur never called for me during the day. "Yes, of course," I stammered. As I left the garden, I looked back toward Erik. He stood straight and tall. I hated that we had been interrupted, but he gave no hint as to his thoughts.

Felix eyed me warily as we walked toward the library. I didn't have to read his heart to know his thoughts. He was commanding and determined in his pace. "You are concerned and wish to warn me," I said, sounding small behind him.

Felix exhaled and shook his head but didn't stop walking. "Among other things."

"What other things?" I asked, quickening my pace.

"He saw you kissing Erik."

"Is that why he sent you?"

"No."

"Have I done something wrong?" I asked, unsure of why he felt the need to warn me.

Felix shook his head. "No. He has allowed it. You are within your rights to spend time with Erik, and I suppose you may kiss him if you choose." Felix's tone sounded oppositional to my rights. He disapproved, but I was unsure if it was of my behavior or of Erik.

I moved ahead of him and stopped, determined to understand. Felix stopped when I put up my hand. "Are you disappointed in me?" I asked.

"No, Phina."

"So, why must you warn me that he saw us kiss?" Felix hesitated. "Tell me, Felix. I want to know."

Felix took in a deep breath and exhaled slowly. "He doesn't want you to go."

"I'm not going anywhere," I argued, but that wasn't it entirely. "There's more, isn't there?" I asked.

Felix hesitated again and tightened his jaw, resisting his urge to answer me. I stubbornly crossed my arms over my chest. I didn't care if Astur was waiting; I refused to move until Felix told me. Felix could have lifted me easily and carried me to the library, but he didn't. Instead, he exhaled through his pointed nose and rolled his eyes. Felix lowered his voice and leaned in toward my ear. "He cares for you, Phina. It pains him to see you with another man," he said.

I was shocked. I shook my head quickly, denying his words, and yet, I was conflicted that my actions pained Astur. It was never my intention to harm anyone; it was not the healer's way.

"You are mistaken, Felix. Lucia warned me. He is kind and indulgent; that is all," I whispered. My stomach tightened, and tears pricked my eyes. I was forced to blink back the emotion, flooded with insecurity that, either way, I'd misread his heart. Surely, I would be able to know.

Felix put his hands on my shoulders and forced me to pay careful attention to him. He looked directly into my eyes and spoke his words purposefully.

"Lucia has not had an easy life and has many misgivings of men in authority. She warned you because she cares about you, but I know Astur."

I swallowed. The truth of Felix's words flowed from his hands. He knew his friend, indeed. I thought about Erik's kiss that was still fresh on my lips. I remembered the comfort of both Erik and Astur's arms. Even Felix's touch, at that moment, felt safe. Their care for me was all similar.

"I know that you speak the truth, Felix, but I don't know what power this knowledge gives me."

He scoffed slightly but didn't release me. "Power? Don't you see? You hold all the power. You make him a better governor; you make him a better man."

"I cannot take credit for what gifts the great spirit has given him."

"I know nothing of your great spirit and gifts. I do know that your presence has made all the difference."

I thought of the way Astur was when I first arrived at the palace. So many things had changed. He laughed and sang with me. I had not heard him argue with his advisor, Marcus, in months. He managed his interactions with the senators and his army well. The region was at peace.

When he was heavily burdened, I played softly and allowed him to reason through his thoughts aloud. Occasionally, I would suggest a solution or interject an observation, but I was not an advisor in any official capacity. I just reasoned that it helped him sort his thoughts so that he could rest peacefully.

Felix's compliment delighted me, and I smiled beneath my veil. It pleased me that my presence was a blessing to Astur. Then fear struck my gut, and I placed my hand on my middle. The gossip, Erik's accusations, and what was presumed of the governor played over in my mind. My age was known to him, my womanhood, and my dependence.

"Will he require more than my music?" I asked.

Felix cocked his head to one side. "What do you mean?

"Does he wish for me to be more than a healer and minstrel in his palace?"

It was well within the governor's right to take any woman he desired. According to the histories I had read, many governors had both wives and mistresses. Astur kept neither. He only kept me.

I steadied myself and lifted my chin assertively. I lowered my veil so that Felix could hear me clearly. "Now that I'm of age, will he take me as a mistress?" I whispered in Felix's ear.

Felix stepped back, and his eyes widened. He was angered at the prospect. He shook his head, but not in a way that denied the possibility. I stood proudly, waiting for Felix to answer me. If he knew something, then I wanted to know, too.

"I don't know, Phina." Felix's eyes looked sad. "I know nothing of his intentions." He sounded disappointed, but I wasn't sure if it was in Astur or himself for not knowing.

I replaced my veil and turned. "I will go to him."

"Phina, wait," Felix called after me.

I shook off his words. "No, Felix. There's nothing more you need to say. We neither know, so I refuse to waste my time speculating. He will make his mind known in time."

It was Felix that had to keep with my pace as I hurried toward the library. The guards opened the door for me as Felix and I approached. Astur looked up briefly at my arrival but returned to his work. He didn't look at me directly.

"Will you be needing me, sir?" Felix asked.

"No, thank you," Astur said with polite command.

I caught Felix's eye, and he nodded once encouragingly. As soon as Felix was gone, Astur looked down at the papers on his desk. I stood waiting for him to acknowledge me.

I watched him write something on a bit of parchment. He rolled it up and set it to the side. He concentrated on his papers, so I looked out the window. The view of the garden was clear. Felix was right; Astur could see everything. I wondered if he watched Erik and me during our visits. I wondered if he watched me in the garden often. Other than his chamber and my room, the garden was where I spent most of my days.

The kiss replayed in my mind, and I felt the warmth of Erik's touch and how I had leaned into him. I looked back toward Astur. He had yet to look up at me. I closed my eyes and sketched Erik's heart against my own. He'd confessed his love for me before he kissed me.

Erik's heart was layered with mine. He'd loved my child's heart and only recently had begun to love my woman's heart. His heart's colors were vibrant, bright oranges and reds, fiery like a sunset or a flame. His heart's shape was angular and sharp. The fractures in his heart had only begun to heal, leaving dark and unknown areas.

Felix's words interrupted my sketch, and I tried to deflect their distraction. I took a deep breath, but Astur's presence pressed in against my thoughts of Erik. I sketched Astur's heart to compare. I smiled a little because Astur's heart didn't need to be drawn. I already knew it well. His heart was rounded and solid, strong, and filled to the brim with deep greens and the blue of the sky. His fractures were evident, too, but time had rubbed them smooth like the shiny pebbles in the river.

Felix's words were true. Astur did care for me, but he cared for many. He cared for his citizens. He cared for his household. He cared for Lucia and Felix, and especially Traian. At the sound of rustling paper, I opened my eyes.

"Phina," he said and gestured for me to come closer. I approached his desk. He motioned for me to lower my veil. It bothered him as much as it bothered Erik not to see my mouth when I spoke to him. His expression softened. Returning to his thoughts, he picked up a letter and unfolded it. He cleared his throat before he said, "We will have guests soon."

"Your mother plans to return?"

"No."

"More soldiers?" I guessed. Astur shook his head. "Then, who?"

"Cato's sister, Livia, and her maid, a cousin, I think." My eyes widened at Cato's name. I understood why Astur wished to see me. "He says his apartments aren't fit for guests. My mother thought it best Livia stay here during her visit."

"What does that have to do with me?" I asked.

He tilted his head to one side and considered his words carefully. "It means that Cato will be at the palace more often to see his sister. I know how that affects you, so I wanted to prepare you." He gave me a moment to let that sink in. "I also ask that you make Livia and her maid feel welcomed. I've asked the same of Lucia and Myrtle. They thought it best that I speak with you as well. Our families, mine and Cato's, have strong ties to the capital, and I am expected to show them every consideration. I want them to feel at home."

I understood. "Will I be expected to play for them?" I asked.

He nodded. "Most likely, but I will give you notice when and if that is asked of you."

"When do they arrive?"

"Tomorrow."

"Do you know Livia well? Is she much like her brother?" I asked cautiously.

"When we were children, Cato was not as he is now. I considered him a friend. Livia is the youngest of his siblings, and we were thrown together often." He smiled at the memory. "She and I visited briefly during my meetings at the capitol. Mother hosted a dinner with many of my old acquaintances. I saw nothing of Cato in her demeanor."

"You speak of your mother. Does she intend for Livia to be your mate, your wife?" I corrected.

Astur stiffened and blinked, and his gaze hardened. I jumped when he released a hard chuckle. He stood and paced a few steps. "Oh," he said. "I had not thought." He muttered several curses. "The woman is cunning. How did I not see?" He returned to the desk and reread the letter. "You see it differently. Thank you, Phina. Thank you for showing me." His tone was full of gratitude.

I lowered my gaze and offered a slight bow of my head. "Will that be all?"

"Yes," he said distractedly. I could tell that he felt trapped, and if I didn't know better, afraid. I couldn't leave him like that.

"Astur," I began. He looked up at his name. His eyes were conflicted. "Please let me know if I may be of any assistance."

"You already have," he said with an appreciative smile. "If you aren't careful, I'll make you an advisor before long," he teased.

"I will do everything to make them feel welcomed, and thank you for considering me."

His eyes softened, and he gave a nod towards me. I knew I was dismissed.

Chapter Nineteen

The next day arrived, but our guests did not. The day after that, they still had not come, so I spent time in the garden with Traian and Erik. It was the first visit since he'd said he loved me and our kissing. Traian was unusually restless and demanded that I stand and walk with him. As long as I was moving, he was content. Erik was patient, yet I could tell he wanted to kiss me again. My feelings were much the same as his.

When Lucia came to get her fitful son, she eyed Erik as if he were the cause of Traian's agitation. "Your supper's ready, Phina," she said in her commanding way.

"Thank you, Lucia. I will be in shortly."

Once we were alone, Erik took my hand and led me to the edge of the garden. It was private there, but I knew we could still be seen from the library. He laid his cloak on the grass and gestured for me to sit down before he joined me.

He retook my hand and traced my fingers with his. He then placed our palms together. His fingers towered over mine. He put his other hand on the other side and hid mine between his. I liked the warmth of his hands and the pressure of our palms as he held them together.

"I have a surprise for you," he said.

His eyes flickered with familiar mischief. At the cottage, he had said those words to me numerous times, but his *surprises* came in the form of creepy, crawly things that tended to jump out of his hands when he opened them.

"I don't remember much liking your surprises," I teased.

He kissed my hand. "I think you'll like this surprise," he said confidently.

I felt giddy at the prospect of a gift. I had not been given one in quite some time, other than my silver tunic and headwrap and my stool, but I didn't think those were gifts as much as they were conveniences.

"Do you have it with you?" I asked.

"No, it's far too big to carry."

"When may I see it?"

"Soon, but I need for you to leave the palace for a day."

I withdrew my hand from his and lowered my gaze. "I don't know if that is possible. I have not left it since I was brought here." Erik lifted my chin and searched my eyes. Their deep blue drew me in and held me fixed. "He doesn't wish for me to go," I whispered, repeating Felix's words.

Erik's expression hardened slightly. "I may make it so that he doesn't have a choice," he said, and then he kissed me. Before I left him, Erik encouraged me, "Ask. I doubt he will refuse you."

That evening when I played for Astur, I asked after his guests' arrival. He commented that they had been delayed but would arrive within a week. I was nervous to ask to leave the palace with Erik. I had never made such a request, and I didn't want to be disappointed.

After Astur finished his supper, I mustered up the courage to speak before he readied himself for bed. "Astur, may I leave the palace with Erik?" Astur set his glass of wine on the table and looked up at me. "He said he has a surprise for me but that it was too big to carry." Thankfully my voice remained steady.

"Where will he take you? How long will you be away?"

I shook my head. "I do not know where, but he said it would just be for the day."

"You wish to go?" he asked.

"Yes." I nodded enthusiastically.

"Do you like surprises?" he asked curiously.

"I did when I was a child, and I suppose that hasn't changed for me. The great spirit surprises me often in the garden, but those gifts are not for me specifically. I look forward to Erik's surprise." I couldn't hide the smile at the anticipation. "That is if you allow me to go." I looked up eagerly, hopeful that he would say yes.

Something passed through his eyes. "Would my consent be a gift to you?" he asked solemnly.

"Indeed." Astur watched me for several heartbeats. He simply nodded but said nothing else for the remainder of the night.

The following afternoon, Erik passed through the garden briefly before a meeting with Felix and his captain. Two soldiers were with him, so I left my veil in place as he approached. He turned and spoke to the men. They stayed near the entrance to the garden.

"I only have a moment. Are you able to go?" he asked but didn't raise his voice.

"Yes, but when?" I matched his tone.

"Tomorrow. I will be here early, so be ready. Meet me outside the kitchen." He smiled and winked. I smiled beneath my veil, and he could read the eagerness in my eyes.

***

I hardly slept. I played for Astur late into the night, thinking it would help settle me, but it only made me more excited. I ate quickly, packed some bread and wine, water, cheese, and fruit for the day, and then waited at the kitchen's entrance. It was the same door that I'd entered with Felix. Erik's arrival was prompt, probably as eager as I was to begin our day together.

Erik rode through the back gate on a tall, black mare. He dismounted and walked purposefully toward me; I was already walking to meet him. He took the basket of food, but he didn't touch me.

"Will we be riding?" I asked, looking up at his horse.

"Yes. Do you mind?"

"No, but except for Grandfather's old mule, I've never ridden."

"Don't worry," he said. "She's gentler than she looks."

Erik helped me onto the beast before he handed me the basket. He then mounted behind me. He took the reins and guided the horse out of the gates.

I had not left the palace in two years; I'd had no reason to. Leaving the palace felt decidedly odd, and I looked up toward my window. The height of the walls made me feel small. The city hadn't changed from what I could tell, but I wasn't paying much attention to it. I was eager for an entire day with Erik. I liked the warmth of him at my back and the closeness of his breath behind me. Erik's eagerness to be rid of the city heightened as he took the closest road from the palace that led out of town. Erik's arms and legs maneuvered the horse confidently.

"When did you learn to ride?" I asked.

"I rode as a boy before I came to live at the cottage. It wasn't that hard to relearn."

"She's beautiful. Have you had her long?" I patted her mane.

"Yes, she's been with me since the beginning. She was my first captain's horse. After he fell in battle, she was skittish. Thankfully, I was able to work with her before she was terminated. It would have been a terrible waste. She's well trained, and the army cannot afford to lose men or horses."

Once we were away from the city's center, I recognized the direction he was going. My stomach tightened, and I was afraid. "Where are you taking me?" I asked.

"You'll see."

"The cottage?" I asked cautiously. I turned to see his face over my shoulder.

"Yes," he replied.

"No." I shook my head and fidgeted in the saddle. "I cannot, Erik. Please, no," I said in a breathy whisper. Tears flooded my eyes, and I couldn't see the road ahead.

Erik slowed his horse's pace and wrapped an arm around my waist to hold me steady. He put his chin on my shoulder and whispered soothing sounds into my ear. "It's okay, Phina. You don't need to be afraid. You are safe with me."

He spoke the truth, but my body shook uncontrollably. "Stop!" I demanded. Erik halted the horse and wrapped both arms around me. The memory of the last time I saw the cottage was too much. Ragged breaths and sobs wrenched my body. Erik held me tightly against his chest. I ripped the veil from my face so that I could breathe. "I do not want this surprise, Erik! Take me back!" I demanded.

"I'm sorry, Phina. I didn't think, but trust me; I would never hurt you like that." He tenderly kissed my temple, and I was distracted by his lips and his strong arms that held me together. "Please allow me this indulgence." I shook my head defiantly. "I promise it will please you." He kissed my cheek and leaned me back, almost cradling me in his left arm so that he could see my face.

His lazuli eyes pierced me through, and I could read the sincerity of his words and feel the promise of his heart. I was safe with him, and I trusted his heart and his words. After a few calming breaths, I begrudgingly nodded my agreement.

He smiled and kissed my mouth, anticipation returning to his expression. "Thank you," he said, and with a kick, spurred his horse to move faster before I changed my mind.

Erik held me close for what remained of our trip. He hummed tunes and whisper-sang into my ear. Before long, his excitement got the better of him, and as he rounded off the road onto Grandfather's property, he was whistling a happy tune.

The path wasn't as overgrown as I'd expected it to be. I could see the roof to the cottage and the side of the barn. The worn path of stones welcomed us. The fields lay fallow, and there were no chickens or goats or cows, but the gardens near the cottage had been weeded recently.

Erik halted the horse. Tears fell again, but in joy, this time. Erik squeezed me gently and quickly kissed my temple before he dismounted.

"Here," he offered, helping me down from the horse.

He removed the horse's saddle and left her to graze in a patch of grass. He took my hand and led me toward the cottage; I strolled behind him, taking it all in. I didn't want to miss anything.

I marveled to see that Grandfather's garden had survived. The plants had been tended to recently. They were not what they had been, but they had somehow survived after all that time.

"Did you do this?" I asked.

"Yes." He smiled proudly. "Is this a *happy* surprise?" I blinked, filled with even more emotion. I didn't trust my words, so I nodded quickly.

He opened the door and stepped back to let me enter. I hesitated, hoping there would be no trace of Mother's rape and murder. I took a deep breath and stepped over the threshold. The cottage was almost empty except for a few pieces of furniture. The floors were swept, and the space was tidy and clean.

"How did you manage it?" I asked.

"I have stayed here many times. Even after I thought you were dead, I couldn't leave it in the state I found it. This is the only home I've ever claimed. Each time I was stationed nearby, it was convenient, but since I've spent my free time with you at the palace, I confess that I paid a few men to help me make it especially inviting."

I walked around the kitchen and placed the basket on the table. The sound was welcoming like I'd just come in from the garden. I let my hand trace along the table and the hearth. I closed my eyes, remembering Grandmother and Grandfather, hearing their laughter and mother's voice calling us to supper. The walls remembered the music and their singing. Joy bubbled up through my chest, and my smile and tears weren't enough to express it. Erik followed me as I walked through each room. He didn't say anything or interrupt my thoughts, but I knew he was watching me. He waited patiently for me to make my way through the cottage.

In Grandmother and Grandfather's room, I noticed that the bed was made with different blankets. Grandfather's chest was still under the bed, but a second chest was next to it. Erik had claimed the cottage and this room.

"May I?" I asked tentatively toward Grandfather's chest.

He nodded once, but I couldn't read his expression. I pulled it out and opened it. There, lying on top of Grandfather's few belongings, was my braid. I reflexively felt the back of my head through my headwrap. I still missed the feel of my hair. It was barely past my shoulders. I touched the braid longingly, but I didn't linger there. I closed the chest and slid it back under the bed.

In the room that I shared with Mother, I knelt down beside her trunk. I opened it carefully and found her skirts and boots. Sprigs of lavender had been laid with them. I lifted a less-faded skirt from the top and pressed it against my chest. I had never worn women's clothes. I had worn skirts and dresses as a child and then spent years in boys' clothing. I looked down at my tunic with the palace symbol, and I suddenly wanted to change out of it. My palace clothes did not belong at the cottage.

"Will you allow me a moment alone?"

Erik cleared his throat. "Of course," he stammered and backed out of the doorway.

I loosened my headwrap and veil and laid them across the top of the chest. I pulled the tunic off over my head. Mother's blouse was a little loose in the shoulders, but the skirt fit well, even if it was a bit too long. I ran my fingers through my hair. It was still short by healers' standards, but I was thankful not to cut it anymore. I tucked the sides behind my ears and checked my appearance. I put on Mother's boots and giggled when my feet slid into them – a perfect fit.

Erik waited for me at the kitchen table. He turned when he heard me enter. He had changed his clothes, too, and was wearing breeches and a linen shirt. His eyes widened when he saw me. He stood formally, acting like a soldier even without a uniform.

"Your hair," he whispered. I tugged at it self-consciously. My cheeks flushed, and I looked down. "No, it is beautiful, Phina. You are beautiful."

129

"Thank you," I said, turning to face him, but it wasn't just for the compliment. He understood that it was for everything.

"Seeing you like this is thanks enough." He smiled admiringly at my appearance. My changes pleased him, and he knew his efforts had been a great gift.

Just like when I'd seen him at the palace, I ran to him and hugged him. This time, he was not surprised, and he returned my embrace, allowing me to settle there in his arms. For the moment, we were free from our obligations. There were no veils, no palace symbols emblazoned on our chests. No one was going to interrupt our privacy or watch us from balconies or libraries. We were Erik and Phina, together again in the cottage.

I heard him sigh as he let his hand stroke down my hair to the small of my back. My hands moved from around his waist, and I could feel his smooth muscles under his shirt. His heartbeat increased, and he took in a deep breath. I sensed his caution to hold me there.

"Let's walk the horse down to the pool and water her," he suggested as he released me. He took the basket from the table and called to his horse with a whistle.

Chapter Twenty

The bathing pool was only a short distance from the cottage. The scent of fresh flowers assailed my senses. "Lilacs!" I exclaimed and ran ahead to gather them in my arms. How I had longed for their familiar aroma. Lilacs did not grow in the palace garden; there were none to be had. Erik chuckled as I smothered my face in their blooms. "Oh, Erik, this is a happy surprise!"

Erik spread his cloak over the ground and inspected the basket that I had packed for us to share. I opened the water and took a sip. Erik uncorked the wine. The horse watered herself at the edge of the pool and then meandered back to a shady spot of grass.

The lilacs were in full bloom, and we were hidden behind their protection. We ate but only spoke a little. It was pleasing, together in the silence between us. The sound of water flowed nearby.

A light breeze lifted my unbound hair, and it tickled my face. Erik reached over and moved a loose strand. "This is nice, even more pleasant than I hoped," he commented.

After we ate, I removed Mother's boots and sat at the edge of the pool, letting my feet dangle into the water. It was tempting to strip down and dive in and bathe. I bit my lip, considering.

Erik removed his boots and joined me. When he offered me bloom from the lilacs, I sniffed it appreciatively. He propped his hand behind me, allowing me to lean into his arm and shoulder. He moved his foot underneath mine in the water, lifting it with his. His feet were considerably larger.

"What do you desire for your life?" he asked.

That was an easy question to answer. "I wish more than anything to be of service through the great spirit, and I wish to be a healer like Mother and Grandfather, but you already know that."

"I have less than a year left with my current enlistment and obligations to the army," he began. I kept my attention on the pool and his foot. I liked the way he touched me, but he hadn't kissed me since we'd arrived at the cottage. "I have been thinking a great deal about what is next for me."

I could feel his eyes watching me again. I leaned into his chest and rubbed my head under his chin. He kissed my hair, and his warmth consumed me. "Where will you go?" I asked. I hoped that his *next* would not be too far away and might somehow include me.

"Not where I will go, but where I will stay."

I liked that. "May I *stay,* too?" I asked.

Erik sat back and laughed. "What do you mean?"

"I don't know; now that you've returned, and you are not misjudging me, I do not want to be without you again."

My words delighted him. "I was hoping you would feel that way. You already know how I feel about you and my intentions to ask the great spirit to join us. Our reunion only makes that purpose stronger, but I must know your heart. Do you want that? Do you love me, Phina?" he asked seriously.

My stomach tightened at the intensity of his question. His lazuli eyes drew me in, but he did not kiss me. He waited for my reply.

I had been flattered by his telling me how he imagined his return from the army. When he'd said that he loved me in the garden, I was honored. He honored me, but I was suddenly unsure of myself. I did not want to be without Erik; I had just said so, but I also felt a pull and conflict toward the palace.

When I did not reply, he doubted me again as he had that first day. "Is your heart divided?" he asked.

I took in a quick breath, and my eyes widened. I assessed my thoughts and feelings. "I am not entirely sure, but I do not think it is divided." I smiled reassuringly. "I never imagined a future with you, and now that you present that possibility, I am hoping for it more and more. I have never professed love to a man; I have never sung for a man. I do not know yet how that is to be; you would be the first."

The fire in his heart flashed with my words. "I would like nothing more than to join our paths and, with a great deal of practice, live here together as healers. It is my greatest desire to be your mate and partner in all things. I wish to claim you. Would you be my mate?"

Grandmother's gift of sight flooded in from behind my eyes. I could see it; I could see clearly the future Erik proposed. We were there, together in the cottage. The garden flourished with everything needed for healing. The hearth was lit and warmed the interior. The scent of sweet cakes lingered in the air. I held a child at my breast, and Erik bounced two others on his knees. Their hair was as black as ravens' wings. Their eyes were their father's. That was most assuredly the future I wanted.

"Yes, Erik, I will be your mate," I whispered in the space between us.

I anticipated that he would lean in and kiss me, but he did not. He allowed the words to linger there, absorbing the declaration as something sacred. He took my face in his hands and ran his long fingers through my hair. I sighed at his touch and pressed myself against him.

"Oh, Erik," I panted through a smile, wanting him to kiss me and hold me close, yet still, he did not.

I had made a revelation about myself since the kiss in the garden and Felix's warnings. When my emotions ran, it was more challenging to read a man's heart. When I was consumed by my own thoughts and feelings, I was unable to use my gift. I pressed myself away from Erik, but he held me, unwilling to let me go. We'd just declared ourselves, but I needed space to breathe.

"Let me go, Erik," I demanded.

"No," he said flatly and tightened his arms.

"Erik, release me. I need space to read your heart," I panted and pressed to get away.

He released me and eyed me cautiously. "You have the gift to read men's hearts?" he asked accusingly. I wrapped my arms around myself and nodded. He jumped to his feet and paced a few steps away from me. "How long have you had this gift?"

I shrugged. "I do not know exactly, but since I arrived at the palace, it has been easy. Except when my emotions blind me, or when I am surrounded by many men, men's hearts are clearer than even the great spirit's song."

"Do they know?"

"Who?" I asked.

"The governor and the commander, do they know?" His voice rose with worry.

"Yes, of course." I shook my head, confused, and sighed in exasperation. Erik paced some more and ran his hands through his short hair. "I do not understand. Are you angry with me? Have I done something wrong?"

Erik took in a deep breath and sat next to me again. "No, Phina, you have done nothing wrong, but do you know what this means?" I shook my head. I had no idea what he was asking me. "You are not safe under the care of men. They will use your gift to their advantage and exploit you."

I shook my head again and laughed. I refused to believe such a thing concerning Astur and Felix. "No, Erik. The governor teases that he will make me an advisor, but he is only teasing. Felix knows because I felt the need to warn him for our master's sake. One of the senators, Cato," I began.

"You know Cato?"

"Yes," I said, unsure of his tone. "Do you?"

He nodded. "Yes, he has recruited several soldiers for his personal security. What do you read in *his* heart?"

"What do *you* read?" I asked, cautious and unwilling to confide my own perceptions of the vile man.

"He is eager and ambitious. His sight is set on greatness. He has a keen perspective on the region. I have heard him speak many times, and I believe his intentions are for the common good."

Even without reading his heart, I could tell that Erik revered Cato, almost admired him. "You respect him?"

He did not answer my question but read my expression. "You do not."

I shook my head. "No." I stood then and walked along the edge of the pool.

"Do you care to explain?" Erik asked.

I allowed the silence to grow between us, separating myself from my emotions and from Erik. I drew on the great spirit's presence at the bathing pool. It was a sacred place for me.

"From my first acquaintance, I have distrusted him. He desires things that are not rightfully his."

"What do you mean?" Erik asked.

I chose my words carefully. "I know nothing of him outside the palace. Because of the way he makes me feel and my warnings to Felix and the governor, he has been given only limited access." I considered for a moment. "I suppose that will change once his sister arrives."

"His sister?"

"She's coming to visit and will stay at the palace."

"Did he… Did Cato do something to you?" he asked protectively.

"No, nothing physical, but he covets the governor's power and undermines him." That pained me to say, but Erik knew there was more. "I do not trust his cunning and manipulation. He desires my music and gift of song."

Jealousy flickered in Erik's eyes. "How many men have heard you sing?"

I shrugged my shoulders. Erik stood and raised his arms in exasperation. I had been careful with my song, and I didn't understand his fury. "You are so naive!" Erik accused. "You are exceptionally gifted, Phina; you always have been. You know the power of a healer's song."

"I know the power, Erik," I defended. "I have been careful." He glared at me, unconvinced. "I have only sung for the women and the flowers. That's how

Cato heard. He snuck into the garden after I'd played at the Governor's Feast. He overheard me and demanded that I sing for him. Thankfully, Felix arrived and took him away. My room is adjacent to the governor's chambers, making it impossible for him not to hear me sing my prayers." Then the truth came forward, the truth Erik was waiting to hear. "I have, on occasion, joined my song with Astur's. I knew no reason to deny him when he requested it and agreed to sing with me."

"He sings," Erik said with derision.

"Yes, he sings. He has a pleasant voice, and I think he enjoys the distraction. Sometimes he even sings before I have chimed in." Erik frowned. "Please do not be disappointed in me. Before Traian, Astur was my only companion. I have had no friends and very little attention. I know that he is my master and not my *friend*, but until you arrived, you understand."

Erik's expression softened, and he walked toward me. He placed his hand on my hair again. "I am sorry, Phina. I am sorry that your life has led you there and that you are subject to a powerful man, a man who might claim you in any way he desires."

"That is not his nature, Erik. He will not."

Erik's eyes examined mine, knowing that I spoke the truth, but much like Lucia, he had a distrust for men in authority. It was then that Erik took me in his arms. His mouth was on mine, and he lowered us to the ground and continued to kiss me. One arm wrapped around my waist, and the other held my neck as Erik gently lay me down beside him. He kissed my mouth, my cheek, and my neck.

The fresh lilacs surrounding the pool penetrated my senses. The great spirit's song swelled in my heart and threatened to bubble up and out of my throat. Instead of a song, I released a sigh, and for the first time in my woman's life, I could see how easy it would be to sing for a man, a man I loved.

The physical touch I had been denied for so long urged my arms and legs around Erik, and I pressed myself against the length of him. I could read his heart clearly as it beat against my own. The jagged, vibrant pieces were emblazoned.

"Erik," I moaned, desiring more. I wished I had the power to crawl inside of him. He hesitated at the sound of his name and the plea in my voice. "Erik," I repeated, allowing my hands to move along his shoulders and back.

"Phina," he whispered in reply, but his tone sounded less like pleading and more like a warning. He stiffened and cooled his lips against my neck before he removed my hands from around him. He took my hands in his and kissed my fingertips. I didn't want him to stop kissing me, and I frowned petulantly when he caught my eye. He smirked and rolled his eyes before he rolled over onto his back beside me. He kept one of my hands firmly in his.

"Phina," he exhaled. "I had no idea my love for you would stir such passion between us."

"What *did* you expect?" I asked.

He chuckled low in his chest. "I see you as you are, but I'm cautious because somewhere in my mind, you are still a child. I know you are not," he added quickly when he read my disapproval, "still, I will be more careful the next time I kiss you."

"Why careful?" I asked.

"Because I refuse to get carried away physically. That is until you have sung for me, and we've prayed together under the full moon. Do you understand?"

I understood. I had seen numerous women taken when I lived on the street, whether against their will or not. For a time, I lived along a back alleyway at the edge of the city. It was dark there. One woman that I remembered well because she was kind to me met her men there. She brought me bread and sometimes would leave me wine.

She would wait every evening at nightfall, the time men sought her out. She knew I was hidden, but maybe she felt safer knowing someone was close by. Soldiers, merchants, and even senators found her there. I wondered what Astur would think about such a woman and how men used her. She may have defended her actions and refused to believe herself used at all. From all I had read and seen, there were many degrees between rape and mating for life. I refused to fall somewhere undesirable.

"Is that what you meant when you said you might make it so that the governor would have no choice?"

Erik rolled over onto his side and propped himself up with his elbow. "Yes, Phina. As your mate, I would trump even your beloved governor." His own words pleased himself; he kissed the tip of my nose, and I giggled.

"When might we make it so?" I asked.

"As soon as I am able, but you will have to wait for me." I did not like the idea of waiting. I had waited long enough for Erik's return, and another year seemed too far to imagine.

The rest of the afternoon, we talked and dreamed and planned our life together as healers. Before we left the pool, I gathered lilacs to plant in the palace garden. I also collected cuttings from some of Grandfather's healing herbs to transplant. My focus was on the palace once again and my life and garden.

I wrapped my head in one of Mother's scarves, but I was not yet ready to change out of Mother's clothes. Erik donned his cloak and soldier's tunic. He called for his horse with a whistle and saddled her. I looked back at the cottage as we made our way toward the city. Erik held me tightly and whisper-sang into my ear. I hummed with him, and before long, our voices mingled sweetly in the dusky light. Our parting at the kitchen door was sweet and filled with hope.

Chapter Twenty-One

I took the lilacs straight to the garden to plant them in the soil. I spaced the cuttings a few feet apart and lovingly whispered a prayer of thanks for the memory of Mother. The great spirit was powerful to keep even transplanted things alive. I was proof of that.

I also added some of Grandfather's herbs to the healer's garden. I introduced them all to one another and sang over them as I had heard Mother and Grandmother do. Grandfather's plants would make an excellent addition to the old healer's garden.

I looked down at Mother's skirt pooled around my knees. I liked the feel of the fabric and the familiar pattern in the cloth. Beginning at the top of my head, I closed my eyes and allowed my hands to follow the contours of my body under her healer's clothes. I felt the shape of my breasts and waist and hips and thighs down to my knees. Under Mother's clothes, I felt more like a woman than I did beneath my palace tunic and veil.

I remembered the intensity of mine and Erik's kisses and the way my heart sang when he held me close. I lifted my face toward the setting sun and raised my hands to take in all the joy of the day. I stood and twirled around, allowing the fabric to lift and swirl.

When I stopped and opened my eyes, I noticed Astur on his balcony watching me. Somehow, I knew he'd been there all along. I stared into his dark eyes and smiled broadly, releasing a joyful giggle at being caught dancing around the garden. His features softened, and his indulgence shown in his eyes. I was too happy to be self-conscious. Even Cato's presence could not have dampened my joy.

Once up the back stairs, I begrudgingly replaced Mother's skirt and blouse with my palace uniform. I folded her clothes and placed them on the shelf between Grandfather's cap and Erik's boots. I stuck sprigs of dry lavender in the folds of the fabric.

***

"Welcome back," Astur said when I entered his chamber.

"Thank you."

"Where did Erik take you?" he asked, but I sensed that he already knew. He wouldn't be a good governor if he didn't.

"The cottage."

"How did you find it?" he asked with genuine curiosity.

"Much like I remembered. Erik has been looking after it all this time."

Astur nodded knowingly. "What is that?" he asked, lifting his nose into the air.

"Lilacs."

"The scent suits you."

I blushed a little at his compliment. "I am glad you like it. I brought some back with me, and I planted them in the garden."

He smiled wryly. "I heard your singing and stepped onto the balcony to find a stranger there. Your appearance took me by surprise. You looked nothing like yourself. It's a wonder the guards didn't apprehend you," he said teasingly.

I smiled at his playfulness. "I found Mother's things at the cottage. Today was the first time I've worn women's clothes, healer's clothes," I corrected. He didn't scoff at the idea of my being a woman or a healer.

The look in Astur's eyes darkened slightly, and he swallowed before he spoke. "They also suit you."

"Thank you, Astur. Thank you for allowing me this day." I beamed and took my instrument to play.

The night was comfortable between us, and I could tell that Astur was pleased I had returned. I did not mention the plans Erik and I had made. He still had a year before his release from the army, and I did not want to do anything to jeopardize either of our positions. Besides, I did not want to give Astur any reason to worry. That night, I only remembered playing a little while. The day caught up with me, and I yawned several times. I may have fallen asleep mid-song.

***

I was eager to see Erik again, but he did not come to the garden for two days. On the third evening, I returned to my room, disappointed that he had not joined me.

"Phina, there's a letter for you," Astur said, handing me another small envelope.

"May I assume that it is from Erik?" Astur nodded once. "May I read it now?" I asked.

"Of course." I left my instrument and eagerly moved toward the light to read.

My Dearest Phina,

I have been sent away – sudden orders. Please understand. I promise to return to you soon.

Love, Erik

My heart sank at the words. I was saddened not to see him. I blinked back the emotion that threatened to leak out behind my eyes. I took a deep breath before I turned to face Astur.

"Did Felix send him away?" My tone sounded accusatory.

Astur snapped his chin up, and his jaw tightened at my tone. He did not like to be challenged. His dark eyes flashed and then softened, and he cocked his head to one side curiously. His words were careful and pacifying, like he was speaking to a child. "Yes, but for army business, not to hurt you intentionally."

Astur's words were true, and I hung my head, ashamed that I had misdirected my disappointment. "Forgive me; I spoke out of turn." I hurried to my instrument and fumbled with the strings on the dulcimer to keep from making eye contact. I was afraid I might cry if I saw pity in Astur's eyes.

Astur interrupted my sullen song. I couldn't manage anything livelier. "Phina," his voice was warm and comforting, with only a hint of reproof.

"Yes, sir?" I whispered low over my instrument as I strummed.

"Why are you sad at his departing?" I shook my head, refusing to answer. "Erik is a soldier, and he must follow his captain's orders. Do you understand that?" I nodded, but I did not lift my head. "Phina, look at me." I looked into Astur's dark brown eyes and wondered why he even bothered to speak with me about it, but I wasn't able to block out his heart's concern. He stared into my eyes for a few heartbeats before he asked, "What happened at the cottage between the two of you?"

My eyes widened, and I shook my head, denying his insightfulness. His tone was protective, and the cool hues of his heart darkened and swirled beneath his chest. My silence concerned him.

"Did you?" he asked, insinuating that I had done something indecent. I understood his meaning.

"No," I said, lifting my chin proudly, challenging him to misjudge my time with Erik. Astur's brows creased together as he examined me.

"Do you love him?" I nodded. "You wish to be with him." Astur didn't say it like a question. I nodded again. The pain that flashed in Astur's eyes was nothing compared to the way the light in his heart faded.

"I am sorry that you disapprove of my choice," I said. My words were heartfelt and sincere. Astur's opinion was important to me.

"It's not that, Phina," he said, and I read something different from his heart.

"Felix said that you don't wish for me to go." Astur pursed his lips and considered his commander's comment. He tilted his head, giving a nod to my words.

"Do you wish to go?" he asked.

"I cannot," I stated flatly, "but once Erik's commission is served, perhaps."

I was shocked by Astur's reaction. He glared and stood in a huff. He was angry; he was hurt. *Rejection.* I definitely felt rejection, yet he had offered me nothing to accept.

Felix's inability to answer whether or not Astur intended to make me his mistress irritated me, so I stood and blurted out the question without thinking. "Do you expect me to stay here and play for you forever? What are *your* intentions for me, Astur?"

Astur's eyes flashed again, and I knew I had provoked him, but he did not say anything. His head raised to face my challenge head-on. I knew that look; conflict poured off of him. He did not know himself, nor did he know his intentions. That was unacceptable to him.

He took a deep breath and walked toward me. His height and shoulders blocked the flickering candlelight, and I was in shadow. He stared down into my eyes.

I refused to be intimidated by him or his stature. I looked up into his eyes boldly. "Will you deny me my future as a healer?"

He shook his head. "That is not my intention. Your music and your presence comfort me. For the first time in my life, I see clearly who I am and how to lead, and for that, I do not wish for you to go." The intensity of his words carried something else. *Selfishness? Regret? Anguish?* No, *Desire.*

I took in a shaky breath, overcome by the surety of his feelings for me, even if he was not. I spoke slowly to keep my breathing steady. "Astur, I need to understand your intentions. Will I remain your minstrel, or do you wish for me to be your mistress?"

He lowered his gaze, ashamed that I had asked. He was honorable. His integrity was one of his greatest attributes, but the conflict in his heart was greater. I understood that conflict. I'd felt it leaving the palace. I felt it standing in his library after Erik's kiss. My mind was divided between the security of the palace and my calling as a healer.

When Astur refused to answer me, I stepped back and turned to go, but before I could get away, he grabbed me by the shoulders forcefully and turned me to face him. He inspected my eyes, but when he found no protest there, he pulled me in and kissed me.

Warmth, deep penetrating warmth enveloped me. Astur's strong arms were around me, holding me close. His breaths were steady, but his heart, his heart was the most transparent, most vibrant blue. The blue of a cloudless sky. The blue of the bathing pool with lilac around the edges.

I was overcome by our closeness and returned his kiss with near-matched ferocity. It was nothing like the kisses I shared with Erik. I received no gift of sight, no clear future.

Astur was not careful nor protective of his feelings. He was no longer the governor and master; I was no longer his minstrel and servant. He was Astur, and I was Phina. No song threatened to escape my throat because Astur's moan when I kissed him back was deep and melodious and matched my own heart's song. Erik had no song when he kissed me.

Our lips parted, and Astur hugged me close to his chest, refusing to let me go. Our hearts beat strongly. "Please don't leave me," he whispered into my ear. "Please, Phina, I need you."

His words were neither desperate nor pleading. They flowed from the depths of him, and I could not refuse him or his need. I nodded and clung to him, allowing my body to absorb all of his color and warmth. He gently kissed the top of my head and down to my cheek. He kissed my mouth again softly, and I returned his affection in kind.

We both jumped at the loud knock on his door. He cursed at the interruption. "What?" he bellowed.

I heard Felix's voice muffled through the door. "Sir, you're needed," he commanded.

Astur turned back, torn to leave me. "Go," he whispered and released me. I took my instrument, wide-eyed and flushed, and left him.

"What is it?" Astur asked as he opened the door.

"Cato sent a messenger. His party was attacked on the road leaving the capital. They made it to the region's border, where they sent word. His party will arrive before midnight."

I had forgotten that Cato's sister was due to arrive. My disappointment at Erik's absence had blinded me. At that moment, I had the added confusion of Astur's kiss. Distractedly, I dressed for bed, but where Astur held me, sandalwood and myrrh clung to my skin.

Astur said nothing of love, only that he *needed* me. If we hadn't been interrupted, would he have taken me? *No, he would not.* I felt horrible that, in Astur's embrace, I'd temporarily forgotten my promise to Erik, and I was confused by the intensity of Astur's need.

I lay in my bed, but I was not tired. I tossed and turned. Every time I was the least bit comfortable, my body would remember how it felt to be held and kissed. My skin recalled Astur's hands and burned where he'd taken me forcefully. I had not resisted; I had not refused him.

I called out to the great spirit, but I was ashamed of my wanting. I longed for Mother; she would have guided me. I was alone and vulnerable and felt the weight of confusion. Tears pooled and clouded my vision; I was powerless to see my way.

I rose from my bed and tiptoed back into Astur's chamber. I took a bottle of wine and returned to my room, sipping the contents straight from the bottle as I gazed out the window. The night was clear.

Chapter Twenty-Two

In the morning, I rose early and left my room. Astur was already about his daily business. I had little appetite but managed some tea to settle my stomach and a sweet roll from Cassia. I was thankful not to see Lucia or Myrtle. Their gazes would have suspected. My eyes were puffy from crying and lack of sleep.

I went to the garden and checked the lilacs that I'd replanted. There was no change in them, yet I felt altered. As the warm sun rose overhead, I sleepily tended to the healer's garden.

I have no memory of falling asleep there, but when I opened my eyes, a stranger stood over me. Her eyes were wide with concern. "Oh, good, I was about to call the guard; I thought you were dead!" she exclaimed in a frantically breathy voice.

I blinked and pressed myself up into a sitting position. The young woman smiled behind her veil. Her eyes were friendly and welcoming. "Hello, I'm Marilla," she said as she offered her hand to me. I took it and rose to face her. She was only a few inches taller than me, curvy and slightly plump.

"I am Phina," I replied.

"Phina. That's a nice name. Wait, Phina, Phina," she repeated to herself. "That's right, you're the minstrel. Cato spoke of you. He says the governor keeps you for his amusement. You are quite a curiosity. Would you play for me?

I'd love to hear you play. Perhaps you would play for Livia, too. She could surely use something to calm her."

I marveled at Marilla's ability to babble on. She spoke rapidly, barely taking a breath.

"You arrived in the night," I remarked and pressed against the thoughts of what I had done with Astur just moments before Felix knocked on the chamber door.

"Yes, it was only a few hours before daylight. We were all exhausted, but the governor and his staff welcomed us and saw us to our rooms. Cato was so brave when we were attacked on the road. His guards were at the ready; they protected us. Livia was upset. She begged to go home, but Cato refused to turn around. She cried for a long time. Cato consoled her, and finally, she settled down for what remained of our journey." Marilla's gestures and voice were light-hearted and expressive at her retelling.

"Do you live in the capital?" I asked.

"Oh, no. I live in the country. Livia lives in the city with her mother and her mother's second husband. Livia's father died soon after she was born. Her mother's husband is a senator like Cato, but much older, of course," she giggled. "Livia prefers the city, but her mother sends her to the country for long visits. She says Livia needs the distractions of fresh air, but my mother suspects it keeps unwanted suitors from paying too much attention to Liv. Mother says the capital is swarming with cads and scoundrels, but I have yet to meet any," Marilla said, liked she hoped to.

"Welcome. I am glad you arrived safely. If you need anything, please let me know. I will do what I can to be of assistance." I looked around but only saw a guard at the garden's entrance. I was curious about him but supposed that Astur and Felix would require their guests to be looked after. "Where is Livia?"

"She is still sleeping. I don't expect her to wake until after midday."

I rallied after my nap and returned to my duties in the garden. For the lack of anything else to do, Marilla asked if she could stay with me. Marilla was pleasant company. She eagerly recounted every detail of their journey and the attack near the border.

"Mother will be frantic when she receives the news." Marilla didn't sound bothered about their attack, except that she couldn't tell her mother herself. "Livia's mother begged my mother to let me accompany Liv. When the governor's mother, Lady Gaius, proposed the visit, I was delighted. Where we live in the country, nothing exciting ever happens."

The guard approached us. "Pardon me. Your meal awaits you in your chambers."

The idea of a meal pleased Marilla, and she rose and tilted her head and curtsied quickly before following the guard back to her room. "I'll see you," she called back with a smile in her voice.

Later that afternoon, Marilla returned. I was with Traian, and I read to him from a small book of poems. It was a silly little book, but he enjoyed the rhythm and rhyming of the words as I read. The poems weren't specifically for children, but I could see their benefit. I had memorized a few of them already.

At Marilla's approach, I tucked the book inside my tunic. Erik had warned me about my gifts and my ability to read. I did not wish to draw unwanted attention to myself in the company of other young ladies.

The guard waited at the garden entrance again. When she saw Traian, Marilla ran to him. "Oh, my goodness!" she exclaimed. "He's beautiful. Those curls! Ah, and that dimple in his chin," Marilla prattled over the baby. "May I hold him?"

Marilla clapped her hands and made silly sounds and faces to get Traian's attention. She held out her hands to welcome him, and surprisingly, he leaned in and kicked his little legs to get closer to her. She scooped him up in her arms and giggled. Traian smiled and nuzzled himself into Marilla.

"I just adore babies," she gushed. "Are they not the most wonderful things? I cannot wait to have my own," she said longingly. "I hope my husband adores children as much as I do. I want an entire house full of them."

"Are you intended?" I asked.

"Oh, no, but Mother is hopeful. Father will arrange it. I hope he is a young officer or a young senator like Cato." She giggled, delighted at the prospect.

I thought about how different healers' lives were from the women of the regions. Young ladies were rarely joined in love. The wealthy were joined to secure property and to protect their family's assets. I believe that the women grew to love their husbands in time, but I wondered about such things.

Female healers ultimately made a choice. We were only promised or betrothed if it were to a man we loved and chose. The great spirit made it easy to fall in love with a male healer, but, again, female healers could not join themselves fully until they had sung for their mate in the presence of the great spirit. Then, and only then, would we become one, united.

Mother and Grandmother died before they could pass along all of their knowledge. With no elder, I was left to make my own way. I was too young to know and still too naive to figure it all out on my own. I was thankful I had chosen Erik; he would ensure that things were done right for me.

I glanced over at the guard. Marilla followed my gaze. "That's Alexander. He's to accompany me everywhere I go."

"By whose authority?" I asked.

She looked back at me. "I don't exactly know. Cato wishes for Livia to be watched constantly, but I think that's more their mother's doing than his. I am here to keep her company and see that she's never alone, but I was surprised that a guard would accompany *me*. I suppose that's the governor's doing or his commander's." She shrugged. "Either way, I wonder if he's a cad," she giggled.

She glanced back at Alexander. "I don't think he's a cad. If he were, he wouldn't be at the palace. He's most likely terribly honorable and devoted to his governor," she said wistfully. She then leaned in conspiratorially. "He is rather handsome, though, don't you think?"

I looked back at Alexander. He was handsome, but his uniform only made me think of Erik. Marilla's attention was drawn back to Traian, who was not interested in soldiers or guards or anything that didn't amuse him.

***

I returned to the kitchen later for supper. With guests, the kitchen had a different rhythm, much like it had been when Lady Gaius visited, except that the governor's ball was over a month away. I overheard some of the women and Lucia.

"Be sure that gets out first. It needs to be hot."

"No, Cassia, they only need one sweet cake each night. Save that one for tomorrow."

"I don't know anything about either one of them. Pay attention. Learn what they like, but keep the master's preferences first and foremost."

Chapter Twenty-Three

I left the bustle of the kitchen and found myself idle in my room. I busied myself at the table with my herbs, but my mind was too distracted, waiting and listening for Astur's return. My stomach ached at the prospect of facing him again and, yet, fluttered with excitement. I had so many questions.

I tried to read, but I was too agitated to focus on the words. I paced before I settled at the table; I straightened my stores and tidied the space. When the sky was heavy with the night, I checked the dulcimer's tuning, anticipating Astur's return.

I closed my eyes and felt his arrival even before I heard him. His heart's presence consumed his chambers and followed his scent. It wasn't overpowering, but it was familiar to me. Everything about Astur was familiar to me.

I stood in the shadow outside his chamber. I was nervous, and it was difficult to swallow. I fidgeted, holding my instrument. I considered if I should wear my veil now in his presence.

"Phina, I know you're there. Please come." I stepped into his chamber. He removed his cloak and placed it over the back of a chair. "Will you join me?" He motioned for me to sit on the small sofa where he'd offered me wine. "Have you had a good day?" he asked politely. He did not appear nervous or insecure, but then again, he was accustomed to having difficult discussions. He was the governor, after all.

"Yes," I answered tentatively.

"Would you like a glass of wine?" he offered.

"No, thank you, Astur."

At the sound of his name, he grinned. "I'm glad that remains." I looked up questioningly. "If you were upset with me, I think you might only call me *Sir* or *Governor*."

I was not angry with him, but I was confused. His playful tone was at odds with the intensity of his kiss and the way he'd held me before Felix interrupted us. I lowered my chin and diverted my gaze. I felt self-conscious and small.

"Astur, I cannot see my way," I confessed. "Erik *loves* me and has asked me to wait for him until his conscription is served. When he kisses me, I see our future clearly."

"What did you see when *I* kissed you?"

"I saw nothing," I whispered and tried to hide the rest, but I could not lie. My emotions were intense.

"*Nothing*," Astur repeated, sounding offended that his kiss had not given me sight. "But, there was *something*," he coaxed. He sat down next to me on the sofa and took my hand.

His warmth fixed me to the spot, and it took considerable effort not to touch him. I needed to remember Erik and my promise. "Astur, you say that you *need* me and desire for me to stay, but Erik understands my calling as a healer. He will give me children, and together, we will live a healer's life."

"That is all well and good, but that does not answer my question. If you did not *see* anything, what did your other senses and abilities tell you? You, better than anyone, can read my heart," he mused.

I looked up into Astur's eyes and did not look away. He let go of my hand and stood suddenly, realizing that I had read his heart clearly. I waited patiently as he paced back and forth in front of me. He stopped twice to examine me. I expected him to speak, but he just placed his hands on his hips and huffed a breath. I closed my eyes and tried to settle myself so that I could reread his heart. Perhaps during the kiss, emotion distorted my abilities. That was not the case; the colors and intensities were much the same as when he'd kissed me. His song was there, too.

When I opened my eyes, he was staring at me. I was unsure of his expression. Still, his heart desired me, desired for me to do more than stay; of that, I was sure.

"Alright, tell me everything; I'm ready." He braced himself.

"It is true; I read your heart. I see your intentions, and I hear its song."

Astur scoffed. "A song? You think my heart sings?" He did not believe me. I nodded, but he shook his head.

"You doubt me, again, but yes, Astur, your heart sings, and I admit that it is both beautiful and compelling."

He raised his eyebrow. "Does *your* heart sing?" he asked with a wry smile. I shrugged, unwilling to give myself away. "Phina, I asked you a question that only you can answer."

His words were gently commanding in our close proximity. I caught my bottom lip between my teeth and looked away. I anticipated his touch when he stroked my cheek with the back of his hand. "You have grown into a beautiful young woman." I closed my eyes and swallowed. "Will you please answer me?" he coaxed.

"May I ask the same of you?" I asked instead.

"But, you already know the answers."

I shook my head. "No, Astur, I only know your heart. How you proceed is another matter entirely. What will you make of me? What will I become?"

Astur took my face in his hands and stared into my eyes. His touch was gentle yet firm. Again, the warmth that was Astur permeated my flesh, and I mustered no resistance. "I will never take you or make you do anything beyond your will. If it is a healer you desire to become, then I will not stop you. You have my word." He leaned in and kissed me, and I closed my eyes and allowed it. The kiss felt premeditated.

"Stay here and continue to do your work," he whispered. I was confused. He had just promised me free will to pursue my work and rights to refuse him, but his words were neither a question nor a command. "Do I have your assurance that you will stay?"

"As far as I can give it, yes."

"What does that mean?"

"Only the great spirit has the power to keep promises. I can only do what is in my own ability and follow the great spirit's leading."

"Do I not have any say against your great spirit?" I shook my head solemnly. "If I have no power to fight it, is it best if I never try?"

He was teasing. I smiled. "That would be wise of you."

"What does your great spirit say about kissing me?"

"The great spirit is silent on kissing yet clear on the differences between mates and mistresses."

"Hmmm," Astur mused. "Does it please you – the kissing?"

I looked down, embarrassed. It did please me, yet I felt conflicted by my promise to Erik and Astur's need. In Astur's presence, his need was greater.

He tilted my chin up with his finger. He was smiling, satisfied by my silence. He kissed me again and again. I was dizzy when he released me. "Play for me, Phina. Play from your heart."

I moved to my stool and closed my eyes. I had to take a deep breath before I settled myself enough to play. An unfamiliar chord strummed across the strings, and the melody flowed from my fingers. My heart's song did not bubble out but in harmony with Astur's.

Chapter Twenty-Four

The following afternoon, I took Traian from Lucia and made my way to the garden. I heard voices and was curious to meet Livia. I passed by Marilla's guard, Alexander, but stopped when I saw Cato with a young woman at his side. Their likenesses were subtle, but I knew it must be his sister. She was tall and graceful.

"Phina," Marilla called and waved as she was drawn toward Traian.

Cato and Livia looked over, and Cato whispered something into Livia's ear. Livia's eyes were hard to read. They didn't look like she was smiling.

I stiffened as Cato and Livia approached me. I cut my eyes back at Alexander, and he strode toward our gathering. If Felix assigned Alexander to this post, I trusted Felix would warn him to keep a careful eye when Cato visited. Cato eyed the soldier as he positioned himself a protective distance behind me.

"Phina, you already know Cato. This is his sister, Livia," Marilla said excitedly.

I ignored Cato and focused only on Livia. "Welcome. It is a pleasure to make your acquaintance," I said and smiled behind my veil.

"Thank you. Marilla has told me many things about you and the garden. It's beautiful." Her voice was sweet but cautious, like she might be timid.

Marilla took Traian from me, and I was left with nothing to do with my hands. I watched as Marilla walked him toward the grassy spot where he liked to crawl and play. I looked back at Livia, who was staring at me.

"Your eyes!" Livia commented. "I've never seen such eyes." She peered at me, fascinated and curious. It was my turn to be timid.

"Neither have I. I told you she was fascinating. Just wait until you hear her play, but I'm holding out for a song," Cato said. His tone of superiority irritated me.

I turned my attention toward Marilla and Traian. He squealed happily as she lifted him up into the air.

"Cato, you embarrass her." Livia's tone sounded sincere in the reproof of her older brother.

A second guard approached. "Sir, the governor will see you now."

Cato looked at his sister. "I am summoned. You must fend for yourself." He kissed his sister's hand and bid the two of us a good day. Alexander followed Cato and the other guard and took his place at the garden's entrance. After Cato's exit, Alexander didn't pay particular attention to us. I looked toward the library and wondered if Astur watched as he worked.

I looked at Livia again and tried to think of what to say to make polite conversation. She, too, found herself at a loss for words. Thankfully, Marilla called us over. "Livia, Phina, come and see." Marilla swung Traian around in a circle and sat down. Traian giggled, and Marilla nuzzled his neck.

"Marilla likes babies," Livia said.

"Yes, and from the looks of Traian, he finds her equally as likable." Livia smiled then, and her high cheekbones rose above her veil.

The three of us sat together and laughed at Traian. Marilla was the first to lower her veil. She kissed Traian and made silly faces at him. In the company of women, we were allowed more freedom. Livia and I did the same. Livia's smile was friendly, although she remained distracted by my eyes. She held only a slight resemblance to Cato. I was relieved by that. Her cheekbones were high, and her neck was long and slender. Her lithe movements were graceful and refined.

When Traian fussed, I stood and hummed a tune to soothe him. As was our habit, I walked him and rocked him until he fell asleep in my arms. Marilla walked over and asked if she could hold the sleeping child. I followed her back toward Livia and passed Traian over to Marilla. She smiled and closed her eyes.

"Holding a sleeping baby is the most wonderful feeling in the world," Marilla sighed.

"You say that about everything," Livia whispered.

"I can't help it," Marilla confessed. "I can't help it if things feel wonderful."

"I hope your father finds you a virile man who gives you loads of the little things. Then, maybe you'll be satisfied."

"Livia," Marilla said soothingly. "Don't be like that. How can you resist them? They're so sweet."

"Yes, when they're settled and sleeping, but how often does that happen?"

"You'll love them when you have your own," Marilla said confidently.

"If I must, I will have one. I will give my husband a son and be done with the business."

I listened intently to their exchange. "But what if you like the business?" Marilla asked teasingly. "Some women do, you know. They like kissing and hugging and making babies." Marilla sighed longingly.

"As if you know anything about that," Livia chided.

Marilla shrugged. "Maybe I could convince Alexander to give me my first kiss. He looks more than capable."

All of our eyes looked back toward Alexander. He stood straighter and wondered at our gaze. Marilla fell into a fit of giggles, and Livia and I joined her. Traian stirred, and Marilla sobered and settled him back into sleep.

***

Astur ate his suppers downstairs with his guests. Each night, he came to his chambers later and later, and it felt odd, throwing off our routine. A few evenings, he kissed me, but when I returned his affection, he quickly released me and demanded that I play the dulcimer instead. It wasn't that I felt rejected, but I liked his attention and his touch.

Not only were my nights adjusted, but my days were no longer solitary. Marilla met me in the garden each morning, eager and ready for the day. Livia preferred to sleep late and begin her days in leisure. Marilla was a pleasant distraction from my wavering thoughts between Astur and Erik. I had received no word from Erik and wondered how things would be between us when he returned. I would have to tell him everything.

Marilla followed me around the garden. She knew the names of all the flowers and was curious about the other plants. She was eager and learned quickly. She donned a gardening apron and spoke of her gardens at her home in the country.

"Kyle keeps Mother's gardens. He prefers his solitude, but as long as I'm quiet, he lets me tag along."

I didn't ask Marilla to be quiet or to allow me my solitude. She intrigued me. When she spoke, it was like opening a book, a new page every day, and the words spilled out into my ears. Marilla described her home in the country so well that I thought I'd been there myself. She talked about being a wife and the duties of a wife. She spoke about the running of the house and seeing after the children and servants. Marilla happily anticipated the time when she would be claimed.

"A wife is for duty and to give her husband a son, an heir. Mistresses are for pleasure. A wife is to manage the home. It would be the greatest of honors to present him with the gift of a house full of sons. I hope that my husband is young and that I please him enough so he doesn't take a mistress right away."

"You *expect* him to have a mistress?"

"In time, or if he is older, he most likely has one already."

"But what would he have with a mistress? Cannot a wife do both, please her husband and perform the duties required of her?" Healers mated for life. A healer's mate never chose to find pleasure beyond their union.

Marilla grew somber. "You do not know of these things, do you?"

I shook my head. "The ways of the regions are strange to me. I am still becoming accustomed to them." I had read many things, but they did not give personal accounts, only historical ones.

"I suppose that it is different from the servants and common folk. Father says it's a privilege of the wealthy. Ladies and senators and many officers have different expectations," Marilla explained. "The daughters aren't given much choice in the matter. We know what is expected of us." Her smile faltered a bit, but then she trudged on, "Livia understands. I hope that things are arranged quickly for her. Cato will make it so."

"What do you mean?" I asked.

Marilla covered her mouth with her hand. "I'm sorry. I shouldn't have said anything."

"I don't understand. What is being arranged for Livia?"

Marilla cocked her head. "You don't know?" I shook my head. "Oh, I thought the governor would have told you, you being his muse and mistress. According to Mother, mistresses know all of a man's secrets," she giggled. "If everything goes well, and the governor agrees to the terms, he will claim Livia."

I blinked and swallowed back my body's response. Then, it was to be. I was right to assume Astur's mother had sent Livia for that purpose. I cleared my throat, and Marilla turned to face me. She placed her hand on my cheek. "Phina, you're all flush. Are you well?"

I blinked quickly to hide my tears. "Marilla, I am not the governor's mistress," I clarified. "I've heard the rumors, but you are mistaken to assume. He keeps me for the music."

Marilla smiled, relieved for me, relieved for her friend.

Chapter Twenty-Five

It wasn't too many nights more before I was called to play for Astur's guests. Livia and Marilla were both curious, but it was at Cato's urging. I sat as I had the final night of Lady Gaius's visit. Unlike that night, the guests clamored around me after they finished their meal.

Marilla, Livia, and I spent our afternoons together in the garden with Traian. They were familiar with me, and their curious eyes were not an intrusion. Cato's eyes, on the other hand, were. I was thankful for Astur occupying his attention before Cato could make his way toward me.

Marilla liked to sing and knew many songs. After a glass or two of wine, Livia joined her. Marilla jested, "She needs to loosen her tongue." Marilla didn't need anything to loosen her tongue. I did not sing with them, but then again, they didn't ask. I missed the times that Astur joined his voice with mine.

On several nights, I played for his guests, but Astur did not call for me. He did not require that I play to ease him into sleep. He had not kissed me, either. He was attentive to Livia, and she smiled in his presence. His heart was content, and I thought him to be happy.

In the weeks that followed their arrival, I found that I enjoyed Marilla and Livia's company. I knew my place, but I was drawn into their friendship and lively banter. I also found that I liked playing for them.

"How do you know so much about the flowers?" Livia asked.

"Mother and Grandfather taught me."

"Did they keep the gardens here, too?" Marilla asked.

"No, they kept their own garden. They were healers."

"Alexander says that the guards come to you sometimes. Are you a healer, too?" Marilla asked.

"In time, and with much study and practice, I will be."

"I don't recognize many of these plants. We have different varieties in the capitol's gardens," Livia commented and gestured toward the healer's garden.

"Those are not for admiring; they're for healing." There was warning in my voice.

I had been careful not to work in the healer's garden with Marilla in the mornings. Medicinal plants needed special handling, especially when it came to harvesting.

Marilla looked curiously over the plants. She'd not cared to pay much attention to them because they didn't captivate her like the roses and lilies and lilacs. Much like the bees, Marilla was attracted to floral scents and vibrant colors. She was like a bee in other ways, too, rounded, plump, and full of energy.

Marilla reached to pluck a bud from the poison plant. "No, Marilla, not that one." My tone was sharp. Marilla jumped and jerked her hand away. "Forgive me, but I must insist that you not touch these plants. That bud is lovely but equally as deadly. Each of these holds powerful properties." I took Marilla's hand and looked into her eyes. Mother's words flowed from my mouth with her same gentle instruction. "Ask and understand before you proceed." Marilla nodded solemnly.

"The governor lets you keep something so dangerous?" Livia asked.

"It's only dangerous if you don't know how to use it," I defended. "The healing potential is greater than the threats. The governor has allowed it."

My words sounded final, as if I issued the decree myself. Livia stood to her full height and huffed a breath. "But that one, there. Why wouldn't you pluck out that hideous thing?" She asked, pointing to the healing plant.

"That *hideous* thing has the greatest healing powers of them all. Be mindful not to judge something's outside. You might miss an opportunity to gain a new appreciation." Livia set her shoulders proudly and looked away. Thankfully, Marilla distracted us and drew Livia back to the flowers Marilla most admired. The days flew by quickly. Traian grew, Marilla and I gardened, and Erik returned.

From the corner of my eye, Alexander stood at attention and saluted an approaching soldier. I thought it might be Felix, but I was mistaken. "Erik!" I exclaimed when he walked past Alexander into the garden. I ran to him, losing myself. His broad smile and arms welcomed me. After a brief embrace, he released me and was painfully aware that we were not alone.

I introduced Erik to Livia and Marilla. "It is a pleasure to meet you," Erik said. Livia marveled at the intensity of Erik's eyes, but she did not comment as she'd done when we were first introduced.

Erik returned his attention to me. "May I speak with you, alone?" he asked formally.

I looked at Marilla and Livia. "Will you excuse us?" I asked politely. Marilla's eyes widened and glistened playfully. She smiled behind her veil. Livia was slower to respond. Marilla hooked her arm around Livia's elbow and pulled her away.

"Come, Liv, let's see what adventures we can find with Alexander. If nothing else, he can lead us to refreshments. Proper soldiers know how to find food." Marilla peaked back at me and winked.

Erik took my hand and led me to the bench near the wall. He wasted no time before he kissed me. Solidly, I felt his joy. His heart glowed at our reunion. It had been weeks since Astur had kissed me, and much of that conflict had disappeared. In Erik's arms, I felt secure and knew my path.

When I sat back to better look at him, I noticed a different trim on his cloak and tunic. "Alexander saluted you. Were you promoted?" I asked.

"Indeed." He kissed me again.

"Erik, that's wonderful. When?"

"Just after I left."

"What does this mean?"

"That means that I have the command of my own men, now. I'll be leading them when we return to the front."

"Is that not at odds with being a healer?"

Cautiously, Erik looked at me. "Phina, I am a soldier; I must do as I'm commanded."

"Governing men, having authority over their lives, leading them into battle, is that not in direct contrast to your oath to do no harm?"

"I see it that I'm doing a greater good to secure the region and its inhabitants. You, Phina, are one of those whom I have sworn to serve and protect."

I nodded humbly, thankful for Erik's service. "How do the battles go?" I asked.

"They go well, for now."

"How long will you be here?"

"A few days. The governor is hosting a feast for our troops. Our captain will be awarded his next rank, then, too. My captain agreed to have you play with me."

"Together?"

"Yes, since I left you, I've been practicing. I've played for the men; I think it would please everyone."

"I don't know, Erik; I don't want to be a spectacle."

"You won't be, and we'll be together." Again, Erik's joy was enough for both of us.

The next night, I readied myself to play for Astur and his guests. I corrected myself; Astur continued to pay little attention to me. I was playing for Erik and his fellow soldiers. Livia, Marilla, and Cato were also in attendance. The gathering was not as formal as the Governor's Feast, but the food and wine flowed the same.

Astur was comfortable with Felix and Erik's captain. Astur's position as governor commanded respect, but his heart was more settled among the soldiers than senators and citizens. Livia and Marilla stayed at Cato's side. They looked elegant and lovely in gowns befitting their station. Their hair was unbound, and under the governor's protection, they were allowed to be unveiled. Marilla smiled and spoke with the soldiers who introduced themselves to Cato. She smiled at Cato, too.

I watched everything from the shadows, unobtrusive, waiting to be called forward to play. I closed my eyes and read the hearts of each man present. My ability seemed keen, but I regularly encountered the same men. Maybe it was because the men in the palace were familiar to me that it was easy to read them. The soldiers' hearts as a whole were honorable, with only a few whose motives I would question. I was nervous about playing in front of so many, but I felt more at ease after reading their hearts.

When they had concluded their meal, several men were called to receive awards and marks of distinction from Felix. Erik was among them. I watched proudly as Astur thanked each one of them for his service.

When the ceremony was completed, Erik's captain introduced the entertainment. "Men, many of you have heard Erik play and sing in camp, but tonight, it is my pleasure to reward each of you with a special treat. Erik assures me that we will not be disappointed."

Erik smiled and raised his hand in greeting. Another soldier handed him a dulcimer; Erik thanked him and turned toward where I was waiting. He motioned for me to join him, and I stepped out of the shadows to the applause and jeers of his comrades. I blushed at their comments.

"Settle down, men," Erik's captain commanded, but the men took little head to it.

Ignoring the soldiers, Erik positioned our chairs together. I sat down and waited for his cue. "When did you get an instrument?" I whispered.

"Before I left. I couldn't let you play better than me, now could I?" Erik teased. "We'll begin with Grandfather's songs," he suggested. I nodded and kept my eyes on his. He played the first chords, and I joined in. We'd never played together, and I found that I liked it very much.

Erik sang out as we played. After a few songs, he asked me to sing with him. I looked around the room. I had only ever sung with Erik and Astur, and I did not want to give Cato the satisfaction of hearing my voice. I also did not understand Erik's intentions. He had warned me to be careful with my song and not to reveal my abilities.

I looked up into Erik's eyes, ready to refuse him, but they were bright and focused. "Please, Phina, sing with me." The jagged pieces of his heart were less angular, more rounded. The fiery colors burst into flame at the prospect. I lowered my veil and closed my eyes, following Erik's lead in song.

The murmurs of the crowd ceased, and the room fell quiet. We played and sang three more songs. Each was received with cheers and applause. Erik reveled in the praise and accolades, and I reveled in Erik's joy.

After we played, Erik escorted me to the stairs that led to my room. He looked around to make sure that we were alone. "Thank you," he whispered into my ear. He leaned back and looked into my eyes. *Love. Desire. Longing.* He pressed me against the wall and kissed me then. His hands stroked down to my waist, and he pulled me closer into him.

My stomach tightened, and my heart raced, and it took my entire will not to take Erik's hand and run away with him. Grandmother's sight returned, and I was swept away in the future.

"Can you see it?" I panted as Erik kissed down my neck. "Can you see them?"

I felt Erik's breath against my skin. "Yes, clearly," he whispered. "Hold fast to the vision, Phina. It's ours."

Chapter Twenty-Six

Astur's chamber door slammed and shook the walls around me. "What was the meaning of that?" Astur bellowed from his chambers into mine.

It was the first words he'd spoken to me in weeks. His heavy footfalls thudded towards my room. I gathered my robe and covered myself, but I didn't have time to wrap my head. Astur's broad shoulders blocked the doorway. I stood facing him, but we were both cast in shadow. I trembled in fear. *Humiliation. Disappointment. Jealousy. Rage* poured from his heart.

"Answer me," he demanded, but I made no reply. He cursed and stepped toward me. I looked away, ashamed. He grabbed me by the shoulders and shook me. "How could you?" he growled as he lifted me from the ground.

"Astur, you're hurting me." I wriggled to get away. "Please, put me down." My words stammered.

Astur huffed a deep breath and gathered himself. He stepped forward and set me down, and I stumbled back out of reach. Reflexively, my arms wrapped around my trembling body.

"Who gave you permission to sing?" he asked, releasing his words with a measured pace.

"Erik asked me to." I lifted my chin and refused to be intimidated again. "*I* gave myself permission."

"Do you know what that did to me?" I shook my head. "To watch as you closed your eyes and joined your voice with his was the most excruciatingly painful thing I've ever heard. My ears are still burning. It's one thing to see him kiss you and put his hands on you, but your song does not belong to him. It was like watching you naked and exposed; it drove me to madness."

Astur ran his hands through his hair, exasperated. I shivered in response to his tirade, and I was saddened that I had caused him pain. "Promise me that you will never force me to witness that again." I swallowed, too nervous to speak. "Phina, promise me that you will not join your voice with another man, especially Erik."

I shook my head. "I cannot."

"Do you have so little regard for me?" he growled.

"No. My voice is my own, and my songs belong only to the great spirit."

Astur huffed again and stepped toward me, but this time he did not grab me forcefully. He gently placed his warm hands on my shoulders and whispered, "I cannot watch that again. I need you, Phina. I need you like I need breath."

His lips were on mine, gentle and sure, possessive and pleading. I allowed him to kiss me, unable to refuse his warmth and desire. The moan of his heart's song carried me away to an unknown place. He lifted me gently and brought me to my bed.

Again, there was no sight beneath his kisses, and without sight, there was no future. I had no future with Astur. I stiffened, controlling myself, refusing to react to his touch. I shook with the effort that it took to hold myself together.

"Please, Astur, no. Please, I beg you not to take me, not like this."

Astur calmed himself with a deep breath. His heartbeats thundered against my breasts. He glared, and his eyes flashed. He left me there without another word.

***

I went to the garden early the next morning to meet Erik. I felt tired and edgy from the long night, but I wanted to see him before he left again. Alexander stood guard in his usual post. It only added to my emotions because I wanted to be alone with Erik. I stopped when I saw Cato and Marilla. She smiled up at him, her wide eyes inviting. She hung on Cato's every word as he looked over the healer's garden.

Marilla turned and called to me. I begrudgingly walked toward them. "Marilla has been telling me about your little garden. This is where I found you singing. Do you remember?" I did not answer him. "She says that you can explain their usefulness."

"I know a little," Marilla confessed, "but I'm sure I'll learn more. Phina is an excellent teacher."

"Last night proved she's excellent at many things, wouldn't you agree? Remind me to give your soldier friend my deepest gratitude."

Marilla beamed. "Yes, and all this time, she put up with mine and Livia's singing, encouraging us while she played. We had to wait for Erik to come before she showed her true talents." Marilla smiled indulgently at me like she did Traian when he did something new.

Erik arrived then. He greeted Marilla and Cato and then asked if he might speak to me alone. Cato kissed Marilla's hand and asked if she'd like to walk him out. Marilla happily agreed.

I was unsure of Cato's intentions towards Marilla. He was not warmed or softened by her presence. I wondered if my disdain for Cato marred my ability to read his heart. Marilla's eyes and smile gave herself away. She obviously liked Cato's attention. I thought briefly about how I could caution her without offending her or Livia.

Erik looked at me and traced my puffy eyes with his fingertips. "Was last night too much for you? Did our performance exhaust you?"

"No." I rested my face in his palm and closed my eyes.

"I have some news," Erik began. I opened my eyes to read his expression. "We've been called away. My captain, I mean my major," he corrected, "has been called away to the capital. From there, we will join the battle."

"When do you go?"

"We break camp tonight."

"Tonight? I thought we had another day."

"Our circumstances changed. I only have a moment."

"But Erik, I have so much I want to say."

"Can it wait until I return?" he asked impatiently.

"I don't know." Erik sighed and took me into his arms. "I'm afraid, Erik."

"Do not worry after me. I'm a competent soldier. I will return to you." I shook my head against his chest. He misunderstood.

"No, I'm afraid you were right; my heart is divided," I confessed. Erik pushed himself back to look at me. "But, I think perhaps yours is as well." He cocked his head to one side, considering my words. "You like your position, and you find purpose in your service. You want to go into battle and the glory it will afford you. That's not a healer's way." Erik's face stiffened at my challenge. "Please," I begged, "stay with me. Take me back to the cottage and remain there with me."

"I need to do this, Phina. They need me," he said with the same tone he used when he first returned to me.

"I need you!" I pleaded.

"The governor will take care of you and see after you. Please, don't make me regret leaving you."

"You're going to be gone again for months!" I argued. "This isn't fair!"

"What you're asking of me isn't fair, either. I love you, Phina. I will return, and we will see what the future holds for us."

"We will *see*?" I asked, and then I did see. I saw it all clearly. All of my hopes and visions for the cottage shattered into a million tiny slivers. He had no intention of returning there with me; his heart hungered for battle.

The pain in my chest crushed me, and I lowered myself to the ground. Erik knelt beside me and took my hands. He kissed my fingers and then my mouth. "I'm sorry, Phina. For now, this is my path." His blue eyes held me fixed. He kissed me once more, rose, and hurried back to camp.

***

I cried and cried after Erik's departure. I took bottles of wine from Astur's chamber and drank until the wine numbed me enough to sleep. Myrtle came to check on me first. "Are you ill, child?" she asked. "That Marilla has been asking after you, and don't get me started on the garden and Traian."

"I'm sorry, Myrtle, I can't."

"Alright, I'll send up a tray. I'm too old to be making it up those stairs. I'll send Cassia."

Lucia came the next morning, bringing another tray and some wine. It was morning, but she thought the wine might thicken my blood and give me strength. Little did she know that my blood was thick enough.

"Drink," she demanded. I sat up and took the cup she offered. The wine tasted heavy and sweet on my tongue. I'd eaten little more than some bread. Even Cassia's sweet roll couldn't tempt me.

Lucia sat on the edge of my bed and took my hand. "This is the price we pay."

"The price of what?"

"For letting our hearts be carried off by a soldier."

"Erik didn't carry my heart away. He simply filled it with hope and a dream, and then he took that away."

Lucia nodded. "That will take some time to heal, but at least you're still in one piece."

"Barely."

"The Lady Gaius arrives tomorrow. I need the palace at its best. That includes you."

"Will I be expected to play?"

"Can you muster that?" she asked, but it wasn't exactly a question. I was expected to play.

"I suppose I can. How many days?"

"Two." I sighed. I had lost track of time.

"I won't sing."

"I dare say. If the governor's word holds, you may never sing again. It's a wonder he didn't remove your tongue."

I looked down at my lap and felt ashamed of the pain I had caused Astur. "I didn't know it would hurt him."

Lucia lifted my chin and patted my cheek tenderly. "I wish I had the answer for you. I truly do." She searched my eyes as if she could find the answer there. "Felix hasn't seen him in such a fit since his wife and child died. I haven't seen him in a rage since before you arrived. Your music settled and refined him. The night you sang, you drove him half-mad."

I nodded and took another sip of the wine. "Where is he? I haven't heard his footsteps."

"Except for suppers with his guests, he keeps to himself. He sleeps in the library. He says he's working, but I suspect he doesn't trust himself to be alone with you. Do all of your kind have this power over men?"

"I don't know, and the great spirit has yet to guide me."

"Well, then, for now, you eat and bathe and dress. Don't waste any more time wallowing in misery. Prepare yourself for the day and make the best of whatever comes."

Even in her sternness, Lucia's words comforted me. They came from a place of concern. Her presence comforted me, too. "Thank you, Lucia. I won't disappoint you." She patted my knee and returned to her duties.

It was afternoon before I made it outside. Alexander gave me a brief nod as I entered. Had he witnessed Erik's departure? The sun shone brightly, and the gardens were tended. Livia sat next to Marilla, who was singing to Traian. He squealed when he saw me, and my heart leaped inside my chest. It was the first feeling my heart had stirred in days. His tiny fists wrapped around my neck, and I smothered him with kisses. I had missed my time with him.

"How are you?" Marilla asked sympathetically.

"I'm well," I said. It wasn't quite a lie.

"Will you be attending the Governor's Feast?" Livia asked.

"I will play, but I will not attend."

171

"Lady Gaius arrives tomorrow. I look forward to it." Livia said, lifting her chin proudly.

"I do not," Marilla sighed. "She always tells me to stand up straighter. I can't; I'm just not that tall."

I covered my mouth, but the giggle escaped. It was the first time I'd laughed. "Thank you, Marilla. I needed that."

Marilla smiled. "If it helps, I can make you laugh."

Chapter Twenty-Seven

Lady Gaius arrived, and the preparations for the feast forged ahead. Marilla and I minded Traian. Along with Lucia's other responsibilities, he was a handful and too much for Lucia to manage. Lady Gaius and Marcus put the final touches throughout the palace and gardens. Livia didn't leave the lady's side.

I didn't hide and peek from Astur's balcony as I had done the year before. I wasn't curious about the guests and their finery. I knew my place, and I would play in the garden.

Myrtle brought me a new tunic and slippers for the occasion. It was resplendent. The fabric's weave glistened in the sunlight; hints of silver and blue formed an intricate pattern. It gave the illusion of moonlight over water as I moved. In the garden, it would reflect every flicker of torchlight.

I waited downstairs until I was called. Marcus came and motioned for me to follow him. Although he hurried, he never rushed his steps. I walked into the garden and assumed my position. Last year, I wore my palace tunic; this year, I looked nothing like I had before and was veiled.

Last year, I had played to please my master. Without Erik, I played to please myself. I took in a settling breath and strummed the first chord. The garden fell silent, and everyone's attention turned toward me. If there were comments, I paid no heed to them. I blocked my ability to read the men's hearts, save one. I tried, really, I tried, but no matter what, Astur's heart shined brightly, the colors and its song.

I played through my selections and bowed my head, receiving their applause. It was not as heartfelt as the soldier's cheers, but I received it just the same. Cato and Lady Gaius stepped forward and demanded the audience's attention.

"Thank you, dear, for that lovely interlude," Lady Gaius said.

"Isn't she fantastic?" Cato said in his most charming voice. He clapped his hands loudly, and the guests followed his lead.

"Yes, indeed. Now, if I might hold your attention for a moment more," Lady Gaius began. "I believe we have an even greater delight." She took Cato's hand.

"Yes, my lady, we do."

"Come, Astur. Come, Livia." The lady and Cato each extended a hand to summon them. Livia lowered her gaze and fluttered her eyes when everyone turned to look at her. She and Astur walked toward Cato and Lady Gaius. Astur took Livia's hand and presented her to the gathering. "For some time, I have hoped for my son, your governor, to be happily joined, and it is with utmost pleasure that I now announce the uniting of our two families."

Cato kissed Lady Gaius's hand before he released it. He then turned to his sister and kissed her cheek. The guests applauded and voiced their good wishes. Astur and Livia were swarmed by those who wanted to be first to congratulate them. Livia smiled radiantly. Astur looked pleased, but I was too stricken by the news to read his heart. I stepped back into the shadows to make my retreat, but Marilla caught me by the arm.

"Phina, isn't it fantastic? Livia is claimed!" Marilla gushed. I blinked hard and nodded, but I couldn't press down my feelings enough to speak. "They make such a handsome couple." Marilla looked over her shoulder. "I couldn't ask for a better night. Everything is lovely. And you, just look at you; you looked beautiful playing. You're all shimmery like the ocean."

"Thank you, Marilla, but I must go."

"Please, won't you stay? Now that Livia is with Cato and the governor, I have no one to stand with me."

"I will stand with you," a male voice said from behind us.

I turned to see Alexander there. Marilla's eyes fluttered up at him. "Yes, but Phina will talk and laugh with me. Will you do that, too?"

Alexander smirked. "Yes, I can stand and talk, but you will have to try very hard to make me laugh."

Marilla considered his offer and then looked back at me. "I'll see you tomorrow, Phina. Have a good night." She pulled me into a hug and whispered, "I'll let you know if he is honorable." She didn't need to waste her efforts. I already knew Alexander's heart; he was both honorable and protective of Marilla.

I ran up the stairs and made it into my room before I broke down. I had prayed from the beginning that Astur would find comfort in a mate. I sang to the great spirit on his behalf for a woman to come into his life and give him a son, an heir. They were the prayers of an innocent child. I had meant no harm in praying them, so why was my heart aching?

I held myself as tightly as I could and rocked myself on the edge of the bed. First Erik, now Astur. Grandfather, Grandmother, and Mother. The loss and heartbreak were unbearable. With agonizing gasps, I cried out to the great spirit. I had no song. I had no words.

I watched as the night moved into the day. I observed the dark sky awaken to its vibrant blue. My desperate cries conveyed my pain to the great spirit until only murmurs and hums remained. With or without Erik, I decided on my course.

**

I was determined to leave. I told no one of my plans but waited patiently for my opportunity. I went about my routine so that no one would suspect.

When Marilla told me all about their plans to return to the capital, I happily received her news. "The governor will go ahead, and then the rest of us will meet him there for the governors' meetings." Once Astur and his guests were gone, I would make my escape.

Chapter Twenty-Eight

A few nights later, I woke to Astur's boots clomping into his chambers. I sat up and strained my ears to hear their words, but it was Lucia's voice that I heard instead.

"We have to tell her."

"It's the middle of the night. Can't it wait until morning? She'll be devastated," Felix argued in a whisper.

"We'll be gone by morning," Astur said.

"Phina, wake up; we need to speak with you," Lucia said. I gathered my robe and stood from the bed, turning to cover myself and adjust my head covering.

"I'm awake; come in," I said in a whisper, but they were already there.

Lucia led the party. She stepped forward and took my hand sympathetically; Felix placed his hands on my shoulders and looked into my eyes. He offered no pretense before he delivered the news. "Phina, Erik is dead." My eyes were wide with shock. I shook my head, denying his words.

"It's true, Phina," Lucia added.

I pulled my hand from Lucia angrily and faced Astur, pointing my finger up at him. "This is all your fault!" I screamed. "You didn't want me to go, so you sent Erik away! You did this!" I ducked from Felix's hands and thrust myself toward Astur. I beat against him, but my fists were no match for his broad chest.

"Phina!" Lucia and Felix called together, but it was too late. I was already in Astur's arms. He held me securely so that I didn't hurt myself. I screamed in agony; my heart was breaking. My entire body was breaking in two.

"Leave us!" Astur command to Lucia and Felix over my shoulder.

I screamed and wriggled and fought him until my body was spent. The rage left me, but soon the overwhelming grief and sorrow flooded in. I collapsed in his arms and wailed. Astur lowered us down onto the floor and carefully cradled me in his arms.

"He only had a few more months!" I sobbed. I knew he would most likely reenlist, but I still held out hope that he might reconsider, and we could be together. "The cottage was ready, and we …" My voice choked. "My hope in that future is gone," I cried.

Astur whispered soothing sounds over me. He rocked me back and forth against his chest. "Oh, Phina, I am sorry for your loss. I feel responsible for every soldier who falls in battle, but for your pain, I feel this loss more deeply than the rest."

Astur continued to hold me as I sobbed quietly. Erik was the last member of my family to leave me. I had thought him lost before, but this was different. I was abandoned once again in this life. Astur breathed steadily, calming me; his lips grazed my temple. He rubbed his chin against my head and hummed a familiar tune over me.

The song was one that I had taught him and played for him often. It was a song that Grandfather had sung over me as he rocked me to sleep. Astur's throat vibrated with the sound. His chest reverberated, and the fissures in his heart darkened as his heart's song poured out over me with love and comfort.

Everything about Astur settled me, and in what might have been the final blow to break me, I felt strangely peaceful. I looked up into his eyes in astonishment. How had a song, a simple song, sung by a man who had no connection to the great spirit, how had that song, Astur's song, embraced me entirely?

Astur wiped the tears from my eyes and kissed my eyelids. His lips moved down my cheek and briefly across my lips. He eased back and looked into my eyes, assessing my reaction. Like before, when we kissed, he found no protest. Our breaths were steady, his determined, mine resigned.

He desired me; he needed me. His wants were the same as mine, and I leaned in and kissed him, gradually releasing my emotions, fears, and confusion. I had missed his touch and attention.

"Phina," Astur moaned as my hands roamed over his back.

"Astur," I sighed as he kissed down my neck.

My voice pleaded, but not in protest. His heart's song was loud in my mind. The vibrant colors of his heart washed over me like the bathing pool, except they were warm. His song grew from a melody into a chorus.

In his embrace, I escaped from the pain, all the pain of my life. Layer upon layer, he lovingly removed. He carried me, kissing me all the while, and laid me gently across my bed. His intentions were clear, his heart and mind aligned. Astur lay down beside me.

My eyes were wide, but I was not afraid. I kissed him again and tugged to remove his shirt. Astur eyed me cautiously. I wanted nothing more than to smother myself against his chest and crawl inside his heart. I tugged at his shirt again.

Understanding, Astur sat up and pulled his shirt over his head. I loosened my robe and unwrapped the fabric around my head, allowing my hair to fall. And that was where it began. His hands were on me, leaving traces of fire where he touched my skin.

Our hearts' colors mingled and bled into one another's. Free from the pain, I left my thoughts and turned myself over to him. Astur's efforts rekindled my heart. He stoked the dying embers until they were a roaring flame. Beneath him, I forgot my pain. Beneath him, I was sheltered. Thankful for his kindness and indulgence, I took all of him into me. He gave me exactly what I asked for.

***

179

Spent from his exertion, he smothered me down into the pillows until his breaths steadied. The intensity of his heart had cooled, but his embrace was warm. Sensing his release, I prepared myself for his reaction to the intimate moment we shared.

Astur rolled over onto his side and looked at me, assessing my reaction. His eyes were cautious as he stroked down my hair, removing a few strands from my face. I dared not speak, unsure of what he read in my expression, uncertain of what words might proceed from my mouth, and I didn't want to cry.

I lowered my gaze and focused on the dip in his chest; my fingers traced down his sternum. He wrapped his arms around me and held me close. He kissed the top of my head and sighed.

His heart's song remained steady and vibrant, but with his sigh came remorse. He was intended for Livia. I had been promised to Erik. Erik was gone, but Livia lay in her bed, unaware. I wondered if his remorse would soon turn to regret.

"You may go," I said and eased from his arms.

"I regret that I must." Was that the regret I sensed? The regret that he must leave me?

"Where are you going?" I asked.

"I ride with Felix. I need to address the troops."

I sat up and covered myself. "You will be joining the battle?" I asked. Concern clouded my mind. I had just lost Erik, and I was afraid I might lose Astur, too. Would everyone be taken from me? I felt even greater disappointment because Astur was not mine to lose. I pulled the covers around myself for protection.

"If I must, but I have no idea until I see for myself. Reports from the front can change in a moment." Astur grabbed his shirt and looked over at me. "Will you be alright?" Concern for me washed over him.

"Yes," I said.

He placed his hand at the back of my head and kissed my forehead. The kiss was neither dismissive nor was it passionate. He had comforted me in a moment of confusion. We had not promised ourselves; he had given me no assurances. I knew my place, and I reminded myself that this was not my home and that, although I had just given myself to Astur, he was still my master.

I heard his determined footfalls leave his chambers. I covered myself the best I could and breathed in his scent; sandalwood and myrrh clung to my sheets and my skin. I closed my eyes and cried myself to sleep.

Chapter Twenty-Nine

The sun was hot on my face when Lucia came to my room. Myrtle breathed heavily beside her. "Oh, child, if Lucia keeps forcing me to tend to you, I'm finding you a new room."

Lucia frowned when she picked up my night dress from the floor. She laid it beside me before she sat on the edge of my bed and looked into my eyes. "Good morning," she said, assessing me.

I sat up and secured the covers around me with one hand self-consciously and pressed down my hair with the other. Did Lucia suspect anything? Could she smell the heavy musk in the room? To me, Astur's scent was everywhere.

"It's time to get up," Myrtle said.

"Yes, Erik has caused you pain enough," Lucia agreed.

"But, I don't want to," I argued.

Lucia's eyes flashed at my refusal, and she crossed her arms. "Phina, you're a woman, now, and women such as us don't have the luxury to mourn. Get up; let the dead be dead and begin anew."

Lucia wasn't cold and unfeeling. She'd had a hard life and had suffered her own losses. Her instructions told me how she coped and moved on, but that was not a healer's way. I had to follow my own path of grieving.

Erik and I were not joined. He was not my mate, so I could not sing the grieving song and close my heart to men. I could only offer a song of thanks and remember his friendship, his love, and the time we shared.

Lucia instructed me to come downstairs as soon as I was dressed. There were matters to which I must attend. Myrtle bathed my face and helped me dress. She then brushed through my matted hair and wrapped my head, placing the veil over my mouth. Myrtle stepped back and examined her work. She offered me a pained smile and hugged me hard.

"Child, get through the best you can," she soothed.

I followed Myrtle to the kitchen, where Cassia placed a bowl of stew in front of me. I had no appetite. I ate a few bites, but my stomach rejected it. "Try the bread," Cassia urged when she placed a cup of hot tea next to my plate.

"May I have some wine?" I asked.

Cassia poured me a cup and patted my shoulder. I looked around the kitchen. The women's eyes darted back and forth to me. They were all widows and had suffered a loss; they wouldn't be there if they hadn't. My eyes filled with tears at their kindness.

They had all had mates, mates who they had given themselves to, but now their mates were gone, snatched away. Erik had not been my mate. I had not given myself to him, but I would have; a thousand times, I would have. Last night, I had given myself to Astur, but he was not my mate. Either way, I had no claim.

"Are you finished?" Lucia asked.

"Yes, ma'am."

"Come." I followed Lucia outside, where a soldier stood holding onto the reins of Erik's black mare. My heart sank when I saw the beast. "He'll settle the details for you."

"Ma'am," the soldier said to me in greeting, "Erik left all of his belongings to you." He offered me a satchel and the reins.

"What am I to do with a horse?" I asked.

"I don't know; I was told to bring her here. The major says she's bad luck. She's survived two riders and refuses to go back into battle. No one dares claim her."

I walked toward the towering beast and placed my hand on her neck. Her dark eyes looked tired and pained. Maybe she and I were destined. I, too, had survived and was left unclaimed.

The young soldier offered me the satchel again. I took it and placed it over my shoulder. It was heavier than I expected. "Thank you," I said.

"If you have no more questions, ma'am, I need to be on my way."

"Does she have a name?" I asked. The soldier shrugged. I turned my attention back to the horse. "Raven, I think I'll call you Raven. Do you like that name?" The horse whinnied and snorted.

I clicked my tongue and led Raven to the stables. There, I met another soldier who took the mare and assured me she'd be cared for. I followed Raven into her stall. The soldier returned and filled her watering trough and feed bucket. He handed me a brush, so I smoothed down her coat. Her black hair was as dark as mine, if not darker.

While Raven chomped loudly over my head, I sat down against the wall and opened Erik's satchel. It contained a few tools, a flute, some medicinal herbs, and a journal. Although it was empty, the bag still felt heavy. I pressed my hand along the bottom and sides and found a pocket sewn into the lining. I pulled out a piece of cloth and discovered where Erik had sewn coins so that the satchel's contents didn't jingle.

Always the prankster, he'd hidden his wealth. Without knowing it, he'd also left me with provision to escape the palace. I had a horse to carry me and plenty of coins to buy some hens and seeds. Maybe it would be enough to buy a goat. I repacked the bag, carefully securing the coin-laden cloth. I patted Raven gently and assured her that I'd return to her soon. Once upstairs, I hid Erik's satchel behind Mother's clothes.

Astur was away for a fortnight. From Marilla's account, he would return in time to take them back to the capital himself. Livia and Lady Gaius busied

184

themselves with plans for the marriage feast. Marilla and I spent time together in the garden and with Traian. The little scamp learned to walk and was everywhere. I visited Raven in the stables every day and walked her in the paddock. My days were labored and heavy, but I forged on following Lucia's example.

Chapter Thirty

The nights were long, and grief snuck into my room and took up residency. Nearly every night, I joined it there with a bottle of wine. Crying again over Erik's death, I couldn't get a handle on my emotions, and the wine only exasperated my efforts to grieve. The hope of being together at the cottage allowed my heart to dream of a future as healers. I didn't bother to wipe the tears from my face.

Guilt impeded my ability to pray, and I found little comfort in the great spirit's songs. In my grief, I had given myself to my master. I had been consumed with lust, mingled with sorrow, comforted by his warm touch and kisses, carried away to a place that protected me from the pain. I no longer had that in his absence, and the wine only numbed the pain a little.

Astur had not slept in his chambers since the soldier's feast. The last time he'd been there was to tell me about Erik. The last I'd seen of him was his back when he left my room. I didn't know what to expect when he returned, so I was alarmed when I heard his boots on the stone. What would he expect from me?

He didn't call for me or demand that I play for him. I listened carefully from my darkened room as he went through his routine. Once he was settled, I forced myself to go back to sleep. If everything went according to plan, it might be one of the last nights I spent at the palace.

Astur's thrashing woke me suddenly. He muttered and cursed and moaned. It was much like the first nights I'd spent there. Without thinking, I grabbed the dulcimer and ran into his chamber. My fingers tingled to be on the instrument. It had been weeks since the Governor's Feast.

My hand strummed the first chords that led into Grandfather's lullaby. Why was that the first song to mind? It was the song Astur had sung to calm me before I offered myself to him. It was the song that stirred our hearts.

"Phina." Astur's voice was deep and strained as he stood over me. I hadn't heard him get out of bed.

"Yes, Astur." My voice was timid and small.

"I need you."

"I know; I'm here."

"No, I want you next to me." Astur offered me his hand. I hesitated. "Please, Phina, will you lie with me and keep the dreams away?"

He didn't demand; he asked. This time, I wasn't crying or sad or overwhelmed by grief. It was my decision, mine alone. I had the power to comfort him as he'd done for me.

I took his hand and allowed him to lead me to his bed. We lay together, but no passion passed between us. "Tell me about the dreams," I said.

Astur shook his head. "They're too painful to recount."

I searched his eyes and let my fingers stroke through his hair. He sighed at my touch. "It will help to release the memories," I whispered.

He pulled me into his side and lowered his head onto my shoulder. His warm breath huffed out over me. I let my hands stroke down his neck and shoulders, easing the tension, and he relaxed into my embrace.

"Are they memories of your time as a soldier?" I guessed. He nodded. "Was it too much to be so close to the front?"

He groaned in response. "The smell of blood, their wounds, the desperation in their eyes, I can't bear to look at them."

"And yet, you must."

"I carry the responsibility for each of their lives. It's too much, especially the losses."

The fissures in his heart spread wide open with his confession, and I wrapped my arms around him, securing him to me. I nodded, rubbing my cheek against his hair. I understood. I pressed my lips onto the top of his head and whispered a prayer of encouragement over him. When he asked me to call him by name, I prayed that my words would be a balm to him. There beside him and the way he clung to me, I knew it was more than my words. My lips and my body held the same power. Perhaps that is why he had kissed me often.

I lay with him, settling him, coaxing him toward sleep. I hummed low into his ear, and his breaths settled before he drifted off. I considered many things lying there with him. I wondered if Livia would have the same ability to comfort him once they were joined, and for a flash, I imagined what it would be like if I stayed. Would Livia be aware of me? Would Astur want us both? Then, I chuckled low in my chest and knew Astur could never manage that. He was faithful and would honor his promises to Livia, and I could not bear the thought of Livia sharing his bed. I was determined to go.

Sometime before daylight, Astur stirred and pulled me closer still. He cupped my face in his hands and stared intently into my eyes. There was no denying his desire for me. Knowing he would forever be without my music, and I would be forever without his heart, I allowed him to have whatever he wanted, and he took it all from me.

Astur was gentle and unhurried. Nothing pulled him away. Beneath him, filled with his warmth, I surrendered myself to his heart's song. The melody and cadence of its beating absorbed me. There was no vision, yet there was no other music but his.

"Thank you," he whispered. *Gratitude.* I smiled and let him kiss me. "You are a wonder, Phina, and I am thankful that your great spirit brought you here."

I accepted his words with a smile but made no declarations of my own. I stroked his hair and gazed into his dark eyes, memorizing their shape and hue.

There was much about him that I would miss. Astur drifted back into sleep, and I left his bed, bathed and dressed. I was in the garden before he began his day.

***

Lady Gaius requested for me to play their last night. I overheard her speaking with Livia in the garden that morning; Marilla wasn't with them and had not joined me, either. It was odd, but I didn't pay much attention to my thoughts of Marilla once I heard Lady Gaius's sharp words.

"You will dismiss her as soon as you are his wife. There will be no discussion on the matter."

"But what if Astur refuses me? I don't know him like she does. He doesn't look upon me with the same eyes."

"You will have to gain your own loyalties, Livia. Woo him; build trust between you. Find what delights him and make him happy. Do only what pleases him."

"Dismissing her will not please him. He adores her music, and I am no minstrel."

"As Lady Gaius, you will have the authority of the running of this palace. That little thing will not have a place under your management; Astur will accept that. I will help him see reason."

Fuming, I almost interrupted them and told them my plan to leave; Livia wouldn't need to bother with me at all.

Chapter Thirty-One

I played my best for their small gathering, a fond farewell. Marilla sat close to me, but Livia did not join us. She sat between Lady Gaius and Astur. I was relieved that Cato was not present. Felix and the guards would escort them all to the capital the following day. After their departure, I would thank Lucia and Myrtle and layer kisses on Traian's cheeks and brow. He would be missed most of all.

The dinner party broke up, and everyone turned in early. Astur and I did not speak of what had happened between us. We had each found comfort, but I did not want to give Astur the wrong impression or appear too eager. He was intended for Livia, and I must respect that. I didn't dare look into his eyes all evening.

Avoiding my room until I was absolutely sure Astur was asleep, I slipped into the library one last time. I would pay my final respects to the garden in the morning. I poured myself a glass of wine; it was quiet, sitting in the dark among all the books. I gave thanks to the great spirit for all the knowledge I had gained there. I sang prayers for Astur and his future as governor. I sang blessings over his mind and asked the great spirit to give him discernment and insight for his region's people. I prayed for him a son, an heir. I raised my glass to the great spirit before I drank the last of it.

"Phina!" I heard Felix bellow my name. I did not like the tone. "Phina! Girl, where are you?"

Something was wrong. I ran and opened the large wooden door. "What is it?" I asked.

"Come!" he demanded. When I wasn't in my room, had Astur sent Felix to find me? Felix grabbed my elbow and hastened me up the stairs. His size and strength were no match for me. From the look on his face, I dared not challenge him.

Felix pulled me toward the bed. Panic washed over me, but it wasn't from the memory of the night we'd shared. Instead, Astur thrashed and writhed; he moaned and finally choked in a fit of seizures. Lucia and Myrtle were there with him. Myrtle wiped his brow with a damp cloth, and Lucia held his head as he heaved and vomited.

I hurried toward them and felt Astur's face; his skin was clammy, and his lips were pale. I opened his eyes to examine them. Their dark centers were enlarged. His breaths were shallow, and he moaned in gulps.

"Phina," he gasped and grabbed hold of me. I pried his hand away and examined his fingertips.

"Poison," I said and heard Lucia's gasp. "How was it ingested?" I asked. Felix shook his head; he didn't know.

I ran to my room and found my stores. The healing plant struggled to produce, but I managed to harvest bits and pieces. I ground the contents of the bottle into a paste. Its sweet aroma wafted around me.

I returned to Astur's side. "Myrtle, I need to make a tincture. Will you fetch me some water from the pitcher? Felix, I need clear, undiluted spirits. Would there be any in the cellars?" Lucia nodded, and the two of them left together.

I mixed some of the paste with the water and then stirred it gently, releasing its properties. I placed the cup to Astur's pale lips and bid him drink. He gagged and turned his face away.

"Astur, please. It will help." Myrtle stared at my calling him by name. I did not respond to her. "Open your mouth and let me pour it onto your tongue." His lips barely parted. The poison was strong.

I pulled at my head covering and wrapped the paste inside the edge. I folded it over and dipped it into the water. I placed the cup next to Astur's face and allowed the saturated fabric to drip into the corner of his mouth.

Astur didn't fight me, but his body was rigid as he fought the waves of nausea and tremors that racked his body. His eyes were wide and pleading. He was consumed by fear and agony.

"You are going to be fine, Astur," I whispered as I dipped the poultice back into the cup. "Suck," I urged, and his lips puckered against the cloth. His neck tightened as he swallowed.

Just then, Felix entered Astur's chambers with a bottle of clear liquid. He uncorked it with his teeth and passed it over to me. I poured it onto the remaining paste and stirred, careful not to waste any of it. It was all that I had.

"Let that set," I said, handing it to Felix. He placed it on the table next to Astur's bed. "Myrtle, can you please?" I asked and offered her the cup and poultice. "I need to harvest more." She nodded and moved to take my place. I unwrapped the rest of my head covering and handed it to Myrtle.

Felix was the only one who had never seen my head unbound. He stiffened at my side, but, as a seasoned commander, he revealed nothing else. His eyes held a million questions, and he doubted himself. I could hear the incredulity roll off his heart. Lucia and Astur had held that fact from him. I was even stranger than he suspected.

"Where are you going?" he asked.

"To the garden. I need the healing plant," I said as I made my way to the door.

He was a step behind me. "You cannot go like that alone," he said. "I'll go."

It was dark, and the palace was lit only by sconces along the corridors. Felix lifted a torch from outside of Astur's chambers and held it high above our heads to light our path. I stopped and gasped. Felix bumped into me from behind.

"What is it?" he asked, alarmed.

"It's gone! The healing plant is gone!" I kneeled down and ran my hands into the loosened dirt. "Someone's dug it up!" Felix kneeled down beside me and moved the torch over the healer's garden. The soil was freshly upturned. Someone had deliberately poisoned Astur and had taken the only way to save him. "The poison plant is gone, too. They were here this morning." I ran my hands over the soil again, but even the roots were gone. "They've taken everything."

My mind raced. If the root of the poison plant had been used, Astur would have died instantly. There was some hope in that. If the poison was extracted from the flowers or leaves, there was a good chance the healing remedy would work, but if it was taken from the stalk, then he might die of dehydration and fever. The side effects would be brutal on his body. I grabbed some leaves from the nausea plant and a few more from the fever plant.

My eyes blurred with tears. "Felix, without the healing plant, I may not be able to save him." My voice sounded small and helpless.

Felix grabbed me by the shoulder and shook me. "No! You will," he commanded. His harsh tone was laced in fear. He was afraid for Astur's life, too. "Come!" I stood, and we raced together back up the stairs.

In my absence, Myrtle had continued my ministrations. The poultice was nearly dry. Astur's eyes were closed, but he was rigid with pain. His hands were clasped in tight fists at his sides. Lucia had also returned and was wiping his brow with a cloth.

"Is he still vomiting?" I asked. Lucia shook her head.

I walked past them into my room and gathered my jars of medicinal herbs. With my meager stores, I was no healer. I was an embarrassment to the calling.

I poured the distilled liquid over the fever and pain medicinals' contents and set them aside; I would need them later. The clear spirits would help their properties absorb more quickly on the tongue. "Myrtle, pour a bit over what you can salvage from the cloth." She took the bottle and stepped away from the bed.

I examined the spirit solution with the healing paste, stirred it gently, and then tasted the slightest drop with my little finger. It was ready. I dipped my fingertips into the liquid and dabbed Astur's lips with it. I repeated the gesture, parting his lips. The clear spirits would burn the blisters that were sure to have formed on his tongue and gums. His vomit bowl held traces of blood, but I wasn't sure if it was from his stomach or mouth. I hoped it wasn't from his stomach.

"Hold him. This will be uncomfortable," I said to Lucia. She cut her eyes toward Felix, who joined her to secure their master and friend.

I coated the inside of Astur's mouth, and he moaned and struggled to move away. "Shhh, I know it burns, but I promise it will help." Astur fought me and made me jostle the contents of the healing paste, nearly spilling it all.

I moved out of his way, saving what little remedy remained. "Astur! If you want to live, you will not fight me!" Everyone jumped at my tone. "Hold him," I commanded.

Felix restrained Astur, and I climbed over the two of them and straddled Astur's chest. Lucia held his head and forced his jaw open. Blood pooled at the corner of his mouth.

After a deep breath, I continued. Astur's guttural cry shook me to my core, but I tightened my knees and thighs over him and held on as he battled against the pain.

I scraped the bottom of the bowl and used every bit of the paste. What little Myrtle was able to gather would need time to steep. Astur shook with pain. The tremors were too much for him to contain.

"Hand me the second jar to the left," I said.

Myrtle uncorked it. The pungent odor wafted out of the jar, and Astur's eyes looked horrified. "I know you don't like this one, but it will help." He shook his head wildly to free himself from Lucia's hold.

Felix cursed and doubled his efforts. Lucia climbed over Astur and knelt down, placing his head between her knees. She held him and nodded once, ready for whatever came next. Astur was a strong man, and it took all three of us to keep him in place.

If I gave him a regular dose, it would ease the pain, but would it be enough? Given Astur's size and the infusion of distilled spirits, my mind was muddled with how much to administer. I hesitated and placed my hand on my forehead.

"What is it, Phina?" Lucia asked.

"I don't know how much to give him."

"Give him all of it!" Felix grunted from behind me.

"It's alright, Phina, you can't do more harm. Can you give him enough to sleep?" I nodded once and doubled the dose.

The pain extracts worked, and Astur gradually eased. His breathing settled, but he was still rigid. I placed my hands on either side of his face; our eyes locked. Lucia was the first to move. She and Myrtle gathered the vomit bowl and cloths.

"I'll return with fresh linens and water. Will you need anything else?" I shook my head but didn't release Astur's gaze. I stroked his temples and whispered soothing words over him.

As Astur relaxed, Felix moved and stood beside the bed. He didn't say anything but watched his friend and our shared intensity. Astur's eyelids fluttered, and I knew it wouldn't be long before he passed into sleep. Still holding his head in my hands, I lowered my forehead down and rested it on Astur's. I whispered words of healing and protection over him. I called on the great spirit to fortify my efforts. I felt drained and inadequate.

"Sing for him," Felix whispered.

"I cannot," I whispered in reply. If I sang, I would never be able to give myself to another man. I only knew the consequences for a female healer; for all I knew, it might curse Astur and Livia's union if I sang for him.

"It worked for Lucia and Traian. Why won't you do it for him?"

"It's different."

"It works for your precious flowers," he grumbled.

So as not to disturb Astur, I gently removed myself from his bed. I stood and faced Felix. "It doesn't work the same for men."

"You sang for Erik; what's the difference? Aren't they both men, or can you only love your kind?"

I glared up at Felix. "I sang *with* Erik, just as I have sung *with* Astur, but without his voice, it will be my undoing." Felix didn't understand. "My song will bind me to him." Felix looked down. His heart was full of fear and sadness. I put my hand on Felix's and forced him to look back at me. "I will do all I can; I promise."

***

Torn between grief and duty, I relied on my calling as a healer. Astur's pain was still present, and the fever soon followed. I had time to mix the pain and fever tinctures so that they would work simultaneously.

After dawn, Felix notified Lady Gaius of the events of the night. She demanded to see Astur, but Felix refused to let her in. He also made her promise not to breathe a word to anyone else in the palace.

Myrtle brought me bread and tea and sat with Astur while I changed and bound my hair. I dozed between doses and watched for any changes. Felix's worry for his friend flowed off of him with every breath. Felix's heart was anxious.

Astur moaned from the pain. At times, he thrashed and cried out like he was being attacked. His eyes were open, but he didn't see any of us clearly. When Astur's fits were violent, Felix held him down so that he wouldn't hurt himself or accidentally strike me.

As the second night passed, Felix's worry for his friend increased. Nothing I did reduced Astur's fever. Lucia and Myrtle brought me everything from my stores, but nothing worked. I had used all that remained of the healing plant.

Felix and I were alone with Astur in the darkness of a moonless night. Myrtle had taken her exhausted old body to bed, and Lucia had Traian and her palace duties. Felix and I watched Astur's labored breaths. "He's worse, Phina. He needs you," Felix said, kindly commanding me to do something.

"I've done everything I know. Without the healing plant, I am helpless."

"Sing for him." I looked up into Felix's eyes. We had already been through that. Felix's voice was barely above a whisper, but his heart begged. "We both know you have the power to save him with your song."

I shook my head. "I have no power. The power comes from the great spirit."

"Well, it's your voice that summons the healing. Sing for him, Phina. You're his only hope."

"I cannot."

"You will not."

Tears stung my eyes. Was I strong enough to give Astur my song and then leave him? He would heal and marry Livia. He was a good governor; he was good for the people and the region. If he died, what would become of us? My heart ached at the prospect of forever being alone, but I cared too much for Astur to allow him to die. My loneliness would be nothing compared to his death.

"Please," Felix begged.

I was afraid that Astur would die, and I knew withholding my song would do more harm than I could bear. I stroked Astur's fevered brow. My heart ached, and tears welled in my eyes. I knew it had to be done. This was personal and private. If I sang for Astur in anyone's presence, I would be self-conscious, which would lessen the power.

"Leave us," I said.

"Thank you, Phina," Felix whispered, but his relief at my words flooded his heart. He hastened from the room.

Chapter Thirty-Two

As I stared at Astur, my song would not come. I sat close to him on the bed and stroked his brow. I cried out to the great spirit to hear my words and save him. Soon, I was swept up into the great spirit's presence, the tears passed, and the words flowed out. I sang until my mouth was dry and hoarse. I sipped tea to soothe my throat and poured small sips of the healing liquids into Astur's mouth to keep his fever under control.

My singing soothed him. His breaths steadied, and he settled into a deep sleep. I placed my hand over his heart and willed it to be healthy. The hues swirled and mingled under my touch. I sang every healing song I knew.

Drawn even closer to Astur, I laid across his chest and melded my heart with his. I prayed to the great spirit in song and then directed the words over Astur. I carefully wove the melodies and words. I called on all the powers of the great spirit to heal him. I dropped tinctures onto his tongue and made him sip infusions from a small cup.

The hours passed, and I sang. Caught up in the great spirit, the binding song flowed out as effortlessly as the rest. When I heard the words, I wept because it no longer mattered; I had already given him my body and gift of music. I would be bound to him forever.

Exhausted from two nights of healing, I collapsed on Astur's chest. I continued to sing until the sun's rays made their appearance, lifting the haze in the room. My throat was parched, and my eyes were puffy. Astur moaned but didn't wake. I closed my eyes and whispered one more prayer of healing before I, too, fell asleep.

An unfamiliar hand stirred me awake. I opened my eyes and found myself lying next to Astur. His arm was over me. I rolled over, and Lady Gaius stared down at me. Her eyes were sharp with concern.

Felix rushed in and stood a few paces behind Astur's mother. He apologized with his eyes for allowing me to be found sleeping on the governor. I stood suddenly and gathered myself.

Lady Gaius looked at Astur, and lines of worry crossed her face and aged her. Had she seen him suffering after he was wounded in battle? The lady composed herself enough to address me.

"Will he live?" she asked.

I felt his forehead. It was warm but not feverish. I had to clear my throat before I could speak. "I have done everything I can. It is up to his body now. He is strong. I believe he will."

Lady Gaius's pride returned. "Then you are dismissed."

"Yes, ma'am," I said but didn't want to leave Astur unattended. "Please call me if there are any changes."

Lady Gaius sat on the edge of Astur's bed and took his hand. "No, child, you misunderstand. You are free to *go*."

"Pardon me?" I asked.

"You've done your part."

"But, ma'am, I need to stay until he improves."

"We can manage," she said. "You have served the purpose of entertaining him, but your music will no longer be needed. You have no place here; you do not belong." She turned to Felix. "See that she's given provision and escorted from the palace immediately."

I looked into Lady Gaius's eyes but did not argue. She was right. I had done everything in my power to heal Astur, and it was my opportunity to leave. Felix looked as though he would intervene, but I shook my head. It wasn't worth his efforts.

I went to my room and packed my few belongings, but I left the herbs that remained at Astur's bedside. I changed into my healer's clothes and left my palace tunic behind forever. I packed Mother's book and secured the dulcimer in Grandfather's hat before I slung Erik's satchel over my shoulder.

Felix was waiting for me outside my room. I did not return to Astur's chambers and followed Felix down the back stairs. When Astur awoke, Livia and his mother would be at his side.

Felix walked me toward the kitchen. He had been the instrument of the great spirit who found me, and he was also the one who escorted me out of the palace. I sensed his regret and his deep sorrow at my departure.

"Please do not worry about me. I will be alright, Felix. You may leave me here."

"Phina, she is wrong to do this. Astur will come for you."

I shook my head, denying his words. "No, Felix. That is not my future."

"How can you know that?"

I shrugged. "I must return to my home. My calling is to be a healer, not a governor's minstrel."

He knew that *minstrel* was not the whole truth. I had once asked Felix if Lucia was his mate. His eyes asked me the same unspoken question. After watching me for the better part of two days, he already knew. Felix had been the first to notice Astur's changes, and he had witnessed my protection for our governor.

Felix lifted his chin. "I'm sorry, Phina. I'm sorry." His voice was strained. His heart poured out regret. He regretted that his friend had misused me, but it had not been like that.

I looked away and blushed. "Please thank Lucia for me. I will miss Traian most of all." My voice caught, and I was unable to continue.

"You'll tell her yourself," he said gruffly. "Lucia," he hollered into the kitchen and grabbed a basket. He handed it to Cassia and asked that she pack it full of food, water, and wine.

"What is it?" Lucia looked at both of us. "Who is with the governor?" she asked accusingly.

"His mother," Felix replied. "She dismissed Phina."

"Dismissed? But she saved him. She needs to stay."

"No, Lucia. I must."

Lucia shook her head. "Where will you go?"

"I'm going home. I'm going back to the cottage." The truth of my words fell solidly. I smiled through my tears. "Thank you, Lucia. Thank you, Felix. Please tell Traian how much he's loved."

Unexpectantly, Lucia hugged me, and Myrtle brought me the basket that Cassia had packed. "Oh, child, watch after yourself," Myrtle said.

"Yes, ma'am. I will." Myrtle hugged me then, too.

I turned quickly and walked to the stable to find Raven. Felix followed me. The black horse was easy to spot among the dapples and the grays. Raven eyed me warily when I approached her stall. "Come here, girl," I coaxed, clicking my tongue to entice her. She lifted her head proudly and huffed air through her lips. "Want to go home? Want to go with me to the cottage?" I whispered.

As if she understood, she lifted her head in a nod and stomped her hoof. Felix eased the bridle over her head, but I didn't bother to saddle her. Felix held the basket while I climbed onto her back with Erik's satchel.

Felix's eyes were nearly as dark as Astur's, and with that brief reminder, I let my eyes wander up toward his chambers. Felix placed his hand on my knee, forcing my attention back to the present. He handed me the basket.

"Thank you for sharing your song." I nodded, accepting his words. "I wish you all the best."

"Thank you," I whispered but couldn't say anything else. Without another glance, I tapped my heels into Raven's side and rode through the palace gate.

Part Two

Chapter Thirty-Three

My time at the cottage was busy. I bought a goat for milking and seeds to plant vegetables. As soon as I was able to make cheese, I traded it for two hens. I drew fresh water from the spring, and I fished along the river. My heart was content there, but it was lonely, and I missed the books, all of the books.

I wondered about Marilla and her return home. I thought about Traian every afternoon, but by evening, my thoughts went to Astur. I sang songs of healing to the great spirit every night on his behalf. I prayed for his life to be blessed, and as difficult as it was, I even prayed for Livia. They would be joined as soon as he was healed. I prayed for him a son.

It was warm the morning that everything changed. I felt a wave of dizziness pass over me as I dropped the bucket down into the spring. I cooled my hands in the water and patted my face and neck. I tried to eat some bread, but it tasted off. Even the wine at supper tasted bitter. My symptoms continued for a couple of days, and then the exhaustion crashed down over me. I brewed some tea and slept.

A week later, the moon showed brightly, but my bleeding did not arrive. It was then that I noticed the changes; I had been too distracted to pay attention to myself. From then on, I knew that I had conceived Astur's child. I had only lain with him twice: once, the night the news of Erik's death threatened to take me under, and next, the morning after his return when I comforted him.

I went to the cupboard where I kept my stores. I held the bottle of seeds and rolled them around, examining each one. They had the power to expel the child. It was early; I still had time. I considered my choice for three days. Each day, I picked up the bottle, examined the seeds, and placed it back on the shelf. One day, I even went as far as to allow one to steep, but I couldn't drink it. The child inside of me was repelled by its scent, and I heaved and vomited.

On the fourth day, I opened the jar decidedly and hurled its contents out the window. There would be no more regard for the matter. I had not mistaken Astur's presence for love. Neither had I sang for him; that had come later. Astur was solid and warm, and I had needed him, just as he needed me. Although I feared and had had my share of abandonment, the great spirit, once again, provided for me and blessed me with a child.

Before two moons passed, my body transformed, round and curvy. My hips expanded to accommodate a baby. I marveled at all the changes and continuously sang thanks and protection over my unborn child.

***

I had become a healer in my own right because it wasn't long before the needy sought me out. My days were focused as I settled into my old home that was now my new home. I practiced healing and helped all that I could.

Grandfather's garden thrived under my hand. The months passed, and my breasts and belly rounded carrying my child, Astur's child. Grandmother's gift of sight was strong, and I dreamed nightly that it was a boy, a son. His eyes were like mine, but his hair was dark brown like his father's. I could never give my son his father's name, and since he would have no father to name him, I decided early in my pregnancy to share my father's name, Mendel.

As the baby grew, so did my hair, full and black as ravens' wings. I let it fall loose around my shoulders. When it was long enough to braid, I nearly wept. Finally, I had the look of a healer, except for the eyes, which remained a silver-gray.

The cycles of the moon passed. I was healthy and strong. The garden flourished, and I lived contentedly until my child's arrival.

***

I was restless the entire night, and I couldn't get comfortable. The moon was full, and I felt the waves of labor increase before the sun rose in the morning. Slowly, I made my way to the bathing pool. The lilacs were in bloom, and their scent was heady. I lowered myself into the water and floated as my body worked to birth the child.

Mendel was large and active, and the past few weeks had been uncomfortable. I breathed and sang. I panted and rested between the waves of labor that thrashed from the inside. I prayed to the great spirit. I sang for mercy on my child and the life that I promised to provide for him. I prayed for forgiveness that, like me, he would never know his father.

When the pressure intensified, I knew my time was close. I gripped my fingers into the grass at the side of the pool, held my cries, and pushed the baby out. I gathered him from between my legs and floated him up into my bosom. I leaned back against the side and rested as I held my newborn son.

Through tears of joy and pain, I sang songs of blessing and thanksgiving. The memory of Mother's voice joined mine. Her love flooded my heart and flowed from me onto my son. I named him and claimed him. "Mendel," I whispered over him. His hair was not the color of raven's wings but a rich brown like his father's. His complexion was fairer, much lighter than mine.

I took my time walking back to the cottage. I drank water and ate bread. I slept and nursed my son. For days, I ate only what I could gather fresh from the garden and what I had managed to save in the root cellar. Mendel was strong like his father, but I did not linger on the thoughts of Astur. My mind stayed fixed on my son.

Chapter Thirty-Four

Mendel slept in the basket at my bedside while I kneaded bread in the kitchen. I used the time he napped in the afternoon wisely. He was a large baby and did not enjoy being worn all day. He preferred to be swaddled when he slept, and my back appreciated the breaks, too.

From a distance, the sound of hoofbeats thundered toward the cottage. I was unable to tell if it was one horse or two. As the hoofbeats came closer, I wiped my hands on my apron and walked toward the door. The afternoon sun cast them in shadow, but then I realized that there were three riders.

I wasn't alarmed. I acknowledged the risk of living alone, but I refused to allow it to control my destiny. I claimed my calling as a healer, and I dismissed any thoughts to the contrary. I reasoned that I had only myself and Mendel to protect. With the great spirit's help, I would do my best.

The palace insignia blazed silver on their tunics, and I braced myself for the arrival of soldiers. It was then that I recognized Felix's bearing. He turned from the road, and the two soldiers at his flanks followed his lead.

Why were they there? Were they looking for me? They must require a healer. Was it Traian or Lucia? Was Astur ill again? The thought of Astur brought pain to my heart.

My heartbeat increased, and my mouth went dry. I raised my chin and braced myself for whatever might come. I had sung prayers of protection over my son, and I knew that no matter what, the great spirit would honor those requests.

As soon as they saw me, Felix motioned for the soldiers to stay back. Felix dismounted his horse and walked toward me. His smile was warm and triumphant, but I could not return his greeting.

Sensing my apprehension, Felix stopped. He assessed our surroundings, but there was no threat from the cottage. I cut my eyes toward Felix in a warning. *Fear.* He knew I was afraid.

"Phina, you look well. It is good to see you," he said like he was relieved to find me. "We've been scouring this section for two days! None of the locals would tell us how to find you. You'd think they'd have more sense than to lie to soldiers."

"They didn't lie to you. One may only find a healer when a healer is needed." His brow furrowed, but he dismissed the distraction of my statement.

Lady Gaius's words returned and washed over me, reminding me of my place. I bowed my head. I was a commoner, an ordinary citizen, subject to the governor and the region's laws. As the governor's representative, I needed to welcome Felix appropriately. I lifted my chin again and mustered a friendly smile.

"Now that you have found me, what do you need? What brings you to the cottage?" I asked.

Felix's expression changed, and his excitement waned. "We found you," he said like that was enough of an explanation.

"Why were you looking for me?" I asked.

Felix hesitated. "He can't sleep. He's irritated, and the pain lingers. Nothing will settle him."

It would soon be a year since Astur had been poisoned. "Is it lingering effects of the fever?" I asked.

"Physically, he's healed. He's regained his strength, but sleep eludes him. It's taken longer than anyone expected."

"Did he send you?" I asked.

"Yes and no, but I found you on my own. He needs you, Phina. He needs you body and soul."

A wave of unfamiliar emotion flooded over me. I placed my hand to my chest to catch my breath. My thoughts moved in different directions, and my breasts tingled, bringing me back to the present. Mendel would awaken soon. I dismissed Felix's words with a wave of my hand and stepped down onto the path, further away from my sleeping child.

Felix ignored my reaction and continued to press his assertions. His voice was soothing and low. "What little he's able to sleep, Astur dreams about you. He says that you're dancing in the garden with Traian, but when he approaches you, it's not Traian." Felix took a step toward me and whispered, "He swears the child is his. He's quite convincing."

I lifted my chin even more proudly but dared not look into Felix's eyes. I batted back tears and contained the emotion that threatened. I swallowed before I spoke. "His and Livia's," I suggested.

Felix shook his head smugly. "No, that's not possible."

I looked up, surprised by his words. "What happened? Does she not please him?" I asked, but I knew I had no right to know. Neither did I have time for idle chatter. He needed to be on his way.

Felix startled me with a laugh. "I should say not. She pleased herself and his mother's intentions. Livia was quite put off when it was your name that he called from the fever."

I stepped back and covered my mouth with my hand, shocked. My song had cursed their union. Felix stepped toward me again with pleading in his eyes. "I can't stand to watch him suffer. It's only a matter of time before he comes to find you himself, but that is not only what brings me here. The child he describes has your eyes, Phina. You will give him a son," he insisted.

My heart sank, and I reflexively grabbed my middle where Astur had planted his seed and where that seed had grown and lay sleeping at the back of the cottage. Astur's sight was clear; his son indeed had my eyes.

"But what will become of us, the child and me?" I asked.

Felix shook his head, confused by my question. Before he had a chance to respond, it was too late. Heat rushed into my breasts; I had ignored Mendel too long. He was likely thrashing against his bindings, searching for his next meal. I stepped back into the doorframe, anticipating his cry. My breasts hardened, and within seconds, Mendel bellowed out in frustration and hunger. That was when he reminded me most of his sire.

Felix responded instantly and gave me an incredulous look. I braced my hands on the doorframe to block his entrance. I glared at him, daring him to go past me.

"Phina, let me in," Felix commanded. He was a man of authority who could easily lift me out of the way.

Mendel's scream was insistent, and my body ached to appease him. Tears pooled in my eyes, unable to contain the rush of guilt and fear and need to protect my son. Looking into Felix's eyes, I had no choice but to step aside.

Felix ran toward the sound of the distressed child. I followed him, unsure of what his reaction might be. As I entered the room, Felix froze when he looked into the basket. Carefully, he scooped up the screaming baby and looked him over. Shock and amazement showed in Felix's expression.

He looked at me and then back at the baby in his hands. He inspected him. Surprised, Mendel opened his eyes and stared at the stranger. Felix blinked, knowing Mendel was the same child Astur had seen in his dreams.

"Aren't you full of surprises?" he marveled. Felix examined the baby for Astur's contribution. There was no denying Astur in Mendel's features. The only attribute I had managed to give was the color of his eyes. "He's big," Felix assessed, impressed. "What do you call him?"

"Mendel, for my father."

"Mendel," Felix repeated. "Your father will be eager to meet you. Would you never have told him?" There was an accusation in his tone.

"I do not know," I confessed. Mendel stretched and rooted; his little mouth opened and searched. I anticipated his impatience and the unnerving scream that would surely follow. "I need to feed him," I said and gestured. Felix passed him over to me. I loosened my blouse and eased the fidgety baby onto my breast.

Felix stepped back and diverted his eyes. He took in a deep breath, clearing his mind and perhaps taking in the reality of what he'd found. I sighed in relief as the milk rushed down, and Mendel suckled voraciously.

Felix paced around the room, taking it in. He stood in the doorway, looking into the small living space and the kitchen.

"Will you tell him?" I asked.

"I cannot withhold this from him. It is his right to claim his son."

I nodded. I understood, but I could not speak. The region's laws were explicit, and I knew the consequences. If a child, especially a son, was conceived and later claimed, it was a man's right to take a son from his mother. My stomach ached at the thought.

Felix waited until Mendel was satisfied. He then opened his hands, asking to hold my son. I sensed no deceit from Felix. I trusted that he wouldn't run from the cottage with Mendel. He was curious and wanted to examine him more closely. Felix held Mendel securely in his arms and smiled down into his little face. I'd seen Felix do the same with Traian a hundred times. I imagined Astur would hold our son with the same pride and affection if given a chance.

"He will take him," I said. I didn't recognize my own voice.

Felix's jaw stiffened before he turned to face me. "Yes, he will want the child with him. As the governor's son and heir, he will lack for nothing."

"He's still so young; can we not wait until he's weaned to make it known?" I asked. My voice was far away, and my breasts ached at the thought of being separated from my baby.

Felix walked back toward me. "Phina, are you well?" he asked, putting his hand to my cheek. Tears spilled out of my eyes at his tenderness.

"I'm sorry, Felix. I'm not ready to give him up."

"What?" he asked, and then realization crossed his face. He took me by the arm and sat me on the edge of the bed. He held Mendel in one arm and put his other arm around my shoulder, securing me. His concern for me was familiar.

"I came here to find *you*, Phina. It's you he wants. He doesn't yet know anything about the child. He's miserable. He was unsettled before I brought you to the palace. Since you left, he's unrecognizable. I came, hoping to convince you to return to him."

"I cannot return as I once was," I asserted. "I am a mother and healer now. I have responsibilities. I can no longer be his *minstrel*."

Felix looked at the baby and shook his head. There was no denying his relief at finding me. "It will not be like that for you, again." Felix said the words, but his heart meant it as a promise.

"We neither have that say," I said.

"No, but you will read Astur's heart for yourself," he mused.

I lowered my gaze, unprepared to see Astur. "I do not know my thoughts on the matter."

Felix stroked Mendel's tiny forehead with his thumb and watched as his eyelids fluttered. Felix was determined to tell Astur everything he had found. *Relief. Anticipation. Delight. Pride.*

"You need to figure that out," he said. *How long do I have?* I looked at Felix with the unspoken question and braced myself for his reply. "I will return here tomorrow for your answer, but I hope that your decision will please us both." He unceremoniously kissed Mendel's crown of dark brown hair. "The guards will remain behind."

"That's not necessary, Felix. I have no intention of fleeing."

Felix furrowed his brow. "That is not why," he said. "I leave them to protect you, not to watch you."

I regretted my words. "I'm sorry, Felix. I forget myself. Thank you, but Mendel and I are safe enough." I tried to appease him, but there would be no convincing him. The guards would remain whether or not I could see them. "What time might I expect you?" I asked like we were setting an important meeting.

Felix chuckled then, easing the tension between us. His eyes were filled with fondness. "Phina, it is a good thing that I found you. I understand your apprehension; truly, I do, but this is not how I expected to find you."

"It is not how I expected to find myself." I returned Felix's warm smile. Felix passed Mendel back into my arms, and his eyes lingered on the baby's face. "May I ask you a favor?" I asked. Felix nodded once. "I would like to be the one to tell Astur about his son," I said, barely above a whisper.

Felix searched my eyes as he considered my request. "Regardless of whether or not I tell him, he will be eager to see you once he knows where you are. He won't waste a moment." I placated Felix with a smile, but I could not muster the confidence required to face the near future. I followed Felix back through the kitchen. He hesitated at the door and looked into the lowering sun in the sky. "Expect me before midday."

Chapter Thirty-Five

That night, neither Mendel nor I slept very well. He was fussy and wanted to nurse all night. He approached his third month of life and was growing rapidly. I comforted him the best I could, but my thoughts were elsewhere. I thought about the palace and Astur. I let myself linger on the memories of our nights together. There were so many nights spent listening, playing, and sharing. He was always kind.

I loved Astur; there was no denying that. I had given him everything: my music, my voice, my body, and finally, a son. Would he still desire me? Would he know his own mind?

Mendel fell into a deep sleep just before the sunrise. I was exhausted after wrestling with him and my thoughts all night. I washed my face, put on a clean skirt and blouse, and brushed and braided my hair. I bound it with a blue and silver scarf.

I stoked the fire in the kitchen to bake the bread that had risen overnight. I gathered mint from the garden and steeped the leaves for tea. I had just put the bread in the oven when hoofbeats thundered nearby. I had not seen or heard the soldiers after Felix left the cottage.

I rolled my eyes in annoyance. Felix had said midday, but it was not even midmorning. Like the day before, I hastened toward the door to meet them.

Three men's tunics displayed the palace insignia, and the lead rider had Felix's bearing. The fourth wore a deep blue cloak. I knew that cloak, and my breath caught.

Astur. Astur had come to see me himself.

Astur spurred his horse toward the cottage. Felix was right behind him. "Sir," Felix warned as Astur dismounted. Felix was at his master's heels. He placed his hand on Astur's forearm.

"What?" Astur asked, angry to be restricted.

"Sir, caution," Felix said.

"Curse caution, Felix." Astur jerked his arm away and turned toward me. "Phina," he said like he'd just discovered a hidden treasure.

I was immovable, but my heart delighted at the sound of my name. The part of me that wanted to rush into his arms battled against reason. I was bound to him, but I did not know his heart. *His heart.* I batted back the threatening tears of joy. A slight smile formed at the corner of my lips at the sight of his healthy body walking toward me. He was well and alive; he was healed. My expression softened; I could not deny my joy and thankfulness at that. The great spirit had answered my prayers.

Astur hesitated before he continued, but he was genuinely pleased to see me. I hoped he would be as equally delighted once he met his son. He shook his head like he didn't know where to begin. "I can't sleep; what little I do, I see you dancing around in the garden. You keep singing to me." His tone was accusing like I was doing it intentionally to torment him.

I nodded. "Yes, Felix told me." I turned to face Felix. "I thought I had until midday." My voice was more impatient than I intended.

Felix shrugged. "Our governor had another agenda."

I guessed as much. I returned my eyes to Astur's. He was a sleep-deprived and impassioned man, yet, from what I could read, his heart was clear. Felix cleared his throat and interrupted the intensity of the moment.

"Excuse me, sir; I will wait with the men," Felix said.

214

Bewildered, I turned to face Felix again. He gave an approving nod; he was right to leave us alone. After all, this was between Astur and me. I had asked Felix to allow me to be the one to tell Astur about Mendel, but I thought I would have more time to prepare myself. I thought I would give Felix an answer and make plans to return to the palace on my own, but that is not how it would happen.

Remembering my manners, I gestured my hand toward the door. "Won't you come in?" I offered. I stepped aside to allow Astur admittance. Astur examined Felix for a brief moment and wondered at the tone of our voices.

"Thank you," I mouthed to Felix. He lifted his chin and took in a deep breath. He looked toward Astur and then back to me before he smiled and gave a nod of encouragement.

Standing behind Astur, I followed his eyes around the kitchen as he took everything in. The aroma of baking bread wafted toward us. A block of cheese and a knife lay on the table, too. My steeping tea had cooled.

"So, this is your cottage?" he asked.

"Yes. It is no palace, but it offers its own comforts."

"You live here alone?" he asked, but there was something in the tone of his voice that was irritated.

"Yes." He scoffed his disapproval. "I'm quite happy here, sir."

He cocked his head to one side. I was unsure if I had the right to call him Astur again, but *sir* was not the word he wished to hear.

The scent of the baking bread alerted me that it was done. I hurried past Astur to the oven and removed the bread; it was ready. In my distraction, I had completely forgotten about it.

"We've interrupted your morning," he said.

"I wasn't expecting *you*," I agreed. I glanced toward my bedroom. Mendel slept soundly, but I knew it might not last. "May I offer you some refreshment?"

He shook his head, but his eyes stayed fixed on me. "No, but eat, if you like."

I had no appetite. "Thank you," I said awkwardly. "Please, won't you sit?" I asked.

"If you'll join me." He pulled out a chair.

I shook my head. "No, thank you; I prefer to stand. I have something to tell you, and," I stammered and held the back of a chair to ground me. I stumbled over my thoughts to find the words to tell him about his son.

"I, too, have something to say, so perhaps we should both sit or both stand," he teased.

Astur's words passed over my ears; I had missed his voice and the presence of his heart. Warmth rose to my cheeks, and I looked away.

"May I begin?" he asked. I nodded, and Astur stepped toward me. "You have been away for a long time. Your presence and music are missed." My eyes soon returned to his. I could not resist the sight of him.

"Felix told me that your healing took a long time."

"Yes." Astur's jaw tightened. *Weakness. Frustration.* He did not want to speak of that. He shook off the painful thought and then returned to the present. "That is not what brings me here." He lifted his chin and spoke with authority, "Phina, I wish for you to return to the palace with me. I wish for you to be at my side as I govern."

It was as though he offered me a position. Would he finally make good on his jest to make me an advisor? "In what capacity?" I asked, matching his tone. Like before, Felix was not aware of Astur's intentions, and I was too nervous to read Astur's heart. My own pulse quickened, awaiting his reply.

Astur shook his head, confused by my question. "Felix told me what you did. He said you didn't leave me for two nights." I nodded. "He told me how you sang for me, but he didn't need to. I can't remember much about that time, but I do remember that." His eyes pierced me, searching mine for answers. He already knew some of the consequences of singing for a man.

I closed my eyes but couldn't offer any reply. My heart ached to be near him. I worked desperately to forget his comfort, and in such close proximity, I battled against my longing. I belonged to him; I was bound, but I could not return as I once was.

"I knew you were gone, but when I went into you your room and found your tunic lying there, it was like you had evaporated into the air. The first time I left my chambers, I went to the garden. Except for the lilacs, nothing of you remained. I couldn't bear the thought."

The cadence of Astur's words was paced as though he'd rehearsed them. "Phina, we searched; Felix searched," he clarified. "When he returned yesterday and said he'd found you, I needed to see for myself. Please, return to the palace with me and be at my side."

"I am a healer now. I have responsibilities." I didn't care to mention that one of those responsibilities was our son.

"Yes, I know that, and at my side, you will perform them well."

"You said that you would never force me to do anything against my will. I wish not to return to the palace as your minstrel. That is no longer my calling." I lowered my eyes because it was easier to refuse him that way. I knew too well that my refusal might anger him.

"My *minstrel*," he scoffed. "No, Phina, not as a minstrel. Of course, you may play for me anytime. Your music, the silence in my chambers is deafening." The longing of his heart mirrored mine. "Please, look at me." I lifted my eyes and looked into his. He was smiling, and his excitement and relief from earlier returned. *Curse caution, indeed.* "Would you consider returning under different circumstances?"

I eyed him warily. "What circumstances might that be?" Would he make me his mistress?

"As my lady," he said, explaining to me like I was a simpleton.

"You wish to be joined? You wish to be my mate?" I asked disbelievingly.

"Of course, Phina. What else would you expect?" I shook my head. I didn't know.

I shook my head again, denying his desire for me. "No. It's the song, the binding song. I was carried away, praying every healing song I knew," I confessed. "Your heart has been wooed by my song." Grandmother's warnings settled over me, and I felt her remonstrance for misusing my song.

Astur considered my denial. "Do you regret singing for me?"

"No." I did not regret singing for him or for singing the binding song. "But it has ruined me for all other men," I confessed. Surprisingly, that pleased him.

"You doubt my intentions," he said. I nodded. He considered my words. "Have you lost your ability to read my heart?" he asked.

"No, but it is more difficult because I must tell you something, something that I kept from you."

Caution. "What is it, Phina? What have you kept from me?" His tone was steady, but his heart's colors shifted. He would not tolerate deceit.

It might be better to show him rather than to tell him. "Will you excuse me?" He stepped forward to follow me, but I put up my hand. "Please, just one moment; I will be right back."

Chapter Thirty-Six

I walked into my bedroom and eyed my baby, our son. I cradled Mendel in my arms and kissed his sweet face. I wondered if he had any idea in his little head that our lives were about to change dramatically.

"I love you, my sweet boy. I'm taking you to meet your father." Tears welled in my eyes, and I whispered a prayer to remain calm no matter Astur's response. My heart raced, yet my pace and breaths were measured.

Astur peered out the window over the field toward the barn. "Where does that path lead?" he asked, not looking at me.

"To the bathing pool," I said.

"It's very peaceful here," he remarked but didn't turn around.

"Yes, it is," I whispered, not wanting to disturb Mendel. I took a deep breath to settle my voice and looked into Mendel's face for courage. I set my shoulders and lifted my chin. It was time. "Astur," I began. Astur's shoulders rounded at the sound of his name as though a weight had been lifted from them. "I would like you to meet my son."

Astur turned to face me. His eyes briefly met mine and then fell onto the baby in my arms. Astur blinked and staggered back. His expression was unreadable.

"Is he mine?" Astur asked, bracing himself for confirmation, but he already knew the truth.

"Yes."

Astur was in front of me in two long strides. His heart's colors shone brightly but different than before. Had Felix not found me, Astur would never know about his son. That saddened him. I wanted him to understand.

"Your mother made it clear that I was no longer welcome there, and Felix, too, knew it was best I go."

I touched his forearm and looked into his eyes, willing him to understand. The simple pleasure of touching him sent fire straight to my belly. "Please, Astur, do not blame her. She planned for you and Livia, and I was a distraction." Astur shook his head, angered by his mother's interference.

"Did you know?" he asked.

"No, I didn't. It was too soon." Astur blinked and took a deep breath, clearing his mind and perhaps taking in the reality of his dreams. "My leaving, your son, I never intended for them to hurt you."

Astur swallowed back his emotion. "May I hold him?" he asked.

"Of course," I said, relieved, and placed Mendel into his father's outstretched arms.

"What do you call him?" he asked.

"Mendel. I named him for my father." I hoped that Astur would approve.

"Mendel," Astur repeated. His eyes glistened with awe. "You were alone. How did you manage it?"

I remembered how his young wife had died bringing their son into the world. There had been no healers present to sing the baby forth, and the great spirit had not been called upon.

"I have just recently come to accept that I am never alone; I never have been. The great spirit is always with me, and even if Mendel is unaware of it, he was with me, too." I stroked my hand down the infant's back. "He is the embodiment of your comfort, of the comfort we shared."

My apprehension at Astur's arrival was strangely absent. He reached his hand over and followed mine, gazing affectionately over his son. "When you knew of him, why did you not send word to me?" There was an accusation in his tone. Concealing the truth from Astur hurt him most of all.

I smiled soothingly. "If you remember, we were consumed with loss. You comforted me, and I, in turn, comforted you. There were no declarations made between us. You were not my mate, Astur." Astur looked down and nodded once, but he made no apology. My words were the truth, but they still caused him pain.

"I have a son," he said. The words got stuck, tamped down by the awe. "You cannot withhold my rights to be his father," he said sternly, intensifying the shades of his heart. *Protection. Possession.*

"It was not my intention, Astur. Please forgive me."

Astur looked at me, and his heart softened and flowed its cool blue. My own heart swelled under his gaze. I had missed his presence. "There is nothing to forgive," he whispered. Astur's expression was kind, and he almost smiled.

"I am thankful. The great spirit made way for me to have a family again," I whispered.

When Astur spoke, his voice was gruff with emotion. "You and your music comforted me from the beginning. Your great spirit has given me a family, again, too."

Our gaze fell back onto Mendel, and heat rushed to my breasts. Sure enough, Mendel wriggled, and his eyelashes fluttered. When Mendel woke, Astur stiffened.

"His eyes, he has your eyes," he marveled.

Astur loosened the swaddling and examined Mendel's fingers and toes. Mendel stretched and rooted at the loosening of the binding and turned his head, searching for his next meal. Mendel appeased Astur's inspection for a moment or two more before his bottom lip quivered.

"I need to feed him," I said, offering out my hands.

Astur hesitated a moment too long, and Mendel bellowed out a cry of frustration. Astur passed Mendel back into my arms. I sat in the chair that Astur had offered me earlier. I loosened my blouse and adjusted Mendel in my lap.

Unlike Felix, Astur did not look away. Instead, he sat in the other chair and watched the two of us, fascinated and curious.

Once we were settled, Astur's questions began. "How old is he?"

"Nearly three months."

"Has it been difficult managing it all on your own?"

I shook my head and smiled. "He's big and heavy, and he likes to eat often, but that is not a difficulty unless I don't get to him soon enough. His cry a moment ago was just a taste of his real impatience."

When Mendel was finished with his meal, Astur stood and reached out his hands to retake Mendel. Astur stepped away and turned toward the window to get a better look.

"You've given me a son, Phina. You know what this means." I thought there was teasing in his voice, but I was too frightened to acknowledge it. I nodded solemnly but refused to look him in the eye.

"If you claim him, how will you remain as governor?" I whispered toward the ground.

He scoffed. "I won't be the first governor to claim a son after his birth. Even the king has two sons by his mistress."

Mistress, I repeated in my mind. Astur stroked Mendel's face and outlined his lips with his fingertip. He was charmed by our son. Astur smiled and mimicked Mendel's expressions.

"When will you claim him?" I asked. My voice was unrecognizable.

"Immediately." His reply both pained and delighted me. Mendel would always know his father. "I claim Mendel, but it was you that I came here for." It was hard for me to accept the offer to be his lady. He was under no obligation to me, but I was already bound.

Astur read my expression clearly. He then looked down at Mendel, whose eyes were alert and curious. "Your mother doubts me, son." Astur smiled wryly. "I wonder what it will take to convince her." He winked playfully at Mendel.

Mendel squirmed and was restless. Astur walked him a few paces and bounced the baby in his arms; he looked natural, holding our son. The movement settled them both. Astur organized his thoughts before he spoke.

"Phina, it took a long time before I was strong enough to ride, too long, but the dreams have haunted me for months. Your absence has been painful and prolonged my healing." He shook his head like he regretted something. All of his jests were gone. "I never should have agreed to marry Livia." He pursed his lips like the words tasted bitter. "But that is beside the point. I denied my heart. I should have made it clear the night you sang with Erik. As angry as I was, I denied my feelings for you. Even before you sang your healing songs, I knew you were the one I most desired."

My lips pulled a bit at the edges, accepting his words. Astur passed Mendel back into my arms before he sat down next to me. He took my face in his large, warm hands. "Phina, I love you. I came here today to tell you that. We sent scouts all over the region to find you. Felix finally tracked Erik's conscription. I kicked myself for never asking where your cottage was."

I felt the familiar tension of desire, the longing. Astur looked into my eyes, searching for a reply. Maybe it wasn't the binding song, after all. Although it had been nearly a year since he'd kissed me, I knew it was his intention.

I stiffened and rambled questions, breaking his concentration. "What of your mother? The rumors? Your reputation?"

He lowered his hands onto my shoulders, willing me to understand. "My mother is of little concern. The day I fell ill, my mother suspected that I was backing out of the engagement." He smirked before he continued, "I will relish the sight of her face when I give her the news. She will be delighted that I have an heir. As far as the rumors, I believe it will only enhance my reputation as governor. Political scandal usually does," he chuckled. "I also won't be the first governor to choose a commoner, a citizen."

I blushed a little and lowered my gaze, but there was no denying the sincerity of Astur's words. He intended to claim me. He lifted my chin with the tip of his finger and forced me to look into his eyes.

"Teach me the song." I had not expected that request. Huskily and with emotion, he explained, "The song, Phina. The binding song. I know the tune; you sang it over me in the fever, but I want to know the words so that I may sing them to you."

I swallowed, unsure of how to proceed. I had lost myself in worry, singing every healing song that I knew. In my exhaustion, the binding song came forth. It was all I had left to give.

"I will teach you the words, but it is best to be bound under a full moon."

"Was it a full moon when you sang it to me?" I shook my head. "Did it bind you?" I nodded. "Then, I don't think it matters when I sing it." I smiled at his reasoning.

The warmth of his hands flowed all the way through me. He leaned in, and I anticipated his kiss. I did not distract him or refuse him. Even before our lips touched, I heard the melody pour off his heart in a wave. I closed my eyes and saw all the colors, more vivid than in my memory. Astur loved me, and his intentions were clear.

Mendel squirmed in my arms and demanded my attention. His little feet kicked out and pressed us apart. Astur laughed. "He's going to have to learn to share you," he said, putting his arms around the two of us. *Contentment. Joy. Love.*

"Will you?" Astur asked formally. "Will you be my wife, my mate?" he tagged on the healer's term. I was carried away in the moment. My heart was already bound to him, and his son fidgeted in my arms. I loved Astur; I loved our son. Would it be enough to return with him?

"Yes, Astur," I began, but before I could say anything else, his mouth was on mine. I was pulled into his arms and lifted onto my feet. Astur was triumphant at my acceptance.

Chapter Thirty-Seven

Astur released me and took Mendel in one arm. He nuzzled the baby's full head of brown hair under his chin and kissed his cheek. Securing me to his side, Astur took my hand and led me back outside.

"Felix," Astur called.

Felix hastened toward the cottage, but as soon as he saw Astur holding Mendel, a smile spread across his face. He looked at the baby and shook his head. There was no denying the pride Felix felt for his friend and the relief at finding me.

"May I?" he asked tentatively, offering his hands out to take Mendel from Astur. Astur passed his son off proudly for inspection and then placed both arms around me. I stiffened a little, unaccustomed to the affection.

Mendel seemed to like the attention. He was attentive to the men in his presence. "What's your plan, sir?" Felix asked but did not take his eyes from Mendel's.

I looked up at Astur. Would he expect me to leave immediately? I was not prepared to go. "Please, may I have a few days?" I asked.

Felix waited for Astur to answer. Astur's thoughts worked behind his eyes. "I will stay with Phina and the child; we will return together," Astur said.

"What will you have me do?" Felix asked. He was a contrast of authority and tenderness holding Mendel.

"Station men and notify Lucia of our plans to return. Ask Lucia to prepare my chambers and a room for the child." Astur glanced over me. "She'll need clothes," he sighed. "I trust Lucia and Myrtle can sort that out."

I looked down at my skirt and blouse, and I was suddenly made aware of my appearance. Mine were the clothes of a healer, but as his lady, I would be expected to wear finery and paint my eyes.

Felix and Astur sorted through a few more details before Felix handed Mendel back to Astur. Felix took my hands and kissed both of my cheeks. I gasped. He had never shown any affection like that toward me before.

"Thank you for accepting him. Traian needs a playmate." Felix's expression gave me hope that I might be doing what was best for my child and me, not to mention what was right for Astur.

I watched as Felix rode toward his men and then away to the palace. Astur's attention was on Mendel but soon turned to me. My stomach tightened at the prospect of us being there together, alone.

Astur passed Mendel back into my arms and whistled for his horse. He removed the saddle and leaned it against the cottage stoop. He then folded the blankets neatly before he patted his horse's backside, sending him over to a patch of grass to graze.

"What keeps you?" I asked. "What made you stay?"

"If you aren't ready to return to the palace, then neither am I. I've been apart from you for too long; it's time we become reacquainted."

Astur touched my cheek with the back of his hand. He could read my apprehension. He took my hand and kissed it before he led me back into the cottage.

"I need to change Mendel. Please, make yourself comfortable."

I took the baby into my room, cleaned his tiny bottom, and changed his clothes. He would want to be fed again, and I had eaten nothing the entire morning. When I returned to the kitchen, Astur placed slices of bread and cheese on a plate. He also heated the kettle for tea and pulled out a chair at the table and served me. I thanked him.

"What else do you have here?" His question was pointed as though I had meager means.

"I eat mostly from the garden and the orchard. I milk the goat in the afternoons, and I fish when I want meat for the table. Since Mendel arrived, I haven't fished often," I confessed.

"Then we'll have fish for supper," Astur decided.

He pulled out the second chair and ate with me. We'd never shared a meal together. I played for him while he ate, but I ate alone in my room or the kitchen. I watched as Astur spread the soft cheese across his bread; he complimented the food.

"What do you wish to do before we return?" he asked.

I looked around the cottage. Mendel and I would want for nothing at the palace. "I would like to transplant my healer's garden, Grandfather's plants."

"Would you like me to assign men for the task?" he asked. "They could have your garden moved in a matter of hours."

"No, thank you, a healer's plants are much too delicate to trust to an untrained hand. I will have to do it myself." Astur considered that.

"Where's the best fishing spot? Will you take me there?" he asked.

I smiled at the thought of fishing. "Of course. I keep my pole and net in the barn."

I placed Mendel in a sling and strapped him securely to my chest. Astur followed me to the barn. He noticed the goat and Raven; his eyes took in everything.

"That's a fine mare; how'd you come by her?" he asked, admiring the tall horse who preferred to shelter in the back of the barn. "She carries the region's brand."

"I didn't steal her; she was Erik's. She'd lost two riders and didn't have the heart to fight. Erik left instructions for me to receive everything upon his death. A young soldier brought her to me while you were away. I was thankful. Raven provided transportation for me when I left the palace, and Erik's coins afforded for me to buy seeds and animals."

"Mother sent you away with nothing?" he asked.

"No, Felix and the women packed a basket for me."

"A basket? You were sent away with a day's rations? I'm sorry, Phina. I can't believe she would do that?"

"Astur, I was fine. Please, don't regret what you had no control over. I knew my way home, and I had more than enough to get me by."

"She didn't know that, though, did she? Mother sent you away as punishment, with little regard for your safety."

"Even before I sang for you, I was resigned to leave. Your mother's dismissal did me a favor."

His expression hardened. "Why were you planning to leave me?" he asked. Anger rose to his eyes. "It was not *I* who dismissed you."

"Don't you see? I had no choice. Livia and your mother were making plans for your wedding feast. I knew that you would be leaving for the capital, and with the palace empty, I would make my escape."

"Escape? You make it sound as though you were my prisoner."

I laughed once. "No, Astur, it was not like that. Truth be told, it was more a retreat. I had to surrender to Livia's claiming. I could not endure it. Even after I lay with you, I had no way to secure your affections. I would not share your bed."

"Still, it should have been managed differently."

I handed Astur the fishing pole and basket and net, and we walked together up the path past the bathing pool toward the river. Astur scooped up a few minnows with the net, baited the hook, and tossed the line out into a calm place near the bank. I sat under a tree and laid Mendel between my legs on top of my skirt.

I divided my attention between Astur and Mendel. I noted their similarities: the shape of their noses, the slant of their eyes, and the curve of their ears. I wondered if Mendel would have his father's bearing or favor Grandfather's lean stature.

Astur triumphed over a couple of small perch but didn't seem satisfied. He rested the pole against the tree and moved a couple of rocks around on the bank until he returned with a handful of fat worms.

"These will do," he said.

I watched as he fished and pondered that I knew very little about him or his abilities outside the palace. I clapped my hands together and cheered when he landed a bass the length of his forearm.

"When did you learn to fish?" I asked.

"I don't recall. From the time I was a boy, I fished the ponds and streams near my home. Once my studies were completed, my tutors would accompany me. As a soldier, I had to do my share of hunting and fishing."

"You seem to enjoy it."

"Very much, but I prefer the sport of hunting."

"Do you set traps or use a bow?" I asked.

Astur chuckled. "What sport is there in a trap?" he asked.

I shrugged. "I suppose none, but I like to roast a rabbit or squirrel and dry the meat."

All of this talk of food was making me hungry. I looked up into the sky; it was past midday, and Mendel would require his nap. I still needed to tend to Raven and the goat.

"Are you finished, or would you like to stay?" I asked. "I have work to do."

Astur looked at me curiously. "Ah, I forget. Of course, let me help you." He secured the basket with a rock and left the fish until later. He freed the minnows and worms that remained before he washed his hands in the water. I wrapped Mendel back in the sling, and Astur offered me his hand.

Once on my feet, he smiled at me. "What?" I asked, self-consciously yet happy with his smile.

"I've missed you, but it's more than that. I feel as though I've missed Mendel, too. I can't explain it." So, he kissed me instead.

Astur took my hand and led me back toward the cottage. He hesitated as we passed the bathing pool and the lilacs. He inhaled their fragrance. "This is the

229

scent that reminds me the most of you. I demanded that Lucia bring me cuttings from the garden. Is there any way to bottle it so that it's always with me?"

"We could bring more to the palace," I suggested. Deep inside, I still felt hesitant about returning, unsure how everything had changed in a single day. Astur read my expression and nodded.

Astur returned the pole and net to the barn and then joined me as I collected eggs from the hens and picked a few apples. Upon entering, I sliced more bread and buttered it. I was thirsty, but the water jug was nearly empty.

"I can get that," Astur offered and took the pitcher from my hand. "Do the animals need watering, too?"

"Yes, but I do that while Mendel naps. Besides the early morning, it's the only time in the day when both of my hands are free."

I did not intend to complain, nor was I looking for sympathy, but Astur's expression hardened again. Something displeased him, but I did not want his pity. I lived simply, and I was accustomed to doing everything myself. The great spirit provided for my every need and gave me abilities too. Although I knew him capable, except for his time as a soldier, Astur had had servants to command.

"What displeases you, Astur?" I asked.

"A woman shouldn't have to work this hard."

I laughed at his reasoning. "All women work this hard."

His brow furrowed. "No, they don't."

"They may not all be doing the same kinds of work, but almost every woman is occupied from daylight until dark."

My boldness took him by surprise. I had rarely laughed at him; I never dared, but things were different between us. I wasn't the girl he knew; I was a woman, a healer, a mother, and soon, I would be his mate. Astur didn't say anything else. He took the water jug from me and walked out toward the spring.

After we ate, I swaddled Mendel and nursed him to sleep. I walked out to the barn, but Astur tended to the animals. He forked hay into the stalls and watered the horses while I milked the goat. The silence between us wasn't awkward, but Astur's keen eyes watched my every move.

I mixed bread dough before our supper. Astur retrieved the fish and cleaned them outside. I gathered vegetables, and he used fresh herbs to season the fish. The aroma wafted through the cottage. Mendel stirred and joined us; our evening was a pleasant one.

After supper, we sat on the floor together with Mendel, thoroughly entertained by him. "Would you play for us?" Astur asked, including Mendel in the request.

"It would be an honor," I said. How could I refuse them?

Astur took my wrist as I made my way to rise. "No, not for *honor*, Phina. For pleasure or not at all."

"Well, then, it would be my *pleasure*," I corrected.

I went into my room to get the dulcimer. I played little since arriving back at the cottage and even less since Mendel's arrival. I tuned the instrument before I returned.

"What would you like me to play?" I asked. "But I warn you, I'm in much need of practice."

"Anything. What is Mendel's favorite?" he asked.

"I have no idea."

"Do you sing for him?" he asked, concerned that I was in some way neglecting his son.

"Of course, I do; he is not without music entirely. It's just too much to hold him and play at the same time."

I strummed over the strings and played a simple tune to limber my fingers. Astur leaned back and smiled while Mendel cooed and kicked his little legs. Astur turned his attention to Mendel and hummed along, holding the baby's hand and stroking his cheek.

As I played another song, Astur scooped Mendel into his arms and stood, moving gently around the room like a dance. The joy and affection between them lightened the mood. The sun lowered in the sky, casting the cottage in deep shadows. Only the firelight shone in the room.

I took a break to nurse Mendel. He yawned and stretched. "He's sleepy," Astur observed. "Play him the lullaby."

I resumed playing, and Astur eased down on the floor next to Mendel and nuzzled the baby into the warmth of his chest. For a moment, I wondered if I might be allowed to do the same. Where would Astur sleep? Would he expect to share my bed?

Those questions were quickly answered. I played the lullaby, as Astur requested. I didn't sing, but instead, Astur began. His deep voice sung the sweet words over Mendel in a hushed tone. He didn't ask me to sing with him. It was a special moment between father and son. There was nothing but an endearment between them, and my heart melted at the site.

By the second chorus, Astur's eyes were as heavy as Mendel's, and they mirrored a yawn. When Astur's voice lowered to a hum, I watched as the two of them drifted off to sleep. I blinked in disbelief. The warmth wasn't just from the fire in the kitchen; it was as if the entire cottage exhaled. I watched them as they slept. I didn't have the heart to disturb either one of them. I rose silently and put myself to bed.

Chapter Thirty-Eight

I woke to find Mendel beside me, rooting for his next meal. The sun was just coming up, but I did not see or hear Astur. Someone whistled a happy tune. Then, I heard the whack of an ax splitting firewood.

I went through my usual routine, dressed, entered the kitchen, and baked the bread. Astur came in with an armload of firewood and placed it near the hearth. He smiled at the two of us.

"Good morning. How did you sleep?" Astur asked.

"I slept well; thank you. When did you bring Mendel to me?" I asked.

He shook his head and shrugged. "Not long ago. He didn't stir all night. Neither did I, for that matter."

He dusted off his hands on his trousers and came to stand near me. He placed his arms around my waist and drew the two of us into an embrace. He kissed the top of Mendel's head before he leaned in and kissed me, too. As much as I craved Astur's touch, I was still uncertain of his affection. I wondered if it would be like that once we returned to the palace? Would I be free to express my own desires toward him once we were joined?

"It's quiet here; I like your cottage, too. So many things feel right. Do you feel it?"

His smile was content, and I knew exactly what he meant. I returned his smile. "Healers have lived here for generations. That's what you feel. You feel the great spirit's presence."

"Maybe, but I also know that it's your presence that I most desire." My stomach tightened, and my cheeks warmed. Astur watched the color rise. "That pleases you," he teased. I smiled, lowered my gaze, and blushed deeper still. It did please me; it pleased me more than I cared to admit.

I leaned my head against Astur's shoulder. "It doesn't seem possible," I said. "Nothing of my life has been what I expected. To suffer loss and yet gain. It is a constant tugging at my heart. You, here with me, desiring me and your willingness to claim Mendel; it doesn't seem real. It may take some time before I can accept it."

Astur agreed. "Yet, here we are. Speaking of time, when can you be ready to return with me?"

I let out a deep breath and stepped from Astur's embrace. I placed my hands protectively around Mendel. The garden was a priority, but there were other things. "I wish to know what will be expected of me." My eyes were wide. "I know very little about the ways of a lady, and I do not want to disappoint you." Astur listened to my words but did not reply. "I once had a great deal of freedom to read and tend to the garden. I was allowed to heal your guards and watch after Traian." He nodded but sensed there was more. "I need to know."

Astur took Mendel from me and sat down at the table. He reached and grabbed an apple, biting into it with a loud crunch and dabbing the juice at the corner of his mouth with his thumb. His eyes were on Mendel.

I turned to check the bread, distracting myself with our morning meal. I wasn't frustrated with Astur's silence and preoccupation with his son, but I wondered if he'd considered all of my lacking. Many young women in the region were better suited to be the next Lady Gaius. Young women like Livia and Marilla had been groomed from birth to be ladies. They were expected to carry themselves in society and supervise their servants and estates. I managed myself and the cottage, but I had no idea how to manage the palace.

Lucia and Myrtle would help. Even Marcus would guide me. Lady Gaius continuously spoke to Livia about how things should be done. I bristled at the thought of Astur's mother instructing me about the way of things.

After we ate, Astur replied to my questions. "As my lady, you will have the running of the palace, the servants, and the grounds. You will be expected to be at my side for all social gatherings, feasts, and perhaps occasionally for meetings with senators and dignitaries."

"What else of my duties?" I asked.

"Duties?" Astur clarified.

"My duties as your wife. What will you expect of me?" Did he not understand? "Where will I stay? Where will you keep me? Do you expect me to paint my eyes and dress as the other women do?" My voice rose as my concern flowed out between us. "By the great spirit's blessing, I am a healer first and foremost. All else falls behind. Although they may coexist, being your mate and Mendel's mother must wait in line. Healing will always be at the forefront of my heart and mind."

Astur's brow furrowed. I was unsure he approved of my words. He had experienced my healing and song first-hand, but would he accept that about me? Would he allow me to share my gifts with others?

"What freedoms do you desire?" he asked.

I was surprised by that being what he asked. "To read, of course. To heal when and where it's needed. To dress as a healer and not paint my eyes. I will bind my hair, except when I am alone with you, but I do not desire all of your ways."

Astur nodded once. His jaw tightened, and his expression grew serious. "I think we can come to a compromise on those points. I understand your calling and desires. You may maintain your freedoms with the garden and the books. I would never limit those areas that give you the greatest pleasure." I smiled, unable to hide my delight at returning to the library, remembering all that I could share with Mendel as he grew. "So, please, answer my first question. When may we return?"

I thought about what it would take to prepare the plants and pack my healers' stores. "I will need help, but I can be ready in three days," I said.

***

Astur fished again and constructed a few crates to help transport the plants. I sorted through all of my belongings. One trunk contained mine and Mendel's clothes, and another chest held everything I needed for healing, Erik's flute, and Grandfather's dulcimer. I admired Erik's flute for a moment before packing it in the trunk. I would honor Erik by teaching Mendel to play it.

The day was warm. I had opened all the windows, but the cottage still felt stuffy. Tiny beads of perspiration formed on Mendel's forehead as he nursed. Once he was settled for his nap, I decided to go to the bathing pool. I gathered my towel and soap and walked down the hill toward the pungent scent of lilacs that hung in the warm air.

I removed my skirt and blouse and stepped into the refreshing water, running the bar of soap over my skin. Astur must have seen me from the barn and followed me. He watched as I removed my head covering and loosened my braid. He smiled approvingly. "May I join you?" he asked but was already pulling off his boots. His clothes were drenched in sweat.

I hesitated to answer, but I didn't know why. The lure of the bathing pool was hard to resist. "Of course," I stammered, nervous and self-conscious. I had only ever been with Astur at night in dimly lit rooms. There in the daylight, surrounded by lilacs, he undressed and jumped feet-first into the pool. I turned so that the splash hit my back. He broke the surface of the water and swam to the edge, gathering his clothes and motioning for me to pass him the soap.

He scrubbed his shirt and wrung out the dampness before he spread it out on the ground to dry. He then did the same with his trousers. He bathed and washed his short hair. Before he returned the soap to me, he gathered a handful of lilacs, rubbed them together, and took in the scent from his hands. Astur swam over and rubbed his hand on my neck and sniffed.

I leaned my head back into the water to dampen my hair. A healer's locks were rarely seen, but I was even more exposed with it splayed around my shoulders. Astur lathered his hands with soap and lilacs and ran them through my hair. I closed my eyes and soaked in the implicit gesture.

"I want to make something clear," Astur said. His tone was commanding yet not severe. I looked into his brown eyes, eager to know. "Your role as my lady is different from being my wife, my mate, and your responsibilities lie on both sides of our chamber door. The most important part will lie within and between the two of us."

I took in a quick breath when he grabbed my waist and pulled me into him. He'd just said that the most important part lay between us, but there was no space with his body aligned with mine. My full breasts pressed against his chest, feeling his heartbeat.

He took my hand and kissed it. "I will bind myself to you, Phina, and as long as it pleases you, you will share my bed. I hope to find pleasure there for the remainder of our days. Mendel is my son and heir, but I wish for a family, children, grandchildren, and to live long enough to see great-grandchildren," he laughed at the thought. I had rarely seen him so exuberant.

Gathering my wits, I asked, "Do I have the right to refuse you?" I had once before, but if he pressed his advances any further, I wouldn't, but I did not know the realm of mates. I knew very little about marriage. Grandmother and Grandfather were the only married couple I had ever lived with. I supposed I would need guidance in marriage, too.

"Why would you want to do that?" He kissed my neck, breathing in the scent of lilacs.

I shrugged my reply. "Will I have the freedom to disagree with you?"

He faced me again, reading my expression. "Why would you ask such things? Do you think me so domineering that I would not consider you?"

"I know how you are, and I know what displeases you. I do not wish to disappoint or embarrass you."

"Oh, Phina, I don't think you're capable, but yes, you may *respectfully* disagree with me," he laughed, lightening the mood. "But, you may never *refuse* me," he teased.

His mouth went up in a grin before he winked. I bit my lip and rolled my eyes at his playfulness. I wasn't sure I would ever be able to refuse him. Again, Astur kissed me long and tenderly, and I lost myself in the pool, contrasting cold water and warm flesh. The images of his heart were brighter than the lilacs.

"Teach me the song, Phina," Astur whispered against my ear.

I closed my eyes and took a deep breath. When I'd sung it before, I was drained and spent. At that moment, I was neither and sang the binding song, strong and clear. Astur echoed the lines until, together, we repeated them. The great spirit bound us in those promises. I was no longer tethered to Astur, alone, dangling. His heart's song burst forth and grounded me. *Love. Dedication. Promise. Bound.*

Astur and I were carried away in the great spirit's presence, consumed by joy. He ran his fingers through my hair as he kissed me. We were bathed, washed clean, renewed, and made one. The physical pleasure that followed was more extraordinary than I remembered. I cried out at our combined release. Panting from the exertion of our joining, Astur and I clung to one another. He held me tightly as our breaths settled. Suddenly, my breasts hardened, and I felt the milk rush forward.

"Mendel," I whispered.

Astur lifted his head to listen. "I do not hear him."

"He'll awaken soon." I pressed my hands against Astur's chest, torn between my desire for Astur and Mendel's needs. "I must go to him," I said apologetically.

Astur lifted my chin. "There are no apologies for what is natural and necessary." I put my arms around his neck and pulled myself up to his height. I thanked him for understanding but could not explain that my regret was not in Mendel's tending but in having to leave Astur's arms.

Chapter Thirty-Nine

The old bed creaked under Astur's weight. "Will it hold the both of us?" he asked skeptically.

It held my mother and me and had supported the weight of my father for a brief time. I ignored Astur's question and focused on settling Mendel for the night. Astur's bed was large, much larger than mine, and would easily accommodate the two of us.

Astur's long body curled around my back. He stroked my hair and sang the lullaby while Mendel nursed to sleep. My eyes grew heavy as Astur sang, but I was aware of his intentions. An evening breeze blew through the cottage, and I cuddled into Astur's warmth.

Once Mendel was settled in his basket at the side of my bed, I turned to embrace Astur. Except for a few creaks of the bed, we silently expressed our affection. Neither of us wanted to be interrupted by Mendel's waking. I slept soundly, filled with hope that our binding would forever be blessed.

The next morning, Astur helped me prepare the plants for transport to the palace garden. Carefully, we pulled the roots from the soil and wrapped them in dampened cloths to protect them. I sang over each one, asking the great spirit for their safe transfer.

"Do you have to take all of them?" Astur asked.

"If I am to make my home there, then yes. I want all of them."

"You have enough here to heal the entire region," he complained.

"I wish I had had more when you were poisoned. You would have been healed in days instead of months." He snorted derisively, but Astur didn't complain about the work after that.

That day and the next were much the same. The garden was nearly ready. Astur inspected the Lilacs and was doubtful that the two of us could uproot them. I took some cuttings, and he assured me that he would send men to dig them up if I desired. I would decide once we were settled.

On the second evening, I took Mendel to the bathing pool. He was thrilled to be in the water with me. Astur did not linger long on the bank. He jumped in again, and Mendel laughed as the water splashed around us. Astur moved Mendel back and forth in the water; Mendel's little legs kicked out happily. He liked the water as much as I did. The tug on my heart was sharp, remembering all the times I'd bathed with Mother. Would this be the last time that I bathed among the lilacs? Would I be the last healer to reside there?

Watching Astur with Mendel tugged at my heart, too. Astur was captivated by our son; his love and affection poured out over both Mendel and me. Leaving the cottage and every other sacrifice would be worth Mendel being raised by his father. My doubts vanished when Astur turned to me and smiled. It was all the assurance I needed.

That night Astur and Mendel slept soundly, but I could not settle. Astur sensed my unease. He said that my cottage would be watched from then on, and I could visit if I wished. I walked through each room, remembering the happier times, the music, and the laughter. I remembered the lessons, all the lessons. Consumed by fear, I had no idea where I was going when I fled the cottage after Mother's murder. I knew where I was going this time, but I was still concerned about what was to come.

"Why did you leave the bed?" Astur asked. His words came in a whisper behind me. I turned to face him.

"I couldn't sleep." He heard the worry in my voice.

"What distresses you?" Astur asked, taking me in his arms.

"I am thankful for many things: your healing, our reunion, Mendel, and most especially our binding. Yet, I find myself unsettled, unsure of what tomorrow brings."

"How can I assure you?" he asked.

I shook my head; I did not know. "In time, the consequences of this decision will reveal themselves. Leaving here is the hardest. I love my home and thought I would live out the remainder of my days as a healer. Felix's finding me has once again changed everything."

"Do you regret leaving?"

It was too soon for regret. Hesitant and conflicted, yes. I shook my head again. "No. There are no apologies for what is natural and necessary," I said, repeating his words. "I belong with you, Astur. Mendel and I both do, but it does pain me to leave this place."

Astur hugged me tightly, securing me to the spot. "You will be fine, Phina. You'll see." His presence encouraged me more than his words. "What does your great spirit say on the matter?" he asked, but there was no teasing in his voice.

"I have been bound to you for a year and days. My heart is secure, tied to you. Since your arrival, I have sung many prayers and offered thanks, but I have no sight when it comes to you. The great spirit is silent on the matter."

Astur had no more words. He stroked my hair and exhaled deeply, releasing his own apprehension. The sound of his breath brought me back to a simpler time between us. He lifted me into his arms and kissed me before he carried me back to bed.

***

Felix and a half-dozen soldiers arrived early. They brought with them a wagon to transport the animals along with all of my belongings. The men set to loading my few possessions, and we were ready to leave within two hours of their arrival. They even had time to dig a few of the lilacs from around the pool. Most of the plants remained; I couldn't bear to leave the place barren of its hedge and protection.

Days before, Astur offered a carriage for Mendel and me, but I refused the offer. I was capable of riding Raven, and I would feel more confident on horseback than in a stuffy box pulled by horses. Astur didn't press his opinion, but I could tell he would prefer I be carried back to the palace. I had no need for such things.

I walked through the cottage one last time with Mendel. I whispered songs of thanks and protection as I walked through each room, but I did not linger. I was nervous about returning to the palace, but I refused to delay. The simple comforts of the cottage no longer held me. My heart was bound to Astur's, and I had fought the attachment long enough. It was time to go.

Chapter Forty

Felix set a comfortable stride, and Raven kept pace. Astur looked over several times to ensure that Mendel and I were safe by his side. I smiled, but my body was in knots; Mendel slept, oblivious.

My stomach sickened slightly, realizing that we approached the front entrance. I had always come and gone from the back of the palace. The streets were crowded, yet the people made way for the procession of soldiers. The citizens greeted their governor warmly, but their curious gazes fell onto Mendel and me. Astur dismounted and offered his hands to assist. I handed Mendel to his father before I slid down Raven's side.

I eyed the staircase, too petrified to take the first step. Astur held a sleeping Mendel. He looked around and acknowledged those who had gathered with a wave. He commanded something to the men, but I didn't pay attention. I looked down when Astur took my hand. He smiled and kissed it, bringing me back to the present.

I was neither veiled nor were my eyes painted. My dress was not that of the palace, either. I heard the murmurs of curious citizens. Speculation and gossip would run rampant through the streets like wildfire. I wondered if that was Astur's intention. He would want everyone to know he had returned to the palace with a woman and child. A formal announcement had yet to be made, but a feast would be expected once it was. There would be a celebration and revelry.

Hand-in-hand, Astur and I ascended the stairs. Felix and the guard surrounded us, as was their duty when the governor entered the palace. The group moved slower with me, but I didn't feel rushed when it took me two steps for each of their strides. Astur kept a firm hand on mine. His other arm cradled Mendel. Encircled by once-familiar hearts, I relaxed. *Purpose. Duty. Protection.*

I looked up to see Astur's profile. His jawline exuded confidence. At his side, I had to hold myself higher. To see his face, I had to lift my chin. He glanced over and winked. I smiled back at him.

"Welcome home, Phina," he whispered. *Triumph.*

As soon as the palace doors closed behind us, the soldiers took their posts. Their familiar faces acknowledged me with nods and bows. A couple of them muttered the words, "Ma'am and my lady."

Myrtle was the first to approach us. "Welcome back, my lady," she said with a curtsy.

"Not *my lady*, Myrtle, simply Phina."

"As you wish," Myrtle conceded and embraced me. She then made over Mendel. "Oh, my goodness, what a precious child," she cooed. She placed her hands on her cheeks and stepped towards Astur. "You've done right, sir. He's a fine lad." Astur beamed at the old woman's remarks.

"Phina, I must return to my duties. Myrtle and Marcus will tend to you," Astur said and handed Mendel back to me. "Get settled, and I'll see you at supper."

"Marcus?" I asked, confused. Marcus was the governor's advisor. What business would he have with me?

"He'll see to everything," Astur said, dismissing me.

Myrtle motioned for me to follow her. I looked back at Astur, who was already rounding into the library. He had stayed with me at the cottage for three days. I had not considered what his absence meant to the region. I was selfish to keep him all to myself.

I knew the way to Astur's chambers, but Myrtle insisted on seeing me there. "Lucia's seen to the changes. The men brought your things up when you arrived.

We didn't have much time, but I think you'll find it welcoming. The governor never needed many comforts. Simple, he is. Curse these blasted stairs," she complained.

I laughed. "I've missed you, Myrtle," I said.

"Child, the missing was mutual."

I entered Astur's chambers to find Lucia and Marcus. Lucia hugged me and took Mendel into her arms in one swift motion. Marcus stepped forward and bowed his head. "Lady Gaius, it is a pleasure to be at your service."

"Please, Phina," I corrected.

"My deepest apologies, ma'am, but that will not be acceptable. You are to be addressed by your title. It would be best if you become accustomed to it." I felt his gentle reproof.

Mendel stirred, and Lucia recognized his need for me. "Would you kindly excuse us, Marcus?" I asked.

"But I was directed to see to your needs. I have many things for you to consider."

"I need to tend to my child," I said, but Marcus did not understand.

Lucia interrupted, "She needs to feed the boy."

Marcus jerked and stammered. "Yes, ma'am. Of course, I will be waiting." He ducked out of the chambers in fits and bows.

Lucia and Myrtle laughed. "He isn't easily ruffled. I'm not sure he knows what to make of it." Lucia said.

"Neither do I," I confessed.

"It's good to have you back, Phina," Lucia said. Her smile was warmer than I'd ever seen it. "Your Mendel will be a perfect addition to the palace. We're all delighted to have you back."

While Mendel nursed, I noticed the changes that had been made to Astur's chambers. Bedding, tapestries, a second wardrobe, and even a cradle furnished the large room. My little stool sat in front of a rocking chair that was large enough for Astur.

Myrtle offered me some water, and Lucia continued cleaning an already spotless room. "Please, sit with me. Tell me about Traian and the palace. What news do you have?" I asked.

Myrtle and Lucia exchanged a glance. "The scamp is everywhere, and keeping up with him is no small fete. He's climbing and running, and, thanks to you, he sings all the time," Lucia said like it was a complaint, but the pride for her son won out.

"I cannot wait to see him. I hope he remembers me."

Lucia laughed. "*Phina* was one of the first words he spoke. Not long after you left, Felix and I were speaking of you. Traian was playing on the floor, not paying any attention. He popped up his little head from his toy and said, 'Phina,' plain as day."

When Marcus returned, he carried a stack of fabric, and a meek little man scurried behind him who was encumbered by dresses that he cradled in his arms like limp bodies. I exhaled. They were there to dress me.

Myrtle took Mendel and occupied him while I paid attention to Marcus. Lucia had the running of the palace, and in the meantime, she could keep it. The little man laid the dresses out for my viewing. Marcus did the same with the ornate fabrics and asked me to choose which I preferred for my dresses. They were all lovely. I liked the way the threads shimmered throughout the brocades and damasks. I shook my head; they were all too fine.

"Do these not suit you, Lady Gaius?" Marcus asked, making sure to use my title.

"They're lovely, but I've never worn such finery. Do you have anything less ornate?" I asked.

The little man's eyes opened wide at my request. Marcus clasped his hands together and took in a calming breath before he spoke. "Ma'am, you are Lady Gaius Julianus Astur, are you not?" I nodded. "Excellent. This is Forest, and he has been instructed to see that you are clothed. Once the announcement of your marriage is made public, there will be a feast in your honor, and the governor has asked that you be made ready."

246

I felt overwhelmed at the thought of being under such scrutiny. Marcus's eyes softened as he read my expression. "I know you do not like any of this attention, but for my master's sake, would you consider at least one of these? Please, this man is a skilled tailor." Marcus gestured toward the man at his side. "I'm sure, together with Forest, you and I will find what is right for you. Neither of us wishes to disappoint him." Marcus smiled then, and his heart was sincere. They were beautiful fabrics, and, at his urging, I reconsidered.

I chose the one that was the least ornate. Forest and Marcus were pleased or probably more relieved. It would get me by until the rest were ready. I changed into the new dress and described what I wanted. Forest inspected my skirt and considered it before he asked if he could take it with him. Astur and I agreed to compromise, but I felt like I was the one making the most concessions. He hadn't been plucked from his home, nor was he being dressed by strangers.

Once they were gone, I went into my old room and realized it had not been altered in the least. My tunic lay over the bed just as I had left it. How odd to see it there. The room was clean, but nothing had been disturbed. I picked up my little jars and inspected each one. It felt like a lifetime ago. In some ways, it was – Mendel's lifetime.

"Master refused to allow us to move anything," Myrtle said.

"It's odd to be back," I said.

"Don't let it fret you." She handed Mendel back to me and patted my hand. "You belong here, child. Claim it, and make it your own." Her eyes were brightened by her smile.

"Thank you, Myrtle."

Myrtle composed herself and let her attention fall back onto Mendel. "It's been many years since I've looked after a young'un, but I'd be honored if you'd allow me. The governor wasn't a child for long, but I did right by him." I looked at Myrtle with new eyes.

"You were Astur's maid?"

She laughed her hearty laugh. "Indeed."

"I didn't know; he never spoke of it."

"I've served his family for a long time. When Lady Gaius took me on, I was a young widow with two boys. They were apprenticed, and I needed to find a way to feed myself. Soon afterward, she brought our master into the world. I was moved from the kitchen to the wee one's chambers and then back to the kitchen. I will happily resume the duty of caretaker if you'd like me to."

"I would be honored for your assistance, Myrtle, but I do not know what is expected of my time. I do not wish to leave Mendel."

"I can tell; that's what makes you a good mother," she encouraged.

"Do you know if my plants are in the garden?" I asked. She nodded. "I'll need an apron and my tools. Are they still there?" I asked.

She laughed again. "He wouldn't let us move anything that you'd touched. Everything should be exactly where you left it."

Chapter Forty-One

I donned a healer's skirt before I went to inspect the garden. My apron hung in its usual spot near my table. I wrapped Mendel securely to my chest and went downstairs, where I found the crates stacked in the garden.

I watered them all liberally and set to work. The healer's garden was again overgrown but not as bad as it was before. I needed to get the plants in the ground soon if I hoped for a successful transplant. I cleared a small patch of soil and went to work.

I worked all afternoon with only a couple of breaks to nurse Mendel. The rest was welcomed, but it gave my mind time to consider the neglect around me. It had taken months before the healer's plants gave me a healthy yield.

As I lifted each plant from the crates, I lovingly spoke its name. I called on the great spirit and introduced the roots to the soil and leaves to the sky. I paid careful attention to the neighboring plants. "This is your home now. Grow, produce your fruit, and prosper." It became my mantra in rhythm to the task. The words were not just for the plants. Mendel and I needed to be reminded, too.

I whisper-sang as I worked, and the afternoon slipped into the evening. Mendel dozed off and on but did not fidget or demand to be released. He sensed the changes around him, and his eyes widened as I worked like he was taking it all in for the first time. I told him several times that we were doing important work. He understood.

**

I changed back into Forest's dress for supper. I begrudgingly admitted that I liked the blue fabric with its deeper blue stitching. Mendel nuzzled his face into the soft ruffle at my neckline. I think he liked it, too.

Astur said that he would meet me for supper, but I had no idea where that would be. I had always taken my meals in the kitchen. He often took his meals in his chambers. Would I be expected to eat there with him? My question was answered when Astur came back upstairs. He smiled approvingly at my dress.

His hand lingered on my cheek as he kissed me and then walked toward the cradle where Mendel lay, happily kicking his legs, free from the confines of the sling. "You look beautiful, nothing like the woman from the garden."

"You saw me working."

"I admit it was a distraction, a challenge to keep my focus on Marcus and Felix. Along with my other correspondence, I had to compose a letter to my mother."

I stood next to Mendel's cradle and watched Astur. Mendel held tightly to Astur's finger, but Astur's smile for his son did not indicate his thoughts about his mother. His heart was happy in our presence. I did not want to waste our evening speculating about his mother's response. If she desired, Lady Gaius would write and speak for herself. Then the fear that she might not be satisfied with a letter washed over me, and I saw it clearly.

"She will come for the marriage feast," I said.

Astur chuckled. "Her own death could not keep her away. She'll be curious and eager to meet her grandson," he cooed.

"Have you made the announcement?" I asked.

Astur turned to look at me then. "Marcus will take care of everything. The official announcement will be made in the morning, but news of your arrival has already spread in several circles. Our banquet will be held in a fortnight. I refused to hold the annual Governor's Feast under the guise of my healing. It will bring joy to the people, but not as much joy as it brings me." He smiled and drew me to his side. I smiled back at Astur. He was a good governor and cared for the citizens; he was a good mate and father and cared even more for us.

There was a knock on the chamber door. One of the maids brought in our supper, but I did not recognize her. "Hello, I am Phina," I said, introducing myself. I moved to help her with the tray.

The tall woman smiled but did not let me touch the tray in her hands. "Yes, ma'am. I am Raya." Her voice was raspy and deep. She placed the tray on the table. I thanked her, and she curtsied. I dipped my head, unaccustomed to being served. I felt like a guest rather than the lady of the palace.

Astur chuckled after she left. "You might want to get used to that."

"Used to what?"

"Being ignored when you insist that people call you Phina. Only a select few will be allowed the honor."

"Felix, Lucia, and Myrtle?" I asked.

"Perhaps when they are alone with you, but I doubt they will very often." That displeased me. "I'm sorry, Phina, but you've risen to a place of position."

I disagreed with his reasoning. "No wonder you grew weary of hearing *master*, *sir*, and *governor*. Hearing *ma'am* and *my lady* will grow just as tiresome."

"Lady Gaius," Astur teased. I rolled my eyes.

"That title fits your mother much better, and I doubt she will find pride in sharing it." I crossed my arms stubbornly.

He moved toward me then and took me into his embrace. "Lady Gaius," he teased, refusing to release me. I looked away, trying not to smile and give into him. "Lady, lady, lady," he repeated. I shook my head, refusing it. "Laaaddy." He dragged out the word before he kissed my stubborn mouth. "My lady. My Lady Phina," he said possessively.

The sound of my name and the warmth of his body distracted me. His lips pressed against mine, gently urging a response. His persistence paid off, and I smiled. "May we make *that* a compromise?"

He considered for a moment and then nodded once. "Lady Phina," he repeated. He would set a precedent. The title suited me, and I thrilled in the relief of maintaining my name. I thought briefly that Marcus and Lady Gaius might disapprove, but Astur would honor me.

Astur's bed was nearly double the size of mine at the cottage, but we did not need that much room. He held me against his side all night. When I rose to check on Mendel in the cradle, Astur barely stirred. Mendel nursed, and I closed my eyes and sang as I rocked him in the oversized chair. When I opened my eyes, Astur was awake, leaning on his elbow. His eyes were bright, and mine mirrored his. *Love. Protection. Satisfaction.*

***

My reunion with Traian was a delight beyond words. It seemed impossible, but he knew me. He gently patted Mendel. "Phina and Mendel," Traian repeated in his child's voice.

I did not correct him; I would forever be Phina to him. He was a sweet child, and, within a day, I found him at my side in the garden, curious. He, too, sang to the flowers and liked the way the soil felt in his chubby, little hands. We spent our mornings together in the garden, and I spent my afternoons reading in our chamber while Mendel napped. Our son liked it when I read aloud equally as much as being sung to.

It only took a few days before Astur asked me to play for him. He rocked Mendel and joined his voice with mine. Mendel enjoyed our combined voices, or perhaps he basked in our joy. Mine and Astur's nights and days set a predictable rhythm between duty and desire. Astur was right; my responsibilities lay on both sides of our chamber door.

The plants were all getting along, but I had a great deal of weeding and trimming to do. I felt it when Astur watched me from the library. I also sensed his absence from the palace. Thankfully, he was not called away in those early days of our union.

Marcus consulted both of us about the feast's plans, and within a week, Forest returned with my new clothes, slippers, and headwraps. The timid man presented each skirt and blouse and dress with flair. The fabric billowed out; the folds of the skirts twirled around. The blouses were sewn from the finest linen. Instead of full dresses and tunics, he had made matching vests and cloaks.

I was delighted with his designs. He was indeed a master tailor and had interpreted my desires correctly. "You approve?" he asked, but it was an unnecessary question. He could read my delight.

"Yes, Forest. Thank you. You have a genuine gift."

"I have one more to show you, ma'am. I thought it might be appropriate for the feast."

He unfolded the silk damask dress delicately. The silver fabric glistened in the sunlight, but the fine blue stitching caught my eye. The outline of tiny blue flowers had been woven into the fabric. I gasped and covered my mouth with my hand. Tears welled in my eyes.

"It reminded me of the color of your eyes, and it represents the colors of our region. I thought you might want to make an impression," Forest stammered at my emotional response to the dress.

I smiled and nodded, unable to speak. I batted back the tears that threatened. Once again, Grandfather's presence would be with me. I took a deep breath and thanked Forest.

***

Lady Gaius's letter arrived a day ahead of her carriage and two days before the feast.

My Dearest Astur,

 Make ready for my arrival.

 Mother

Astur had never spoken of his father, and I had never asked. Astur's account was filled with fondness. "Father was a great deal older than Mother. He was set in his ways, terribly indulgent, but he was good to me. I wish he would have lived longer; he died shortly after he arranged my marriage." Lord Gaius had been an advisor who served at the capital, but Astur and his mother resided at their family estate.

253

"He raised me more like a grandson than a son. Still, I think he would be proud of me. I will need to recall his wisdom so that I can share it with Mendel."

Astur and Felix were away from the palace when Lady Gaius arrived. She was accompanied by her manservant and a maid. Myrtle welcomed her and made her comfortable until supper.

A part of me wanted to go to her and meet her on my own terms, but Astur asked that I wait until we could introduce Mendel together. I honored his request because he wanted to buffer any condemnation or hostility towards me. He was not worried exactly, only cautious for mine and Mendel's sakes.

I did not know what indications he had written. He said that his letter was brief and to the point. "I invited her to the feast. I told her that I had claimed you and the child. There was nothing else I chose to elaborate on. She will see my happiness for herself."

It would be my first time eating in the dining room. Lucia made all the preparations and was sure to serve Lady Gaius's favorite wine. I chose a linen skirt and blouse that were the color of lilacs. Astur smiled his approval.

He took Mendel from me and carried him downstairs. I walked at his side; my nervousness increased with every step. Lady Gaius arrived just as we entered.

"Lady Gaius," I said and curtsied. Her eyes were wide, but she did not say anything to me.

"Mother," Astur said in greeting and walked forward to kiss her cheek.

"Astur," Lady Gaius replied and then turned all of her attention on Mendel. She lifted her chin proudly. "So, this is the child." The lady covered her mouth with her delicate fingers. She blinked several times to contain her emotion, and I watched as her lips formed a pained smile. "He has your likeness," she whispered and reached to touch Mendel's face.

Lady Gaius did not speak to me at supper. She hardly acknowledged me. She had dismissed me, sent me away. I was unable to read her expressions regarding me. She delighted in Mendel and Astur. That's all I could ask.

Chapter Forty-Two

Astur smiled as he entered our chamber. "That went better than I expected," he commented. Astur stayed for a long while after supper with his mother. I could tell she had things she wished to discuss with her son, and I needed to put Mendel to bed. "It's all sorted. Her concerns were easily dismissed."

I did not like that word. "*Dismissed* or laid to rest?" I asked.

"She had many questions, Phina, and I answered each one of them. In her way, I think she's happy for me."

"She spoke very little. I cannot read her. Does she hate me?"

Astur shook his head and almost laughed. "No, Phina, she does not hate you. You are a stranger, but in time, she will see you. She owes you a great debt, and her pride interferes."

"She owes me nothing," I argued.

"On the contrary, she owes you my life, and thanks to you, our family land is secure in Mendel. I know it might be hard for you to accept, but it's the truth."

The following morning, the lure of Mendel coaxed Lady Gaius from her chambers. He was irresistible to her, and she found herself in the garden, timidly approaching.

"Please, won't you join us?" I offered.

She walked forward and sat on the bench near where Mendel played happily on a blanket. We neither said anything; our attentions were all on the baby. Lady Gaius smiled and leaned forward, trying her best to get a reaction from her grandson. He appeased her with a smile.

"You know, I watched him the first time you played. At the feast," she clarified. I looked up but did not reply. She was talking about Astur, not Mendel. "All I could think about was that if you brought him that much pleasure in a crowded feast, what must you do alone for him, night after night, in his chambers? You were a child, yet your music was not that of a child."

I looked away. "He supposed me much younger."

She made a soft snort of disbelief. "I should have seen that you were a woman in the making. Did you know that you carried his child when I sent you away?" Lady Gaius asked.

"No, ma'am, I did not know for a while."

"Why did you not send word?"

"I presumed that he and Livia were joined. I did not want to disrupt their union. Astur was a kind master, and I did not wish for him to be obligated to me in any way."

Lady Gaius watched me for a moment, considering my words. She returned her gaze to Mendel. It was easier for her to speak when she wasn't looking at me. "I have never seen him in such a rage as when he found out that I had dismissed you. I thought I was doing what was right for him and Livia, but there was no relief from his pain. His heart was broken, and he did not know how to find you. My heart broke watching my son's pain. You, as a mother, may already understand that."

"You were doing what you thought was best," I soothed. "Besides, I wanted to go, and you provided my release. Child or no, I needed to be away from the palace. I have loved your son for a long time, and I would have never been able to watch him with a wife. Until recently, I didn't know his feelings for me; perhaps he didn't either."

"He's happier with you. He's freer, more confident, more at ease." I smiled at her compliment. "Watching him writhe in pain after I dismissed you, I resolved to never manipulate him again. I knew that I had somehow done wrong. I am content that he is settled and that you've given him an heir. I am not here to meddle in your marriage; I only ask that you count me in Mendel's life."

"Of course, Lady Gaius. You are welcome to know your grandson. I harbor no ill towards you. Like I said before, I needed to go, and now is my time to return."

"You are very different, Phina."

"Yes, ma'am, I know."

***

Lady Gaius and Marcus took command of the preparation for the feast. Mendel would make a brief appearance at the beginning of the evening, and once he was settled, I would return to our marriage celebration.

Myrtle helped me dress. The silver gown shimmered from every angle, and the blue flowers were the exact color of Grandfather's eyes. This was an important night. To help ease my nerves, I tucked lilacs and lavender in the headwrap to keep Mother and Grandmother with me, too.

Astur and Lady Gaius greeted the guests. Once most of them were gathered, Astur presented Mendel and me in the great hall. Astur stood tall at my side. He took Mendel in his hands and lifted him so that more guests could see. They oohed and aahed and applauded.

When I returned to the feast, I was greeted and congratulated. Astur kept me close by his side. A few times, he took my hand and kissed it. It was a simple gesture that drew my attention back to him. Each kiss was laden with a promise that the evening would soon be over. After the meal, toasts were offered in our honor. He introduced me as Lady Phina, but there was no playfulness or teasing in his eyes.

I should have known that the evening would not have been all merriment. Astur was focused on a guest who was retelling a humorous story. I sensed the arrogant heart before he made his way through the crowd. I took Astur's hand. He turned and looked at me; I had never been so bold to touch him in public. He read my widened eyes.

"Cato," I mouthed.

Astur stiffened and lifted his chin to find him. He carefully smoothed his features and assessed the guests. He was a picture of serenity, yet his eyes were keen.

Cato approached us, oozing charm and assurance. Astur put his arm around me and drew me closer to his side. "Governor, Lady." Cato dipped his head and greeted us in turn.

"Cato," Astur said, but I remained silent while they exchanged pleasantries. Cato congratulated me, but his words did not penetrate my mind. I did not offer him my hand in greeting. I couldn't get past his heart. *Conceit. Betrayal. Covetousness.* Cato tried to catch my eye, so I looked past him and into the eyes of another man, a stranger.

This man's stare was piercing, and his heart overshadowed Cato's and pressed against me. He tilted his head to the side and concentrated; there was recognition in his eyes, but I did not know him. I could not read his thoughts, but his heart was a dark place. *Deceit. Murder. Treachery.* Cato's companion made me even more cautious than Cato. He posed no immediate threat, but his association with Cato felt uncomfortable. I would warn Astur and Felix of this man's heart.

"Come along, Dolon. I see the elder Lady Gaius. You must make her acquaintance." Dolon acknowledged Cato's words and dipped his head respectfully toward me and then toward Astur. Dolon said nothing before they walked away.

I gestured for Astur to come closer. He inclined his ear to listen. "Do you know him?" I whispered.

Astur shook his head. Other guests approached then, and I returned to the present, but I was shaken by the brief encounter. I dared not leave Astur's side for the rest of the evening. I even stayed late enough to wish the guests a safe journey home.

My breasts ached; I had been away from Mendel too long. I heard him crying as I climbed the stairs, and although I was exhausted from the long evening, I ran to him. Astur was at my heels. Myrtle offered me an apologetic smile. She rose from the rocking chair and forced Mendel into Astur's arms, relieved to be rid of the screaming baby, but then I realized that she had passed Mendel over so that she could help me out of the dress.

"How do ladies tend to their babies?" I asked, frustrated. Myrtle had me out of the dress and in my nightdress in a flash. Mendel's screams rose to a panic at the sound of my voice.

"Shhh," Astur soothed and jostled him back and forth.

It took a few attempts to convince Mendel that he wanted to eat. He had forgotten why he was upset. Myrtle hung up my dress and turned down the bed before she left. I was too befuddled to thank her, but Astur did it for both of us.

"They have wetnurses," Astur said as he undressed.

"What? Who?" I asked.

"The ladies. They have servants. Would you like one?"

"No," I said. My tone was impatient. Astur bristled. I eased back into the chair and closed my eyes. Mendel settled, too. "I'm sorry. I forgot to *respectfully* disagree."

Astur chuckled. "I would prefer it, and I will try to be more sensitive to Mendel's needs. This evening's demands and my desire to be near you kept you apart." Mendel sucked voraciously like he didn't believe he'd ever be fed again.

"Bring him to bed and lie with me," Astur said. "I want to be near you both." It was a secure feeling, lying between Astur and Mendel. Their combined need enveloped me, and my heart was guarded on all sides by their love.

In my exhaustion, I couldn't settle. Several of the evening's events played through my mind. Astur's hand stroked down my shoulder to my waist and hip and back up to my neck. He moved my hair and kissed the tender skin below my ear. I thrilled at his touch. Lying next to Astur, the evening faded into a memory.

Chapter Forty-Three

Back at the palace, my days were predictable. I read, I tended to the healing plants in the garden, and I mothered Mendel. Lady Gaius, Traian, and Mendel were my constant companions. Lady Gaius was stern, but she enjoyed the children. I overheard her several times mimicking silly rhymes with them. My afternoons were solitary, and after supper, my evenings, well, they took on a life of their own.

I often played for Astur and Mendel, but once Mendel was sleeping soundly, Astur would woo me to bed with him like it was his most important appointment of the day. I did not need much convincing. Most every night, we pleased one another.

One afternoon, I overheard two maids gossiping. They seemed relieved that Astur was happily joined. "It's a wonder how Master's made a full recovery."

"Perhaps Lady Phina exhibits healing powers in their bed," another maid giggled.

"The delights of youth," the first maid sighed. I blushed.

***

Cato came to the palace under the guise of visiting his *dear* friend, Lady Gaius. Thankfully, I didn't have to make excuses for my absence. Mendel was the priority. I slipped into the library to find a book of poems that I had read to Traian. I thought Mendel might enjoy the rhymes.

I stopped short and ducked back into the library when I saw Cato and Dolon walking down the hall toward the sitting room where Lady Gaius received her guests. Something about Dolon pricked at my memory, but I still couldn't place him. I'd never read a heart so foul.

Later that evening, Astur wooed me with kisses. "What's on your mind?" he asked, sensing my distraction.

"I was thinking about Cato," I said.

"It's rather off-putting to know that my *mate* is thinking of another man in my bed," he teased.

I shook my head. "It's not that. I saw him today with that man, Dolon. He came to see your mother. They make me uneasy."

"Did he say or do something to upset you?"

I shook my head. "No, I stayed in the library."

Astur's eyes were concerned. "I don't want you frightened. Cato has no right to make you uncomfortable. Is there anything else?" Astur asked.

"Did you ever find out what happened?"

"With what?"

"When you were poisoned."

"Nothing we could prove, but we found traces of the plants in Marilla's room."

"Marilla? Are you sure?" My surprise could not be concealed.

Astur nodded. "Myrtle found them while she was cleaning. We suspect that she slipped it into my drink at dinner. It was the most logical scenario."

I shook my head, denying that possibility. Marilla was sweet and caring. I never detected any deceit in her; she wasn't capable. Sure, she was interested in the plants and asked many questions, but did she use that knowledge against Astur?

"I would have suspected Cato before Marilla."

"If you remember, Cato was not in attendance. He was with a few other senators; he had an alibi."

"What did you do with her?" The punishment for an attempt against the governor would be death.

Astur's reply was curt and dismissive. "I didn't have the heart to kill her. She'll rot in the dungeon unless I decide to do otherwise."

"Did she offer a defense?" I asked.

"Felix questioned her at length. She denied it but then confessed that she knew the properties of the plant. The proof was found in her room; there was nothing more to it."

"Except that she had no motive."

"She was jealous of Livia's claiming. We wondered briefly if she also planned harm against Livia. Livia was ill, too. Not to the same degree, but she must have been exposed."

"Where is the dungeon?"

"Not far from the palace. It's where I keep all the prisoners."

"How many prisoners are there?"

"A dozen or more at any given time. Most are soldiers who are punished for unruly conduct and insubordination. Some are citizens who have not paid their taxes. Marilla is an exception; there are few women so bold or so ignorant."

His words disturbed me; Marilla was neither bold nor ignorant. I had trusted Marilla and remembered only affection and companionship. Had she used me ill? No, but I was unsure of the circumstances.

"Did *you* question her?"

He shook his head. "I could not. Felix and Marcus handled almost everything. There were more pressing matters for the region. Until now, I have not thought of her." I wondered at his ability to be so unfeeling.

"May I see her?" I asked.

"No, that is not your place."

Astur's reproof was gentle, but I wanted to disagree. Still, I did not. I would have time to consider it and seek guidance from the great spirit before pressing my appeal.

***

It seemed as though Cato visited the palace whenever Astur was away. Lady Gaius received him each time he called. Dolon was with him, but he lurked outside the sitting room rather than going in to visit. I did not want the guards and maids to become accustomed to his presence.

Lady Gaius planned to stay a month after the marriage feast, but she delayed her departure when Cato offered to escort her back to the capital. She was expected to visit friends there but was not in any hurry to leave Mendel.

Astur was obligated to go away, so I did not mind Lady Gaius's distraction. I was deeply saddened as Astur's time to leave approached. I mustered my courage, but he knew my feelings. I clung to him and released my song, emploring the great spirit's protection over us while we were apart.

Astur rose early. He lifted a sleeping Mendel from the cradle and laid him beside me for comfort. Astur stroked my hair and kissed each of us goodbye.

"I will be back before you know it," he promised. His heart didn't want to be separated from us either, but his mind governed him, and his duty determined his steps as they led him away from me.

Chapter Forty-Four

I made significant progress in the garden before the maids and soldiers sought me out. With Lady Gaius, Traian, and Mendel, I once again tended to the residents' healing needs. Even soldiers who did not serve at the palace found me there.

Lady Gaius observed everything I did, but she reserved her comments until we were alone. "I have never met a healer," she confessed, "but my father, the former king, spoke of them as if they were a product of fantasy. He was among the first to conquer this region. Did you know that?"

"No, ma'am."

"Are there others like you?"

I shook my head. "I do not know. I am the only one of my family who remains. I may be the only one in this region, but I know nothing about any others."

"Astur is most fortunate. You healed him even before he was poisoned."

"That was the great spirit's doing, not mine."

"If that is what you believe, but I see otherwise. You have unique abilities, Phina. Don't be so modest." I looked at Lady Gaius, reading her expression. She lifted her chin proudly. "Claim your position. You have risen to a place of influence; use it to benefit others." Her instructing tone was the same she used with Livia. "You can make a difference."

I wasn't sure how to take Lady Gaius's guidance, so I let it settle in the back of my mind for another time. I would consult the great spirit about her meaning and determine if the great spirit used Lady Gaius as a messenger or if her words were her own.

During Astur's absence, my thoughts returned to Marilla. I sang prayers on her behalf, and the next day, the guard, Alexander, found me in the garden. It was a rare moment that I was alone. Mendel napped, and I wanted to harvest some ingredients without the distraction of his tiny hands grasping at everything within reach.

"Lady Phina," Alexander said humbly and dipped his head forward in a bow.

"Alexander," I said, but I wasn't surprised to see him. As I knelt by the healer's garden, my thoughts returned to Marilla, but when I stood, I realized it was not my mind but Alexander's heart that screamed Marilla's name.

"I'm sorry to disturb you," he said, warming up to the topic. He came seeking healing, but what ailed him was not physical. He needed more than herbs and medicinal plants.

"How may I be of service?" I asked, dusting off my hands on my apron.

Alexander was caught off guard by my question. "It is I who wish to be of service, my lady. Marilla," he said aloud.

"How is she?"

"You know?" he asked.

"Only a little. Would you tell me what you know?" I asked.

"She counted you among her friends. She asked for you to testify on her behalf, but you were no longer at the palace." His news saddened me; my escape had many consequences. "I would have looked for you, but I was arrested and taken to the dungeon."

"Upon what grounds?" I asked.

"For not protecting the governor. For abandoning my post." *Failure.*

"How was it found?"

"Lady Gaius took command and demanded the guards and maids search the entire palace. They found traces of the poison in Marilla's room, but she couldn't have done it because she wasn't there all day and all that night."

"And you believe her innocent."

"Yes, ma'am." He almost smiled, relieved that I might believe him.

"What lured you away from your duty, soldier?" I asked, softening my tone.

Alexander cleared his throat. "Marilla's a silly girl, but she doesn't have a malicious bone in her body. She was upset; Cato hurt her feelings, and she was confused and crying, but she managed to go to supper. Afterward, I followed Marilla out for some fresh air, but then she didn't want to go back inside, so we slept together on the balcony of the great hall. She was with me the entire time, ma'am," Alexander explained.

"Alexander, why didn't you come forward with the truth sooner?"

"I tried, ma'am, but the palace was chaos. Cato rushed in, afraid for his sister. He is a powerful man and accused everyone; he even accused you. I remained silent because I didn't want to taint Marilla's reputation. Livia knew we were together, and she swore Marilla to secrecy." Alexander hung his head. *Remorse.* "By the time I knew they'd taken her, I was punished, too. I held out hope that she would be released. I served my time and was sent away. When I returned months later, I heard from a guard that Marilla remained in prison." *Pain.*

"Have you seen her?" I asked.

"Yes, ma'am, but she has not faired well; she sent me away." *Rejection.*

"Can you get me inside?" I asked.

"Yes, my lady, I can, but you must not go as you are." Alexander hesitated. "Would you be willing to dress a commoner? Perhaps say that you are sent by her family?"

"It is difficult for me to convincingly deceive anyone, but I will wear my healer's clothes and find a way."

Chapter Forty-Five

Alexander thanked me before he left. He was still troubled, but even a glimmer of hope does wonders for the hopeless. I went straight to the kitchen. A couple of the women gasped when I entered.

"Lady Phina, what brings you?" Cassia asked, surprised. She wasn't unwelcoming, but I felt out of place. I checked myself.

"I'm sorry, Cassia. I came to find Myrtle. Is she here?"

"Yes, ma'am. She's out back." Cassia pointed with her head because her hands mixed a bowl of ingredients up to their wrists.

"Thank you, Cassia," I said and hurried out through the door. Myrtle stood with an ax in one hand and a limp chicken in another. She flopped the dead bird onto the chopping block and severed its head with a dull thump against the wooden board.

"Myrtle," I called.

"Watch yourself, my lady; there are blood and feathers everywhere."

I looked down and watched my step. "Would you come upstairs when you're finished? I have a favor."

Myrtle tilted her head, curious. "Of course, ma'am. It will be a while unless you need me sooner."

"No, it's nothing urgent. I'll wait in our room. I need to get to Mendel."

***

In the hours before Myrtle arrived, I sorted through my stores, packed Erik's satchel, and aired my healer's clothes. I had only kept them for sentimental sake, but I was thankful I hadn't discarded them. I considered what I might need to make Marilla comfortable.

Myrtle found me rocking Mendel and singing to him. She smiled and didn't look winded from her hike up the stairs. "I don't think I'll ever find more delight than in hearing your voice in the palace again."

"Funny you should mention it. Was it terrible when I was away?" I asked.

"You were dismissed; Master was hanging on by a thread. None of us could do for him what you could. I warned Lady Gaius that she'd made a grave mistake, but she wouldn't listen to reason. The palace was in turmoil."

"Can you tell me about how you came to find the poison in Marilla's room?" I asked.

Worry creased Myrtle's brow, and she caught herself on the sofa at the foot of our bed. She sat down and shook her head. "Oh, child," she began, forgetting herself. "That sweet girl. She never did anyone any harm, but I found that cursed plant in her room, hidden under a stack of linens."

"Was Marilla there when you found it?"

"Yes, ma'am."

"What was her reaction?"

"What could she say? The answer would have been the same, regardless. If she was guilty, she would have denied it; innocent, she would have said the same."

"I'm going to see her tomorrow. I want to get to the bottom of this."

"My lady, I don't think that's wise. What would Master say?" she asked.

"He would most likely forbid it, but he's not here to ask. Besides, I need to go alone. Would you be so kind as to tend to Mendel? I don't plan to be away for long, and I need to know he's safe so I can focus on Marilla." Myrtle disapproved, but she agreed to watch him.

***

Alexander and I rode together toward the dungeon. He thought it might be too conspicuous if I were seen riding Raven. He walked me through the prison gates and escorted me to one of the guards.

"She wishes to visit a prisoner." The guard eyed my satchel and gestured to inspect it. I placed it before him, and he examined each item, lingering on the food and blanket. It was evident that he intended to keep those items. "I wouldn't if I were you," Alexander whispered to the guard. The guard shifted uneasily and reconsidered before he replaced each item.

Alexander then led me to another guard who he knew by name. "Back to see the wench?" Craugis asked in a gruff voice. Alexander didn't reply. "Who's this?" he asked, gesturing toward me.

"A friend," Alexander said. "She's come on behalf of the family."

Craugis grunted and led us into the prison. "Don't make her cry again. We can't stand the wailing."

"It wasn't my intention last time," Alexander said with a huff.

The stone walls were lower than I expected, but that was because all of the cells were underground. As we entered, the odors reviled my senses, and my instincts recoiled. Heavy, dank earth mingled with the stench of blood and human waste. I covered my mouth reflexively.

"You'll get used to it," Craugis said.

We walked deeper and deeper underground. There was little light, except for the torches that Alexander and Craugis carried. The corridor was long; heavy wooden doors sealed each cell.

Craugis stopped and hefted the ring of keys from his hip. He fumbled around the circle until he found the one he was looking for. "Visitors," he announced. He unlocked the door with a loud click. The sound was quickly absorbed in the earthen walls.

There was a faint squeal and scuffling; the sound of a chain clinked. Craugis pulled the door open for us to enter. Alexander was eager to enter first. He held up the torch, and Marilla retreated to the far corner of the room.

"Marilla?" Alexander asked in a whisper. The tone was in opposition to the way his heart cried her name.

"I told you not to come!" she whimpered and hovered against the wall, keeping her face in shadow.

Alexander moved toward her. I placed my hand on his arm and shook my head. "Marilla, it's Phina."

Marilla shook her head and cowered. "No. No, go away."

I motioned for Alexander to light the candle with his torch. "Leave us," I whispered. Alexander looked confused; he did not wish to go. "Wait outside. Please." He nodded once, but his eyes lingered on Marilla for a moment longer.

I placed my satchel on a small table next to a couple of candles and a basin of water, but we'd found Marilla in darkness. There was a low pile of hay in the corner that I imagined was her bed. A bucket stood in the corner, heavy with the scent of urine. I removed the contents of my bag.

"Marilla, I've come to see you."

"I don't want to be seen."

I inched closer to her in the small space. "Please, Marilla, I'm here to help you."

Marilla lifted her gaze toward the light but could not look directly at it. She blinked, adjusting to the candlelight. Her face was gaunt, and dark circles shadowed her once-bright eyes. Pity replaced my shock.

"I'm hideous," Marilla whispered and stroked down the tattered dress that hung loosely over her. Her formerly plump cheeks pulled at her expression.

"Are you hungry? I brought you some bread and one of Cassia's sweet rolls. I remembered how much you liked them." Marilla looked confused at the words, like they were foreign to her ears.

I gathered her hands into mine and lowered her onto the floor beside me. Her eyes were wide. I rose then, dampened a small cloth in the basin, and lathered the lavender soap to wash her face and hands. She marveled at the tender gesture. I then handed her the sweet roll. She closed her eyes and sniffed it but did not eat it right away.

"How are you so kind to me?" she asked.

"I did not know you were here. I assumed you had returned to your home, safe with your family, perhaps even claimed by now."

Marilla scoffed. "That will never happen, even if I am released, not with this, I won't." She removed her sleeve to show a brand above her wrist, the mark of a criminal. "My family has abandoned me; they must despise me. I suppose I should be thankful for two meals and an hour of sunlight each day. I thought by now, I would be hung, but I'm still here. There is no claiming or babies in my future," she said with deep sadness. Then she returned to the present, "How are you here, Phina?"

"Alexander."

Marilla lowered her gaze onto her lap and picked at the roll's crust. She tasted the morsel, and tears leaked from her eyes. "He's a fool."

"No, he only appears to be foolish; he acts out of love and concern for you."

She dismissed that thought. "I didn't touch your plants, Phina. You warned me not to, and I didn't. I would never harm the governor or anyone."

"I know that, Marilla. That's why I'm here. Who? Do you know?" She shook her head. "Was it Cato?" I asked. She shrugged her bony shoulders.

"I'm sorry, Phina. I do not know. I wasn't in the garden or my room all day. I thought Cato's attention was sincere, but he was only using me to get to you. After the night you sang with Erik, he sought me out and asked me everything about you. I thought maybe he fancied me enough to claim me, but I was misled."

I wiped Marilla's face again. She leaned into my hand, craving human touch more than food. "I am going to have you released."

Marilla laughed, disbelieving my words. "Are you back at the palace? Are you playing for the governor again? Do you think he would do that for you?"

"Yes, I am back at the palace, but it is very different. After I left, I bore a son, Astur's son. Felix found me, and Astur claimed both Mendel and me. I cannot wait for you to see him for yourself."

Concern flashed across Marilla's face. "You lied to me. You said that you were not his mistress."

"I was not, Marilla. I found comfort in him after Erik's death, and he found solace in me."

"You're Lady Gaius!" she exclaimed.

"Lady Phina," I corrected.

"You shouldn't be here. What were you thinking? Alexander," Marilla called. Alexander opened the door, relieved to hear Marilla's voice. "What do you mean by bringing her here? The governor will be furious! I'll be hanged for sure!" She placed her hands on her throat.

"Marilla, please, lower your voice. It was her idea. She asked to come," Alexander whispered. "She wants to help you." He moved closer to her and lifted his hand to comfort her. Marilla shied away, wrapping her arms around herself. A heavy chain clanked with each step. Alexander fisted his hand and lowered it to his side. "Marilla," he repeated, but she shook her head and moved away.

Alexander turned then and walked toward the door. "We should go," he said and lifted his tightened jaw. He held the door open for me.

I offered Marilla the blanket and left the bread and lavender soap on the table with the cloth. I looked back at her before I ducked under Alexander's outstretched arm. I thought I saw hope in her eyes. I would not disappoint her.

Before we left the prison, I turned to our escort. I remembered Lady Gaius' words; I would use my position to help Marilla. "Craugis, I'm sending provision for the prisoner. See that she gets everything I send."

"Yes, Lady Gaius." He bowed his head. He'd overheard everything.

"Lady Phina," I corrected again.

"Yes, ma'am," he said. "Get the lady out of here, or we'll all be swinging from the gallows," he warned Alexander.

Chapter Forty-Six

I hurried up the back stairs into our chambers, relieved that Mendel wasn't crying. I heard the rocking chair squeak in a steady rhythm. Myrtle knew how to comfort him in my absence; thankfully, I was only away a few hours.

I rounded into our chamber, but it wasn't Myrtle rocking Mendel. It was Astur. He set his jaw and blinked, taking in my healer's clothes and boots. He pursed his lips and disapproved of everything.

"Where were you?" he asked, pacing his words in time with the chair. Mendel lay against Astur's shoulder, and Astur patted his tiny back.

My eyes widened, and I swallowed before I spoke. "I went to the dungeon to see Marilla."

Astur rolled his eyes and took in a settling breath. Considering his words carefully, he said, "I told you not to go."

"No, you told me it was not my place. Those are two different things." My tone remained respectful.

Mendel squirmed at the sound of my voice and the tension between us. Astur frowned and stood to hand Mendel to me. He didn't touch me or welcome me with a kiss.

I sat in the rocking chair and prepared to nurse Mendel; Astur's warmth lingered in the wood. I looked down into Mendel's eyes and stroked his head.

"She's innocent," I said. Astur grunted. "She's been wrongly convicted, and I ask that you pardon her."

"Can you read women's hearts now, too?" he asked, mocking me.

I met his gaze. "No, Astur, but I can read Alexander's. She was with him."

"Did *he* take you there?"

"Yes, but it was all my doing." I didn't want Astur to take out his frustration with me on the young soldier. "Please, release her and allow Alexander to bring her here." Astur's incredulous expression needed no explanation. He turned from me in a huff and slammed our chamber door behind him.

I took Mendel down to the baths with me before supper. He splashed and squealed with delight as I moved him back and forth in the water. I bathed him and held him against my bare breasts. I sang and let my voice echo around us. I prayed for Marilla's release and for her to be made whole again. I prayed for the ability to soften Astur's heart, knowing that would be the great spirit's doing, but perhaps I could help him see reason.

Lady Gaius and I ate supper together, but she did not ask after her son. I wondered if she knew he had returned. I put Mendel to bed and fell asleep reading, waiting for Astur to join me.

I woke to the clean scent of sandalwood and Astur's beckoning heart. He took the book from my hand and extinguished the candle. He sat on the bed beside me and placed his hand on my stomach. "Where did you go?" I whispered.

"I think you can guess," he breathed.

"The baths?"

He chuckled once. "Yes, among other places."

"Do you believe me?" I asked.

"Yes." There was a smile in his voice. "I spoke with everyone myself, even Marilla."

I sat up and searched his eyes in the dark. "You did? You believe me." I hugged him tightly and wept. "Thank you, Astur. Thank you. I'm sorry I worried you and that I wasn't here to welcome you home."

"I'm sorry, too. I should trust your judgment. The guards are processing Marilla's release. Alexander will bring her to you in the morning; she will need time to recover from this ordeal."

"I will see to her care," I whispered.

"Good. That will relieve some of the guilt."

I didn't thank Astur with words; I thanked him with kisses. He pressed himself against me and lay down beside me. "Would you welcome me home now?" I wrapped myself around him and welcomed him with everything.

***

Alexander wasted no time bringing Marilla to the palace. I handed Mendel to Myrtle and gave her instructions to leave him with his grandmother in the garden. I took Marilla straight to the baths. Her sallow skin hung on her bones. She moved like she was in a sad dream. The year in prison had altered her. She wept as I brushed the knots from her hair, following her hand down the smoothed locks.

"They cut it, you know, all of it, down to my scalp," Marilla said.

I comforted her with a knowing glance. The feel of my stubbled head wasn't easily forgotten. I hadn't been allowed to grow my hair for three years, and I understood the shame Marilla carried.

Myrtle clipped Marilla's nails and rubbed scented oils over her skin. Marilla winced at the touch. Myrtle and I pulled a dress over her head, and Marilla delicately traced the trim on the cuff, covering the brand on her wrist.

Marilla barely ate anything. I mixed an herb tincture into her tea to stimulate her appetite and another to help her relax. She asked to rest, so I settled her in a guestroom. When I left her room, Alexander approached me from across the hallway.

"Thank you, ma'am," he said earnestly, but his heart's gratitude rolled off of him in waves. *Relief.*

I smiled and received his words. "Be patient with her. She's suffered unknown agony."

"I can be patient," Alexander said in his soldier's voice. Still, he was eager to see her. I needed to caution him.

"I am hopeful that Marilla will return to herself, but it will take time." That pained him.

"May I see her after she's rested?" he asked.

"Yes. I will bring her to the garden this afternoon for some fresh air."

***

Lady Gaius and Mendel were in the garden. She held him in her lap and clapped his hands in rhythm to a song. I sat next to them, careful not to disturb their time.

"You brought her here?" Lady Gaius asked.

"Yes, ma'am."

"You believe her innocent?" she asked, lifting her chin.

"Yes, ma'am," I repeated.

"What makes you so sure as to ask Astur to pardon her?"

Without going into detail, I said, "She's not capable. She wasn't in the garden all that day, and she has an alibi."

"You mean an accomplice," Lady Gaius retorted.

"No, ma'am. Alexander, her guard, was with her. She was with him the entire time."

"Are you sure you believe him? Is he not covering over other indiscretions?" Lady Gaius was a shrewd woman. She understood the way of things much better than I did, but she was blinded by her pride and protection over her son.

"Lady Gaius, it is not as you presume." She did not believe me.

"Livia spoke of Marilla's jealousy more than once. The girl has always been in Livia's shadow, not only in beauty but in status and intellect. Perhaps you are right; she's not capable, except she knew all about your plants." Lady Gaius directed her chin towards the healer's garden.

"No, ma'am. That's not what I mean. Marilla is sweet and caring. She knew the plants, but she did not know how to use them, not as you suppose."

"I hope you're right, Phina. For all our sakes, I hope you're right."

Chapter Forty-Seven

Once Mendel was down for his nap, I went to Marilla's room. She was sitting up in the bed, sipping a cup of tea. The maid, Raya, stood over her like a guard, watching Marilla's every move.

"I'll see after that," I said, dismissing Raya.

"Yes, ma'am, but Lucia said to watch her."

"I'm sure she did, but I can manage it." Raya moved away from the bed and dipped her head in a bow. "Please inform Lucia that I'll be with Marilla for a while."

When Marilla and I were alone, I asked, "How was your rest?"

"Brief," Marilla confessed. "I kept waking up, unsure of where I was. Each time I dozed off, I could smell the dungeon. I looked out the window, and I could hear the chain as I walked. This doesn't seem real." Tears pooled in Marilla's eyes, but she didn't have the strength nor the will to hide them.

I patted her hand. "You're safe, and you're free. You will never return," I assured her. She offered me a wan smile. "Would you like to join me in the garden?" I asked.

Marilla hesitated. "I don't know."

"Come outside and get some fresh air."

I put my arm around Marilla's waist and ambled toward the garden. Marilla walked, dragging one leg like it weighed more than the other. She also kept her eyes on the floor, conditioned not to look into the jailers' eyes.

Alexander brightened as we approached, but soon concern clouded his vision. He wanted to help her but did not want to suffer her rejection. He was also bothered that she kept her eyes diverted.

Alexander and I waited for Marilla to sit. She closed her eyes and inhaled the scent of the flowers. "They're lovely," she whispered. I motioned toward the lilacs. Alexander picked a bloom and offered it to her. She looked up but refused to look into Alexander's eyes.

"Thank you," she whispered and took the lilacs. She sniffed them and then lowered her hands to her lap.

This continued for a few days. Marilla preferred to stay in her room. She said that open spaces made her uneasy. Lady Gaius spent time with her in the mornings, and I coaxed her to the garden in the afternoons.

Astur was called away again, and Cato returned with Dolon. I asked Alexander to keep an eye on them. I had no interest in them myself, but knowing they visited often made me leery.

When Marilla was unwilling to leave her room in the afternoons, I brought the dulcimer and played for her. She apologized for being unable to do more than eat and sleep.

"It will take time to recover from your confinement."

"How long?" she asked, impatient with herself.

"I do not know, but we will be with you."

"You and the governor are most kind."

"I meant Alexander," I said.

Marilla's lips twitched, and I noticed color rise to her cheeks. "Is that a smile?" I teased.

Marilla covered her mouth self-consciously and looked away. The brazen, man-crazed girl that arrived at the palace was mostly gone, but perhaps some of her liveliness remained.

Looking for ways to draw Marilla out, I brought Mendel to see her one morning. She was sitting in a chair near the window. Her eyes shined brightly when she saw me with my baby. "He's beautiful," she sighed. "May I hold him?" she asked. Marilla held Mendel like he was breakable. "I see the governor," she said. I smiled at that, thankful that Astur's likeness was mirrored in our son.

I sat quietly and allowed Marilla time to rekindle her joy of babies. Instead, it had the opposite effect. Marilla nuzzled her face into Mendel's head affectionately and then pulled him into her chest. The sudden movement startled me.

"Marilla?" I asked, and my voice rose with concern.

"I'm sorry, Phina," she gasped in a sob. "I'm so sorry." She loosened her grasp on Mendel and stroked his head soothingly. She rocked him back and forth, but Mendel wasn't bothered, so Marilla's motions only soothed herself. I followed her shaking hand along Mendel's back, supporting him in case she wasn't strong enough to hold him. "You're the luckiest girl. You have been claimed, and you've given your husband a son. What greater pleasure could there be?" Tears fell down Marilla's cheeks. "I will never know that joy."

"Marilla, please do not give up hope. Perhaps one day…" I began, but Marilla's eyes flashed.

"No!" she said. "You gave me hope in the dungeon and saw to my release, but you cannot fill my heart with hope for something that's impossible!" She looked into Mendel's face before she placed him solidly in my lap, refusing to allow herself the hope of a child.

She stood, walked toward the window, and crossed her arms around herself. "I will forever be known as a criminal." Marilla pulled up the sleeve of her dress to show me the brand. "I am a disgrace to my family. My parents despise me; they've written me off. My father's plan to arrange my marriage will never be. All that they invested in me is wasted; I will never bring honor to my family."

"Do they know you've been released? Do they know you've been pardoned?" I asked.

"I have not heard from them since before I was taken. Livia promised to tell them on her way home, but when I asked to send them a letter, the guards only laughed at me. Once I was branded, I lost all my rights. Even if my parents did send word to me, I doubt the guards would have been able to read any better than me."

Marilla's parents must be notified. "We will send them word. I will be right back. Can you manage Mendel?" I asked. Marilla nodded, too surprised to refuse me.

I ran from the library with parchment and ink. I stopped short when I heard Cato's voice. "Come along, Dolon. Lady Gaius is waiting."

I was trapped in the hallway. This section of the corridor had no doors or recesses. I stood with the parchment in one hand and the quill and ink in the other. I lifted my chin and stood tall, but it took a great deal to keep my expression neutral.

"Lady Phina," Cato greeted me with a bow.

I swallowed. "Cato," I said, knowing it would reflect negatively on Astur and the palace if I disrespected a senator. Dolon frowned when he saw the parchment.

"Do you draw?" Cato asked like he hoped to uncover an unknown talent.

"No," I said without thinking. In close proximity, their hearts pressed against my mind – *Curiosity* on Cato's part. *Danger* and *Distrust* flowed from Dolon. He thought I was a danger to them. I almost laughed. I supposed being seen as a threat was better than insignificant or something Cato coveted.

"Why would a woman need parchment?" Dolon whispered suspiciously. The man's heart was filled with shadows. "Do you care to answer my question?" Dolon dared ask.

I leveled my eyes to his and refused to indulge his unspoken accusation. I could both read and write. My ability to read was known only by a few. I would not dare let Cato and this insolent, arrogant man know.

"Dolon, you've offended her. Apologize to the lady, or we'll be banished," Cato said, lightening the mood but not quite teasing. Dolon continued to stare at me. There would be no apology.

"Lady Phina," Alexander called, and I was relieved to hear his measured pace hasten behind me. "The governor and Felix have returned, ma'am," he lied smoothly. Cato eyed Dolon.

"Thank you, Alexander. I appreciate your news."

I dipped my head in the same way Lady Gaius had when dismissing someone from a conversation. It felt feeble, but it worked. Dolon and Cato left my presence immediately. Perhaps they were eager to find Lady Gaius before Felix or Astur found them in the palace.

"Thank you, Alexander," I sighed when we were alone.

"I'm sorry, ma'am. You asked me to keep my eyes on them, but I was detained when I saw them arrive. It won't happen again." I smiled at his eagerness to please me. "Except for the day Erik left you in the garden, I've never seen you so pale. I wish I had gotten to you sooner." Alexander was observant. I fanned myself with the parchment. "May I escort you?" he asked.

That was perfect. "Yes, would you write a letter for Marilla?" I asked.

"Yes, ma'am. It would be an honor to assist her in any way I can."

Marilla was surprised when I returned with Alexander, but she didn't offer Mendel back to me right away. She was settled with him. I was thankful that I allowed them time to become acquainted.

Alexander sat at the desk and uncorked the ink. He dipped the quill and waited for the words. Marilla hesitated. "I do not know how to begin," she said.

Alexander smiled encouragingly and suggested, "How about *Dear Mother and Father*?"

Marilla lowered her eyes, but her lips turned upward in a slight grin. She nodded. Alexander repeated the words as he wrote, "Dear Mother and Father." She watched his hand as he formed the words. The script was fine, like Erik's. He paused, waiting for Marilla to continue.

When she said nothing, I chimed in, "I am writing to tell you that I have been pardoned. I currently reside at the palace under the governor's protection until other plans can be made for me." Marilla exhaled, but her relief was short-lived because her future was still unknown. What plans would be made for her?

Chapter Forty-Eight

Alexander and I didn't linger in Marilla's room. She needed rest after the emotional exertion of writing her letter. She thanked me, and her eyes stayed fixed on Alexander for a moment before she focused back on the safety of Mendel's face. She perceived no judgment or pity there.

Alexander walked me back down the corridor toward my chamber stairs. "I forgot the ink and quill," I said and turned around toward Marilla's room. My haste and forgetfulness broadsided me again, and we were met by Dolon and Cato on their way out of the palace. Cato stopped to greet me with a bow. Dolon shifted his cloak and did the same. I was unprepared for their formality after the suspicion I had encountered before. I dipped my head, acknowledging their gesture before my eyes fell on the dagger at Dolon's side.

I blinked and drew in a quick breath. I recognized the curve of the hilt and the glint of steel. A wave of dizziness washed over me, and I was unable to keep my footing. Simultaneously, I was washed over by the shadows of Dolon's heart. The darkness consumed me, and I was taken under. Cold, suffocating air rasped my lungs. I held tightly to Mendel and leaned against the wall.

Alexander's strong arms braced me, but I continued to fall. "Lady Phina!" Alexander exclaimed. His voice was muffled through the shadows. Mendel cried out. Had I dropped him? No, I felt him solid against my chest. "Ma'am, ma'am." I heard Alexander's voice through Mendel's cries, but I couldn't answer him before everything went black.

***

Images of my child-self ran in the field toward the cottage. I clutched wildflowers in my fat little child's hands – the light of midday shown around me. Everything glistened.

"Phina," Mother called. She smiled when I presented her with my offering. Her love radiated from her lazuli eyes.

Then the scene of Mother shifted. "Watch yourself, Phina. Be mindful of your surroundings. Be sure to thrust confidently with the blade. Hold it securely in your hand. Remember the death points of your assailant. An attacker will be larger and stronger than you but not smarter. As long as you're calm, your weapon will be your defense." Mother wrapped her hand around mine, forming the proper grip with my fingers. "Hold it securely," she repeated. "In the moment, courage will replace fear."

"Who taught you this, Mother? Are these hidden ways of a healer?" I asked.

"Your father taught me. He didn't want me to be defenseless."

"But, Mother, this feels unnatural to protect myself and accidentally harm someone."

Mother's eyes hardened. "No, Phina, if you are ever threatened, you will not harm accidentally, but with purpose. Your life is more valuable than anyone who would do you harm." I dared not question Mother. Her tone was firm, and I knew to pay attention and heed the truth of her words.

Voices mumbled in my ears. Mother's face moved like a mist through my mind. "Mother?" I whispered.

"No, child, it's Myrtle." She patted my face with a cool cloth.

My eyes fluttered open, and I focused on Myrtle's concerned eyes. I was in my bed. "Mendel!" I exclaimed in a breathy whisper and sat up suddenly, but I regretted moving so quickly. I groaned and rested my aching head back onto the pillows.

"He's fine. Been sleeping for the better part of an hour."

"How long have I been here?" I asked.

"Only a little longer than that." Myrtle laid the damp cloth in the basin. She offered me a cup of water.

"What happened?" I asked.

"Alexander sent a guard to the kitchen. He said you fainted. He carried you up here."

"We were with Marilla," I whispered.

"Drink," Myrtle encouraged. I sipped the water; it soothed my parched throat.

"You gave that young man a terrible fright, not to mention the guards."

"The guards?" I asked. Then it all came back to me in a flash. I shook my head to disagree, but it pounded at my temples. "No, Dolon and Cato were in the hallway."

"I don't know, my lady; they weren't there when I arrived. I came up here to tend to you and the baby."

Mendel woke up and demanded that I feed him. I couldn't remember my afternoon clearly, especially the time after Alexander and I left Marilla's room. Myrtle instructed me to keep to my chambers and stay in bed to rest.

I made myself a tincture for the headache and rested until supper. Raya brought up my tray and asked if I needed anything. I shook my head and thanked her. The remainder of the evening, I was restless and called upon the great spirit for answers and protection. When it was Mendel's bedtime, I let him sleep next to me. His presence comforted me, and in Astur's absence, I needed the comfort. When he was in a deep sleep, I found Grandfather's dulcimer and played, singing low over the strings. The thoughts of my family and Erik trickled in. The years' events passed in waves of color and light. Music played in my mind, and chords formed from my fingertips. My mind took me back – so far back to simpler times and safety, innocence, and the security of the cottage.

I was reminded that the palace was not my home, but neither was the cottage. When Astur was away, I missed him. I never felt scared, but the events of the day disturbed me.

When I opened my eyes, Astur stood at the foot of the bed, watching me. His expression was filled with pleasure and longing. I was so absorbed in the music that I hadn't sensed his heart. I was too wrapped up in memories to notice anything else.

"Don't stop," he whispered. "Keep playing. Please," he added. The song settled him, too, but with him home, I wanted to rush into the warmth and allow his hard body to hold me close. I wanted to feel the rhythm of his heartbeat against my breasts and hear his heart's song. I played through the chorus once more and ended the song with a final chord.

My eyes stayed fixed until the sound dissipated into the stillness of the night air. It was dark, except for the moonlight streaming in from the balcony. Astur walked around the bed and cradled my face in the palm of his hand before he kissed me. The relief at his touch released the tears that I didn't know were waiting behind my eyes. Astur kissed my tear-stained cheeks.

"What's wrong?" he whispered. "Aren't you happy to see me?" he teased.

I laid the dulcimer to the side and wrapped my arms around Astur, holding tightly to him. His arms pulled me closer. He kissed my hair and rubbed his hands down my back, comforting me; his heart's colors were bright. I wept harder, but he didn't know why.

"What's upset you?" he asked, but I couldn't explain it.

"Hold me," I whispered.

He moved in closer and scooped me up into his lap. He soothed me with sweet shushing sounds that soon transitioned into a hum. Astur's deep voice and heart's colors washed everything away. I swam in the dark blues and soared through the lighter hues of the morning sky.

"Do you want to talk about it?" Astur whispered.

I shook my head. "No, I just want you," I said, sounding small. My voice was muffled by his neck and chest. I did want him; I desired nothing more than his presence and his comfort. I wanted to give myself to him; I eased my mind with his song. "Lie with me and be one."

It was the first time I asked for his physical love with words. He knew I loved him and that I was bound to him, but the joy my request brought him exploded into new colors. His heart rejoiced in victory. Yellow and pink like a sunset contrasted against the calming blue and indigo. His pleasure consumed me as our mutual desire intensified. I released my longing and discovered another layer of our binding. I gave thanks to the great spirit for revealing another dimension of our union.

Chapter Forty-Nine

Astur still lay in the bed when Mendel stirred. I nursed him quietly, but Astur woke, too; a governor's day began early. He was curious as to the mood he'd found me in the night before. His unspoken questions needed answers before he would leave me.

"I'm better," I said. "You don't need to worry."

"Yes, you're better, but that doesn't remove my concern." There was a smile in his voice, and I basked in his gaze. Mendel and I were his, and he wanted to do everything in his power to protect and provide for us, not just as the governor but as a mate and father.

"I fainted yesterday," I said.

Astur's concern increased. "Are you ill?" he asked.

"No. I rested, and, other than a slight headache, I felt fine." He examined me, searching for any signs of injury. "I'm fine, Astur," I repeated.

"Did you hit your head?"

"No, Alexander was there. He called the guards and maids, and they took care of me."

"Where were you?"

"In the corridor. We'd written a letter to Marilla's parents."

"You can write?" he asked.

"Yes," I said, bothered that my story was interrupted. "Of course, I can. If I can read, then I can write." But then, I supposed they weren't one and the same. "I didn't write the letter; Alexander did." That eased Astur's tension, but I still didn't appreciate his response. I considered him.

"You know that if I ever give you a daughter, she will know. I will teach her just like I will teach Mendel."

Astur bristled at my boldness. There would be no compromising on that point. Whether or not Astur consented, our daughters would be educated as thoroughly as our sons. Mendel did not have a healer's markings, but he would know the great spirit's ways and understand all of the plants and their properties.

"Tutors," Astur corrected me. "Mendel will have tutors."

"Perhaps later, but surely not before he's ten. I am his mother; it is my responsibility."

"You are a lady now. It no longer befits your station."

"Besides the dungeons and my son's education, what else does not *befit* my station?" Astur took a calming breath through his nose. I shook my head, not wanting to engage in an argument so early in the morning. "I'm sorry, Astur. We can discuss Mendel's training later; I doubt we will settle anything this morning."

He nodded once. We were learning more about each other with each day of our union. Our upbringings were different, and our expectations were drastically opposed. "I'm sorry, too. I don't mean to disqualify your abilities. It comes as a surprise. I know better; please continue. I want to know about yesterday." I settled back and told him how Cato found me. "Did he upset you?" Astur asked.

"No, they saw me with the parchment."

"They?"

"He was with Dolon again. The shadows of that man's heart are the darkest I've encountered." I shuddered, and the memory chilled my blood. "He did something with his hand, and everything went black."

Astur moved toward me to comfort my distress. "Has this ever happened?" I shook my head.

My thoughts went away again into memories—thoughts of Mother and the cottage. Memories of cutting woody stems before we boiled them, laying each one out and measuring it carefully. They were the length of Mother's dagger's hilt, my father's dagger.

I asked about the shapes that were carved into it. Mother explained that my father had etched symbols of love into it. She rubbed the letters with her thumb fondly.

"Do they hold the great spirit's power?" I asked in my child's voice.

"No, my little one, no power, just bittersweet memories."

"Phina," Astur called from a distance. I blinked and focused on his anxious face. He wiped tears from my cheeks. "You said something about a dagger. Did he threaten you?"

I shook my head, confused by his words. When I found the memory again, I said, "I think Dolon has Mother's dagger."

"How do you know?"

"I don't. Dolon pressed me with questions that I didn't answer. His dark heart consumed me, and then I noticed the dagger at his side."

"How did your mother come by such a weapon? Is it commonplace for a healer to be armed?"

"No, but she felt exposed after Erik left and Grandfather died. There were more soldiers, and she knew we were vulnerable. My father gave it to her before he left, but it never protected her. It protected me, or I wouldn't be here."

"You said your father was a soldier. Was it a soldier's blade?" I shrugged. "Dolon is Cato's guard. Like Cato and I, he is a former soldier. I have one of my own." He rose from the bed and opened a box at the bottom of his wardrobe. "Look, was your mother's dagger like this?"

My hand trembled as I took Astur's dagger in my hand. It was nearly identical. "No, this one is different. See, there are no markings here." I pointed to the unmarked steel. "Mother's had etching in the blade. I rolled Astur's dagger over and traced it with my fingertip. Dolon's dagger had that marking."

Astur hesitated. "Are you sure? That's a serious accusation."

I looked back at him with a blank expression. "I'm aware of that, Astur, but I need to know how he came to be in possession of Mother's dagger or if he's the man who killed her."

***

"Marilla," I said as I entered the garden.

"Good morning," she said and blinked up at me.

"I'm happy to see you. How are you this morning?" I asked.

"I'm well. Thank you."

"How did you get here?"

"Alexander," she whispered. I should have known that she wouldn't come on her own.

She sat down and plucked weeds alongside me. She moved slowly, yet deliberately. I was thankful for her presence and any help tending the garden. I was even more grateful to see her outside in the fresh air. When Mendel demanded to be freed from the sling, Marilla entertained him. Later, Lady Gaius arrived. She stopped and stared. Lady Gaius's pride for her grandson far outweighed her distrust of Marilla.

"Phina. Marilla. I'm glad I found you together." Marilla's gaze lowered onto her lap. Lady Gaius continued, "I've just received word that Livia will arrive in two days." Marilla lifted her chin, surprised by the news.

"Why?" Marilla asked before I could.

"She's coming to see you, dear."

"Me?" Marilla asked.

"Yes, you."

"But how does she know? We only sent a letter to Mother and Father yesterday."

Lady Gaius's sympathetic smile allayed Marilla. "News travels fast from the regions to the capital. Cato sent word to his sister as soon as you were released. According to Cato, she wasted no time coming to see you," Lady Gaius said, evident that she admired Livia's concern for Marilla.

I stopped weeding long enough to listen but returned to the task and focused on a patch an arms-length away. "Phina, do you have anything to say?"

"No, ma'am. I'm surprised, that's all."

"Why Livia?" Marilla asked.

"Cato said that your father's been ill, and your mother must stay with him. They've been beside themselves with worry," Lady Gaius said.

The little bit of color that had risen to Marilla's cheeks faded as Lady Gaius shared her news. Lady Gaius patted Marilla's shoulder gently. "There, there, Marilla, it will be fine. You'll see."

Marilla didn't say anything else, and when it was time for our midday meal, I saw her back to her room, where she would remain for the rest of the evening. She had yet to join us for supper.

***

"Livia is returning to the palace," Lady Gaius announced when she'd finished her wine. Astur bristled beside me.

"Upon whose invitation?" he asked.

"I suppose mine," Lady Gaius said.

"Why can she not stay with her brother?" Astur asked.

"She's not coming to see her brother but to see Marilla. As long as that young lady resides here, within the palace walls, I suppose her guests are your guests."

I read Lady Gaius's expression. I wasn't sure if she still disagreed with Marilla's pardon. She didn't challenge Astur, but he was not pleased with her logic.

"What is her plan?" Astur asked, referring to Marilla. "Do her parents wish for her to go home?"

"I have no idea. It all happened suddenly. Cato came in and announced the news, and then he and his guard left me almost immediately."

At the mention of Dolon, a chill ran down my spine. Astur was preoccupied with his mother, so he didn't notice me. I took in a breath through my nose and released it slowly, dabbing my mouth and neck with my napkin—a light sheen of moisture through the pallor of my skin.

Astur cursed. "Barely a mention is made of the man, and you're all clammy," he said.

"What man?" Lady Gaius asked.

"Dolon."

"Cato's Dolon?" Lady Gaius's voice rose as they argued over me.

"Yes! Cato's Dolon!" Astur snapped. I was sinking into the memory again. "Hold Mendel, Mother. I'm taking Phina to bed." I felt Mendel being taken from me while Astur's strong arms lifted me from my chair. My head lolled against his chest just before everything went dark.

***

The scent of lilacs was heavy around me. The birds called their own from the trees. The critters made their night sounds. I wrestled with the memories of Mother and couldn't shake free of their hold. The darkness of her rape and murder pressed against my heart. I couldn't catch my breath. The stones I used to weigh Grandmother pulled and tugged at my skirt. No matter how I kicked my legs, I wasn't strong enough to break the surface of the water. The river's current worked against my arms. My lungs burned, and I gasped against the pressure. My head throbbed at my temples.

"Phina!" Astur's worry bordered on anger. He stroked my face tenderly. "Phina, come back to me," he pleaded.

I opened my eyes to see everyone was there; Astur, Felix, Myrtle, and Lucia stood around my bed, staring at me. Lucia moved forward and did her own assessment.

Myrtle fussed over me too. "What ails you, child?" Myrtle asked.

"I'm alright," I said. "May I have some water?"

Lucia poured me a glass. "You look dreadfully pale. What remedies do you have in your stores?" Lucia asked.

"Nothing. I just need some water; then, I'll figure it out. Where's Mendel?" I asked.

"He's with Mother," Astur said gruffly. "We need to get to the bottom of this," he said, and I could hear the worry in his voice.

"Astur, please. Don't do anything rash." I touched his hand.

"Rash," he repeated, but he softened his tone before he spoke again. "The mere mention of his name sends you reeling. I won't disqualify your abilities this time. I will send Felix to bring him in for an interrogation. Describe the marking we're looking for."

"I want to be there when you question him," I said.

"No," Astur and Felix said at the same time. "If he's as dark-hearted as you say, I don't want him anywhere near you," Astur said protectively.

I looked from Astur's eyes to Felix's. "But I can help. I'll know if he's deceiving you. I'll know if he's telling the truth." Felix turned to look at Astur.

"You know she's right," Felix said.

Chapter Fifty

When I refused to stay in bed, Alexander was stationed as my guard. He walked me to and from the garden. He only left me to escort Marilla. Myrtle was told to check in on me often, and it all felt ridiculous. I was fine, but Astur would not be satisfied.

Dolon could not be brought in right away for questioning because Cato and Dolon had gone to meet Livia at the border. She would arrive the next day. That night, Astur and I talked.

"You haven't said anything about Livia. Does it bother you?" Astur asked as he combed his fingers through my hair. I shook my head. "It would bother most women." I searched his eyes for understanding. He smiled and kissed my mouth. "But it doesn't bother you because you can read my heart."

"Not exactly," I said between kisses.

Astur smiled again over my lips. "Then why?" he asked. "Don't you know the threat of another woman?"

"I am not jealous of Livia because I am secure in our union. We share a child. We've sung the binding song, and the great spirit has made us one. We are not perfect, and we must learn to love one another, but I have no reason to doubt you."

The colors of his heart swirled around, and he relished in my trust. "I was afraid her coming for Marilla would hurt you."

"There are many things that have hurt me and many more that could, but Livia is no longer one of them."

Astur held me tightly, tucking me into his side. His warm hands moved over my body, reclaiming me and sending chills across my flesh. We shared our physical love more intentionally than before, but I was only beginning to understand the love between mates.

The day was bright when Livia arrived. Cato and Dolon came to the palace with her. Lady Gaius greeted them and directed Dolon and Cato to wait in her sitting room while she took Livia to see Marilla. Astur was in meetings all morning but promised me that I would be called as soon as Felix inspected the dagger.

I left Mendel with Myrtle and waited with Marilla. She was nervous and uneasy to see Livia. Marilla fidgeted with her dress and the long sleeve she insisted on tugging low over her wrists.

"You look beautiful, Marilla," I said to encourage her, but her pale lips only went up a little in a timid smile.

"I'm still thin and weak. She may not recognize me."

"She'll know you. She's your friend and relation. You cannot deny one's attachment."

When Lady Gaius opened Marilla's door, Livia rushed past me, making over Marilla. She hugged her cousin and friend, and tears of relief flowed down both of their faces. "Marilla, it's good to see you. We were worried sick. Your mother and father, too, were devastated when they heard about your arrest and conviction," Livia whispered. Her emotions made it hard to speak.

"Oh, what a happy reunion!" Lady Gaius gushed with satisfaction.

Livia released Marilla from their embrace yet kept her arm around Marilla's frail shoulders. Livia dipped her head towards me and offered me a curtsy. "Lady Gaius," she said, remembering her place and my position.

"Lady Phina," I corrected and offered her a cordial smile. Livia was just as beautiful as I remembered. Her graceful gestures and long neck accentuated her beauty.

"Lady Phina," she repeated. "Thank you for allowing my visit. You have no idea how hard it was to leave Marilla behind. Cato was determined to get me home. Then to be the bearer of bad news and watch her father's health decline." Livia dabbed tears from the corner of her eyes with a lace-edged handkerchief. Livia smiled at Marilla and cupped her cheek affectionately. "Thank you for seeing to our dear Marilla's pardon."

Livia's speech was timely and well-versed, but I couldn't help but think it sounded stilted and rehearsed. Had Cato or Lady Gaius told her what to say? She was probably unsure of herself and my reaction to her. After all, she had been chosen, and had things been different, she would have stood in my place, and I would have been far away.

"How is my father?" Marilla asked.

Livia led Marilla to a chair and sat her down before she spoke. "He's better but too weak to travel. They look forward to seeing you. You know your mother would leave him if she could. She felt torn and regretted that she must send me in her stead. He will be fine once you're home." Marilla's eyes fluttered with joy at the prospect.

Alexander waited outside Marilla's room for me. When he knocked, I felt a solid pang at the bottom of my stomach. Felix had sent for me. Lady Gaius opened the door. He stuck his head in and said, "Lady Phina, it's time."

I offered the women a pensive smile. "I must be going," I said. "I hope to see you all at supper." They nodded and smiled as I excused myself.

Alexander moved to allow me to go past him, but his eyes searched for a glimpse of Marilla. She didn't smile, but her eyes thanked him. He cherished the sight. She looked at him; she actually looked at him. He smiled, and his heart burst into color, seeing Marilla. His heart filled with happy pink and deep burgundy, like the garden flowers she loved.

Alexander's joy carried me part of the way to the library; then, the colors of his heart darkened. "When will she leave?" he asked. *Pain. Longing.*

"I don't know, Alexander." He nodded once, maintaining his soldier's stance. I had no words to comfort him; I had no sight as to their future.

Alexander escorted me to Lady Gaius's sitting room instead of the library. There were guards stationed outside the door. "Please wait here, ma'am," one of the soldiers said. He opened the door and went inside.

"Are you alright, ma'am?" Alexander asked. I was unable to speak.

Felix came out, and his jaw tightened as he faced me. I swallowed, and my eyes widened, waiting for Felix's response, but I already knew.

"Where is Astur?" I asked.

I could feel myself weakening with the knowledge that lay before me. Felix placed his hands on my shoulders as he'd done numerous times. His care and concern held me in place. I could be strong until Astur arrived. Felix and Alexander would keep me safe. Astur's hand was at my back then, and Felix removed his hands. Astur was the safest of all, and I leaned into him. He and Felix exchanged a glance.

"It's just as she described," Felix said. "Guards are with him. Cato's inside, too. He's not sure what's going on, but he's angry that he's been detained."

Astur frowned. "You don't have to do this, Phina," Astur said, but he knew that was his hope and not the truth.

Felix led us into the room. Astur was at my side, and Alexander was at my back. "What's the meaning of this?" Cato said. His face was flushed, and his heart raged. "Why have we been surrounded by guards?"

Astur lifted his chin and stared at Cato, silencing him. Cato knew his place, and familiar cunning reflected in his eyes. He would observe and bide his time. Astur walked directly to Dolon's blade and lifted it for closer examination.

"Is this your blade?" Astur asked Dolon.

"Yes," Dolon said flatly.

"And how did you come by it?" Astur asked.

"It was my soldier's blade—standard issue." He looked around at all the other soldiers in the room. "I dare say we all have one."

"What about these markings? These aren't standard."

"That's how I know it's mine," Dolon said, revealing nothing in his expression, but his heart was a different matter.

"Can you tell me what they represent?" Astur asked.

"It's my family's markings," Dolon lied.

Astur handed me the dagger for inspection. My hands shook, and I closed my eyes, rubbing my thumb over it as I had done as a child. I clutched the weapon close to my heart, feeling Mother with me again. I opened my mind to the great spirit for words and strength.

"Do you have anything to say?" Astur asked.

I nodded and found my voice. "Were you ever on patrol near the river?" I asked. When he didn't answer, I continued, "Let me be more specific. Did you and another soldier ever come to a small cottage and find a woman alone?" Dolon's eyes dulled, skeptical of my presence. He was bothered that he was being questioned by a woman, a small, insignificant woman.

"What's the meaning of this?" Cato interrupted. He moved forward but was apprehended by one of the guards. "What are you getting at?" Felix nodded toward the guard, and Cato was released. Cato jerked his arm free but remained silent.

"Were you ever wounded as a soldier?" I asked.

Dolon's eyes blazed. He didn't know how, but he knew that I could see into his past. When he hesitated to answer me, Felix cleared his throat.

"The lady asked you a question, Dolon. Be wise," he warned.

Dolon glared back at me. "Yes," he said.

His heart's darkness and guilt poured out around the rage. I took in a deep breath and relied on the great spirit's strength. Sensing the change, Astur placed his hand at the small of my back.

"Were you wounded by *this* dagger?" I asked, staring into Dolon's cold eyes. He gave no reply but tilted his head. *Caution. Threat. Escape.* He was suspicious that I knew what he'd done.

"You have no proof," Dolon said.

Beside Astur and surrounded by so many protective hearts, I knew the great spirit had provided me with this opportunity to confront my fears and Dolon. "So then, how did you come by it?" I asked.

"I won it in a game of chance," he answered.

I shook my head, disagreeing. "No, this was my mother's dagger; I would know it anywhere. You took it from her. Do you remember that day?" Dolon set his jaw, mocking me. "You and another soldier came to the cottage. One of you required a healer, or you wouldn't have been able to find her. When you arrived, finding a woman alone, you took advantage of her. You held her down and allowed her to be raped."

There was an audible intake of breath. Dolon shook his head, denying my words. "Again, you have no proof."

"She stabbed you here," I said and placed my hand on my side just under my ribs, "just before you slit her throat." My voice remained steady, but I could feel the emotion rise in my throat.

"You told me that you were ambushed that day," Cato interrupted again. "You said that you and Nicoli were attacked; you never mentioned a woman."

"We *were* ambushed. She wasn't a woman; she was a conjurer. She sang, luring us in, and then cursed us. Nicoli bled out before I could get him back to the road. The minx got what she deserved." Cato stood aghast, shaking his head, denying the truth of Dolon's words.

The pain and shame of Mother's death could no longer be contained. I stepped toward Dolon, threatening him with my words. "She was no conjurer; she was my mother, and you murdered her!" I said, facing Dolon, challenging him with the point of the dagger.

His eyes were incredulous. "She haunts my dreams, and you look just like her," Dolon spat, cursing me. At the same time, Dolon raised his hand to strike me, but Astur swept me away with one arm and blocked Dolon with the other. Alexander grabbed me around the waist and pulled me out of the way, disarming me at the same time. Astur and Dolon exchanged blows before guards surrounded them. Dolon was apprehended, and Felix and the guards took command.

There was another scuffle, and Dolon broke free from the fray. He turned on Alexander, who stood protectively in front of me. It all happened suddenly.

Before Dolon could reach me, Alexander stabbed Dolon with Mother's dagger—a sure and fatal blow. My hands flew to my mouth, muffling the scream as the vile man stepped back and collapsed to his knees. I stared into Dolon's eyes, and his face paled as guards covered him with his cloak, sealing his fate. He would die in darkness; he would die in pain.

Astur's arms were around me then, and I turned into him, sobbing into his chest. He commanded things to Felix and the guards, but I couldn't hear his words. I retreated into the sound of his heartbeat and the colors of his heart.

Chapter Fifty-One

"Take her upstairs," Astur commanded to Alexander.

"Yes, sir," Alexander said, and I heard his heels click as he saluted his governor.

I buried my face deeper into Astur's chest; I did not want to be without him. He kissed my temple and tightened his embrace. "I must see to this." I shook my head, refusing to let him go. "Please, Phina. Alexander will take care of you. Go to Mendel."

At the mention of Mendel's name, I felt the tingling in my breasts. He would need me; I'd been distracted too long. Astur's warm hands held my face and forced me to look into his eyes.

"You are safe," he whispered and stroked my cheek. "Wait for me; I will be with you as soon as I can." I nodded but couldn't find my voice.

"Ma'am," Alexander stepped forward and offered me his arm to lead me back to my chambers. Alexander's heart was racing, but he was himself. I looked back toward Astur as we left the empty sitting room.

Alexander insisted on walking me all the way back to my chambers. I assured him that I could make it up a few stairs by myself, but he refused to hear me. "I have my orders, ma'am. He commanded me to take you upstairs."

When I opened the door to our chambers, I was surprised to find Lady Gaius standing near Mendel's cradle. Why was she there? I wanted to be alone.

No, that wasn't true; I wanted to be with Astur. Alexander stood stiffly behind me. After what had happened downstairs, I wasn't prepared to see anyone. Lady Gaius turned and smiled, and I followed her eyes toward the other side of the room. I was shocked to find Livia holding Mendel.

"Lady Gaius, Livia, what brings you here?" I asked, but my voice sounded off, breathy and exhausted.

Lady Gaius's smile was pacifying. "Livia asked about Mendel, and since you were otherwise detained, I thought we could come up and see him. We dismissed Myrtle a moment ago."

I took in a shaky breath and feigned a smile. Seeing Livia holding Mendel, something gnawed at my insides. It was innocent enough, but I was still shaken and wanted nothing more than to snatch Mendel from her arms.

"Phina, do you feel faint again?" Lady Gaius asked, noticing my unease.

"No, ma'am. Would you excuse me? I need to feed Mendel."

"Of course, dear," she said agreeably. "Come, Livia, we can visit with him at supper." I took determined steps toward Livia. She bristled and turned slightly, hesitating to give Mendel to me. I'm not sure what she read in my expression, but I did not like the way she held him, like she had to protect him. I must look dreadful. She cautiously relinquished her grasp on my son.

"Drink some wine, Phina. You look pale," Lady Gaius suggested. I didn't answer her and walked toward the rocker to nurse Mendel.

Alexander held the door open for them, and I could hear their voices echo behind them. "Why doesn't she have a nurse?" Livia asked in a tone that sounded like Cato.

"She insists on mothering him herself," Lady Gaius replied, putting an end to the discussion.

Alexander hesitated in the doorway. He was torn between staying and giving me privacy. "Please stay, Alexander. I do not wish to be alone. I will be discrete." He shut the door and chuckled. Something amused him. "What is it?" I asked as I adjusted Mendel and settled him.

Alexander focused on his boots and rubbed the back of his neck. "Sorry, ma'am, but my mum and sisters have never needed privacy. It's just something that's done."

We laughed together. Alexander's heart was at peace, thinking of his family. His presence eased my tension. I marveled at his ability. Had he not just killed a man? He didn't see it that way; it was all duty to him.

I took a deep breath and settled myself, focusing on Mendel's needs. "Thank you, Alexander. Thank you for protecting me."

He looked up into my eyes. "I'm happy to return a favor, ma'am," he said sincerely, and I knew that he was referring to Marilla. "I'm going to miss her," he confessed, but his words weren't necessary. "Would you like some wine as Lady Gaius suggested?"

I nodded and looked back down at Mendel and stroked his head. Alexander's love for Marilla pressed against me, but I couldn't help him with matters of the heart. He poured the wine and brought it to me.

"You could claim her," I whispered.

His expression hardened, and he looked away. He stepped back toward the door before he spoke. "She will refuse me. She says she's not worthy, and I have no way to convince her before she leaves. I don't want her to go," he said, determined. He was young, but there was nothing timid about Alexander.

"When did you know that you loved her?" I asked.

Alexander shook his head, and a broad smile spread across his face. "I don't exactly know. I think it was the first time I heard her laugh. She was full of questions and constant curiosities. I thought I would grow weary of her chatter, but then she laughed at something I said, and I wanted to hear it again."

"What happened that night?" I asked.

"I've told you, ma'am. Marilla was upset and refused to go inside; we slept on the balcony together. Well, she finally cried herself to sleep, and I kept watch."

"You said that Cato had upset her. Do you know what he said to her?"

Alexander shook his head. "Not exactly. Cato is an opportunist and a cad. Marilla was easily manipulated, but I did not like his attention toward her. She naively thought that his intentions were honorable." He blew out a breath. "I told her as much and tried to warn her, but she wouldn't hear it. We quarreled, but when she realized I was right, I felt worse. I didn't want to see her hurt; she was so sad."

***

Astur did not return for a long time. Alexander was relieved by another guard so that he could give his statement. Raya brought up a tray; Myrtle came to check on me, refilled my wine, but didn't stay very long. I tried to read to Mendel, but I couldn't focus on the words. I needed to pray; I needed to sing to the great spirit. I placed Mendel in the sling and walked into my old room. I knelt on the floor and lifted my face toward the light that shone through the window. I sang words of thanks for our safety. I sang words of protection over Astur and Mendel. I sang words of love and comfort over Alexander and Marilla. The birds joined my song, and I closed my eyes and lifted my arms to receive the great spirit.

When I opened my eyes, Astur knelt at my side, head bowed reverently, and his eyes were closed. He had come in and joined me without disturbing my prayers. I had not sensed his heart at all. That surprised me. What did it mean? He opened his eyes and looked at me.

"That was beautiful," he said. His words were tamped down with emotion. "It's the first time I understood every word," he marveled.

I tilted my head and smiled into his eyes. I touched his face and reveled in his comprehension. "The great spirit has opened your mind to understanding." The joy that bubbled up inside of me leaked out of my eyes. "Astur, this is a great honor. You are learning the great spirit's ways." I did not think it possible, yet my love for Astur multiplied at that moment. He believed, and I was humbled by the great spirit's blessing on our union.

"You're right," he said, smiling. "I suppose it had to happen with you singing all the time." I laughed, and we embraced. He lifted me to my feet and asked after me.

"I'm well. I was shaken, but I am relieved to know that Mother's murderer has been brought to justice."

"You are incredibly resilient," Astur said.

"Not of my own accord. The great spirit protects me, and I am surrounded by it. I feel it most in your presence and in those who do your bidding."

Astur watched as I dressed for dinner but didn't say much. He helped me with Mendel, too. I could feel his heart's attraction, and it was distracting, but we did not delay supper for our guests. We would have our time once Mendel was down for the night.

Livia entered wearing a dark green dress; she looked radiant. Lady Gaius walked her toward Astur, who was holding Mendel. Livia curtsied and made over Mendel. She had never expressed interest in babies or Traian when we spent time in the garden. Her response to Mendel seemed genuine; perhaps it was her way of honoring Astur.

Livia and Lady Gaius prattled on excitedly at supper, carrying the conversation. Livia had not been so bold when she visited before, but I had never dined with them or been privy to their private interactions. Livia called upon Astur to chime in with his opinions, and I noticed that she watched him and anticipated his every move. She was ready with a smile and her full attention.

After supper, I politely excused myself. Astur stood to leave with me. "Astur, it's Livia's first night. Please reconsider. It's poor manners to leave your guests," Lady Gaius said.

Astur placed his hand at the small of my back. His eyes narrowed as he considered his mother's words. *Caution.* He dipped his head toward Livia. "Good evening," he said dismissively. "Mother, I hope you sleep well."

Chapter Fifty-Two

"Please, I don't want you to go," I said a day later, clinging to Astur's hand as he left the bed. I did not like the petulance in my voice, but I could not help the way I felt.

"I know, but it doesn't change anything," Astur said as he kissed my hand. He gently released my hold and dressed.

"Then take us with you," I suggested.

Astur's eyes flashed. "That's not your place," he said.

"It could be; you said you wanted me to be at your side as you ruled. Has that changed?" I challenged.

"No, that hasn't changed, but your place is here; your place is here at the palace with Mendel. Besides, you only have a few more days with Marilla. I'll be back before they leave."

I had not been myself since the incident with Dolon. After everything was settled, Astur returned the dagger to me. He assured me that we were safe, but my dreams were fitful, and I sensed danger lurking. I prayed to the great spirit but had no sight.

With Astur away, I was expected to eat with our guests each evening. Thankfully, Lady Gaius took command of the conversation, and Livia followed her lead. Marilla was persuaded to join us but did not participate in their banter. She was satisfied to sit next to me and focus on Mendel. I noticed that she ate well. Her cheeks were filling out and had more color than they'd had when she arrived. Although she seemed content, she still worried about what was to come.

The next evening, Cato joined us. Marilla and I were both uneasy, but there was nothing I could do about it. He had the right to visit his sister and Lady Gaius as long as they received him. Neither of them paid attention to Marilla's response nor mine, but I was better at managing my dislike and distrust.

Alexander stood in the shadows of the great hall, keeping watch over us. He took every opportunity to be in Marilla's presence. He kept guard in the garden; he escorted us to and from supper. I suspected that he even slept outside my chambers, but I had no proof. It wasn't necessary, but I would thank Astur and Felix for that bit of comfort in their absence.

Cato's presence exhausted me each night at supper. He was even so bold as to ask me to play for them. Livia agreed, and Lady Gaius clapped. "Yes, please, dear. It would delight us all." She'd had her fill of wine.

"No," I said flatly.

Livia's haughty eyes disliked my refusal. "You play for Marilla; why won't you play for us?" She asked with a note of superiority.

"I must tend to Mendel," I said and stood to make a hasty retreat. Alexander was behind me, pulling out my chair.

"And Marilla, ma'am," he whispered.

He was right to include her. "Come, Marilla. Will you help me get Mendel ready for bed?" Marilla looked up and nodded in relief. "Goodnight, everyone," I said and dismissed us from their party.

***

"May we walk through the garden?" Marilla asked.

Alexander looked at me for permission, but he desperately wanted to be near her. I could give them some time together since she'd be leaving soon. "That's a wonderful idea. I'd like nothing more than some fresh evening air," I agreed. "Let me find Myrtle so she can take Mendel upstairs for me."

When Myrtle saw the three of us together in the garden, she smiled. "Take as long as you like, ma'am. I'll see that he's readied for bed."

"Thank you," Marilla whispered, but she wasn't thanking Myrtle or me. Her smile was only for Alexander. "I couldn't find a reason to excuse myself."

"You shouldn't have to," Alexander said. "And what right do they have to expect Lady Phina to play for them?" he asked. "They'd never do such a thing, except that the governor's away."

He reminded me of Myrtle. "I agree," I chuckled, "but I suppose we must tolerate them until he returns."

"You're the lady of this palace. What you say is obeyed, not anyone else, not even his mother." Alexander's words rushed out. My eyes widened. "I'm sorry, ma'am," he retracted.

"No, Alexander. Thank you for reminding me. I must be bold."

Marilla passed her hand over a blooming shrub and breathed in its scent. "I, too," Marilla said sweetly. We both looked at her. She rarely interjected an opinion. "I, I do not wish to return with Livia," Marilla stammered but kept her face lowered.

Alexander's heart lept, and he stepped forward, almost losing himself in the joy. I passed a warning glance toward him; we must hear her out.

"You do not wish to go home?" I asked. Marilla shook her head. "What about your parents?"

"I do not believe that they want me back."

"But Livia said so. What would give you that idea?"

"This," she said and pulled some parchment from her sleeve.

"What is that?" I asked.

Alexander exhaled and rolled his eyes. "I should have never read that aloud," he said and snatched it from her hand. Marilla tried to take it, but Alexander hid it behind his back. When she moved in closer, he held it above his head. She jumped, trying in vain to reach it.

"Give it to me!" I said, unamused with their game.

Alexander obeyed and handed me the parchment. I unfolded it and turned toward the light to see its contents. Before he could offer me assistance, I'd already read it, and my heart sank.

"Oh, Marilla. I'm sorry," I said.

"They don't want me; they plan to send me away to find *suitable* work. What does that even mean?" Marilla asked. "Livia said that she would keep me with her, but I do not wish to be her servant. If I have to earn my keep, I'd much rather earn it here."

I did not know how to answer her. Astur would need a great deal of convincing to allow her to stay. "What will you do?" I asked.

"You and the governor have already done more for me than I can ever repay, but I can help you with Mendel and the garden. And with some training, I can assist you with your healing. Please, Lady Phina," Marilla pleaded.

Alexander listened, and except for her request to stay, his heart refuted every word she spoke. He blinked and swallowed. Her words pained him, but I could only smile as their future appeared behind my eyes. It would be so. I relished in the great spirit's gift.

I took Marilla's hand. "Would you considered another option?" I asked and gave Alexander a knowing glance. This was his opportunity to claim Marilla. She shook her head, confused by my question.

"I don't understand," Marilla whispered.

I reached out and took Alexander's hand and placed it over Marilla's. Tears pooled in her eyes, and she shook her head, disbelieving the possibility. This was right; this was good. I pressed their hands together and moved away.

"Ma'am," Alexander began.

"I can find my way," I said, "and I think you can, too." He nodded once like a salute, receiving his orders. They weren't from me but from his heart.

I turned and left the garden but stole one last glance over my shoulder. Alexander's forehead leaned against Marilla's. They were the picture of serenity in the setting sun.

I ran up the back stairs that I rarely used anymore, exhilarated from our time in the garden. I was thankful for Mendel's distraction because it would be hard not to eavesdrop from the balcony. I stopped and offered a prayer of thanks to the great spirit.

Chapter Fifty-Three

The sunset cast deep shadows in our chamber. The sconces had yet to be lit. I heard shushing sounds coming from the corner, and the rocker made its familiar creaking.

"Thank you, Myrtle," I said, but she made no reply. I removed my vest and hung it in the wardrobe. "I'm sorry for not giving you notice sooner," I said, turning to face her, but it wasn't Myrtle in the chair; neither was it Astur. My eyes scanned the room and saw Myrtle lying in a heap at the foot of my bed. It was a wonder I hadn't stumbled over her in the dark.

"Livia, what happened?" I asked in a whisper, cautious and unsettled. I didn't like the look in her eyes, so I walked to the table and scraped the flint against the steel to make a spark. The candle at the center of the table illuminated the room. "What have you done to Myrtle?"

Livia sat up, extending her long neck to peer over the edge of the bed. "I don't think she's dead. She was breathing a moment ago."

I knelt down next to Myrtle and pressed my hand on her back while keeping an eye on Livia. There was no blood, and she was still breathing. I shook Myrtle gently to rouse her, but I stood to face Livia when Myrtle didn't move.

"I don't know why you're here, but I think it's time that you go."

Livia rose from the rocker and walked toward me. She looked down at me and smiled her most demure smile. "No, Phina, it's time for *you* to go."

313

"Leave my chambers, Livia, or I'll call the guards."

"I don't think you will. You wouldn't want anything to happen to your precious Mendel because he's the only reason that Astur claimed you."

That was not the truth, but her words troubled me. "Explain yourself," I said.

"You see, you stole something from me, and I'm here to take it back, and unlike you, I would never do anything to grieve him."

"I haven't taken anything from you," I said, trying to figure out how to get Mendel from her. Hearing my voice, he kicked out his legs and moved his head to see me. "Please, give him to me; he's hungry."

"He won't starve; the wetnurse will be here in the morning."

"What are you talking about?" I asked. "You think that I stole Astur from you?"

Her condescending look told me everything. "Astur was promised to me. He is everything I dreamed my husband would be—young, handsome, and a governor. I thought for sure that I would have to marry an old man to achieve high status, but then Cato and Lady Gaius arranged it." Livia bounced Mendel in her arms and walked around the room. He was not appeased and cried out, impatient to get to me. Livia shushed him and walked some more, turning him away from me.

"I did not steal him from you," I repeated.

"You sang for him; you charmed him with your music and planted seeds of distrust between us."

"Astur made his own choice."

"Yes, he made his choice," she said. "Before we left for the capital, he told Cato and Lady Gaius that he doubted I would make a suitable wife. He said he would disclaim me discretely, but that forced Cato, and I had to take matters into our own hands."

"The poison," I said.

"No, that was Cato."

"And you left the evidence in Marilla's room; you knew she had no alibi because she was with Alexander."

Livia shrugged noncommittally. "Did she tell you that? It doesn't matter; no one will believe her. Marilla's a branded criminal and a liar; you're a liar. Marilla told me you were not his mistress, but what do you call this?" she asked, gesturing her chin toward Mendel.

Livia took a deep breath and walked toward the balcony. I followed her but kept a safe distance away. The garden was dark beneath us, and I saw no guards anywhere. Every part of me searched for a way to get Mendel from her.

"When my beauty failed to woo Astur, Cato decided to eliminate him altogether. He's not satisfied and thinks the king will appoint him as the next governor." Her tinkling laugh was out of place. "But when he lived, I knew that was my second chance." Livia set Mendel on the edge of the balcony and let his feet dangle over the edge. I gasped.

"I watched him, you know, admiring you. Every time I walked through the garden, his eyes were on you from the library, the balcony. His eyes were only for you. As long as you remained at the palace, Astur would never love me, so I had no chance."

She dared me to move closer by dangling Mendel over the side. At first, Mendel laughed like it was a game, but then he cried out, and my heart stopped, stricken by fear.

"No, Livia! Move back!"

Livia smiled with malice. Mendel looked back at me and cried. My breasts ached, and I wanted my baby. Every protective fiber of my being struggled to get to my child.

"Don't worry; I will not harm him. I need him until I have a son of my own. I will be here to comfort them and see to their every need."

"Not their *every* need," I corrected, but she dismissed my words with a wave of her hand. She only had one hand on Mendel, who sat precariously close to the edge of the balcony crying louder.

"Livia, step away from the balcony and give me my son!" I demanded. My chest tightened, and I couldn't breathe.

She shook her head. "Please don't blame me; this is your fault. It's all *your* fault! I had it all planned out with Dolon, and then you had him eliminated." I blinked; I couldn't believe my ears. Was there no limit to that man's treachery?

Marilla rushed into my chamber, panting, "Phina!" But before she could do or say anything more, Cato rushed past her, knocking her out of the way. When he saw Mendel on the edge of the balcony, Cato backed up and tried to convince Livia to make a different choice. He looked at me and then back to his sister.

"You are unwell, Livia," Cato soothed. I took the opportunity and inched closer but could not get to her.

"Livia, stop!" Marilla stepped onto the balcony, too.

Sensing the danger to Livia, Cato grabbed me to protect his sister. "Move away, Marilla," Cato grunted. I fought to break free, but he tightened his hold on me.

"Let them go!" Marilla demanded. I'd never heard her speak so boldly. Mendel's cries continued in the chaos.

"Unhand my wife, Cato," Astur bellowed from the door.

The ferocity in Astur's words wasn't frightening; it was a comfort. His eyes darkened. His commanding presence made everyone react.

Cato released me and ran to his sister, and Marilla drew a dagger, slicing through Cato's sleeve and drawing blood as he ran past her. Her boldness startled everyone.

"Give me the baby, Livia!" Marilla demanded.

Cato drew his own dagger to protect his sister. "Move away, Marilla," Cato warned.

Marilla moved forward anyway. Cato stepped back and stumbled against Livia. Marilla's determined expression was unwavering. She thrust the dagger again, forcing Cato to take the defensive. Marilla pressed forward and made a clean strike to Livia's side.

Livia was cornered, and like a wild animal, her eyes were savage and unpredictable. Marilla reached for Mendel, but it was too late. The horror caught in my throat, along with my scream as I watched. Livia released Mendel's leg. I ran to the edge of the balcony and looked over, nearly losing my footing and following him over. Astur caught me and pulled me back to safety.

I strained my eyes into the darkness. He was gone; Mendel was gone. The crushing reality shattered my heart and sealed my ears until Mendel's impossible cry broke the silence.

"I've got him, ma'am. I've got Mendel," Alexander called up. "He's fine, ma'am," he panted. I squinted in the darkness; Alexander held Mendel with one hand and balanced himself against the garden wall with the other. He'd climbed up the trellis toward the balcony.

Tears fell down my face. "Mendel," I sobbed in relief, and Astur held me in his strong arms.

"He's bringing him straight away!" Marilla exclaimed.

In the space of a heartbeat, we were surrounded by soldiers. Cato relinquished his weapon and held his sister protectively. He held up one hand to keep the guards at bay. Livia was pale and losing blood. Cato whispered over her. "I should have never asked you to hide the plant. You should never have touched it." No recognition hinted in her crazed eyes. "Please, forgive me," he begged. "I never knew it would hurt you," he confessed.

Alexander followed Felix into our chamber and placed Mendel safely in my arms. Thankfully, he wasn't crying. I looked him over for injury. Astur performed his own examination. When he was satisfied, he turned to Felix, whose soldiers took custody of Cato and Livia.

Myrtle stirred and, other than a knot on her head, assured us she was well. Alexander and Marilla helped her into a chair.

"It's all my fault. I told Cato what I knew of the plants. I warned him just like Phina warned me. He took everything I said and used it against the governor," Marilla sobbed into Alexander's chest.

I walked over and placed my arm around her. Marilla lifted her head and smiled at Mendel through her tears. Poor thing, it wasn't entirely her fault. I had been right, though; Cato was behind it all. He'd used everyone ill, including Marilla.

Epilogue

"Come, little one; come along, my garden sprite. Let's begin our lessons," I say. Coriander's chubby hands gather the blooms carefully. She is never without the flowers' scents.

Cori arrived before Mendel's second birthday. She was born with the raven's hair and the lazuli eyes. I was not surprised because I dreamed about her every night. Her arrival was a blessing, and she is a delight beyond measure.

It's harder for me to move these days; my belly is round and full with another child. Thanks to the great spirit, I know this daughter will be marked as a healer like her sister. Astur wants to name her Rose.

Traian and Mendel wrestle on the lawn behind us, ever-mindful of the flowers. They take their physical exertions out on one another rather than their sisters and continually get into mischief. Their afternoon lessons with Marcus run smoother when they've worn themselves out in the mornings.

Lucia and Felix have a daughter, now, too. Decima is not much older than Coriander, but she prefers to stay with her mother in the kitchen rather than the garden.

Lady Gaius visits twice yearly. She comes for the Governor's Feast and to celebrate Mendel's birthday. After all, he is the heir of all that she possesses. As their doting grandmother, she enjoys the children and keeps her word not to meddle or interfere in any way.

Alexander and Marilla are expecting, as well. I anticipate their wee one's arrival any day. Alexander's soldiering has taken him away, so Marilla will stay with us throughout her confinement. They were joined soon after Cato and Livia's sentencing. Brother and sister were hanged together, but neither Marilla nor I wished to be present.

I insisted on returning to the cottage with Mendel to avoid any future threats. Astur would not hear of it. "There will always be threats to my position. There will always be threats to the region and to the kingdom. None of that can be avoided, Phina, even threats to our children."

"Then what assurances do we have?" I asked, but I already knew the answer. I could only pray protection over my family and teach them the best I could, so I stayed.

The palace bursts with the joyful sounds of children playing and the promise of more. Each year on the anniversary of our union, Astur asks if I have any sight. He knows good and well that I do not. He is no longer a bystander, and together, we practice the great spirit's ways.

"How can you see our children before they're born, yet you cannot see *our* path?" he teases and swirls his hand around my belly, enticing his daughter to kick and move.

I remind him, "I do not need the great spirit's gift of sight to know that we belong together." His heart's colors respond to my words, and I am surrounded, embraced by their vibrance.

The End

ABOUT THE AUTHOR

Kelda lives in south Louisiana with her beloved
and young adult children, who are all gradually leaving the nest to pursue
their own mates and adventures.
She and her mate have been joined for twenty-nine years.
More than three decades together have taught her much about love and
loss. Traveling with her beloved is her favorite pastime.
When she's not writing, Kelda enjoys knitting, crochet, and quilting.
Kelda has a background in education and counseling and homeschooled
their four children. She shares her experience and encourages parents
through her *Hey, Miss Kelda* vlog, Patreon workshops, and consultations.
Impacting families is one of her greatest joys.
Her non-fiction works, *Call Their Hearts Home* and *TWPH—Insights
Into Living With Teens*, focus on faith and parenting.
Her fictional writing has led her down many new paths, including audio
recording and editing. *Phina* is Kelda's fifth novel, following *IMPACT,
Sweet Caroline, DAWES: A Companion of Sweet Caroline*, and
Autumn's Captive.

Kelda's published works are available on Amazon, Kindle, and Audible.

A portion of the proceeds goes to support the women at
Hope4Burundi.org

To receive bonus material and updates, visit
www.keldalaingpoynot.com

Please consider leaving a review on Amazon, Kindle, and Audible.

Be Embraced!

Ingram Content Group UK Ltd.
Milton Keynes UK
UKHW041055270423
420787UK00021B/27